MA... ...ST—HUNTER AND PREY . . .

Lycon was less than a hundred yards from the hedge, when the blue-scaled killer vaulted over the thorny barrier with an acrobat's grace. It writhed through the air, and one needle-clawed hand slashed out—tearing the throat from the nearest Molossian before the dog was fully aware of its presence. The creature bounced to the earth like a cat, as the last two snarling hounds sprang for it together. Spinning and slashing as it ducked under and away, the thing was literally a blur of motion. Deadly motion. Neither hound completed its leap, as lethal talons tore and gutted—slew with nightmarish precision.

Lycon skidded to a stop on the muddy field. He did not need to glance behind him to know he was alone with the beast. Its eyes glowed in the sunset as it turned from the butchered dogs and stared at its pursuer.

The hunter advanced his spear, making no attempt to throw. As fast as it moved, the thing would easily dodge his cast. And Lycon knew that if the beast leaped, he was dead . . .

—From "Killer"
by Karl Edward Wagner
and David Drake

SPACE GLADIATORS

EDITED BY DAVID DRAKE
WITH CHARLES G. WAUGH
AND MARTIN HARRY GREENBERG

ACE BOOKS, NEW YORK

SPACE GLADIATORS

An Ace Book / published by arrangement with
the editors

PRINTING HISTORY
Ace edition/April 1989

CONTENTS

SPACE
GLADIATORS

INTRODUCTION

LET THE GAMES BEGIN . . .

by David Drake

The classical world knew there were two different species of elephant, the African and the Asian. There was a general tendency to call the eastern variety 'Syrian elephants' rather than 'Indian' as we do, because Syria was the port of entry, but they were talking about the same animal.

Many Romans could tell you that the most striking difference between African and Asian elephants was that the eastern variety was much larger than its African cousin.

That isn't how we learned it in school, because Romans knew nothing of the sub-Saharan species that we think of as African elephants. The Romans meant a northern variety inhabiting the mountains of Mauretania—very similar to the sub-Saharan species, but dwarfed in size.

Whereas we aren't familiar with Mauretanian elephants, because they've been extinct since Roman times. The species was wiped out in the centuries-long slaughter of the Roman Games.

'Games' is a slight mistranslation of the Latin word *Ludus*. The Latin vocabulary is much more limited than that of English, so the same word did duty for dicing in a tavern, a performance of Sophocles—and the slaughter in the arena.

Call them entertainments, then. It's even been suggested there was some socially-redeeming value in them. A city dweller in the Roman world had almost as good an opportunity as an avid viewer of public television today to see varied life forms.

And then watch them die. By the hundreds, by the thousands. . . . By the species.

A Roman also had the opportunity to watch humans slaughtered by the thousands. So far as I know, there hasn't been an attempt to find social benefit in that, though during World War II both the Germans and the Japanese slaughtered prisoners of war in much greater numbers than the Romans managed in their arenas.

The thing is, modern Germans and Japanese made an attempt to hide what they were doing. There were a few Romans (and rather more Greeks under Roman rule) who objected to the Games on philosophical grounds; but they tended to be the folk who objected to slavery also, and slavery was the foundation of classical society. So a few otherworldly philosophers carped, but the citizenry as a whole crammed the amphitheaters.

The human victims of the arena were mostly prisoners of war and criminals (among whom Christians seeking martyrdom amounted to a significant percentage at various times). Sometimes they were armed and set against one another, but only the immediate participants had the slightest interest in who won.

Very often, the prisoners weren't expected to fight: they only had to die. Watching unarmed humans being torn by lions ranked right up there in Roman popularity with seeing antelope shot by archers from high platforms that avoided any risk of the shooters being accidentally gored.

Mass human victims were in a class identical to that of the beasts who died in other events of the day. Professional gladiators were in quite a different category.

A top gladiator was a sports hero who could expect wealth in addition to adulation. He could expect to hobnob with the raffish members of 'the best people'. Very occasionally, he was from a noble family himself.

He *didn't* expect to die in the arena.

Oh, it could happen; the way a wide receiver can get his neck broken in a modern football game. But we have, in the form of graffiti, the Won-Lost records of enough gladiators to know that while it was a tough business, a professional gladiator wasn't simply serving a deferred death sentence.

Gladiators weren't at the pinnacle of their own social class. That place was filled by the charioteers, whose races were an even greater part of the classical social order than gladiatorial combats. (Juvenal's 'bread and circuses' refers to chariot races, not swordfights.)

Since the races were incredibly brutal events themselves—imagine a combination of Demo Derby and Italian-style motorcycle racing—they can be considered combat with a different style of weapon.

Gladiatorial bouts probably began as battles at funerals to achieve a religious purpose: sending the deceased off with a blood offering. Religious motives also underlie the kindred practice of Trial by Combat: the Gods know who is right, who is pure, who is fit. Let the contenders compete under controlled conditions so that the Gods can give the victory where it is due.

Historically, combat by champions hasn't proven a very effective alternative to battle. It's hard to convince an army to go home in defeat simply because one of its members had a bad day against the opposing champion. Indeed, even the semi-legendary accounts—for which David and Goliath can stand for any number of other examples—usually end with the victor's side butchering the army of the defeated champion.

Formal single combat was more effective when it was intended to solve some more personal matter—usually honor, though that was as likely to be 'the honor of winning the tournament' as anything directly involving a lady's name. It did, after all, prove who was the better man that day, and a surviving loser had his bruises as encouragement not to pursue matters further.

If the loser didn't survive, matters had been settled even more firmly.

Violence is a terrible intrusion into the fabric of ordinary society. Formalizing it in the arena has the advantage of controlling what, unchecked, could utterly destroy that society; but it has also the queasy *wrongness* of constituting social acceptance of what is clearly antisocial. That dichotomy makes violence in its most controlled manifestation an interesting subject for fiction.

An interesting arena, if you'll permit me.

The stories we've chosen here explore a number of the aspects of the subject in the context of science fiction. As you go through them, consider the continuum of peace; gladiatorial games; war; and the utter chaos toward which war always tends.

I'd like to live in a world at peace.

But I might settle for a world in which the bloodiest slaughter could be covered as sports news, rather than international affairs.

DIPLOMAT-AT-ARMS

by Keith Laumer

The cold white sun of Northroyal glared on pale dust and vivid colors in the narrow raucous street. Retief rode slowly, unconscious of the huckster's shouts, the kaleidoscope of smells, the noisy milling crowd. His thoughts were on events of long ago on distant worlds; thoughts that set his features in narrow-eyed grimness. His bony, powerful horse, unguided, picked his way carefully, with flaring nostrils, wary eyes alert in the turmoil.

The mount sidestepped a darting gamin and Retief leaned forward, patted the sleek neck. The job had some compensations, he thought; it was good to sit on a fine horse again, to shed the gray business suit—

A dirty-faced man pushed a fruit cart almost under the animal's head; the horse shied, knocked over the cart. At once a muttering crowd began to gather around the heavy-shouldered gray-haired man. He reined in and sat scowling, an ancient brown cape over his shoulders, a covered buckler slung at the side of the worn saddle, a scarred silver-worked claymore strapped across his back in the old cavalier fashion.

Retief hadn't liked this job when he had first heard of it. He had gone alone on madman's errands before, but that had been long ago—a phase of his career that should have been finished.

And the information he had turned up in his background research had broken his professional detachment. Now the locals were trying an old tourist game on him; ease the outlander into a spot, then demand money. . . .

Well, Retief thought, this was as good a time as any to start playing the role; there was a hell of a lot here in the quaint city of Fragonard that needed straightening out.

"Make way, you rabble!" he roared suddenly. "Or by the chains of the sea-god I'll make a path through you!" He spurred the horse; neck arching, the mount stepped daintily forward.

The crowd made way reluctantly before him. "Pay for the merchandise you've destroyed," called a voice.

"Let peddlers keep a wary eye for their betters," snorted the man loudly, his eye roving over the faces before him. A tall fellow with long yellow hair stepped squarely into his path.

"There are no rabble or peddlers here," he said angrily. "Only true cavaliers of the Clan Imperial. . . ."

The mounted man leaned from his saddle to stare into the eyes of the other. His seamed brown face radiated scorn. "When did a true Cavalier turn to commerce? If you were trained to the Code you'd know a gentleman doesn't soil his hands with penny-grubbing, and that the Emperor's highroad belongs to the mounted knight. So clear your rubbish out of my path, if you'd save it."

"Climb down off that nag," shouted the tall young man, reaching for the bridle. "I'll show you some practical knowledge of the Code. I challenge you to stand and defend yourself."

In an instant the thick barrel of an antique Imperial Guards power gun was in the gray-haired man's hand. He leaned negligently on the high pommel of his saddle with his left elbow, the pistol laid across his forearm pointing unwaveringly at the man before him.

The hard old face smiled grimly. "I don't soil my hands in street brawling with new-hatched nobodies," he said. He nodded toward the arch spanning the street ahead. "Follow me through the arch, if you call yourself a man and a Cavalier." He moved on then; no one hindered him. He rode in silence through the crowd, pulled up at the gate barring the street. This would be the first real test of his cover identity. The papers which had gotten him through Customs and Immigration at Fragonard Spaceport the day before had been burned along with the civilian clothes. From here on he'd be getting by on the uniform and a cast-iron nerve.

A purse-mouthed fellow wearing the uniform of a Lieutenant-Ensign in the Household Escort Regiment looked him over, squinted his eyes, smiled sourly.

"What can I do for you, Uncle?" He spoke carelessly, leaning against the engraved buttress mounting the wrought-iron gate. Yellow and green sunlight filtered down through the leaves of the giant linden trees bordering the cobbled street.

The gray-haired man stared down at him. "The first thing you can do, Lieutenant-Ensign," he said in a voice of cold steel, "is come to a position of attention."

The thin man straightened, frowning. "What's that?" His expression hardened. "Get down off that beast and let's have a look at your papers—if you've got any."

The mounted man didn't move. "I'm making allowances for the fact that your regiment is made of up idlers who've never learned to soldier," he said quietly. "But having had your attention called to it, even you should recognize the insignia of a Battle Commander."

The officer stared, glancing over the drab figure of the old man. Then he saw the tarnished gold thread worked into the design of a dragon rampant, almost invisible against the faded color of the heavy velvet cape.

He licked his lips, cleared his throat, hesitated. What in name of the Tormented One would a top-ranking battle officer be doing on this thin old horse, dressed in plain worn clothing? "Let me see your papers—Commander," he said.

The Commander flipped back the cape to expose the ornate butt of the power pistol.

"Here are my credentials," he said. "Open the gate."

"Here," the Ensign spluttered, "What's this . . ."

"For a man who's taken the Emperor's commission," the old man said, "you're criminally ignorant of the courtesies due a general officer. Open the gate or I'll blow it open. You'll not deny the way to an Imperial battle officer." He drew the pistol.

The Ensign gulped, thought fleetingly of sounding the alarm signal, of insisting on seeing papers . . . then as the pistol came up, he closed the switch, and the gate swung open. The heavy hooves of the gaunt horse clattered past him; he caught a glimpse

of a small brand on the lean flank. Then he was staring after the
retreating back of the terrible old man. Battle Commander indeed! The old fool was wearing a fortune in valuable antiques,
and the animal bore the brand of a thoroughbred battle-horse.
He'd better report this. . . . He picked up the communicator, as
a tall young man with an angry face came up to the gate.

Retief rode slowly down the narrow street lined with the stalls
of suttlers, metalsmiths, weapons technicians, free-lance squires.
The first obstacle was behind him. He hadn't played it very
suavely, but he had been in no mood for bandying words. He
had been angry ever since he had started this job; and that, he
told himself, wouldn't do. He was beginning to regret his high-
handedness with the crowd outside the gate. He should save the
temper for those responsible, not the bystanders; and in any
event, an agent of the Corps should stay cool at all times. That
was essentially the same criticism that Magnan had handed him
along with the assignment, three months ago.

"The trouble with you, Retief," Magnan had said, "is that
you are unwilling to accept the traditional restraints of the Service; you conduct yourself too haughtily, too much in the manner of a free agent. . . ."

His reaction, he knew, had only proved the accuracy of his
superior's complaint. He should have nodded penitent agreement, indicated that improvement would be striven for earnestly;
instead, he had sat expressionless, in a silence which inevitably
appeared antagonistic.

He remembered how Magnan had moved uncomfortably,
cleared his throat, and frowned at the papers before him. "Now,
in the matter of your next assignment," he said, "we have a
serious situation to deal with in an area that could be critical."

Retief almost smiled at the recollection. The man had placed
himself in an amusing dilemma. It was necessary to emphasize
the great importance of the job at hand, and simultaneously to
avoid letting Retief have the satisfaction of feeling that he was
to be intrusted with anything vital; to express the lack of confidence the Corps felt in him while at the same time invoking his
awareness of the great trust he was receiving. It was strange how
Magnan could rationalize his personal dislike into a righteous
concern for the best interests of the Corps.

Magnan had broached the nature of the assignment obliquely,

mentioning his visit as a tourist to Northroyal, a charming, backward little planet settled by Cavaliers, refugees from the breakup of the Empire of the Lily.

Retief knew the history behind Northroyal's tidy, proud, tradition-bound society. When the Old Confederation broke up, dozens of smaller governments had grown up among the civilized worlds. For a time, the Lily Empire had been among the most vigorous of them, comprising twenty-one worlds, and supporting an excellent military force under the protection of which the Lilyan merchant fleet had carried trade to a thousand far-flung worlds.

When the Concordiat had come along, organizing the previously sovereign states into a new Galactic jurisdiction, the Empire of the Lily had resisted, and had for a time held the massive Concordiat fleets at bay. In the end, of course, the gallant but outnumbered Lilyan forces had been driven back to the gates of the home world. The planet of Lily had been saved catastrophic bombardment only by a belated truce which guaranteed self-determination to Lily on the cessation of hostilities, disbandment of the Lilyan fleet, and the exile of the entire membership of the Imperial Suite, which, under the Lilyan clan tradition, had numbered over ten thousand individuals. Every man, woman, and child who could claim even the most distant blood relationship to the Emperor, together with their servants, dependents, retainers, and protégés, were included. The move took weeks to complete, but at the end of it the Cavaliers, as they were known, had been transported to an uninhabited, cold sea-world, which they named Northroyal. A popular bit of lore in connection with the exodus had it that the ship bearing the Emperor himself had slipped away en route to exile, and that the ruler had sworn that he would not return until the day he could come with an army of liberation. He had never been heard from again.

The land area of the new world, made up of innumerable islands, totaled half a million square miles. Well stocked with basic supplies and equipment, the Cavaliers had set to work and turned their rocky fief into a snug, well-integrated—if tradition-ridden—society, and today exported seafoods, fine machinery, and tourist literature.

It was in the last department that Northroyal was best known. Tales of the pomp and color, the quaint inns and good food, the beautiful girls, the brave display of royal cavalry, and the fabulous annual Tournament of the Lily attracted a goodly number of sightseers, and the Cavalier Line was now one of the planet's biggest foreign-exchange earners.

Magnan had spoken of Northroyal's high industrial potential, and her well-trained civilian corps of space navigators.

"The job of the Corps," Retief interrupted, "is to seek out and eliminate threats to the peace of the Galaxy. How does a little story-book world like Northroyal get into the act?"

"More easily than you might imagine," Magnan said. "Here you have a close-knit society, proud, conscious of a tradition of military power, empire. A clever rabble-rouser using the right appeal would step into a ready-made situation there. It would take only an order on the part of the planetary government to turn the factories to war production, and convert the merchant fleet into a war fleet—and we'd be faced with a serious power imbalance—a storm center."

"I think you're talking nonsense, Mr. Minister," Retief said bluntly. "They've got more sense than that. They're not so far gone on tradition as to destroy themselves. They're a practical people."

Magnan drummed his fingers on the desk top. "There's one factor I haven't covered yet," he said. "There has been what amounts to a news blackout from Northroyal during the last six months. . . ."

Retief snorted. "What news?"

Magnan had been enjoying the suspense. "Tourists have been having great difficulty getting to Northroyal," he said. "Fragonard, the capital, is completely closed to outsiders. We managed, however, to get an agent in." He paused, gazing at Retief. "It seems," he went on, "that the rightful Emperor has turned up."

Retief narrowed his eyes. "What's that?" he said sharply.

Magnan drew back, intimidated by the power of Retief's tone, annoyed by his own reaction. In his own mind, Magnan was candid enough to know that this was the real basis for his intense dislike for his senior agent. It was an instinctive primitive fear of physical violence. Not that Retief had ever assaulted anyone; but he had an air of mastery that made Magnan feel trivial.

"The Emperor," Magnan repeated. "The traditional story is

that he was lost on the voyage to Northroyal. There was a legend that he had slipped out of the hands of the Concordiat in order to gather new support for a counteroffensive, hurl back the invader, all that sort of thing.''

"The Concordiat collapsed of its own weight within a century," Retief said. "There's no invader to hurl back. Northroyal is free and independent, like every other world.''

"Of course, of course," Magnan said. "But you're missing the emotional angle, Retief. It's all very well to be independent; but what about the dreams of empire, the vanished glory, destiny, et cetera?''

"What about them?''

"That's all our agent heard; it's everywhere. The news strips are full of it. Video is playing it up; everybody's talking it. The returned Emperor seems to be a clever propagandist; the next step will be a full-scale mobilization. And we're not equipped to handle that.''

"What am I supposed to do about all this?''

"Your orders are, and I quote, to proceed to Fragonard and there employ such measures as shall be appropriate to negate the present trend toward an expansionist sentiment among the populace." Magnan passed a document across the desk to Retief for his inspection.

The orders were brief, and wasted no wordage on details. As an officer of the Corps with the rank of Counselor, Retief enjoyed wide latitude, and broad powers—and corresponding responsibility in the event of failure. Retief wondered how this assignment had devolved on him, among the thousands of Corps agents scattered through the Galaxy. Why was one man being handed a case which on the face of it should call for a full mission?

"This looks like quite an undertaking for a single agent, Mr. Minister," Retief said.

"Well, of course, if you don't feel you can handle it . . ." Magnan looked solemn.

Retief looked at him, smiling faintly. Magnan's tactics had been rather obvious. Here was one of those nasty jobs which could easily pass in reports as routine if all went well; but even a slight mistake could mean complete failure, and failure meant war; and the agent who had let it happen would be finished in the Corps.

There was danger in the scheme for Magnan, too. The blame might reflect back on him. Probably he had plans for averting disaster after Retief had given up. He was too shrewd to leave himself out in the open. And for that matter, Retief reflected, too good an agent to let the situation get out of hand.

No, it was merely an excellent opportunity to let Retief discredit himself, with little risk of any great credit accruing to him in the remote event of success.

Retief could, of course, refuse the assignment, but that would be the end of his career. He would never be advanced to the rank of Minister, and age limitations would force his retirement in a year or two. That would be an easy victory for Magnan.

Retief liked his work as an officer-agent of the Diplomatic Corps, that ancient supranational organization dedicated to the contravention of war. He had made his decision long ago, and he had learned to accept his life as it was, with all its imperfections. It was easy enough to complain about the petty intrigues, the tyrannies of rank, the small inequities. But these were merely a part of the game, another challenge to be met and dealt with. The overcoming of obstacles was Jame Retief's specialty. Some of the obstacles were out in the open, the recognized difficulties inherent in any tough assignment. Others were concealed behind a smoke-screen of personalities and efficiency reports; and both were equally important. You did your job in the field, and then you threaded your way through the maze of Corps politics. And if you couldn't handle the job—any part of it—you'd better find something else to do.

He had accepted the assignment, of course, after letting Magnan wonder for a few minutes; and then for two months he had buried himself in research, gathering every scrap of information, direct and indirect, that the massive files of the Corps would yield. He had soon found himself immersed in the task, warming to its challenge, fired with emotions ranging from grief to rage as he ferreted out the hidden pages in the history of the exiled Cavaliers.

He had made his plan, gathered a potent selection of ancient documents and curious objects; a broken chain of gold, a tiny key, a small silver box. And now he was here, inside the compound of the Grand Corrida.

Everything here in these ways surrounding and radiating from the Field of the Emerald Crown—the arena itself—was devoted to the servicing and supplying of the thousands of First Day contenders in the Tournament of the Lily, and the housing and tending of the dwindling number of winners who stayed on for the following days. There were tiny eating places, taverns, inns; all consciously antique in style, built in imitation of their counterparts left behind long ago on far-off Lily.

"Here you are, Pop, first-class squire," called a thin red-haired fellow.

"Double up and save credits," called a short dark man. "First Day contract . . ."

Shouts ran back and forth across the alleylike street as the stall keepers scented a customer. Retief ignored them, moved on toward the looming wall of the arena. Ahead, a slender youth stood with folded arms before his stall, looking toward the approaching figure on the black horse. He leaned forward, watching Retief intently, then straightened, turned and grabbed up a tall narrow body shield from behind him. He raised the shield over his head, and as Retief came abreast, called "Battle officer!"

Retief reined in the horse, looked down at the youth.

"At your service, sir," the young man said. He stood straight and looked Retief in the eye. Retief looked back. The horse minced, tossed his head.

"What is your name, boy?" Retief asked.

"Fitzraven, sir."

"Do you know the Code?"

"I know the Code, sir."

Retief stared at him, studying his face, his neatly cut uniform of traditional Imperial green, the old but well-oiled leather of his belt and boots.

"Lower your shield, Fitzraven," he said. "You're engaged." He swung down from his horse. "The first thing I want is care for my mount. His name is Danger-by-Night. And then I want an inn for myself."

"I'll care for the horse myself, Commander," Fitzraven said. "And the Commander will find good lodging at the sign of the Phoenix-in-Dexter-Chief; quarters are held ready for my client." The squire took the bridle, pointing toward the inn a few doors away.

• • •

Two hours later, Retief came back to the stall, a thirty-two-ounce steak and a bottle of Nouveau Beaujolais having satisfied a monumental appetite induced by the long ride down from the spaceport north of Fragonard. The plain banner he had carried in his saddlebag fluttered now from the staff above the stall. He moved through the narrow room to a courtyard behind, and stood in the doorway watching as Fitzraven curried the dusty hide of the lean black horse. The saddle and fittings were laid out on a heavy table, ready for cleaning. There was clean straw in the stall where the horse stood, and an empty grain bin and water bucket indicated the animal had been well fed and watered.

Retief nodded to the squire, and strolled around the courtyard staring up at the deep blue sky of early evening above the irregular line of roofs and chimneys, noting the other squires, the variegated mounts stabled here, listening to the hubbub of talk, the clatter of crockery from the kitchen of the inn. Fitzraven finished his work and came over to his new employer.

"Would the Commander like to sample the night life in the Grand Corrida?"

"Not tonight," Retief said. "Let's go up to my quarters; I want to learn a little more about what to expect."

Retief's room, close under the rafters on the fourth floor of the inn, was small but adequate, with a roomy wardrobe and a wide bed. The contents of his saddlebags were already in place in the room.

Retief looked around. "Who gave you permission to open my saddlebags?"

Fitzraven flushed slightly. "I thought the Commander would wish to have them unpacked," he said stiffly.

"I looked at the job the other squires were doing on their horses," Retief said. "You were the only one who was doing a proper job of tending the animal. Why the special service?"

"I was trained by my father," Fitzraven said. "I serve only true knights, and I perform my duties honorably. If the Commander is dissatisfied . . ."

"How do you know I'm a true knight?"

"The Commander wears the uniform and weapons of one of the oldest Imperial Guards Battle Units, the Iron Dragon," Fitzraven said. "And the Commander rides a battle horse, truebred."

"How do you know I didn't steal them?"

Fitzraven grinned suddenly. "They fit the Commander too well."

Retief smiled. "All right, son, you'll do," he said. "Now brief me on the First Day. I don't want to miss anything. And you may employ the personal pronoun."

For an hour Fitzraven discussed the order of events for the elimination contests of the First Day of the Tournament of the Lily, the strategies that a clever contender could employ to husband his strength, the pitfalls into which the unwary might fall.

The tournament was the culmination of a year of smaller contests held throughout the equatorial chain of populated islands. The Northroyalans had substituted various forms of armed combat for the sports practiced on most worlds; a compensation for the lost empire, doubtless, a primitive harking-back to an earlier, more glorious day.

Out of a thousand First Day entrants, less than one in ten would come through to face the Second Day. Of course, the First Day events were less lethal than those to be encountered farther along in the three-day tourney, Retief learned; there would be few serious injuries in the course of the opening day, and those would be largely due to clumsiness or ineptitude on the part of the entrants.

There were no formal entrance requirements, Fitzraven said, other than proof of minimum age and status in the Empire. Not all the entrants were natives of Northroyal; many came from distant worlds, long-scattered descendants of the citizens of the shattered Lily Empire. But all competed for the same prizes; status in the Imperial peerage, the honors of the Field of the Emerald crown, and Imperial grants of land, wealth to the successful.

"Will you enter the First Day events, sir," Fitzraven asked, "or do you have a Second or Third Day certification?"

"Neither," Retief said. "We'll sit on the sidelines and watch."

Fitzraven looked surprised. It had somehow not occurred to him that the old man was not to be a combatant. And it was too late to get seats. . . .

"How . . ." Fitzraven began, after a pause.

"Don't worry," Retief said. "We'll have a place to sit."

Fitzraven fell silent, tilted his head to one side, listening. Loud voices, muffled by walls, the thump of heavy feet.

"Something is up," Fitzraven said. "Police." He looked at Retief.

"I wouldn't be surprised," Retief said, "if they were looking for me. Let's go find out."

"We need not meet them," the squire said. "There is another way . . ."

"Never mind," Retief said. "As well now as later." He winked at Fitzraven and turned to the door.

Retief stepped off the lift into the crowded common room, Fitzraven at his heels. Half a dozen men in dark blue tunics and tall shakos moved among the patrons, staring at faces. By the door Retief saw the thin-mouthed Ensign he had overawed at the gate. The fellow saw him at the same moment and plucked at the sleeve of the nearest policeman, pointing.

The man dropped a hand to his belt, and at once the other policeman turned, followed his glance to Retief. They moved toward him with one accord. Retief stood waiting.

The first cop planted himself before Retief, looking him up and down. "Your papers!" he snapped.

Retief smiled easily. "I am a peer of the Lily and a battle officer of the Imperial forces," he said. "On what pretext are you demanding papers of me, Captain?"

The cop raised his eyebrows.

"Let's say you are charged with unauthorized entry into the controlled area of the Grand Corrida, and with impersonating an Imperial officer," he said. "You didn't expect to get away with it, did you, Grandpa?" The fellow smiled sardonically.

"Under the provisions of the Code," Retief said, "the status of a peer may not be questioned, nor his actions interfered with except by Imperial Warrant. Let me see yours, Captain. And I suggest you assume a more courteous tone when addressing your superior officer." Retief's voice hardened to a whip crack with the last words.

The policeman stiffened, scowled. His hand dropped to the nightstick at his belt.

"None of your insolence, old man," he snarled. "Papers! Now!"

Retief's hand shot out, gripped the officer's hand over the stick.

"Raise that stick," he said quietly, "and I'll assuredly beat out your brains with it." He smiled calmly into the captain's bulging eyes. The captain was a strong man. He threw every ounce of his strength into the effort to bring up his arm, to pull free of the old man's grasp. The crowd of customers, the squad of police, stood silently, staring, uncertain of what was going on. Retief stood steady; the officer strained, reddened. The old man's arm was like cast steel.

"I see you are using your head, Captain," Retief said. "Your decision not to attempt to employ force against a peer was an intelligent one."

The cop understood. He was being offered an opportunity to save a little face. He relaxed slowly.

"Very well, uh, sir," he said stiffly. "I will assume you can establish your identity properly; kindly call at the commandant's office in the morning."

Retief released his hold and the officer hustled his men out, shoving the complaining Ensign ahead. Fitzraven caught Retief's eye and grinned.

"Empty pride is a blade with no hilt," he said. "A humble man would have yelled for help."

Retief turned to the barman. "Drinks for all," he called. A happy shout greeted this announcement. They had all enjoyed seeing the police outfaced.

"The cops don't seem to be popular here," the old man said.

Fitzraven sniffed. "A law-abiding subject parks illegally for five minutes, and they are on him like flies after dead meat; but let his car be stolen by lawless hoodlums—they are nowhere to be seen."

"That has a familiar sound," Retief said. He poured out a tumbler of vodka, looked at Fitzraven.

"Tomorrow," he said. "A big day."

A tall blond young man near the door looked after him with bitter eyes.

"All right, old man," he muttered. "We'll see then."

The noise of the crowd came to Retief's ears as a muted rumble through the massive pile of the amphitheater above. A dim light filtered from the low-ceilinged corridor into the cramped office of the assistant Master of the Games.

"If you know your charter," Retief said, "you will recall that a Battle Commander enjoys the right to observe the progress of the games from the official box. I claim that privilege."

"I know nothing of this," the cadaverous official replied impatiently. "You must obtain an order from the Master of the Games before I can listen to you." He turned to another flunkey, opened his mouth to speak. A hand seized him by the shoulder, lifted him bodily from his seat. The man's mouth remained open in shock.

Retief held the stricken man at arm's length, then drew him closer. His eyes blazed into the gaping eyes of the other. His face was white with fury.

"Little man," he said in a strange, harsh voice, "I go now with my groom to take my place in the official box. Read your Charter well before you interfere with me—and your Holy Book as well." He dropped the fellow with a crash, saw him slide under the desk. No one made a sound. Even Fitzraven looked pale. The force of the old man's rage had been like a lethal radiation crackling in the room.

The squire followed as Retief strode off down the corridor. He breathed deeply, wiping his forehead. This was some old man he had met this year, for sure!

Retief slowed, turning to wait for Fitzraven. He smiled ruefully. "I was rough on the old goat," he said. "But officious pipsqueaks sting me like deerflies."

They emerged from the gloom of the passage into a well-situated box, to the best seats in the first row. Retief stared at the white glare and roiled dust of the arena, the banked thousands of faces looming above, and a sky of palest blue with one tiny white cloud. The gladiators stood in little groups, waiting. A strange scene, Retief thought. A scene from dim antiquity, but real, complete with the odors of fear and excitement, the hot wind that ruffled his hair, the rumbling animal sound from the thousand throats of the many-headed monster. He wondered what it was they really wanted to see here today. A triumph of skill and courage, a reaffirmation of ancient virtues, the spectacle of men who laid life on the gaming table and played for a prize called glory—or was it merely blood and death they wanted?

It was strange that this archaic ritual of the blood tournament, combining the features of the Circus of Caesar, the joust of Medieval Terran Europe, the Olympic Games, a rodeo, and a six-day bicycle race should have come to hold such an important place in a modern culture Retief thought. In its present form it was a much-distorted version of the traditional Tournament of the Lily, through whose gauntlet the nobility of the old Empire had come. It had been a device of harsh enlightenment to insure and guarantee to every man, once each year, the opportunity to prove himself against others whom society called his betters. Through its discipline, the humblest farm lad could rise by degrees to the highest levels in the Empire. For the original Games had tested every facet of a man, from his raw courage to his finesse in strategy, from his depths of endurance under mortal stress to the quickness of his intellect, from his instinct for truth to his wiliness in eluding a complex trap of violence.

In the two centuries since the fall of the Empire, the Games had gradually become a tourist spectacle, a free-for-all, a celebration—with the added spice of danger for those who did not shrink back, and fat prizes to a few determined finalists. The Imperial Charter was still invoked at the opening of the Games, the old Code reaffirmed; but there were few who knew or cared what the Charter and Code actually said, what terms existed there. The popular mind left such details to the regents of the tourney. And in recent months, with the once sought-after tourists suddenly and inexplicably turned away, it seemed the Games were being perverted to a purpose even less admirable. . . .

Well, thought Retief, perhaps I'll bring some of the fine print into play, before I'm done.

Bugle blasts sounded beyond the high bronze gate. Then with a heavy clang it swung wide and a nervous official stepped out nodding jerkily to the front rank of today's contenders.

The column moved straight out across the field, came together with other columns to form a square before the Imperial box. High above, Retief saw banners fluttering, a splash of color from the uniforms of ranked honor guards. The Emperor himself was here briefly to open the Tournament.

Across the field the bugles rang out again; Retief recognized the Call to Arms and the Imperial Salute. Then an amplified voice began the ritual reading of the Terms of the Day.

". . . by the clement dispensation of his Imperial Majesty, to be conducted under the convention of Fragonard, and there be none dissenting . . ." The voice droned on.

It finished at last, and referees moved to their positions. Retief looked at Fitzraven. "The excitement's about to begin."

Referees handed out heavy whips, gauntlets and face shields. The first event would be an unusual one.

Retief watched as the yellow-haired combatant just below the box drew on the heavy leather glove which covered and protected the left hand and forearm, accepted the fifteen-foot lash of braided oxhide. He flipped it tentatively, laying the length out along the ground and recalling it with an effortless turn of the wrist, the frayed tip snapping like a pistol shot. The thing was heavy, Retief noted, and clumsy; the leather had no life to it.

The box had filled now; no one bothered Retief and the squire. The noisy crowd laughed and chattered, called to acquaintances in the stands and on the field below.

A bugle blasted peremptorily nearby, and white-suited referees darted among the milling entrants, shaping them into groups of five. Retief watched the blond youth, a tall frowning man, and three others of undistinguished appearance.

Fitzraven leaned toward him. "The cleverest will hang back and let the others eliminate each other," he said in a low voice, "so that his first encounter will be for the set."

Retief nodded. A man's task here was to win his way as high as possible; every strategem was important. He saw the blond fellow inconspicuously edge back as a hurrying referee paired off the other four, called to him to stand by, and led the others to rings marked off on the dusty turf. A whistle blew suddenly, and over the arena the roar of sound changed tone. The watching crowd leaned forward as the hundreds of keyed-up gladiators laid on their lashes in frenzied effort. Whips cracked, men howled, feet shuffled; here the crowd laughed as some clumsy fellow sprawled, yelping; there they gasped in excitement as two surly brutes flogged each other in all-out offense.

Retief saw the tip of one man's whip curl around his opponent's ankle, snatch him abruptly off his feet. The other pair circled warily, rippling their lashes uncertainly. One backed over the line unnoticing and was led away expostulating, no blow having been struck.

The number on the field dwindled away to half within moments. Only a few dogged pairs, now bleeding from cuts, still contested the issue. A minute longer and the whistle blew as the last was settled.

The two survivors of the group below paired off now, and as the whistle blasted again, the tall fellow, still frowning, brought the other to the ground with a single sharp flick of the lash. Retief looked him over. This was a man to watch.

More whistles, and a field now almost cleared; only two men left out of each original five; the blond moved out into the circle, stared across at the other. Retief recognized him suddenly as the fellow who had challenged him outside the gate, over the spilled fruit. So he had followed through the arch.

The final whistle sounded and a hush fell over the watchers. Now the shuffle of feet could be heard clearly, the hissing breath of the weary fighters, the creak and slap of leather.

The blond youth flipped his lash out lightly, saw it easily evaded, stepped aside from a sharp counterblow. He feinted, reversed the direction of his cast, and caught the other high on the chest as he dodged aside. A welt showed instantly. He saw a lightning-fast riposte on the way, sprang back. The gauntlet came up barely in time. The lash wrapped around the gauntlet, and the young fellow seized the leather, hauled sharply. The other stumbled forward. The blond brought his whip across the fellow's back in a tremendous slamming blow that sent a great fragment of torn shirt flying. Somehow the man stayed on his feet, backed off, circled. His opponent followed up, laying down one whistling whipcrack after another, trying to drive the other over the line. He had hurt the man with the cut across the back, and now was attempting to finish him easily.

He leaned away from a sluggish pass, and then Retief saw agony explode in his face as a vicious cut struck home. The blond youth reeled in a drunken circle, out on his feet. Slow to follow up, the enemy's lash crashed across the circle; the youth, steadying quickly, slipped under it, struck at the other's stomach. The leather cannoned against the man, sent the remainder of his shirt fluttering in a spatter of blood. With a surge of shoulder and wrist that made the muscles creak, the blond reversed the stroke, brought the lash back in a vicious cut aimed at the same spot. It struck, smacking with a wet explosive crack. And he struck again, again, as the fellow tottered back, fell over the line.

The winner went limp suddenly, staring across at the man who lay in the dust, pale now, moving feebly for a moment, then slackly still. There was a great deal of blood, and more blood. Retief saw with sudden shock that the man was disemboweled. That boy, thought Retief, plays for keeps.

The next two events constituting the First Day trials were undistinguished exhibitions of a two-handed version of an old American Indian wrestling and a brief bout of fencing with blunt-tipped weapons. Eighty men were certified for the Second Day before noon, and Retief and Fitzraven were back in the inn room a few minutes later. "Take some time off now while I catch up on my rest," Retief said. "Have some solid food ready when I wake." Then he retired for the night.

With his master breathing heavily in a profound sleep, the squire went down to the common room and found a table at the back, ordered a mug of strong ale, and sat alone, thinking.

This was a strange one he had met this year. He had seen at once that he was no idler from some high-pressure world, trying to lose himself in a fantasy of the old days. And no more was he a Northroyalan; there was a grim force in him, a time-engraved stamp of power that was alien to the neat well-ordered little world. And yet there was no doubt that there was more in him of the true Cavalier than in a Fragonard-born courtier. He was like some ancient warrior noble from the days of the greatness of the Empire. By the two heads, the old man was strange, and terrible in anger!

Fitzraven listened to the talk around him.

"I was just above," a blacksmith at the next table was saying. "He gutted the fellow with the lash! It was monstrous! I'm glad I'm not one of the fools who want to play at warrior. Imagine having your insides drawn out by a rope of dirty leather!"

"The games have to be tougher now," said another. "We've lain dormant here for two centuries, waiting for something to come—some thing to set us on our way again to power and wealth. . . ."

"Thanks, I'd rather go on living quietly as a smith and enjoying a few of the simple pleasures—there was no glory in that fellow lying in the dirt with his belly torn open, you can be sure of that."

"There'll be more than torn bellies to think about, when we mount a battle fleet for Grimwold and Tania," said another.

''The Emperor has returned,'' snapped the warlike one. ''Shall we hang back where he leads?''

The smith muttered. ''His is a tortured genealogy, by my judgment. I myself trace my ancestry by three lines into the old Palace at Lily.''

''So do we all. All the more reason we should support our Emperor.''

''We live well here; we have no quarrel with other worlds. Why not leave the past to itself?''

''Our Emperor leads; we will follow. If you disapprove, enter the Lily Tournament next year and win a high place; then your advice will be respected.''

''No thanks. I like my insides to stay on the inside.''

Fitzraven thought of Retief. The old man had said that he held his rank in his own right, citing no genealogy. That was strange indeed. The Emperor had turned up only a year ago, presenting the Robe, the Ring, the Seal, the crown jewels, and the Imperial Book which traced his descent through five generations from the last reigning Emperor of the Old Empire.

How could it be that Retief held a commission in his own right, dated no more than thirty years ago? And the rank of Battle Commander. That was a special rank, Fitzraven remembered, a detached rank for a distinguished noble and officer of proven greatness, assigned to no one unit, but dictating his own activities.

Either Retief was a fraud . . . but Fitzraven pictured the old man, his chiseled features that time had not disguised, his soldier's bearing, his fantastic strength, his undoubtedly authentic equipage. Whatever the explanation, he was a true knight. That was enough.

Retief awoke refreshed, and ravenous. A great rare steak and a giant tankard of autumn ale were ready on the table. He ate, ordered more and ate again. Then he stretched, shook himself, no trace of yesterday's fatigue remaining. His temper was better, too, he realized. He was getting too old to exhaust himself.

''It's getting late, Fitzraven,'' he said. ''Let's be going.''

They arrived at the arena and took their places in the official box in time to watch the first event, a cautious engagement with swords.

* * *

After four more events and three teams of determined but colorless competition, only a dozen men were left on the field awaiting the next event, including the tall blond youth whom Retief had been watching since he had recognized him. He himself, he reflected, was the reason for the man's presence here; and he had acquitted himself well.

Retief saw a burly warrior carrying a two-handed sword paired off now against the blond youth. The fellow grinned as he moved up to face the other.

This would be a little different, the agent thought, watching; this fellow was dangerous. Yellow-hair moved in, his weapon held level across his chest. The big man lashed out suddenly with the great sword, and the other jumped back, then struck backhanded at his opponent's shoulder, nicked him lightly, sliding back barely in time to avoid a return swing. The still grinning man moved in, the blade chopping the air before him in a whistling figure-eight. He pressed his man back, the blade never pausing.

There was no more room; the blond fellow jumped sideways, dropping the point of his sword in time to intercept a vicious cut. He backstepped; he couldn't let that happen again. The big man was very strong.

The blade was moving again now, the grin having faded a little. He'll have to keep away from him, keep circling, Retief thought. The big fellow's pattern is to push his man back to the edge, then pick him off as he tries to sidestep. He'll have to keep space between them.

The fair-haired man backed, watching for an opening. He jumped to the right, and as the other shifted to face him, leaped back to the left and catching the big man at the end of his reach to the other side, slashed him across the ribs and kept moving. The man roared, twisting around in vicious cuts at the figure that darted sideways, just out of range. Then the blond brought his claymore across in a low swing that struck solidly across the back of the other's legs, with a noise like a butcher separating ribs with a cleaver.

Like a marionette with his strings cut, the man folded to his knees, sprawled. The other man stepped back, as surgeons' men swarmed up to tend the fallen fighter. There were plenty of them available now; so far the casualties had been twice normal. On the other mounds in view, men were falling. The faint-hearted had been eliminated; the men who were still on their feet were determined, or desperate. There would be no more push-overs.

"Only about six left," Fitzraven called.

"This has been a rather unusual tournament so far," Retief said. "That young fellow with the light hair seems to be playing rough, forcing the pace."

"I have never seen such a businesslike affair," Fitzraven said. "The weak-disposed have been frightened out, and the fighters cut down with record speed. At this rate there will be none left for the Third Day."

There was delay on the field, as referees and other officials hurried back and forth; then an announcement boomed out. The Second Day was officially concluded. The six survivors would be awarded Second Day certificates, and would be eligible for the Third and Last Day tomorrow.

Retief and Fitzraven left the box, made their way through the crowd back to the inn.

"See that Danger-by-Night is well fed and exercised," Retief said to the squire. "And check over all of my gear thoroughly. I wish to put on my best appearance tomorrow; it will doubtless be my last outing of the kind for some time."

Fitzraven hurried away to tend his chores, while Retief ascended to his room to pore over the contents of his dispatch case far into the night.

The Third Day had dawned gray and chill, and an icy wind whipped across the arena. The weather had not discouraged the crowd, however. The stands were packed and the overflow of people stood in the aisles, perched high on the back walls, crowding every available space. Banners flying from the Imperial box indicated the presence of the royal party. This was the climactic day. The field, by contrast, was almost empty; two of the Second Day winners had not reentered for today's events, having apparently decided that they had had enough honor for one year. They would receive handsome prizes, and respectable titles; that was enough.

The four who had come to the arena today to stake their winning and their lives on their skill at arms would be worth watching, Retief thought. There was the blond young fellow, still unmarked; a great swarthy ruffian; a tall broad man of perhaps thirty; and a squat bowlegged fellow with enormous shoulders and long arms. They were here to win or die.

From the officials' box Retief and Fitzraven had an excellent view of the arena, where a large circle had been marked out. The officials seated nearby had given them cold glances as they entered, but no one had attempted to interfere. Apparently, they had accepted the situation. Possibly, Retief thought, they had actually studied the Charter. He hoped they had studied it carefully. It would make things easier.

Announcements boomed, officials moved about, fanfares blasted, while Retief sat absorbed in thought. The scene reminded him of things he had long forgotten, days long gone, of his youth, when he had studied the martial skills, serving a long apprenticeship under his world's greatest masters. It had been his father's conviction that nothing so trained the eye and mind and body as fencing, judo, savate, and the disciplines of the arts of offense, and defense.

He had abandoned a priceless education when he had left his home to seek his fortune in the mainstream of galactic culture, but it had stood him in good stead on more than one occasion. An agent of the Corps could not afford to let himself decline into physical helplessness, and Retief had maintained his skills as well as possible. He leaned forward now, adjusting his binoculars as the bugles rang out. Few in the crowd were better qualified than Retief to judge today's performance. It would be interesting to see how the champions handled themselves on the field.

The first event was about to begin, as the blond warrior was paired off with the bowlegged man. The two had been issued slender foils, and now faced each other, blades crossed. A final whistle blew, and blade clashed on blade. The squat man was fast on his feet, bounding around in a semicircle before his taller antagonist, probing his defense with great energy. The blond man backed away slowly, fending off the rain of blows with slight motions of his foil. He jumped back suddenly, and Retief saw a red spot grow on his thigh. The apelike fellow was more dangerous than he had appeared.

Now the blond man launched his attack, beating aside the weapon of the other and striking in for the throat, only to have his point deflected at the last instant. The short man backed now, giving ground reluctantly. Suddenly he dropped into a grotesque crouch, and lunged under the other's defense in a desperate try for a quick kill. It was a mistake; the taller man whirled aside; and his blade flicked delicately once. The bowlegged man slid out flat on his face.

"What happened?" Fitzraven said, puzzled. "I didn't see the stroke that nailed him."

"It was very pretty," Retief said thoughtfully, lowering the glasses. "Under the fifth rib and into the heart."

Now the big dark man and the tall broad fellow took their places. The bugles and whistles sounded, and the two launched a furious exchange, first one and then the other forcing his enemy back before losing ground in turn. The crowd roared its approval as the two stamped and thrust, parried and lunged.

"They can't keep up this pace forever," Fitzraven said. "They'll have to slow down."

"They're both good," Retief said. "And evenly matched."

Now the swarthy fellow leaped back, switched the foil to his left hand, then moved quickly in to the attack. Thrown off his pace, the other man faltered, let the blade nick him on the chest, again in the arm. Desperate, he backpedaled, fighting defensively now. The dark man followed up his advantage, pressing savagely, and a moment later Retief saw a foot of bright steel projecting startlingly from the tall man's back. He took two steps, then folded, as the foil was wrenched from the dark man's hand.

Wave upon wave of sound rolled across the packed stands. Never had they seen such an exhibition as this! It was like the legendary battle of the heroes of the Empire, the fighters who had carried the Lily banner half across the galaxy.

"I'm afraid that's all," Fitzraven said. "These two can elect either to share the victory of the Tourney now, or to contend for sole honors, and in the history of the Tournament on Northroyal, there have never been fewer than three to share the day."

"It looks as though this is going to be a first time, then," Retief said. "They're getting ready to square off."

Below on the field, a mass of officials surrounded the dark man and the fair one, while the crowd outdid itself. Then a bugle sounded in an elaborate salute.

"That's it," Fitzraven said excitedly. "Heroes' Salute. They're going to do it."

"You don't know how glad I am to hear that," Retief said.

"What will the weapon be?" the squire wondered aloud.

"My guess is, something less deadly than the foil," Retief replied.

Moments later the announcement came. The two champions of the day would settle the issue with bare hands. This, thought Retief, would be something to see.

The fanfares and whistles rang out again, and the two men moved cautiously together. The dark man swung an open-handed blow, which smacked harmlessly against the other's shoulder. An instant later the blond youth feinted a kick, instead drove a hard left to the dark man's chin, staggering him. He followed up, smashing two blows to the stomach, then another to the head. The dark man moved back, suddenly reached for the blond man's wrist as he missed a jab, whirled, and attempted to throw his opponent. The blond man slipped aside, and locked his right arm over the dark man's head, seizing his own right wrist with his left hand. The dark man twisted, fell heavily on the other man, reaching for a headlock of his own.

The two rolled in the dust, then broke apart and were on their feet again. The dark man moved in, swung an open-handed slap which popped loudly against the blond man's face. It was a device, Retief saw, to enrage the man, dull the edge of his skill.

The blond man refused to be rattled, however; he landed blows against the dark man's head, evaded another attempt to grapple. It was plain that he preferred to avoid the other's bearlike embrace. He boxed carefully, giving ground, landing a blow as the opportunity offered. The dark man followed doggedly, seemingly unaffected by the pounding. Suddenly he leaped, took two smashing blows full in the face, and crashed against the blond man, knocking him to the ground. There was a flying blur of flailing arms and legs as the two rolled across the turf, and as they came to rest, Retief saw that the dark man had gotten his break. Kneeling behind the other, he held him in a rigid stranglehold, his back and shoulder muscles bulging with the effort of holding his powerful adversary immobilized.

"It's all over," Fitzraven said tensely.

"Maybe not," Retief replied. "Not if he plays it right, and doesn't panic."

The blond man strained at the arm locked at his throat, twisting it fruitlessly. Instinct drove him to tear at the throttling grip, throw off the smothering weight. But the dark man's grip was solid, his position unshakable. Then the blond stopped struggling abruptly and the two seemed as still as an image in stone. The crowd fell silent, fascinated.

"He's given up," Fitzraven said.

"No; watch," Retief said. "He's starting to use his head."

The blond man's arms reached up now, his hands moving over the other's head, seeking a grip. The dark man pulled his head in, pressing against his victim's back, trying to elude his grip. Then the hands found a hold, and the blond man bent suddenly forward, heaving with a tremendous surge. The dark man came up, flipped high, his grip slipping. The blond rose as the other went over his head, shifted his grip in midair, and as the dark man fell heavily in front of him, the snap of the spine could be heard loud in the stillness. The battle was over, and the blond victor rose to his feet amid a roar of applause.

Retief turned to Fitzraven. "Time for us to be going, Fitz," he said.

The squire jumped up. "As you command, sir; but the ceremony is quite interesting. . . ."

"Never mind that; let's go." Retief moved off, Fitzraven following, puzzled.

Retief descended the steps inside the stands, turned and started down the corridor.

"This way, sir," Fitzraven called. "That leads to the arena."

"I know it," Retief said. "That's where I'm headed."

Fitzraven hurried up alongside. What was the old man going to do now? "Sir," he said, "no one may enter the arena until the tourney has been closed, except the gladiators and the officials. I know this to be an unbreakable law."

"That's right, Fitz," Retief said. "You'll have to stop at the grooms' enclosure."

"But you, sir," Fitzraven gasped . . .

"Everything's under control," Retief said. "I'm going to challenge the champion."

In the Imperial box, the Emperor Rolan leaned forward, fixing his binoculars on a group of figures at the officials' gate. There seemed to be some sort of disturbance there. This was a piece of damned impudence, just as the moment had arrived for the

Imperial presentation of the Honors of the Day. The Emperor turned to an aide.

"What the devil's going on down there?" he snapped.

The courtier murmured into a communicator, listened.

"A madman, Imperial Majesty," he said smoothly. "He wished to challenge the champion."

"A drunk, more likely," Rolan said sharply. "Let him be removed at once. And tell the Master of the Games to get on with the ceremony!"

The Emperor turned to the slim dark girl at his side.

"Have you found the Games entertaining, Monica?"

"Yes, sire," she replied unemotionally.

"Don't call me that, Monica," he said testily. "Between us there is no need for formalities."

"Yes, Uncle," the girl said.

"Damn it, that's worse," he said. "To you I am simply Rolan." He placed his hand firmly on her silken knee. "And now if they'll get on with this tedious ceremony, I should like to be on the way. I'm looking forward with great pleasure to showing you my estates at Snowdahl."

The Emperor drummed his fingers, stared down at the field, raised the glasses only to see the commotion again.

"Get that fool off the field," he shouted, dropping the glasses. "Am I to wait while they haggle with this idiot? It's insufferable. . . ."

Courtiers scurried, while Rolan glared down from his seat.

Below, Retief faced a cluster of irate referees. One, who had attempted to haul Retief bodily backward, was slumped on a bench, attended by two surgeons.

"I claim the right to challenge, under the Charter," Retief repeated. "Nobody here will be so foolish, I hope, as to attempt to deprive me of that right, now that I have reminded you of the justice of my demand."

From the control cage directly below the Emperor's high box, a tall seam-faced man in black breeches and jacket emerged, followed by two armed men. The officials darted ahead, stringing out between the two, calling out. Behind Retief, on the other side of the barrier, Fitzraven watched anxiously. The old man was full of surprises, and had a way of getting what he wanted; but even if he had the right to challenge the Champion of the

Games, what purpose could he have in doing so? He was as strong as a bull, but no man his age could be a match for the youthful power of the blond fighter. Fitzraven was worried; he was fond of this old warrior. He would hate to see him locked behind the steel walls of Fragonard Keep for thus disturbing the order of the Lily Tournament. He moved closer to the barrier, watching.

The tall man in black strode through the chattering officials, stopped before Retief, motioned his two guards forward.

He made a dismissing motion toward Retief. "Take him off the field," he said brusquely. The guards stepped up, laid hands on Retief's arms. He let them get a grip, then suddenly stepped back and brought his arms together. The two men cracked heads, stumbled back. Retief looked at the black-clad man.

"If you are the Master of the Games," he said clearly, "you are well aware that a decorated battle officer has the right of challenge, under the Imperial Charter. I invoke that prerogative now, to enter the lists against the man who holds the field."

"Get out, you fool," the official hissed, white with fury. "The Emperor himself has commanded—"

"Not even the Emperor can override the Charter, which pre-dates his authority by four hundred years," Retief said coldly. "Now do your duty."

"There'll be no more babble of duties and citing of technicalities while the Emperor waits," the official snapped. He turned to one of the two guards, who hung back now, eyeing Retief. "You have a pistol; draw it. If I give the command, shoot him between the eyes."

Retief reached up and adjusted a tiny stud set in the stiff collar of his tunic. He tapped his finger lightly against the cloth. The sound boomed across the arena. A command microphone of the type authorized a Battle Commander was a very efficient device.

"I have claimed the right to challenge the champion," he said slowly. The words rolled out like thunder. "This right is guaranteed under the Charter to any Imperial battle officer who wears the Silver Star."

The Master of the Games stared at him aghast. This was getting out of control. Where the devil had the old man gotten a microphone and a PA system? The crowd was roaring now like a gigantic surf. This was something new!

Far above in the Imperial box the tall gray-eyed man was rising, turning toward the exit. "The effrontery," he said in a voice choked with rage. "That I should sit awaiting the pleasure . . ."

The girl at his side hesitated, hearing the amplified voice booming across the arena.

"Wait, Rolan," she said. "Something is happening. . . ."

The man looked back. "A trifle late," he snapped.

"One of the contestants is disputing something," she said. "There was an announcement—something about an Imperial officer challenging the champion."

The Emperor Rolan turned to an aide hovering nearby.

"What is this nonsense?"

The courtier bowed. "It is merely a technicality, Majesty. A formality lingering on from earlier times."

"Be specific," the Emperor snapped.

The aide lost some of his aplomb. "Why, it means, ah, that an officer of the Imperial forces holding a battle commission and certain high decorations may enter the lists at any point, without other qualifying conditions. A provision never invoked under modern . . ."

The Emperor turned to the girl. "It appears that someone seeks to turn the entire performance into a farcical affair, at my expense," he said bitterly. "We shall see just how far—"

"I call on you, Rolan," Retief's voice boomed, "to enforce the Code."

"What impertinence is this?" Rolan growled. "Who is the fool at the microphone?"

The aide spoke into his communicator, listened.

"An old man from the crowd, sire. He wears the insignia of a Battle Commander, and a number of decorations, including the Silver Star. According to the Archivist, he has the legal right to challenge."

"I won't have it," Rolan snapped. "A fine reflection on me that would be. Have them take the fellow away; he's doubtless crazed." He left the box, followed by his entourage.

"Rolan," the girl said, "wasn't that the way the Tourneys were, back in the days of the Empire?"

"*These* are the days of the Empire, Monica. And I am not interested in what used to be done. This is today. Am I to present the spectacle of a doddering old fool being hacked to bits, in my name? I don't want the timid to be shocked by butchery. It might have unfortunate results for my propaganda program. I'm currently emphasizing the glorious aspects of the coming war, not the sordid ones. There has already been too much bloodshed today; an inauspicious omen for my expansion plan."

On the field below, the Master of the Games stepped closer to Retief. He felt the cold eyes of the Emperor himself boring into his back. This old devil could bring about his ruin. . . .

"I know all about you," he snarled. "I've checked on you, since you forced your way into an official area; I interviewed two officers . . . you overawed them with glib talk and this threadbare finery you've decked yourself in. Now you attempt to ride rough-shod over me. Well, I'm not so easily thrust aside. If you resist arrest any further, I'll have you shot where you stand!"

Retief drew his sword.

"In the name of the Code you are sworn to serve," he said, his voice ringing across the arena. "I will defend my position." He reached up and flipped the stud at his throat to full pick-up.

"To the Pit with your infernal Code!" bellowed the Master, and blanched in horror as his words boomed sharp and clear across the field to the ears of a hundred thousand people. He stared around, then whirled back to Retief. "Fire," he screamed.

A pistol cracked, and the guard spun, dropped. Fitzraven held the tiny power gun leveled across the barrier at the other guard. "What next, sir?" he asked brightly.

The sound of the shot, amplified, smashed deafeningly across the arena, followed by a mob roar of excitement, bewilderment, shock. The group around Retief stood frozen, staring at the dead man. The Master of the Games made a croaking sound, eyes bulging. The remaining guard cast a glance at the pistol, then turned and ran.

There were calls from across the field; then a troop of brown-uniformed men emerged from an entry, trotted toward the group. The officer at their head carried a rapid-fire shock gun in his hand. He waved his squad to a halt as he reached the fringe of the group. He stared at Retief's drab uniform, glanced at the corpse. Retief saw that the officer was young, determined-looking, wearing the simple insignia of a Battle Ensign.

The Master of the Games found his voice. "Arrest this villain!" he screeched, pointing at Retief. "Shoot the murderer!"

The ensign drew himself to attention, saluted crisply.

"Your orders, sir," he said.

"I've told you!" the Master howled. "Seize this malefactor!"

The ensign turned to the black-clad official. "Silence, sir, or I shall be forced to remove you," he said sharply. He looked at Retief. "I await the Commander's orders."

Retief smiled, returned the young officer's salute with a wave of his sword, then sheathed it. "I'm glad to see a little sense displayed here, at last, Battle Ensign," he said. "I was beginning to fear I'd fallen among Concordiatists."

The outraged Master began an harangue which was abruptly silenced by two riot police. He was led away, protesting. The other officials disappeared like a morning mist, carrying the dead guard.

"I've issued my challenge, Ensign," Retief said. "I wish it to be conveyed to the champion-apparent at once." He smiled. "And I'd like you to keep your men around to see that nothing interferes with the orderly progress of the Tourney in accordance with the Charter in its original form."

The ensign's eyes sparkled. Now here was a battle officer who sounded like a fighting man; not a windbag like the commandant of the Household Regiment from whom the ensign took his orders. He didn't know where the old man came from, but any battle officer outranked any civilian or flabby barracks soldier, and this was a Battle Commander, a general officer, and of the Dragon Corps!

Minutes later, a chastened Master of the Games announced that a challenge had been issued. It was the privilege of the champion to accept, or to refuse the challenge if he wished. In the latter event, the challenge would automatically be met the following year.

"I don't know what your boys said to the man," Retief remarked, as he walked out to the combat circle, the ensign at his left side and slightly to the rear, "but they seem to have him educated quickly."

"They can be very persuasive, sir," the young officer replied.

They reached the circle, stood waiting. Now, thought Retief, I've got myself in the position I've been working toward. The question now is whether I'm still man enough to put it over.

He looked up at the massed stands, listening to the mighty roar of the crowd. There would be no easy out for him now. Of course, the new champion might refuse to fight; he had every right to do so, feeling he had earned his year's rest and enjoyment of his winnings. But that would be a defeat for Retief as final as death on the dusty ground of the arena. He had come this far by bluff, threat, and surprise. He would never come this close again.

It was luck that he had clashed with this young man outside the gate, challenged him to enter the lists. That might give the challenge the personal quality that would elicit an angry acceptance.

The champion was walking toward Retief now, surrounded by referees. He stared at the old man, eyes narrowed. Retief returned the look calmly.

"Is this dodderer the challenger?" the blond youth asked scathingly. "It seems to me I have met his large mouth before?"

"Never mind my mouth, merchant," Retief said loudly. "It is not talk I offer you, but the bite of steel."

The yellow-haired man reddened, then laughed shortly. "Small glory I'd win out of skewering you, old graybeard."

"You'd get even less out of showing your heels," Retief said.

"You will not provoke me into satisfying your perverted ambition to die here," the other retorted.

"It's interesting to note," Retief said, "how a peasant peddler wags his tongue to avoid a fight. Such rabble should not be permitted on honorable ground." He studied the other's face to judge how this line of taunting was going on. It was distasteful to have to embarrass the young fellow; he seemed a decent sort. But he had to enrage him to the point that he would discard his wisdom and throw his new-won prize on the table for yet another cast of the dice. And his sore point seemed to be mention of commerce.

"Back to your cabbages, then, fellow," Retief said harshly, "before I whip you there with the flat of my sword."

The young fellow looked at him, studying him. His face was grim. "All right," he said quietly. "I'll meet you in the circle."

Another point gained, Retief thought, as he moved to his position at the edge of the circle. Now, if I can get him to agree to fight on horseback . . .

He turned to a referee. "I wish to suggest that this contest be conducted on horseback—if the peddler owns a horse and is not afraid."

The point was discussed between the referee and the champion's attendants, with many glances at Retief, and much waving of arms. The official returned. "The champion agrees to meet you by day or by night, in heat or cold, on foot or on horseback."

"Good," said Retief. "Tell my groom to bring out my mount."

It was no idle impulse which prompted this move. Retief had no illusions as to what it would take to win a victory over the champion. He knew that his legs, while good enough for most of the business of daily life, were his weakest point. They were no longer the nimble tireless limbs that had once carried him up to meet the outlaw Mal de Di alone in Bifrost Pass. Nine hours later he had brought the bandit's two-hundred-and-ten-pound body down into the village on his back, his own arm broken. He had been a mere boy then, younger than this man he was now to meet. He had taken up Mal de Di's standing challenge to any unarmed man who would come alone to the high pass, to prove that he was not too young to play a man's part. Perhaps now he was trying to prove he was not too old. . . .

An official approached leading Danger-by-Night. It took an expert to appreciate the true worth of the great gaunt animal, Retief knew. To the uninitiated eye, he presented a sorry appearance, but Retief would rather have had this mount with the Imperial brand on his side than a paddock full of show horses.

A fat white charger was led out to the blond champion. It looked like a strong animal, Retief thought, but slow. His chances were looking better, things were going well.

A ringing blast of massed trumpets cut through the clamor of the crowd. Retief mounted, watching his opponent. A referee came to his side, handed up a heavy club, studded with long projecting spikes. "Your weapon, sir," he said.

Retief took the thing. It was massive, clumsy; he had never before handled such a weapon. He knew no subtleties of technique with this primitive bludgeon. The blond youth had surprised him, he admitted to himself, smiling slightly. As the challenged party, he had the choice of weapons, of course. He had picked an unusual one.

Retief glanced across at Fitzraven, standing behind the inner barrier, jaw set, a grim expression on his face. That boy, thought Retief, doesn't have much confidence in my old bones holding out.

The whistle blew. Retief moved toward the other man at a trot, the club level at his side. He had decided to handle it like a shortsword, so long as that seemed practical. He would have to learn by experience.

The white horse cantered past him swerving, and the blond fellow whirled his club at Retief's head. Automatically, Retief raised his club, fended off the blow, cut at the other's back, missed. This thing is too short, Retief thought, whirling his horse. I've got to get in closer. He charged at the champion as the white horse was still in midturn, slammed a heavy blow against his upraised club, rocking the boy; then he was past, turning again. He caught the white horse shorter this time, barely into his turn, and aimed a swing at the man, who first twisted to face him, then spurred, leaped away. Retief pursued him, yelping loudly. Get him rattled, he thought. Get him good and mad!

The champion veered suddenly, veered again, then reared his horse high, whirling, to bring both forefeet down in a chopping attack. Retief reined in, and Danger-by-Night sidestepped disdainfully, as the heavy horse crashed down facing him.

That was a pretty maneuver, Retief thought; but slow, too slow.

His club swung in an overhand cut; the white horse tossed his head suddenly, and the club smashed down across the animal's skull. With a shuddering exhalation, the beast collapsed, and the blond man sprang clear.

Retief reined back, dismayed. He hadn't wanted to kill the animal. He had the right, now, to ride the man down from the safety of the saddle. When gladiators met in mortal combat, there were no rules except those a man made for himself. If he dismounted, met his opponent on equal terms, the advantage his horse had given him would be lost. He looked at the man standing now, facing him, waiting, blood on his face from the fall. He thought of the job he had set himself, the plan that hinged on his victory here. He reminded himself that he was old, too old to meet youth on equal terms; but even as he did so, he was reining the lean battle stallion back, swinging down from the saddle. There were some things a man had to do, whether logic was served or not. He couldn't club the man down like a mad dog from the saddle.

There was a strange expression on the champion's face. He sketched a salute with the club he held. "All honor to you, old man," he said. "Now I will kill you." He moved in confidently.

Retief stood his ground, raising his club to deflect a blow, shifting an instant ahead of the pattern of the blond man's assault. There was a hot exchange as the younger man pressed him, took a glancing blow on the temple, stepped back breathing heavily. This wasn't going as he had planned. The old man stood like a wall of stone, not giving an inch; and when their weapons met, it was like flailing at a granite boulder. The young fellow's shoulder ached from the shock. He moved sideways, circling cautiously.

Retief moved to face him. It was risky business, standing up to the attack, but his legs were not up to any fancy footwork. He had no desire to show his opponent how stiff his movements were, or to tire himself with skipping about. His arms were still as good as any man's, or better. They would have to carry the battle.

The blond jumped in, swung a vicious cut; Retief leaned back, hit out in a one-handed blow, felt the club smack solidly against the other's jaw. He moved now, followed up, landed again on the shoulder. The younger man backed, shaking his head. Retief stopped, waited. It was too bad he couldn't follow up his advantage, but he couldn't chase the fellow all over the arena. He had to save his energy for an emergency. He lowered his club, leaned on it. The crowd noises waxed and waned, unnoticed. The sun beat down in unshielded whiteness, and fitful wind moved dust across the field.

"Come back, peddler," he called. "I want you to sample more of my wares," If he could keep the man angry, he would be careless; and Retief needed the advantage.

The yellow-haired man charged suddenly, whirling the club. Retief raised his, felt the shock of the other's weapon against his. He whirled as the blond darted around him, shifted the club to his left hand in time to ward off a wild swing. Then the fingers of his left hand exploded in fiery agony, and the club flew from his grasp. His head whirled, vision darkening, at the pain from his smashed fingers. He tottered, kept his feet, managed to blink away the faintness, to stare at this hand. Two fingers were missing, pulped, unrecognizable. He had lost his weapon; he was helpless now before the assault of the other.

His head hummed harshly, and his breath came like hot sand across an open wound. He could feel a tremor start and stop in his leg, and his whole left arm felt as though it had been stripped of flesh in a shredding machine. He had not thought it would be as bad as this. His ego, he realized, hadn't aged gracefully.

Now is the hour, old man, he thought. There's no help for you to call on, no easy way out. You'll have to look within yourself for some hidden reserve of strength and endurance and will; and you must think well now, wisely, with a keen eye and a quick hand, or lose your venture. With a movement stiffened by the racking pain-shock, he drew his ceremonial dagger, a jewel-encrusted blade ten inches long. At the least he would die with a weapon in his hand and his face to the enemy.

The blond youth moved closer, tossed the club aside.

"Shall a peddler be less capable of the *beau geste* than the arrogant knight?" He laughed, drawing a knife from his belt. "Is your head clear, old man?" he asked. "Are you ready?"

"A gesture . . . you can . . . . ill afford," Retief managed. Even breathing hurt. His nerves were shrieking their message of shock at the crushing of living flesh and bone. His forehead was pale, wet with cold sweat.

The young fellow closed, struck out, and Retief evaded the point by an inch, stepped back. His body couldn't stand pain as once it had, he was realizing. He had grown soft, sensitive. For too many years he had been a Diplomat, an operator by manipulation, by subtlety and finesse. Now, when it was man to man, brute strength against brute strength, he was failing.

But he had known when he started that strength was not enough, not without agility; it was subtlety he should be relying on now, his skill at trickery, his devious wit.

Retief caught a glimpse of staring faces at the edge of the field, heard for a moment the mob roar, and then he was again wholly concentrated on the business at hand.

He breathed deeply, struggling for clear-headedness. He had to inveigle the boy into a contest in which he stood a chance. If he could put him on his mettle, make him give up his advantage of tireless energy, quickness . . .

"Are you an honest peddler, or a dancing master?" Retief managed to growl. "Stand and meet me face to face."

The blond man said nothing, feinting rapidly, then striking out. Retief was ready, nicked the other's wrist.

"Gutter fighting is one thing," Retief said. "But you are afraid to face the old man's steel, right arm against right arm." If he went for that, Retief thought, he was even younger than he looked.

"I have heard of the practice," the blond man said, striking at Retief, moving aside from a return cut. "It was devised for old men who did not wish to be made ridiculous by more agile men. I understand that you think you can hoodwink me, but I can beat you at your own game. . . ."

"My point awaits your pleasure," Retief said.

The younger man moved closer, knife held before him. Just a little closer, Retief thought. Just a little closer.

The blond man's eyes were on Retief's. Without warning, Retief dropped his knife and in a lightning motion caught the other's wrist.

"Now struggle, little fish," he said. "I have you fast."

The two men stood chest to chest, staring into each other's eyes. Retief's breath came hard, his heart pounded almost painfully. His left arm was a great pulsating weight of pain. Sweat ran down his dusty face into his eyes. But his grip was locked solidly. The blond youth strained in vain.

With a twist of his wrist Retief turned the blade, then forced the youth's arm up. The fellow struggled to prevent it, throwing all his weight into his effort, fruitlessly. Retief smiled.

"I won't kill you," he said, "but I will have to break your arm. That way you cannot be expected to continue the fight."

"I want no favors from you, old man," the youth panted.

"You won't consider this a favor until the bones knit," Retief said. "Consider this a fair return for my hand."

He pushed the arm up, then suddenly turned it back, levered the upper arm over his forearm, and yanked the tortured member down behind the blond man's back. The bones snapped audibly, and the white-faced youth gasped, staggered as Retief released him.

There were minutes of confusion as referees rushed in, announcements rang out, medics hovered, and the crowd roared its satisfaction, after the fickle nature of crowds. They were satisfied.

An official pushed through to Retief. He wore the vivid colors of the Review regiment. Retief reached up and set the control on the command mike.

"I have the honor to advise you, sir, that you have won the field, and the honors of the day." He paused, startled at the booming echoes, then went on. The bystanders watched curiously, as Retief tried to hold his concentration on the man, to stand easily, while blackness threatened to move in over him. The pain from the crushed hand swelled and focused, then faded, came again. The great dry lungfuls of air he drew in failed to dispel the sensation of suffocation. He struggled to understand the words that seemed to echo from a great distance.

"And now in the name of the Emperor, for crimes against the peace and order of the Empire, I place you under arrest for trial before the High Court at Fragonard."

Retief drew a deep breath, gathered his thoughts to speak.

"Nothing," he said, "could possibly please me more."

The room was vast and ornate, and packed with dignitaries, high officials, peers of the Lily. Here in the great chamber known as the Blue Vault, the High Court sat in silent ranks, waiting.

The charges had been read, the evidence presented. The prisoner, impersonating a peer of the Lily and an officer of an ancient and honored Corps, had flaunted the law of Northroyal and the authority of the Emperor, capping his audacity with murder, done by the hand of his servant sworn. Had the prisoner anything to say?

Retief, alone in the prisoner's box in the center of the room, his arm heavily bandaged and deadened with dope, faced the court. This would be the moment when all his preparations would be put to the ultimate test. He had laid long plans toward this hour. The archives of the Corps were beyond comparison in the galaxy, and he had spent weeks there, absorbing every detail of the facts that had been recorded on the world of Northroyal, and on the Old Empire which had preceded it. And to the lore of the archives, he had added facts known to himself, data from his own wide experience. But would those tenuous threads of tradition, hearsay, rumor, and archaic record hold true now? That was the gamble on which his mission was staked. The rabbits had better be in the hat.

He looked at the dignitaries arrayed before him. It had been a devious route, but so far he had succeeded; he had before him the highest officials of the world, the High Justices, the Imperial Archivist, the official keepers of the Charter and the Code, and of the protocols and rituals of the tradition on which this society was based. He had risked everything on his assault on the sacred stasis of the Tournament, but how else could he have gained the ears of this select audience, with all Northroyal tuned in to hear the end of the drama that a hundred thousand had watched build to its shattering climax?

Now it was his turn to speak. It had better be good.

"Peers of the realm," Retief said, speaking clearly and slowly, "the basis of the charges laid against me is the assumption that I have falsified my identity. Throughout, I have done no more than exercise the traditional rights of a general officer and of a Lilyan peer, and, as befits a Cavalier, I have resisted all attempts to deprive me of those honored prerogatives. While it is regrettable that the low echelon of officials appears to be ignorant of the status of a Lilyan Battle Commander, it is my confident assumption that here, before the ranking nobles of the Northroyalan peerage, the justice of my position will be recognized."

As Retief paused, a dour graybeard spoke up from the Justices' bench.

"Your claims are incoherent to this court. You are known to none of us; and if by chance you claim descent from some renegade who deserted his fellow Cavaliers at the time of the Exile, you will find scant honor among honest men here. From this, it is obvious that you delude yourself in imagining that you can foist your masquerade on this court successfully."

"I am not native to Northroyal," Retief said, "nor do I claim to be. Nor am I a descendant of renegades. Are you gentlemen not overlooking the fact that there was one ship which did not accompany the Cavaliers into exile, but escaped Concordiat surveillance and retired to rally further opposition to the invasion?"

There was a flurry of muttered comment, putting together of heads, and shuffling of papers. The High Justice spoke.

"This would appear to be a reference to the vessel bearing the person of the Emperor Roquelle and his personal suite. . . ."

"That is correct," Retief said.

"You stray farther than ever from the credible," a justice snapped. "The entire royal household accompanied the Emperor Rolan on the happy occasion of his rejoining his subjects here at Northroyal a year ago."

"About that event, I will have more to say later," Retief said coolly. "For the present, suffice it to say that I am a legitimate descendant—"

"It does indeed *not* suffice to say!" barked the High Justice. "Do you intend to instruct this court as to what evidence will be acceptable?"

"A figure of speech, Milord," Retief said. "I am quite able to prove my statement."

"Very well," said the High Justice. "Let us see your proof, though I confess I cannot conceive of a satisfactory one."

Retief reached down, unsnapped the flat dispatch case at his belt, drew out a document.

"This is my proof of my bona fides," he said. "I present it in evidence that I have committed no fraud. I am sure that you will recognize an authentic commission-in-patent of the Emperor Roquelle. Please note that the seals are unbroken." He passed the paper over.

A page took the heavy paper, looped with faded red ribbon and plastered with saucer-sized seals, trotted over to the Justices' bench and handed it up to the High Justice. He took it, gazed at it, turning it over, then broke the crumbling seals. The nearby Justices leaned over to see this strange exhibit. It was a heavily embossed document of the Old Empire type, setting forth genealogy and honors, and signed in sprawling letters with the name of an emperor two centuries dead, sealed with his tarnished golden seal. The Justices stared in amazement. The document was worth a fortune.

"I ask that the lowermost paragraph be read aloud," Retief said. "The amendment of thirty years ago."

The High Justice hesitated, then waved a page to him, handed down the document. "Read the lowermost paragraph aloud," he said.

The page read in a clear, well-trained voice.

"KNOW ALL MEN BY THESE PRESENTS THAT WHEREAS:
THIS OUR LOYAL SUBJECT AND PEER OF THE IMPERIAL LILY
JAME JARL FREELORD OF THE RETIEF; OFFICER IMPERIAL OF
THE GUARD; OFFICER OF BATTLE; HEREDITARY LEGIONNAIRE
OF HONOR; CAVALIER OF THE LILY; DEFENDER OF SALIENT
WEST; BY IMPERIAL GRACE OFFICER OF THE SILVER STAR;
HAS BY HIS GALLANTRY, FIDELITY AND SKILL BROUGHT
HONOR TO THE IMPERIAL LILY: AND WHEREAS WE PLACE
SPECIAL CONFIDENCE AND ESTEEM IN THIS SUBJECT AND
PEER: WE DO THEREFORE APPOINT AND COMMAND THAT
HE SHALL FORTHWITH ASSUME AND HENCEFORTH BEAR THE
HONORABLE RANK OF BATTLE COMMANDER: AND THAT HE
SHALL BEAR THE OBLIGATIONS AND ENJOY THE PRIVILEGES
APPERTAINING THEREUNTO: AS SHALL HIS HEIRS FOREVER."

There was a silence in the chamber as the page finished reading. All eyes turned to Retief, who stood in the box, a strange expression on his face.

The page handed the paper back up to the High Justice, who resumed his perusal.

"I ask that my retinal patterns now be examined, and matched to those coded on the amendment," Retief said. The High Justice beckoned to a Messenger, and the court waited a restless five minutes until the arrival of an expert who quickly made the necessary check. He went to the Justice's bench, handed up a report form, and left the courtroom. The magistrate glanced at the form, turned again to the document. Below Roquelle's seal were a number of amendments, each in turn signed and sealed. The justices spelled out the unfamiliar names.

"Where did you get this?" the High Justice demanded uncertainly.

"It has been the property of my family for nine generations," Retief replied.

Heads nodded over the document, gray beards wagged.

"How is it," asked a Justice, "that you offer in evidence a document bearing amendments validated by signatures and seals completely unknown to us? In order to impress this court, such a warrant might well bear the names of actual former emperors, rather than of fictitious ones. I note the lowermost amendment, purporting to be a certification of high military rank dated only thirty years ago, is signed 'Ronare.' "

"I was at that time attached to the Imperial Suite-in-Exile," Retief said. "I commanded the forces of the Emperor Ronare."

The High Justice and a number of other members of the court snorted openly.

"This impertinence will not further your case," the old magistrate said sharply. "Ronare, indeed. You cite a nonexistent authority. At the alleged time of issue of this warrant, the father of our present monarch held the Imperial fief at Trallend."

"At the time of the issue of this document," Retief said in ringing tones, "the father of your present ruler held the bridle when the Emperor mounted!"

An uproar broke out from all sides. The Master-at-arms pounded in vain for silence. At length a measure of order was restored by a gangly official who rose and shouted for the floor. The roar died down, and the stringy fellow, clad in russet velvet with the gold chain of the Master of the Seal about his neck, called out, "Let the court find the traitor guilty summarily and put an end to this insupportable insolence. . . ."

"Northroyal has been the victim of fraud," Retief said loudly in the comparative lull. "But not on my part. The man Rolan is an imposter."

A tremendous pounding of gavels and staffs eventually brought the outraged dignitaries to grim silence. The Presiding Justice peered down at Retief with doom in his lensed eyes. "Your knowledge of the Lilyan tongue and of the forms of court practice as well as the identity of your retinal patterns with those of the warrant tend to substantiate your origin in the Empire. Accordingly, this court is now disposed to recognize in you that basest of offenders, a renegade of the peerage." He raised his voice. "Let it be recorded that one Jame Jarl, a freelord of the Imperial Lily and officer Imperial of the Guard has by his own words disavowed his oath and his lineage." The fiery old man glared around at his fellow jurists. "Now let the dog of a broken officer be sentenced!"

"I have proof of what I say," Retief called out. "Nothing has been proven against me. I have acted by the Code, and by the Code I demand my hearing!"

"You have spurned the Code," said a fat dignitary.

"I have told you that a usurper sits on the Lily throne," Retief said. "If I can't prove it, execute me."

There was an icy silence.

"Very well," said the High Justice. "Present your proof."

"When the man, Rolan, appeared," Retief said, "he presented the Imperial seal and ring, the ceremonial robe, the major portion of the crown jewels, and the Imperial Genealogy."

"That is correct."

"Was it noted, by any chance, that the seal was without its chain, that the robe was stained, that the most important of the jewels, the ancient Napoleon Emerald, was missing, that the ring bore deep scratches, and that the lock on the book had been forced?"

A murmur grew along the high benches of the court. Intent eyes glared down at Retief.

"And was it not considered strange that the Imperial signet was not presented by this would-be Emperor, when that signet alone constitutes the true symbol of the Empire?" Retief's voice had risen to a thunderous loudness.

The High Justice stared now with a different emotion in his eyes.

"What do you know of these matters?" he demanded, but without assurance.

Retief reached into a tiny leather bag at his side, drew out something which he held out for inspection.

"This is a broken chain," he said. "It was cut when the seal was stolen from its place in Suite-in-Exile." He placed the heavy links on the narrow wainscot before him. "This," he said, "is the Napoleon Emerald, once worn by the legendary Bonaparte in a ring. It is unique in the galaxy, and easily proved genuine." There was utter stillness now. Retief placed a small key beside the chain and the gem. "This key will open the forced lock of the Imperial Genealogical Record."

Retief brought out an ornately wrought small silver casket and held it in view.

"The stains on the robe are the blood of the Emperor Ronare, shed by the knife of a murderer. The ring is scratched by the same knife, used to sever the finger in order to remove the ring." A murmur of horrified comment ran round the room now. Retief waited, letting all eyes focus on the silver box in his hand. It contained a really superb copy of the Imperial Signet; like the chain, the key and the emerald, the best that the science of the Corps could produce, accurate even in its internal molecular structure. It had to be, if it were to have a chance of acceptance. It would be put to the test without delay, matched to an electronic matrix with which it would, if acceptable, resonate perfectly. The copy had been assembled on the basis of some excellent graphic records; the original signet, as Retief knew, had been lost irretrievably in a catastrophic palace fire, a century and a half ago.

He opened the box, showed the magnificent wine-red crystal set in platinum. Now was the moment. "This is the talisman which alone would prove the falseness of the impostor Rolan," Retief said. "I call upon the honorable High Court to match it to the matrix; and while that is being done, I ask that the honorable Justices study carefully the genealogy included in the Imperial patent which I have presented to the court."

A messenger was dispatched to bring in the matrix while the Justices adjusted the focus of their corrective lenses and clustered over the document. The chamber buzzed with tense excitement. This was a fantastic development indeed!

The High Justice looked up as the massive matrix device was wheeled into the room. He stared at Retief. "This genealogy—" he began.

A Justice plucked at his sleeve, indicated the machine, whispering something. The High Justice nodded.

Retief handed the silver box down carefully to a page, watched as the chamber of the machine was opened, the great crystal placed in position. He held his breath as technicians twiddled controls, studied dials, then closed a switch. There was a sonorous musical tone from the machine.

The technician looked up. "The crystal," he said, "does match the matrix."

Amid a burst of exclamations which died as he faced the High Justice, Retief spoke.

"My lords, peers of the Imperial Lily," he said in a ringing voice, "know by this signet that we, Retief, by the grace of God Emperor, do now claim our rightful throne."

And just as quickly as the exclamations had died, they rose once more—a mixture of surprise and awe.

EPILOGUE

"A brilliant piece of work, Mr. Minister, and congratulations on your promotion," the Ambassador-at-large said warmly. "You've shown what individualism and the unorthodox approach can accomplish where the academic viewpoint would consider the situation hopeless."

"Thank you, Mr. Ambassador," Retief replied, smiling. "I was surprised myself when it was all over, that my gamble paid off. Frankly, I hope I won't ever be in a position again to be quite so inventive."

"I don't mind telling you now," the Ambassador said, "that when I saw Magnan's report of your solo assignment to the case, I seriously attempted to recall you, but it was too late. It was a nasty piece of business sending a single agent in on a job with the wide implications of this one. Mr. Magnan had been under a strain, I'm afraid. He is having a long rest now. . . ."

Retief understood perfectly. His former chief had gotten the axe, and he himself had emerged clothed in virtue. That was the one compensation of desperate ventures; if you won, they paid well. In his new rank, he had a long tenure ahead. He hoped the next job would be something complex and far removed from Northroyal. He thought back over the crowded weeks of his brief reign there as Emperor. It had been a stormy scene when the bitterly resisting Rolan had been brought to face the High Court. The man had been hanged an hour before sunrise on the following day, still protesting his authenticity. That, at least, was a lie. Retief was grateful that he had proof that Rolan was a fraud, because he would have sent him to the gallows on false evidence even had he been the true heir.

His first act after his formal enthronement had been the abolition in perpetuity of the rite of the tourney, and the formal cancellation of all genealogical requirements for appointments public or private. He had ordered the release and promotion of the Battle Ensign who had ignored Rolan's arrest order and had been himself imprisoned for his pains. Fitzraven he had seen appointed to the Imperial War College—his future assured.

Retief smiled as he remembered the embarrassment of the young fellow who had been his fellow-finalist in the tourney. He had offered him satisfaction on the field of honor as soon as his arm healed, and had been asked in return for forgetfulness of poor judgment. He had made him a Captain of the Guard and a peer of the realm. He had the spirit for it.

There had been much more to do, and Retief's days had been crowded with the fantastically complex details of disengaging a social structure from the crippling reactionary restraints of ossified custom and hallowed tradition. In the end, he had produced a fresh and workable new constitution for the kingdom which he hoped would set the world on an enlightened and dynamic path to a productive future.

The memory of Princess Monica lingered pleasantly; a true princess of the Lily, in the old tradition. Retief had abdicated in her favor; her genealogy had been studded with enough Imperial forebears to satisfy the crustiest of the Old Guard peerage; of course, it could not compare with the handsome document he had displayed showing his own descent in the direct line through seven—or was it eight—generations of Emperors-in-exile from the lost monarch of the beleaguered Lily Empire, but it was enough to justify his choice. Rolan's abortive usurpation had at least had the effect of making the Northroyalans appreciate an enlightened ruler.

At the last, it had not been easy to turn away forever from the seat of Empire which he so easily sat. It had not been lightly that he had said good-by to the lovely Monica, who had reminded him of another dark beauty of long ago.

A few weeks in a modern hospital had remedied the harsher after-effects of his short career as a gladiator, and he was ready now for the next episode that fate and the Corps might have in store. But he would not soon forget Northroyal. . . .

". . . magnificent ingenuity," someone was saying. "You must have assimilated your indoctrination on the background unusually thoroughly to have been able to prepare in advance just those artifacts and documents which would prove most essential. And the technical skill in the production itself. Remarkable. To think that you were able to hoodwink the high priests of the cult in the very sanctum sanctorum."

"Merely the result of careful research," Retief said modestly. "I found all I needed on late developments, buried in our files. The making of the Signet was quite a piece of work; but credit for that goes to our own technicians."

"I was even more impressed by that document," a young

counselor said. "What a knowledge of their psychology and of technical detail that required."

Retief smiled faintly. The others had all gone into the hall now, amid a babble of conversation. It was time to be going. He glanced at the eager junior agent.

"No," he said, "I can't claim much credit there. I've had that document for many years; it, at least, was perfectly genuine."

IN THE ARENA

by Brian W. Aldiss

The reek and noise at the back of the circus were familiar to Javlin Bartramm. He felt the hard network of nerves in his solar plexus tighten.

There were crowds of the reduls here, jostling and staring to see the day's entry arrive. You didn't have to pay to stand and rubberneck in the street; this lot probably couldn't afford seats for the arena. Javlin looked away from them in scorn. All the same, he felt some gratification when they sent up a cheeping cheer at the sight of him. They loved a human victim.

His keeper undid the cart door and led him out, still chained. They went through the entrance, from blinding sunshine to dark, into the damp unsavory warren below the main stadium. Several reduls were moving about here, officials mainly. One or two called good luck to him; one chirped, "The crowd's in a good mood today, vertebrate." Javlin showed no response.

His trainer, Ik So Baar, came up, a flamboyant redul towering above Javlin. He wore an array of spare gloves strapped across his orange belly. The white tiara that fitted round his antennae appeared only on sports days.

"Greetings, Javlin. You look in the rudest of health. I'm glad you are not fighting me."

"Greetings, Ik So." He slipped the lip-whistle into his mouth so that he could answer in a fair approximation of the redul language. "Is my opponent ready to be slain? Remember I go free if I win this bout—it will be my twelfth victory in succession."

"There's been a change in the program, Javlin. Your Sirian opponent escaped in the night and had to be killed. You are entered in a double double."

Javlin wrenched at his chains so hard that the keeper was swung off balance.

"Ik So! You betray me! How much cajsh have I won for you? I will not fight a double double."

There was no change of expression on the insect mask.

"Then you will die, my pet vertebrate. The new arrangement is not my idea. You know by now that I get more cajsh for having you in a solo. Double double it has to be. These are my orders. Keeper, Cell 107 with him!"

Fighting against his keeper's pull, Javlin cried, "I've got some rights, Ik So. I demand to see the arena promoter."

"Pipe down, you stupid vertebrate! You have to do what you're ordered. I told you it wasn't my fault."

"Well, for God's sake, who am I fighting with?"

"You will be shackled to a fellow from the farms. He's had one or two preliminary bouts; they say he's good."

"From the farms . . ." Javlin broke into the filthiest redulian oaths he knew. Ik So came back towards him and slipped one of the metal gloves on to his forepincers; it gave him a cruel tearing weapon with a multitude of barbs. He held it up to Javlin's face.

"Don't use that language to me, my mammalian friend. Humans from the farms or from space, what's the difference? This young fellow will fight well enough if you muck in with him. And you'd better muck in. You're billed to battle against a couple of yillibeeth."

Before Javlin could answer, the tall figure turned and strode down the corridor, moving twice as fast as a man could walk.

Javlin let himself be led to Cell 107. The warder, a worker-redul with a gray belly, unlocked his chains and pushed him in, barring the door behind him. The cell smelt of alien species and apprehensions.

Javlin went and sat down on the bench. He needed to think.

He knew himself for a simple man—and knew that that knowledge meant the simplicity was relative. But his five years of captivity here under the reduls had not been all wasted. Ik So had trained him well in the arts of survival; and when you came down to brass tacks, there was no more proper pleasure in the universe than surviving. It was uncomplicated. It carried no responsibilities to anyone but yourself.

That was what he hated about the double double events, which till now he had always been lucky enough to avoid. They carried a responsibility to your fellow fighter.

From the beginning he had been well equipped to survive the gladiatorial routine. When his scoutship, the *Plunderhorse*, had been captured by redul forces five years ago, Javlin Bartramm was duelling master and judo expert, as well as Top Armament Sergeant. The army ships had a long tradition, going back some six centuries, of sport aboard; it provided the ideal mixture of time-passer and needed exercise. Of all the members of the *Plunderhorse*'s crew who had been taken captive, Javlin was— as far as he knew—the only survivor after five years of the insect race's rough games.

Luck had played its part in his survival. He had liked Ik So Baar. Liking was a strange thing to feel for a nine-foot armored grasshopper with forearms like a lobster and a walk like a tyrannosaurus's run, but a sympathy existed between them—and would continue to exist until he was killed in the ring, Javlin thought. With his bottom on the cold bench, he knew that Ik So would not betray him into a double double. The redul had had to obey the promoter's orders. Ik So needed his twelfth victory, so that he could free Javlin to help him train the other species down at the gladiatorial farm. Both of them knew that would be an effective partnership.

So. Now was the time for luck to be with Javlin again.

He sank on to his knees and looked down at the stone, brought his forehead down on to it, gazed down into the earth, into the cold ground, the warm rocks, the molten core, trying to visualize each, to draw from them attributes that would help him: cold for his brain, warm for his temper, molten for his energies.

Strengthened by prayer, he stood up. The redul workers had yet to bring him his armor and the partner he was to fight with. He had long since learnt the ability to wait without resenting waiting. With professional care, he exercised himself slowly, checking the proper function of each muscle. As he did so, he heard the crowds cheer in the arena. He turned to peer out of the cell's further door, an affair of tightly set bars that allowed a narrow view of the combat area and the stands beyond.

There was a centaur out there in the sunlight, fighting an Aldebaran bat-leopard. The centaur wore no armor but an iron cuirass; he had no weapons but his hooves and his hands. The bat-leopard, though its wings were clipped to prevent it flying out of the stadium, had dangerous claws and a great turn of speed. Only because its tongue had been cut out, ruining its echo-location system, was the contest anything like fair. The concept of fairness was lost upon the reduls, though; they preferred blood to justice.

Javlin saw the kill. The centaur, a gallant creature with a humanlike head and an immense gold mane that began from his eyebrows, was plainly tiring. He eluded the bat-leopard as it swooped down on him, wheeling quickly round on his hind legs and trampling on its wing. But the bat-leopard turned and raked the other's legs with a slash of claws. The centaur toppled hamstrung to the ground. As he fell, he lashed out savagely with his forelegs, but the bat-leopard nipped in and tore his throat from side to side above the cuirass. It then dragged itself away under its mottled wings, like a lame prima dona dressed in a leather cape.

The centaur struggled and lay still, as if the weight of whistling cheers that rose from the audience bore him down. Through the narrow bars, Javlin saw the throat bleed and the lungs heave as the defeated one sprawled in the dust.

"What do you dream of, dying there in the sun?" Javlin asked.

He turned away from the sight and the question. He sat quietly down on the bench and folded his arms.

When the din outside told him that the next bout had begun, the passage door opened and a young human was pushed in. Javlin did not need telling that this was to be his partner in the double double against the yillibeeth.

It was a girl.

"You're Javlin?" she said. "I know of you. My name's Awn."

He kept himself under control, his brows drawn together as he stared at her.

"You know what you're here for?"

"This will be my first public fight," she said.

Her hair was clipped short as a man's. Her skin was tanned and harsh, her left arm bore a gruesome scar. She held herself lithely on her feet. Though her body looked lean and hard, even the thick one-piece gown she wore to thigh length did not conceal the feminine curves of her body. She was not pretty, but Javlin had to admire the set of her mouth and her cool gray gaze.

"I've had some stinking news this morning, but Ik So Baar never broke it to me that I was to be saddled with a woman," he said.

"Ik probably didn't know—that I'm a woman, I mean. The reduls are either neuter or hermaphrodite, unless they happen to be a rare queen. Didn't you know that? They can't tell the difference between human male and female."

He spat. "You can't tell me anything about reduls."

She spat. "If you knew, why blame me? You don't think I like being here? You don't think I asked to join the great Javlin?"

Without answering he bent and began to massage the muscles of his calf. Since he occupied the middle of the bench, the girl remained standing. She watched him steadily. When he looked up again, she asked, "What or who are we fighting?"

No surprise was left in him. "They didn't tell you?"

"I've only just been pushed into this double double, as I imagine you have. I asked you, what are we fighting?"

"Just a couple of yillibeeths."

He injected unconcern into his voice to make the shock of what he said the greater. He massaged the muscles of the other calf. An aphrohale would have come in very welcome now. These crazy insects had no equivalent of the terrestrial prisoner-ate-a-hearty-breakfast routine. When he glanced up under his eyebrows, the girl still stood motionless, but her face had gone pale.

"Know what the yillibeeths are, little girl?"

She didn't answer, so he went on, "The reduls resemble some terrestrial insects. They go through several stages of development, you know; reduls are just the final adult stage. Their larval stage is rather like the larval stage of the dragon fly. It's a greedy, omnivorous beast. It's aquatic and it's big. It's armored. It's called a yillibeeth. That's what we are going to be tied together to fight, a couple of big hungry yillibeeth. Are you feeling like dying this morning, Awn?''

Instead of answering, she turned her head away and brought a hand up to her mouth.

"Oh, no! No crying in here, for Earth's sake!" he said. He got up, yelled through the passage door, "Ik So, Ik So, you traitor, get this bloody woman out of here!" . . . recalled himself, jammed the lip-whistle into his mouth and was about to call again when Awn caught him a backhanded blow across the face.

She faced him like a tiger.

"You creature, you cowardly apology of a man! Do you think I weep for fear? I don't weep. I've lived nineteen years on this damned planet in their damned farms. Would I still be here if I wept? No—but I mourn that you are already defeated, you, the great Javlin!"

He frowned into her blazing face.

"You don't seriously think you make me a good enough match for us to go out there and kill a couple of yillibeeth?"

"Damn your conceit, I'm prepared to try."

"Fagh!" He thrust the lip-whistle into his mouth, and turned back to the door. She laughed at him bitterly, jeeringly.

"You're a lackey to these insects, aren't you, Javlin? If you could see what a fool you look with that phoney beak of yours stuck on your mouth."

He let the instrument drop to the end of its chain. Grasping the bars, he leaned forward against them and looked at her over his shoulder.

"I was trying to get this contest called off."

"Don't tell me you haven't already tried. I have."

To that he had no answer. He went back and sat on the bench. She returned to her corner. They both folded their arms and stared at each other.

"Why don't you look out into the arena instead of glaring at me? You might pick up a few tips." When she did not answer, he said, "I'll tell you what you'll see. You can see the rows of spectators and a box where some sort of bigwig sits. It's never a queen—as far as I can make out, the queens spend their lives underground, turning out eggs at the rate of fifty a second. Not the sort of life Earth royalty would have enjoyed in the old days.

Under the bigwig's box there is a red banner with their insect hieroglyphs on. I asked Ik So once what the hieroglyphs said. He told me they meant—well, in a rough translation—*The Greatest Show on Earth*. It's funny, isn't it?''

"You must admit we do make a show."

"No, you miss the point. You see, that used to be the legend of circuses in the old days. But they've adopted it for their own use since they invaded Earth. They're boasting of their conquest."

"And that's funny?"

"In a sort of way. Don't you feel rather ashamed that this planet which saw the birth of the human race should be overrun by insects?"

"No. The reduls were here before me. I was just born here. Weren't you?''

"No, I wasn't. I was born on Washington IV. It's a lovely planet. There are hundreds of planets out there as fine and varied as Earth once was—but it kind of rankles to think that this insect brood rules Earth."

"If you feel so upset about it, why don't you do something?"

He knotted his fists together. You should start explaining history and economics just before you ran out to be chopped to bits by a big rampant thing with circular saws for hands?

"It would cost mankind too much to reconquer this planet. Too difficult. Too many deaths just for sentiment. And think of all those queens squirting eggs at a rate of knots; humans don't breed that fast. Humanity has learnt to face facts."

She laughed without humor.

"That's good. Why don't you learn to face the fact of me?"

Javlin had nothing to say to that; she would not understand that directly he saw her he knew his hope of keeping his life had died. She was just a liability. Soon he would be dying, panting his juices out into the dust like that game young centaur . . . only it wouldn't be dust.

"We fight in two foot of water," he said. "You know that? The yillibeeth like it. It slows our speed a bit. We might drown instead of having our heads bitten off."

"I can hear someone coming down the corridor. It may be our armor," she said coolly.

"Did you hear what I said?"

"You can't wait to die, Javlin, can you?"

• • •

The bars fell away on the outside of the door, and it opened. The keeper stood there. Ik So Baar had not appeared as he usually did. The creature flung in their armor and weapons and retreated, barring the door again behind him. It never ceased to astonish Javlin that those great dumb brutes of workers had intelligence.

He stooped to pick up his uniform. The girl's looked so light and small. He lifted it, looking from it to her.

"Thank you," she said.

"It looks so small and new."

"I shouldn't want anything heavier."

"You've fought in it?"

"Twice." There was no need to ask whether she had won.

"We'd better get the stuff strapped on then. We shall know when they are getting ready for us; you'll hear the arena being filled with water. They're probably saving us for the main events just before noon."

"I didn't know about the two feet of water."

"Scare you?"

"No. I'm a good swimmer. Swam for fish in the river on the slave farm."

"You caught fish with your bare hands?"

"No, you dive down and stab them with a sharp rock. It takes practice."

It was a remembered pleasure. She'd actually swum in one of Earth's rivers. He caught himself smiling back into her face.

"Ik So's place is in the desert," he said, making his voice cold. "Anyhow, you won't be able to swim in the arena. Two foot of muddy stinking water helps nobody. And you'll be chained on to me with a four-foot length of chain."

"Let's get our armor on, then you'd better tell me all you know. Perhaps we can work out a plan of campaign."

As he picked up the combined breastplate and shoulder guard, Awn untied her belt and lifted her dress over her head. Underneath she wore only a ragged pair of white briefs. She commenced to take those off.

Javlin stared at her with surprise—and pleasure. It had been years since he had been within hailing distance of a woman. This one—yes, this one was a beauty.

"What are you doing that for?" he asked. He hardly recognized his own voice.

"The less we have on the better in that water. Aren't you going to take your clothes off?"

He shook his head. Embarrassed, he fumbled on the rest of his kit. At least she wouldn't look so startling with her breastplate and skirt armor on. He checked his long and short swords, clipping the one into the left belt clip, the other into the right. They were good swords, made by redul armorers to terrestrial specifications. When he turned back to Awn, she was fully accoutred.

Nodding in approval, he offered her a seat on the bench beside him. They clattered against each other and smiled.

Another bout had ended in the arena. The cheers and chirrups drifted through the bars to them.

"I'm sorry you're involved in this," he said with care.

"I was lucky to be involved in it with you." Her voice was not entirely steady, but she controlled it in a minute. "Can't I hear water?"

He had already heard it. An unnatural silence radiated from the great inhuman crowd in the circus as they watched the stuff pour in. It would have great emotional significance for them, no doubt, since they had all lived in water for some years in their previous life stage.

"They have wide-bore hoses," he said. His own voice had an irritating tremor. "The arena fills quite rapidly."

"Let's formulate some sort of plan of attack then. These things, these yillibeeths must have some weaknesses."

"And some strengths! That's what you have to watch out for."

"I don't see that. You attack their weak points."

"We shall be too busy looking out for their strong ones. They have long segmented gray bodies—about twenty segments, I think. Each segment is of chitin or something tough. Each segment bears two legs equipped with razor combs. At tail end and top end they have legs that work like sort of buzz saws, cut through anything they touch. And there are their jaws, of course."

The keeper was back. Its antennae flopped through the grating and then it unbolted the door and came in. It bore a length of chain as long as the cell was wide. Javlin and Awn did not resist as it locked them together, fitting the bracelets on to Javlin's right arm and Awn's left.

"So." She stared at the chain. "The yillibeeths don't sound to have many weak points. They could cut through our swords with their buzz saws?"

"Correct."

"Then they could cut through this chain. Get it severed near one of our wrists, and the other has a better long distance weapon than a sword. A blow over the head with the end of the chain won't improve their speed. How fast are they?"

"The buzz saws take up most of their speed. They're nothing like as fast as the reduls. No, you could say they were pretty sluggish in movement. And the fact that the two of them will also be chained together should help us."

"Where are they chained?"

"By the middle legs."

"That gives them a smaller arc of destruction than if they were chained by back or front legs. We are going to slay these beasts yet, Javlin! What a murderous genus it must be to put its off-spring in the arena for the public sport."

He laughed.

"Would you feel sentimental about your offspring if you had a million babies?"

"I'll tell you that when I've had the first of them. I mean, if I have the first of them."

He put his hand over hers.

"No if. We'll kill the bloody larvae okay."

"Get the chain severed, the one of us with the longest bit of chain goes in for the nearest head, the other fends off the other brute. Right?"

"Right."

There was a worker redul at the outer door now, the door that led to the arena. He flung it open and stood there with a flaming torch, ready to drive them out if they did not emerge.

"We've—come to it then," she said. Suddenly she clung to him.

"Let's take it at a run, love," he said.

Together, balancing the chain between them, they ran towards the arena. The two yillibeeth were coming out from the far side, wallowing and splashing. The crowd stretched up toward the blue sky of earth, whistling their heads off. They didn't know what a man and a woman could do in combination. Now they were going to learn.

THE KOKOD WARRIORS

by Jack Vance

Magnus Ridolph sat on the Glass Jetty at Providencia, fingering a quarti-quartino of Blue Ruin. At his back rose Granatee Head; before him spread Milles-Iles Ocean and the myriad little islands, each with its trees and neo-classic villa. A magnificent blue sky extended overhead; and beneath his feet, under the glass floor of the jetty, lay Coral Canyon, with schools of sea-moths flashing and flickering like metal snowflakes. Magnus Ridolph sipped his liqueur and considered a memorandum from his bank describing a condition barely distinguishable from poverty.

He had been perhaps too trusting with his money. A few months previously, the Outer Empire Investment and Realty Society, to which he had entrusted a considerable sum, had been found to be bankrupt. The Chairman of the Board and the General Manager, a Mr. See and a Mr. Holpers, had been paying each other unexpectedly large salaries, most of which had been derived from Magnus Ridolph's capital investment.

Magnus Ridolph sighed, glanced at his liqueur. This would be the last of these; hereafter he must drink *vin ordinaire*, a fluid rather like tarragon vinegar, prepared from the fermented rind of a local cactus.

A waiter approached. "A lady wishes to speak to you, sir."

Magnus Ridolph preened his neat white beard. "Show her over, by all means."

The waiter returned; Magnus Ridolph's eyebrows went S-shape as he saw his guest: a woman of commanding presence, with an air of militant and dignified virtue. Her interest in Magnus Ridolph was clearly professional.

She came to an abrupt halt. "You are Mr. Magnus Ridolph?"

He bowed. "Will you sit down?"

The woman rather hesitantly took a seat. "Somehow, Mr. Ridolph, I expected someone more—well . . ."

Magnus Ridolph's reply was urbane. "A younger man, perhaps? With conspicuous biceps, a gun on his hip, a space helmet on his head? Or perhaps my beard alarms you?"

"Well, not exactly that, but my business—"

"Ah, you came to me in a professional capacity?"

"Well, yes. I would say so."

In spite of the memorandum from his bank—which now he folded and tucked into his pocket—Magnus Ridolph spoke with decision. "If your business requires feats of physical prowess, I beg you hire elsewhere. My janitor might satisfy your needs: an excellent chap who engages his spare time moving bar-bells from one elevation to another."

"No, no," said the woman hastily. "I'm sure you misunderstand; I merely pictured a different sort of individual. . . ."

Magnus Ridolph cleared his throat. "What is your problem?"

"Well—I am Martha Chickering, secretary of the Women's League Committee for the Preservation of Moral Values. We are fighting a particularly disgraceful condition that the law refuses to abate. We have appealed to the better nature of the persons involved, but I'm afraid that financial gain means more to them than decency."

"Be so kind as to state your problem."

"Are you acquainted with the world"—she spoke it as if it were a social disease—"Kokod?"

Magnus Ridolph nodded gravely, stroked his neat white beard. "Your problem assumes form."

"Can you help us, then? Every right-thinking person condemns the goings-on—brutal, undignified, nauseous . . ."

Magnus Ridolph nodded. "The exploitation of the Kokod natives is hardly commendable."

"Hardly commendable!" cried Martha Chickering. "It's despicable! It's trafficking in blood! We execrate the sadistic beasts who patronize bull-fights—but we condone, even encourage the terrible things that take place on Kokod while Holpers and See daily grow wealthier."

"Ha, ha!" exclaimed Magnus Ridolph. "Bruce Holpers and Julius See?"

"Why, yes." She looked at him questioningly. "Perhaps you know them?"

Magnus Ridolph sat back in his chair, turned the liqueur down his throat. "To some slight extent. We had what I believe is called a business connection. But no matter, please continue. Your problem has acquired a new dimension, and beyond question the situation is deplorable."

"Then you will agree that the Kokod Syndicate should be broken up? You will help us?"

Magnus Ridolph spread his arms in a fluent gesture. "Mrs. Chickering, my good wishes are freely at your disposal; active participation in the crusade is another matter and will be determined by the fee your organization is prepared to invest."

Mrs. Chickering spoke stiffly. "Well, we assume that a man of principle might be willing to make certain sacrifices—"

Magnus Ridolph sighed, "You touch me upon a sensitive spot, Mrs. Chickering. I shall indeed make a sacrifice. Rather than the extended rest I had promised myself, I will devote my abilities to your problem . . . Now let us discuss my fee—no, first, what do you require?"

"We insist that the gaming at Shadow Valley Inn be halted. We want Bruce Holpers and Julius See prosecuted and punished. We want an end put to the Kokod wars."

Magnus Ridolph looked off into the distance and for a moment was silent. When at last he spoke, his voice was grave. "You list your requirements on a descending level of feasibility."

"I don't understand you, Mr. Ridolph."

"Shadow Valley Inn might well be rendered inoperative by means of a bomb or an epidemic of Mayerheim's Bloat. To punish Holpers and See, we must demonstrate that a nonexistent law has been criminally violated. And to halt the Kokod wars, it will be necessary to alter the genetic heritage, glandular makeup, training, instinct, and general outlook on life of each of the countless Kokod warriors.''

Mrs. Chickering blinked and stammered; Magnus Ridolph held up a courteous hand, ''However, that which is never attempted never transpires; I will bend my best efforts to your requirements. My fee—well, in view of the altruistic ends in prospect, I will be modest; a thousand munits a week and expenses. Payable, if you please, in advance.''

Magnus Ridolph left the jetty, mounted Granatee Head by steps cut into the green-veined limestone. On top, he paused by the wrought-iron balustrade to catch his breath and enjoy the vista over the ocean. Then he turned and entered the blue lace and silver filigree lobby of the Hotel des Mille Iles.

Presenting a bland face to the scrutiny of the desk clerk he sauntered into the library, where he selected a cubicle, settled himself before the mnemiphot. Consulting the index for Kokod, he punched the appropriate keys.

The screen came to life. Magnus Ridolph inspected first a series of charts which established that Kokod was an exceedingly small world of high specific gravity.

Next appeared a projection of the surface, accompanied by a slow-moving strip of descriptive matter:

Although a small world, Kokod's gravity and atmosphere make it uniquely habitable for men. It has never been settled, due to an already numerous population of autochthones and a lack of valuable minerals.

Tourists are welcomed at Shadow Valley Inn, a resort hotel at Shadow Valley. Weekly packets connect Shadow Valley Inn with Starport.

Kokod's most interesting feature is its population.

The chart disappeared, to be replaced by a picture entitled, ''Typical Kokod Warrior (from Rock River Tumble),'' and displaying a man-like creature two feet tall. The head was narrow and peaked; the torso was that of a bee—long, pointed, covered with yellow down. Scrawny arms gripped a four-foot lance; a stone knife hung at the belt. The chitinous legs were shod with barbs. The creature's expression was mild, almost reproachful.

A voice said, "You will now hear the voice of Sam 192 Rock River."

The Kokod warrior inhaled deeply; wattles beside his chin quivered. From the mnemiphot screen issued a high-pitched stridency. Interpretation appeared on a panel to the right.

"I am Sam 192, squadronite, Company 14 of the Advance Force, in the service of Rock River Tumble. Our valor is a source of wonder to all; our magnificent stele is rooted deep, and exceed in girth only by the steles of Rose Slope Tumble and crafty Shell Strand Tumble.

"This day I have come at the invitation of the (untranslatable) of Small Square Tumble, to tell of our victories and immensely effective strategies."

Another sound made itself heard: a man speaking falsetto in the Kokod language. The interpretation read:

Question: Tell us about life in Rock River Tumble.

Sam 192: It is very companionable.

Q: What is the first thing you do in the morning?

A: We march past the matrons, to assure ourselves of a properly martial fecundity.

Q: What do you eat?

A: We are nourished in the fields. (Note: The Kokod metabolism is not entirely understood; apparently they ferment organic material in a crop, and oxidize the resultant alcohols.)

Q: Tell us about your daily life.

A: We practice various disciplines, deploy in the basic formations, hurl weapons, train the kinderlings, elevate the veterans.

Q: How often do you engage in battle?

A: When it is our time: when the challenge has issued and the appropriate Code of Combat agreed upon with the enemy.

Q: You mean you fight in various styles?

A: There are 97 conventions of battle which may be employed: for instance, Code 48, by which we overcame strong Black Glass Tumble, allows the lance to be grasped only by the left hand and permits no severing of the leg tendons with the dagger. Code 69, however, insists that the tendons must be cut before the kill is made and the lances are used thwart-wise, as bumpers.

Q: Why do you fight? Why are there wars?

A:Because the steles of the other tumbles would surpass ours in size, did we not fight and win victories.

(Note: the stele is a composite tree growing in each tumble. Each victory is celebrated by the addition of a shoot, which joins and augments the main body of the stele. The Rock River Stele is 17 feet in diameter, and is estimated to be 4,000 years old. The Rose Slope Stele is 18 feet in diameter, and the Shell Strand Stele is almost 20 feet in diameter.)

Q: What would happen if warriors from Frog Pond Tumble cut down Rock River Stele?

Sam 192 made no sound. His wattles blew out; his head bobbed. After a moment he turned, marched out of view.

Into the screen came a man wearing shoulder tabs of Commonwealth Control. He looked after Sam 192 with an expression of patronizing good humor that Magnus Ridolph considered insufferable.

"The Kokod warriors are well known through the numerous sociological studies published on Earth, of which the most authoritative is perhaps the Carlisle Foundation's *Kokod: A Militaristic Society*, mnemiphot code AK-SK-RD-BP.

"To summarize, let me state that there are 81 tumbles, or castles, on Kokod, each engaged in highly formalized warfare with all the others. The evolutionary function of this warfare is the prevention of overpopulation on a small world. The Tumble Matrons are prolific, and only these rather protean measures assure a balanced ecology.

"I have been asked repeatedly whether the Kokod warriors fear death. My belief is that identification with the home tumble is so intense that the warriors have small sense of individuality. Their sole ambition is winning battles, swelling the girth of their stele and so glorifying their tumble."

The man spoke on. Magnus Ridolph reached out, speeded up the sequence.

On the screen appeared Shadow Valley Inn—a luxurious building under six tall parasol trees. The commentary read: "At Shadow Valley Inn, genial co-owners Julius See and Bruce Holpers greet tourists from all over the universe."

Two cuts appeared—a dark man with a lowering broad face, a mouth uncomfortably twisted in a grin; the other, lanky, with a long head sparsely thatched with red excelsior. "See" and "Holpers" read the sub-headings.

Magnus Ridolph halted the progression of the program, stud-

ied the faces for a few seconds, then allowed the sequence to
continue.

"Mr. See and Mr. Holpers," ran the script, "have ingen-
iously made use of the incessant wars as a means of diverting
their guests. A sheet quotes odds on each day's battle—a pastime
which arouses enthusiasm among sporting visitors."

Magnus Ridolph turned off the mnemiphot, sat back in the chair,
stroked his beard reflectively. "Where odds exist," he said to
himself, "there likewise exists the possibility of upsetting the
odds. . . . Luckily, my obligation to Mrs. Chickering will in no
way interfere with a certain measure of subsidiary profits. Or
better, let us say, recompense."

II

Alighting from the Phoenix Line packet, the *Hesperornis*, Ridolph was startled momentarily by the close horizons of Kokod.
The sky seemed to begin almost at his feet.

Waiting to transfer the passengers to the inn was an overdec-
orated charabanc. Magnus Ridolph gingerly took a seat, and
when the vehicle lurched forward a heavy woman scented with
musk was thrust against him. "Really!" complained the woman.

"A thousand apologies," replied Magnus Ridolph, adjusting
his position. "Next time I will take care to move out of your
way."

The woman brushed him with a contemptuous glance and
turned to her companion, a woman with the small head and
robust contour of a peacock.

"Attendant!" the second woman called presently.

"Yes, Madame."

"Tell us about these native wars; we've heard so much about
them."

"They're extremely interesting, Madame. The little fellows
are quite savage."

"I hope there's no danger for the onlookers?"

"None whatever; they reserve their unfriendliness for each
other."

"What time are the excursions?"

"I believe the Ivory Dune and the Eastern Shield Tumbles

march tomorrow; the scene of battle no doubt will center around Muscadine Meadow, so there should be three excursions. To catch the deployments, you leave the inn at 5:00 A.M.; for the onslaught, at 6:00 A.M.; and 7:00 or 8:00 for the battle proper.''

"It's ungodly early," the matron commented. "Is nothing else going on?"

"I'm not certain, Madame. The Green Ball and the Shell Strand might possibly war tomorrow, but they would engage according to Convention 4, which is hardly spectacular."

"Isn't there anything close by the inn?"

"No, Madame. Shadow Valley Tumble only just finished a campaign against Marble Arch, and are occupied now in repairing their weapons."

"What are odds on the first of these—the Ivory Dune and the Eastern Shield?"

"I believe eight gets you five on Ivory Dune, and five gets you four on Eastern Shield."

"That's strange. Why aren't the odds the same both ways?"

"All bets must be placed through the inn management, Madame."

The carry-all rattled into the courtyard of the inn. Magnus Ridolph leaned forward. "Kindly brace yourself, Madame; the vehicle is about the stop, and I do not care to be held responsible for a second unpleasant incident."

The woman made no reply. The charabanc halted; Magnus Ridolph climbed to the ground. Before him was the inn and behind a mountainside, dappled with succulent green flowers on lush violet bushes. Along the ridge grew tall, slender trees like poplars, vivid black and red. A most colorful world, decided Magnus Ridolph, and, turning, inspected the view down the valley. There were bands and layers of colors—pink, violet, yellow, green, graying into a distant dove color. Where the mouth of the valley gave on the river peneplain, Magnus Ridolph glimpsed a tall conical edifice. "One of the tumbles?" he inquired of the charabanc attendant.

"Yes, sir—the Meadow View Tumble. Shadow Valley Tumble is further up the valley, behind the inn."

Magnus Ridolph turned to enter the inn. His eyes met those of a man in a severe black suit—a short man with a dumpy face that looked as if it had been compressed in a vise. Ridolph recognized the countenance of Julius See. "Well, well, this is a surprise indeed," said Magnus.

See nodded grimly. "Quite a coincidence. . . ."

"After the unhappy collapse of Outer Empire Realty and Investment I feared—indeed, I dreaded—that I should never see you again." And Magnus Ridolph watched Julius See with mild blue eyes blank as a lizard's.

"No such luck," said See. "As a matter of fact, I run this place. Er, may I speak to you a moment inside?"

"Certainly, by all means."

Ridolph followed his host through the well-appointed lobby into an office. A thin-faced man with thin red hair and squirrel teeth rose quickly to his feet. "You'll remember my partner, Bruce Holpers," said See with no expression in his voice.

"Of course," said Ridolph. "I am flattered that you honor me with your personal attention."

See cut the air with his hand—a small petulant gesture. "Forget the smart talk, Ridolph. . . . What's your game?"

Magnus Ridolph laughed easily. "Gentlemen, gentlemen—"

"Gentlemen my foot! Let's get down to brass tacks. If you've got any ideas left over from that Outer Empire deal, put them away."

"I assure you—"

"I've heard stories about you, Ridolph, and what I brought you in to tell you was that we're running a nice quiet place here, and we don't want any disturbance."

"Of course not," agreed Ridolph.

"Maybe you came for a little clean fun, betting on these native chipmunks; maybe you came on a party that we won't like."

Ridolph held out his hands guilelessly. "I can hardly say I'm flattered. I appear at your inn, an accredited guest; instantly you take me aside and admonish me."

"Ridolph," said See, "you have a funny reputation, and a normal sharpshooter never knows what side you're working on."

"Enough of this," said Magnus sternly. "Open the door, or I shall institute a strong protest."

"Look," said See, ominously, "we own this hotel. If we don't like your looks, you'll camp out and rustle your own grub until the next packet—which is a week away."

Magnus Ridolph said coldly, "You will become liable to extensive damages if you seek to carry out your threat; in fact, I defy you, put me out if you dare!"

The lanky red-haired Holpers laid a nervous hand on See's arm. "He's right, Julie. We can't refuse service or the Control yanks our charter."

"If he misbehaves or performs, we can put him out."

"You have evidence, then, that I am a source of annoyance?"

See stood back, hands behind him. "Call this little talk a warning, Ridolph. You've just had your warning."

Returning to the lobby, Magnus Ridolph ordered his luggage sent to his room, and inquired the whereabouts of the Commonwealth Control officer.

"He's established on the edge of Black Bog, sir; you'll have to take an air-car unless you care for an all-night hike."

"You may order out an air-car," said Magnus Ridolph.

Seated in the well-upholstered tonneau, Ridolph watched Shadow Valley Inn dwindle below. The sun, Pi Sagittarius, which had already set, once more came into view as the car rose to clear Basalt Mountain, then sank in a welter of purples, greens, and reds—a phoenix dying in its many-colored blood. Kokod twilight fell across the planet.

Below passed a wonderfully various landscape: lakes and parks, meadows, cliffs, crags, sweeping hillside slopes, river valleys. Here and there Ridolph sensed shapes in the fading light—the hive-like tumbles. As evening deepened into dove-colored night, the tumbles flickered with dancing orange sparks of illumination.

The air-car slanted down, slid under a copse of trees shaped like featherdusters. Magnus Ridolph alighted, stepped around to the pilot's compartment.

"Who is the Control officer?"

"His name is Clark, sir, Everley Clark."

Magnus Ridolph nodded. "I'll be no more than twenty minutes. Will you wait, please?"

"Yes, sir. Very well, sir."

Magnus Ridolph glanced sharply at the man: a suggestion of insolence behind the formal courtesy? . . . He strode to the frame building. The upper half of the door hung wide; cheerful yellow light poured out into the Kokod night. Within, Magnus Ridolph glimpsed a tall pink man in neat tan gabardines. Something in the man's physiognomy struck a chord of memory; where had he seen this round pink face before? He rapped smartly on the door; the man turned his head and rather glumly arose. Magnus Ridolph saw the man to be he of the mnemiphot presentation on Kokod, the man who had interviewed the warrior, Sam 192.

Everley Clark came to the door. "Yes? What can I do for you?"

"I had hoped for the privilege of a few words with you," replied Magnus Ridolph.

Clark blew out his cheeks, fumbled with the door fastenings. "By all means," he said hollowly. "Come in, sir." He motioned Magnus Ridolph to a chair. "Won't you sit down? My name is Everley Clark."

"I am Magnus Ridolph."

Clark evinced no flicker of recognition, responding with only a blank stare of inquiry.

Ridolph continued a trifle frostily. "I assume that our conversation can be considered confidential?"

"Entirely, sir. By all means." Clark showed a degree of animation, went to the fireplace, stood warming his hands at an imaginary blaze.

Ridolph chose his words for the maximum weight. "I have been employed by an important organization which I am not at liberty to name. The members of this organization—who I may say exert a not negligible political influence—feel that Control's management of Kokod business has been grossly inefficient and incorrect."

"Indeed!" Clark's official affability vanished as if a pink spotlight had been turned off.

Magnus Ridolph continued soberly. "In view of these charges, I thought it my duty to confer with you and learn your opinions."

Clark said grimly. "What do you mean—'charges'?"

"First, it is claimed that the gambling operations at Shadow Valley Inn are—if not illegal—explicitly, shamelessly and flagrantly unmoral."

"Well?" said Clark bitterly. "What do you expect me to do? Run out waving a Bible? I can't interfere with tourist morals. They can play merry hell, run around naked, beat their dogs, forge checks—as long as they leave the natives alone, they're out of my jurisdiction."

Magnus Ridolph nodded sagely. "I see your position clearly. But a second and more serious allegation is that in allowing the

Kokod wars to continue day in and day out, Control condones and tacitly encourages a type of brutality which would not be allowed on any other world of the Commonwealth.''

Clark seated himself, sighed deeply. ''If you'll forgive me for saying so, you sound for all the world like one of the form letters I get every day from women's clubs, religious institutes and anti-vivisectionist societies.'' He shook his round pink face with sober emphasis. ''Mr. Ridolph, you just don't know the facts. You come up here in a lather of indignation, you shoot off your mouth and sit back with a pleased expression—good deed for the day. Well, it's not right! Do you think I enjoy seeing these little creatures tearing each other apart? Of course not—although I admit I've become used to it. When Kokod was first visited, we tried to stop the wars. The natives considered us damn fools, and went on fighting. We enforced peace, by threatening to cut down the steles. This meant something to them; they gave up their wars. And you never saw a sadder set of creatures in your life. They sat around in the dirt; they contracted a kind of roup and died by the droves. None of them cared enough to drag the corpses away. Four tumbles were wiped out; Cloud Crag, Yellow Bush, Sunset Ridge and Vinegrass. You can see them today, colonies thousands of years old, destroyed in a few months. And all this time the Tumble-matrons were producing young. No one had the spirit to feed them, and they starved or ran whimpering around the planet like naked little rats.''

''Ahem,'' said Magnus Ridolph. ''A pity.''

''Fred Exman was adjutant here then. On his own authority he ordered the ban removed, told them to fight till they were blue in the face. The wars began half an hour later, and the natives have been happy and healthy ever since.''

''If what you say is true,'' Magnus Ridolph remarked mildly, ''I have fallen into the common fault of wishing to impose my personal tenor of living upon creatures constitutionally disposed to another.''

Clark said emphatically, ''I don't like to see those sadistic bounders at the hotel capitalizing on the wars, but what can I do about it? And the tourists are not better: morbid unhealthy jackals, enjoying the sight of death. . . . ''

Magnus Ridolph suggested cautiously, ''Then it would be safe to say that, as a private individual, you would not be averse to a cessation of the gambling at Shadow Valley Inn?''

"Not at all," said Everley Clark. "As a private citizen, I've always thought that Julius See, Bruce Holpers and their guests represented mankind at its worst."

"One more detail," said Magnus Ridolph. "I believe you speak and understand the Kokod language?"

"After a fashion—yes." Clark grimaced in apprehension. "You realize I can't compromise Control officially?"

"I understand that very well."

"Just what do you plan, then?"

"I'll know better after I witness one or two of these campaigns."

III

Soft chimes roused Magnus Ridolph; he opened his eyes into the violet gloom of a Kokod dawn. "Yes?"

The hotel circuit said, "Five o'clock, Mr. Ridolph. The first party for today's battle leaves in one hour."

"Thank you." Ridolph swung his bony legs over the edge of the air-cushion, sat a reflective moment. He gained his feet, gingerly performed a set of calisthenic exercises.

In the bathroom he rinsed his mouth with tooth-cleanser, rubbed depilatory on his cheeks, splashed his face with cold water, applied tonic to his trim white beard.

Returning to the bedroom, he selected a quiet gray and blue outfit, with a rather dashing cap.

His room opened upon a terrace facing the mountainside; as he strolled forth, the two women whom he had encountered in the charabanc the day previously came past. Magnus Ridolph bowed, but the women passed without even a side glance.

"Cut me dead, by thunder," said Magnus Ridolph to himself. "Well, well." And he adjusted his cap to an even more rakish angle.

In the lobby a placard announced the event of the day:

IVORY DUNE TUMBLE
vs.
EASTERN SHIELD TUMBLE
at Muscadine Meadow.

All bets must be placed with the attendant.

Odds against Ivory Dune:	8:13
Odds against Eastern Shield:	5:4

In the last hundred battles Ivory Dune has won 41 engagements, Eastern Shield has won 59.

Excursions leave as follows:

For deployment:	6:00 A.M.
For onslaught:	7:00 A.M.
For battle proper:	8:00 A.M.

It is necessary that no interference be performed in the vicinity of the battle. Any guest infringing on this rule will be barred from further wagering. There will be no exceptions.

At a booth nearby, two personable young women were issuing betting vouchers. Magnus Ridolph passed quietly into the restaurant, where he breakfasted lightly on fruit juice, rolls and coffee, finishing in ample time to secure a place with the first excursion.

The observation vehicle was of that peculiar variety used in conveying a large number of people across a rough terrain. The car proper was suspended by a pair of cables from a kite-copter which flew five hundred feet overhead. The operator, seated in the nose of the car, worked pitch and attack by remote control, and so could skim quietly five feet over the ground, hover over waterfalls, ridges, ponds, other areas of scenic beauty with neither noise nor the thrash of driven air to disturb the passengers.

Muscadine Meadow was no small distance away; the operator lofted the ship rather abruptly over Basalt Mountain, then slid on a long slant into the northeast. Pi Sagittarius rolled up into the sky like a melon, and the grays, greens, reds, purples of the Kokod countryside shone up from below, rich as Circassian tapestry.

"We are near the Eastern Shield," the attendant announced in a mellifluous baritone. "The tumble is a trifle to the right, beside that bold face of granite whence it derives its name. If you look closely you will observe the Eastern Shield armies already on the march."

Bending forward studiously, Magnus Ridolph noticed a brown and yellow column winding across the mountainside. To their rear he saw first the tall stele, rising two hundred feet, spraying over at the top into a fountain of pink, black, and light green foliage; then below, the conical tumble.

The car sank slowly, drifted over a wooded patch of broken ground, halted ten feet above a smooth green meadow.

"This is the Muscadine," announced the guide. "At the far end you can see Muscadine Tumble and Stele, currently warring against Opal Grotto, odds 9 to 7 both ways. . . . If you will observe along the line of bamboo trees you will see the green caps of the Ivory Dune warriors. We can only guess their strategy, but they seem to be preparing a rather intricate offensive pattern—"

A woman's voice said peevishly, "Can't you take the car up higher so we can see everything?"

"Certainly, if you wish, Mrs. Chaim."

Five hundred feet above, copter blades slashed the air; the car wafted up like thistledown.

The guide continued, "The Eastern Shield warriors can be seen coming over the hill. . . . It seems as if they surmise the Ivory Dune strategy and will attempt to attack the flank. . . . There!" His voice rose animatedly. "By the bronze tree! The scouts have made a brush. . . . Eastern Shield lures the Ivory Dune scouts into ambush. . . . They're gone. Apparently today's code is 4, or possibly 36, allowing all weapons to be used freely, without restriction."

An old man with a nose like a raspberry said, "Put us down, driver. From up here we might as well be back at the inn."

"Certainly, Mr. Pilby."

The car sank low. Mrs. Chaim sniffed and glared.

The meadow rose from below; the car grounded gently on glossy dark green creepers. The guide said, "Anyone who wishes may go further on foot. For safety's sake, do not approach the battle more closely than three hundred feet; in any event the inn assumes no responsibility of any sort whatever."

"Hurry," said Mr. Pilby sharply. "The onslaught will be over before we're in place."

The guide good-naturedly shook his head. "They're still sparring for position, Mr. Pilby. They'll be dodging and feinting half an hour yet; that's the basis of their strategy—neither side wants to fight until they're assured of the best possible advantage." He opened the door. With Pilby in the lead, several dozen of the spectators stepped down on Muscadine Meadow, among them Magnus Ridolph, Mrs. Chaim and her peacock-shaped friend whom she addressed as "Mrs. Borgage."

"Careful, ladies and gentlemen," called the guide, "Not too close to the battle."

"I've got my money on Eastern Shield," said Mrs. Borgage with heavy archness. "I'm going to make sure there's no funny business."

Magnus Ridolph inspected the scene of battle. "I'm afraid you are doomed to disappointment, Mrs. Borgage. In my opinion, Ivory Dune has selected the stronger position; if they hold on their right flank, give a trifle at the center, and catch the Eastern Shield forces on two sides when they close in, there should be small doubt as to the outcome of today's encounter."

"It must be wonderful to be so penetrating," said Mrs. Borgage in a sarcastic undertone to Mrs. Chaim.

Mr. Pilby said, "I don't think you see the battleground in its entire perspective, sir. The Eastern Shield merely needs to come in around that line of trees to catch the whole rear of the Ivory Dune line—"

"But by so doing," Magnus Ridolph pointed out, "they leave their rear unguarded; clearly Ivory Dune has the advantage of maneuver."

To the rear a second excursion boat landed. The doors opened, there was a hurrying group of people. "Has anything happened yet?" "Who's winning?"

"The situation is fluid," declared Pilby.

"Look, they're closing in!" came the cry. "It's the onslaught!"

Now rose the piping of Kokod war hymns: from Ivory Dune throats the chant sacred and long-beloved at Ivory Dune Tumble, and countering, the traditional paean of the Eastern Shield.

Down the hill came the Eastern Shield warriors, half-bent forward.

A thud and clatter—battle. The shock of small bodies, the dry whisper of knife against lance, the hoarse orders of leg-leaders and squadronites.

Forward and backward, green and black mingled with orange and white. Small bodies were hacked apart, dryly dismembered; small black eyes went dead and dim; a hundred souls raced all together, pell-mell, for the Tumble Beyond the Sky.

Forward and backward moved the standard-bearers—those who carried the sapling from the sacred stele, whose capture would mean defeat for one and victory for the other.

On the trip back to the inn, Mrs. Chaim and Mrs. Borgage sat glum and solitary while Mr. Pilby glowered from the window.

Magnus Ridolph said affably to Pilby, "In a sense, an amateur strategist, such as myself, finds these battles a trifle tedious. He needs no more than a glance at the situation, and his training indicates the logical outcome. Naturally, none of us are infallible, but given equal forces and equal leadership, we can only assume that the forces in the better position will win."

Pilby lowered his head, chewed the corners of his mustache. Mrs. Chaim and Mrs. Borgage studied the landscape with fascinated absorption.

"Personally," said Ridolph, "I never gamble. I admire a dynamic attack on destiny, rather than the suppliance and passivity of the typical gambler; nevertheless, I feel for you all in your losses, which I hope were not too considerable?"

There was no reply. Magnus Ridolph might have been talking to empty air. After a moment Mrs. Chaim muttered inaudibly to the peacock-shaped Mrs. Borgage, and Mr. Pilby slouched even deeper in his seat. The remainder of the trip was passed in silence.

After a modest dinner of cultivated Bylandia protein, a green salad, and cheese, Magnus Ridolph strolled into the lobby, inspected the morrow's scratch sheet.

The announcement read:

TOMORROW'S FEATURED BATTLE:
VINE HILL TUMBLE
vs.
ROARING CAPE TUMBLE
near Pink Stone Table.

Odds against Vine Hill Tumble:	1:3
Odds against Roaring Cape Tumble:	4:1

All bets must be placed with the attendant.

In the last hundred engagements Vine Hill Tumble has won 77, Roaring Cape has won 23.

Turning away, Magnus Ridolph bumped into Julius See, who was standing, rocking on his heels, his hands behind his back.

"Well, Ridolph, think you'll maybe take a flyer?"

Magnus Ridolph nodded. "A wager on Roaring Cape Tumble might prove profitable."

"That's right."

"On the other hand, Vine Hill is a strong favorite."

"That's what the screamer says."

"What would be your own preference, Mr. See?" asked Magnus Ridolph ingenuously.

"I don't have any preference. I work 23 to 77."

"Ah, you're not a gambling man, then?"

"Not any way you look at it."

Ridolph rubbed his beard and looked reflectively toward the ceiling. "Normally I should say the same of myself. But the wars offer an amateur strategist an unprecedented opportunity to test his abilities, and I may abandon the principles of a lifetime to back my theories."

Julius See turned away. "That's what we're here for."

"Do you impose a limit on the bets?"

See paused, looked over his shoulder. "We usually call a hundred thousand munits our maximum pay-off."

Magnus Ridolph nodded. "Thank you." He crossed the lobby, entered the library. On one wall was a map of the planet, with red discs indicting the location of each tumble.

Magnus Ridolph located Vine Hill and Roaring Cape Tumbles, and found Pink Stone Table, the latter near an arm of Drago Bay. Magnus Ridolph went to rack, found a large scale physiographic map of the area under his consideration. He took it to a table and spent half an hour in deep concentration.

He rose, replaced the map, sauntered through the lobby and out the side entrance. The pilot who had flown him the previous evening rose to his feet smartly. "Good evening, Mr. Ridolph. Intending another ride?"

"As a matter of fact, I am," Magnus Ridolph admitted. "Are you free?"

"In a moment, as soon as I turn in my day's report."

Ridolph looked thoughtfully after the pilot's hurrying figure. He quietly stepped around to the front entrance. From the vantage of the open door he watched the pilot approach Bruce Holpers and speak hastily.

Holpers ran a lank white hand through his red hair, gave a series of nervous instructions. The pilot nodded sagely, turned away, Magnus Ridolph returned by the route he had come.

He found the pilot waiting beside the ship. "I thought I had better notify Clark that I was coming," said Ridolph breezily. "In case the car broke down, or there were any accident, he would understand the situation and know where to look for me."

The pilot's hands hesitated on the controls. Magnus Ridolph said, "Is there game of any sort on Kokod?"

"No, sir, none whatever."

"A pity. I am carrying with me a small target pistol with which I had hoped to bag a trophy or two. . . . Perhaps I'll be able to acquire one or two of the native weapons."

"That's quite unlikely, sir."

"In any case," said Magnus Ridolph cheerily, "you might be mistaken, so I will hold my weapon ready?"

The pilot looked straight ahead.

Magnus Ridolph climbed into the back seat. "To the Control office, then."

"Yes, Mr. Ridolph."

IV

Everley Clark greeted his visitor cautiously; when Ridolph sat back in a basket chair, Clark's eyes went everywhere in the room but to those of his guest.

Magnus Ridolph lit an *aromatique*. "Those shields on the wall are native artifacts, I presume?"

"Yes," said Clark quickly. "Each tumble has its distinct colors and insignia."

"To Earthly eyes, the patterns seem fortuitous, but naturally and inevitably Kokod symbology is unique. . . . A magnificent display. Does the collection have a price?"

Clark looked doubtfully at his shields. "I'd hate to let them go—although I suppose I could get others. These shields are hard to come by; each requires many thousand hours of work. They make the lacquer by a rather painstaking method, grinding pigment into a vehicle prepared from the boileddown dead."

Ridolph nodded. "So that's how they dispose of the corpses."

"Yes; it's quite a ritual."

"About those shields—would you take ten thousand munits?"

Clark's face mirrored indecision. Abruptly he lit a cigarette. "Yes, I'd have to take ten thousand munits; I couldn't afford to refuse."

"It would be a shame to deprive you of a possession you obviously value so highly," said Magnus Ridolph. He examined the backs of his hands critically. "If ten thousand munits means so much to you, why do you not gamble at the inn. Surely with your knowledge of Kokod ways, your special information . . ."

Clark shook his head. "You can't beat that kind of odds. It's a sucker's game, betting at the inn."

"Hmm." Magnus Ridolph frowned. "It might be possible to influence the course of a battle. Tomorrow, for instance, the Vine Hill and Roaring Cape Tumbles engage each other, on Pink Stone Table, and the odds against Roaring Cape seem quite attractive."

Clark shook his head. "You'd lose your shirt betting on Roaring Cape. All their veterans went in the Pyrite campaign."

Magnus Ridolph said thoughtfully, "The Roaring Cape might win, if they received a small measure of assistance."

Clark's pink face expanded in alarm like a trick mask. "I'm an officer of the Commonwealth! I couldn't be party to a thing like that! It's unthinkable!"

Magnus Ridolph said judiciously, "Certainly the proposal is not one to enter upon hastily; it must be carefully considered. In a sense, the Commonwealth might be best served by the ousting of Shadow Valley Inn from the planet, or at least the present management. Financial depletion is as good a weapon as any. If, incidentally, we were to profit, not an eyebrow in the universe could be justifiably raised. Especially since the part that you might play in the achievement would be carefully veiled. . . ."

Clark shoved his hands deep in his pockets, stared a long moment at Magnus Ridolph. "I could not conceivably put myself in the position of siding with one tumble against another. If I did so, what little influence I have on Kokod would go up in smoke."

Magnus Ridolph shook his head indulgently. "I fear you imagine the two of us carrying lances, marching in step with the warriors, fighting in the first ranks. No, no, my friend, I assure you I intend nothing quite so broad."

"Well," snapped Clark, "just what do you intend?"

"It occurred to me that if we set out a few pellets of a sensitive explosive, such as fulminating mercury, no one could hold us responsible if tomorrow the Vine Hill armies blundered upon them, and were thereby thrown into confusion."

"How would we know where to set out these pellets? I should think—"

Magnus Ridolph made an easy gesture. "I profess an amateur's interest in military strategy; I will assume responsibility for that phase of the plan."

"But I have no fulminate of mercury," cried Clark, "no explosive of any kind!"

"But you do have a laboratory?"

Clark assented reluctantly. "Rather a makeshift affair."

"Your reagents possibly include fuming nitric acid and iodine?"

"Well—yes."

"Then to work. Nothing could suit our purpose better than nitrogen iodide."

The following afternoon Magnus Ridolph sat in the outdoor café overlooking the vista of Shadow Valley. His right hand clasped an eggshell goblet of Methedeon wine; his left held a mild cigar. Turning his head, he observed the approach of Julius See, and, a few steps behind, like a gaunt red-headed ghost, his partner, Bruce Holpers.

See's face was compressed into layers: a smear of black hair, creased forehead, barred eyebrows, eyes like a single dark slit, pale upper lip, mouth, wide sallow chin. Magnus Ridolph nodded affably. "Good evening, gentlemen."

See came to a halt, as, two steps later, did Bruce Holpers.

"Perhaps you can tell me the outcome of today's battle?" asked Magnus Ridolph. "I indulged myself in a small wager, breaking the habit of many years, but so far I have not learned whether the gods of chance have favored me."

"Well, well," said See throatily. " 'The gods of chance' you call yourself."

Magnus Ridolph turned him a glance of limpid inquiry. "Mr. See, you appear disturbed; I hope nothing is wrong?"

"Nothing special, Ridolph. We had a middling bad day—but they average out with the good ones."

"Unfortunate. . . . I take it, then, that the favorite won? If so, my little wager has been wiped out."

"Your little 25,000 munit wager, eh? And half a dozen other 25,000 munit wagers placed at your suggestion?"

Magnus Ridolph stroked his beard soberly. "I believe I did mention that I thought the odds against Roaring Cape interesting, but now you tell me that Vine Hill has swept the field."

Bruce Holpers uttered a dry cackle. See said harshly, "Come off it, Ridolph. I suppose you're completely unaware that a series of mysterious explosions" ("Land mines," interrupted Holpers, "that's what they were.") "threw Vine Hill enough off stride so that Roaring Cape mopped up Pink Stone Table with them."

Magnus Ridolph sat up.

"Is that right, indeed? Then I have won after all!"

Julius See became suddenly silky, and Bruce Holpers, teetering on heel and toe, glanced skyward. "Unfortunately, Mr. Ridolph, so many persons had placed large bets on Roaring Cape that on meeting the odds, we find ourselves short on cash. We'll have to ask you to take your winnings out in board and room."

"But gentlemen!" protested Magnus Ridolph. "A hundred thousand munits! I'll be here until doomsday!"

See shook his head. "Not at our special Ridolph rates. The next packet is due in five days. Your bill comes to 20,000 munits a day. Exactly 100,000 munits."

"I'm afraid I find your humor a trifle heavy," said Magnus Ridolph frostily.

"It wasn't intended to make you laugh," said See. "Only us. I'm getting quite a kick out of it. How about you, Bruce?"

"Ha, ha, ha," laughed Holpers.

Magnus Ridolph rose to his feet. "There remains to me the classical recourse. I shall leave your exorbitant premises."

See permitted a grin to widen his lips. "Where are you going to leave to?"

"He's going to Roaring Cape Tumble," snickered Holpers. "They owe him a lot."

"In connection with the hundred thousand munits owed me, I'll take a note, an IOU. Oddly enough, a hundred thousand munits is almost exactly what I lost in the Outer Empire Realty and Investment failure."

See grinned sourly. "Forget it, Ridolph, give it up—an angle that didn't pay off."

Magnus Ridolph bowed, marched away. See and Holpers stood looking after him. Holpers made an adenoidal sound. "Think he'll move out?"

See grunted. "There's no reason why he should. He's not getting the hundred thousand anyway; he'd be smarter sitting tight."

"I hope he does go; he makes me nervous. Another deal like today would wipe us out. Six hundred thousand munits—a lot of scratch to go in ten minutes."

"We'll get it back. . . . Maybe we can rig a battle or two ourselves."

Holpers' long face dropped, and his teeth showed. "I'm not so sure that's a good idea. First thing you know Commonwealth Control would be—"

"Pah!" spat See. "What's Control going to do about it? Clark has all the fire and guts of a Leghorn pullet."

"Yes, but—"

"Just leave it to me."

They returned to the lobby. The desk clerk made an urgent motion. "Mr. Ridolph has just checked out! I don't understand where—"

See cut him off with a brusque motion. "He can camp under a stele for all I care."

Magnus Ridolph sat back in the most comfortable of Everley Clark's armchairs and lit a cigarette. Clark watched him with an expression at once wary and obstinate. "We have gained a tactical victory," said Magnus Ridolph, "and suffered a strategic defeat."

Everley Clark knit his brows uneasily. "I don't quite follow you. I should think—"

"We have diminished the financial power of Shadow Valley Inn, and hence, done serious damage. But the blow was not decisive and the syndicate it still viable. I was unable to collect my hundred thousand munits, and also have been forced from the scene of maximum engagement. By this token we may fairly consider that our maximum objectives have not been gained."

"Well," said Clark, "I know it hurts to have to admit defeat, but we've done our best and no one can do more. Considering my position, perhaps it's just as well that—"

"If conditions were to be allowed to rest on the present basis," said Magnus Ridolph, "there might be reason for some slight relaxation. But I fear that See and Holpers have been too thoroughly agitated by their losses to let the matter drop."

Everley Clark eyed Magnus Ridolph in perturbation. "But what can they do? Surely I never—"

Magnus Ridolph shook his head gravely. "I must admit that both See and Holpers accused me of setting off the explosions which routed the Vine Hill Tumble. Admission of guilt would have been ingenuous; naturally I maintained that I had done nothing of the sort. I claimed that I had no opportunity to do so, and further, that the Ecologic Examiner aboard the *Hesperornis* who checked my luggage would swear that I had no chemicals whatsoever among my effects. I believe that I made a convincing protestation."

Everley Clark clenched his fists in alarm, hissed through his teeth.

Magnus Ridolph, looking thoughtfully across the room, went on. "I fear that they will ask themselves the obvious questions. 'Who has Magnus Ridolph most intimately consorted with, since his arrival on Kokod?' 'Who, besides Ridolph, has expressed disapproval of Shadow Valley Inn?"

Everley Clark rose to his feet, paced back and forth. Ridolph continued in a dispassionate voice: "I fear that they will include these questions and whatever answers come to their minds in the complaint which they are preparing for the Chief Inspector at Methedeon."

Cark slumped into a chair, sat staring glassily at Magnus Ridolph. "Why did I let you talk me into this?" he asked hollowly.

Magnus Ridolph rose to his feet in his turn, paced slowly, tugging at his beard. "Certainly, events have not taken the trend we would have chosen, but strategists, amateur or otherwise, must expect occasional setbacks."

"Setbacks!" bawled Clark. "I'll be ruined! Disgraced! Drummed out of the Control!"

"A good strategist is necessarily flexible," mused Magnus Ridolph. "Beyond question, we now must alter our thinking; our primary objective becomes saving you from disgrace, expulsion, and possible prosecution."

Clark ran his hands across his face. "But—what can we do?"

"Very little, I fear," Magnus Ridolph said frankly. He puffed a moment on his cigarette, shook his head doubtfully. "There is one line of attack which might prove fruitful. . . . Yes, I think I see a ray of light.''

"How? In what way? You're not planning to confess?''

"No,'' said Magnus Ridolph. "We gain little, if anything, by that ruse. Our only hope is to discredit Shadow Valley Inn. If we can demonstrate that they do not have the best interests of the Kokod natives at heart, I think we can go a long way toward weakening their allegations.''

"That might well be, but—''

"If we could obtain iron-clad proof, for instance, that Holpers and See are callously using their position to wreak physical harm upon the natives, I think you might consider yourself vindicated.''

"I suppose so. But doesn't the idea seem—well, impractical? See and Holpers have always fallen over backwards to avoid anything of the sort.''

"So I would imagine. Er, what is the native term for Shadow Valley Inn?''

"Big Square Tumble, they call it.''

"As the idea suggests itself to me, we must arrange that a war is conducted on the premises of Shadow Valley Inn, that Holpers and See are required to take forcible measures against the warriors!''

V

Everley Clark shook his head. "Devilish hard. You don't quite get the psychology of these tribes. They'll fight till they fall apart to capture the rallying standard of another tumble—that's a sapling from the sacred stele, of course—they won't be dictated to, or led or otherwise influenced.''

"Well, well,'' said Magnus Ridolph. "In that case, your position is hopeless.'' He came to a halt before Clark's collection of shields. "Let us talk of pleasanter matters.''

Everley Clark gave no sign that he had heard.

Magnus Ridolph stroked one of the shields with reverent fingertips. "Remarkable technique, absolutely unique in my experience. I assume that this rusty orange is one of the ochers?''

Everley Clark made an ambiguous sound.

"A truly beautiful display,'' said Magnus Ridolph. "I suppose there's no doubt that—if worse comes to worst in our little business—you will be allowed to decorate your cell at the regional Penitentiary as you desire.''

Everley Clark said in a thick voice, "Do you think they'll go that far?''

Ridolph considered. "I sincerely hope not. I don't see how we can prevent it unless''—he held up a finger—"unless—''

"What?'' croaked Clark.

"It is farcically simple; I wonder at our own obtuseness.''

"What? What? For Heaven's sake, man—''

"I conceive one certain means by which the warriors can be persuaded to fight at Shadow Valley Inn.''

Everley Clark's face fell. "Oh. Well, how, then?''

"Shadow Valley Inn or Big Square Tumble, if you like, must challenge the Kokod warriors to a contest of arms.''

Everley Clark's expression became more bewildered than ever. "But that's out of the question. Certainly Holpers and See would never . . .''

Magnus Ridolph rose to his feet. "Come,'' he said, with decision. "We will act on their behalf.''

Clark and Magnus Ridolph walked down Shell Strand. On their right the placid blue-black ocean transformed itself into surf or mingled meringue and whipped-cream; on the left bulked the Hidden Hills. Behind towered the magnificent stele of the Shell Strand Tumble; ahead soared the almost equally impressive stele of the Sea Stone Tumble, toward which they bent their steps. Corps of young warriors drilled along the beach; veterans of a hundred battles who had grown stiff, hard and knobby came down from the forest bearing faggots of lance-stock. At the door to the tumble, infant warriors scampered in the dirt like rats.

Clark said huskily, "I don't like this, I don't like it a bit. . . . If it ever gets out—''

"Is such a supposition logically tenable?'' asked Magnus Ridolph. "You are the only living man who speaks the Kokod language.''

"Suppose there is killing—slaughter?''

"I hardly think it likely.''

"It's not impossible. And think of these little warriors—they'll be bearing the brunt—''

Magnus Ridolph said patiently, "We have discussed these points at length.''

Clark muttered, "I'll go through with it . . . but God forgive us both if—"

"Come, come," exclaimed Magnus Ridolph. "Let us approach the matter with confidence; apologizing in advance to your deity hardly maximizes our morale. . . . Now, what is protocol at arranging a war?"

Clark pointed out a dangling wooden plate painted with one of the traditional Kokod patterns. "That's the Charter Board: all I need to do is—well, watch me."

He strode up to the board, took a lance from the hands of a blinking warrior, smartly struck the object. It resonated a dull musical note.

Clark stepped back, and through his nose passed the bagpipe syllables of the Kokod language.

From the door of the tumble stepped a dozen blank-faced warriors, listening attentively.

Clark wound up his speech, turned, scuffed dirt toward the magnificent Sea Stone stele.

The warriors watched impassively. From within the stele came a torrent of syllables. Clark replied at length, then turned on his heel and rejoined Magnus Ridolph. His forehead was damp. "Well, that's that. It's all set. Tomorrow morning at Big Square Tumble."

"Excellent," said Magnus Ridolph briskly. "Now to Shell Strand Tumble, then Rock River, and next Rainbow Cleft."

Clark groaned. "You'll have the entire planet at odds."

"Exactly," said Magnus Ridolph. "After our visit to Rainbow Cleft, you can drop me off near Shadow Valley Inn, where I have some small business."

Clark darted him a suspicious sideglance. "What kind of business?"

"We must be practical," said Magnus Ridolph. "One of the necessary appurtenances to a party of war on Kokod is a rallying standard, a sacred sapling, a focus of effort for the opposing force. Since we can expect neither Holpers nor See to provide one, I must see to the matter myself."

Ridolph strolled up Shadow Valley, approached the hangar where the inn's aircraft were housed. From the shadow of one of the fantastic Kokod trees, he counted six vehicles: three carry-alls, two air-cars like the one which had conveyed him originally to the Control station, and a sleek red sportster evidently the personal property of either See or Holpers.

Neither the hangar-men nor the pilots were in evidence; it might well be their dinner hour. Magnus Ridolph sauntered carelessly forward, whistling an air currently being heard along far-off boulevards.

He cut his whistle off sharply, moved at an accelerated rate. Fastidiously protecting his hands with a bit of rag, he snapped the repair panels from each of the observation cars, made a swift abstraction from each, did likewise for the air-cars. At the sleek sportster he paused, inspected the lines critically.

"An attractive vehicle," he said to himself, "one which might creditably serve the purposes for which I intend it."

He slid back the door, looked inside. The starter key was absent.

Steps sounded behind him. "Hey," said a rough voice, "what are you doing with Mr. See's car?"

Magnus Ridolph withdrew without haste.

"Offhand," he said, "what would you estimate the value of this vehicle?"

The hangarman paused, glowering and suspicious. "Too much not to be taken care of."

Magnus Ridolph nodded. "Thirty thousand munits, possibly."

"Thirty thousand on Earth. This is Kokod."

"I'm thinking of offering See a hundred thousand munits."

The hangarman blinked. "He'd be crazy not to take it."

"I suppose so," sighed Magnus Ridolph. "But first, I wanted to satisfy myself as to the craft's mechanical condition. I fear it has been neglected."

The hangarman snorted in indignation. "Not on your life."

Magnus Ridolph frowned. "That tube is certainly splitting. I can tell by the patina along the enamel."

"No such thing!" roared the hangarman. "That tube flows like a dream."

Ridolph shook his head. "I can't offer See good money for a defective vehicle. . . . He'll be angry to lose the sale."

The hangarman's tone changed. "I tell you, that tube's good as gold. . . . Wait, I'll show you."

He pulled a key-ring from his pocket, plugged it into the starter sockct. The car quivered free of the ground, eager for flight. "See? Just what I told you?"

Magnus Ridolph said doubtfully. "It's seems to be working fairly well now. . . . You get on the telephone and tell Mr. See that I am taking his car for a trial spin, a final check. . . . "

The mechanic looked dumbly at Magnus Ridolph, slowly turned to the speaker on the wall.

Magnus Ridolph jumped into the seat. The mechanic's voice was loud. "The gentleman that's buying your boat is giving it the once-over. Don't let him feed you no line about a bum tube; the ship is running like oil down a four mile bore. Don't take nothing else . . . What? . . . Sure he's here; he said so himself. . . . A little schoolteacher guy with a white beard like a nanny-goat . . ." The sound from the telephone caused him to jump back sharply. Anxiously, he turned to look where he had left Magnus Ridolph and Julian See's sleek red air-car.

Both had disappeared.

Mrs. Chaim roused her peacock-shaped friend Mrs. Borgage rather earlier than usual. "Hurry, Altamira; we've been so late these last few mornings, we've missed the best seats in the observation car."

Mrs. Borgage obliged by hastening her toilet; in short order the two ladies appeared in the lobby. By a peculiar coincidence both wore costumes of dark green, a color which each thought suited the other not at all. They paused by the announcement of the day's war in order to check the odds, then turned into the dining room.

They ate a hurried breakfast, set out for the loading platform. Mrs. Borgage, pausing to catch her breath and enjoy the freshness of the morning, glanced toward the roof of the inn. Mrs. Chaim rather impatiently looked over her shoulder. "Whatever are you staring at, Altamira?"

Mrs. Borgage pointed. "It's that unpleasant little man Ridolph . . . I can't fathom what he's up to. He seems to be fixing some sort of branches to the roof."

Mrs. Chaim sniffed. "I thought the management had turned him out."

"Isn't that Mr. See's air-car on the roof behind him?"

"I really couldn't say," replied Mrs. Chaim. "I know very

little of such things." She turned away toward the loading platform, and Mrs. Borgage followed.

Once more they met interruption; this time in the form of the
pilot. His clothes were disarranged; his face had suffered
scratching and contusion. Running wild-eyed, he careened into
the two green-clad ladies, disengaged himself and continued
without apology.

Mrs. Chaim bridled in outrage. "Well, I never!" She turned
to look after the pilot. "Has the man gone mad?"

Mrs. Borgage, peering ahead to learn the source of the pilot's
alarm, uttered a sharp cry.

"What is it?" asked Mrs. Chaim irritatedly.

Mrs. Borgage clasped her arm with bony fingers. "Look."

VI

During the subsequent official investigation, Commonwealth
Control Agent Everley Clark transcribed the following eyewit-
ness account:

"I am Joe 234, Leg-leader of the Fifteenth Brigade, the Fa-
natics, in the service of the indomitable Shell Strand Tumble.

"We are accustomed to the ruses of Topaz Tumble and the
desperate subtleties of Star Throne; hence the ambush prepared
by the giant warriors of Big Square Tumble took us not at all by
surprise.

"Approaching by Primary Formation 17, we circled the flat
space occupied by several flying contrivances, where we flushed
out a patrol spy. We thrashed him with our lances, and he fled
back to his own forces.

"Continuing, we encountered a first line of defense consisting
of two rather ineffectual warriors accoutred in garments of green
cloth. These we beat, also, according to Convention 22, in force
during the day. Uttering terrible cries, the two warriors retreated, luring us toward prepared positions inside the tumble
itself. High on the roof the standard of Big Square Tumble rose,
plain to see. No deception there, at least! Our strategic problem
assumed a clear form; how best to beat down resistance and win
to the roof.

"Frontal assault was decided upon; the signal to advance was
given. We of the Fifteenth were first past the outer defense—a

double panel of thick glass which we broke with rocks. Inside we met a spirited defense which momentarily threw us back.

"At this juncture occurred a diversion in the form of troops from the Rock River Tumble, which, as we now know, the warriors of the Big Square Tumble had rashly challenged for the same day. The Rock River warriors entered by a row of flimsy doors facing the mountain, and at this time the Big Square defenders violated Convention 22, which requires that the enemy be subdued by blows of the lance. Flagrantly they hurled glass cups and goblets, and by immemorial usage we were allowed to retaliate in kind.

"At the failure of this tactic, the defending warriors withdrew to an inner bastion, voicing their war-cries.

"The siege began in earnest; and now the Big Square warriors began to pay the price of their arrogance. Not only had they pitted themselves against Shell Strand and Rock River, but they likewise had challenged the redoubtable Rainbow Cleft and Sea Stone, conquerors of Rose Slope and Dark Fissure. The Sea Stone warriors, led by their Throw-away Legion, poured through a secret rear-entrance, while the Rainbow Cleft Special Vanguard occupied the Big Square main council hall.

"A terrible battle raged for several minutes in a room designed for the preparations of nourishments, and again the Big Square warriors broke code by throwing fluids, pastes, and powders—a remission which the alert Shell Strand warriors swiftly copied.

"I led the Fanatic Fifteenth outside, hoping to gain exterior access to the roof, and thereby win the Big Square standard. The armies of Shell Strand, Sea Stone, Rock River and Rainbow Cleft now completely surrounded Big Square Tumble, a magnificent sight which shall live in my memory till at last I lay down my lance.

"In spite of our efforts, the honor of gaining the enemy standard went to a daredevil squad from Sea Stone, which scaled a tree to the roof and so bore away the trophy. The defenders, ignorant of, or ignoring the fact that the standard had been taken, broke the code yet again, this time by using tremendous blasts of water. The next time Shell Strand wars with Big Square Tumble we shall insist on one of the Conventions allowing any and all weapons; otherwise we place ourselves at a disadvantage.

"Victorious, our army, together with the troops of Sea Stone,

Rock River, and Rainbow Cleft, assembled in the proper formations and marched off to our home tumbles. Even as we departed, the great Black Comet Tumble dropped from the sky to vomit further warriors for Big Square. However, there was no pursuit, and unmolested we returned to the victory rituals.

Captain Bussey of the Phoenix Line packet *Archaeornix*, which had arrived as the Kokod warriors marched away, surveyed the wreckage with utter astonishment. "What in God's name happened to you?"

Julius See stood panting, his forehead clammy with sweat. "Get me guns," he cried hoarsely. "Get me a blaster; I'll wipe out every damn hive on the planet. . . ."

Holpers came loping up, arms flapping the air. "They've completely demolished us; you should see the lobby, the kitchen, the day rooms! A shambles—"

Captain Bussey shook his head in bewilderment. "Why in the world should they attack you? They're supposed to be a peaceable race . . . except toward each other, of course."

"Well, something got into them," said See, still breathing hard. "They came at us like tigers—beating us with their damn little sticks. . . . I finally washed them out with firehoses."

"What about your guests?" asked Captain Bussey in sudden curiosity.

See shrugged. "I don't know what happened to them. A bunch ran off up the valley, smack into another army. I understand they got beat up as good as those that stayed."

"We couldn't even escape in our aircraft," complained Holpers. "Not one of them would start. . . ."

A mild voice interrupted. "Mr. See, I have decided against purchasing your air-car, and have returned it to the hangar."

See slowly turned, the baleful aura of his thoughts almost tangible. "You, Ridolph. . . . I'm beginning to see daylight. . . ."

"I beg your pardon?"

"Come on, spill it!" See took a threatening step forward.

Captain Bussey said, "Careful, See, watch your temper."

See ignored him. "What's your part in all this, Ridolph?"

Magnus Ridolph shook his head in bewilderment. "I'm completely at a loss. I rather imagined that the natives learned of your gambling on events they considered important, and decided to take punitive steps."

The ornamental charabanc from the ship rolled up; among the passengers was a woman of notable bust, correctly tinted, massaged, coiffed, scented and decorated. "Ah!" said Magnus Ridolph. "Mrs. Chickering! Charming!"

"I could stay away no longer," said Mrs. Chickering. "I had to know how—our business was proceeding."

Julius See leaned forward curiously. "What kind of business do you mean?"

Mrs. Chickering turned him a swift contemptuous glance; then her attention was attracted by two women who came hobbling from the direction of the inn. She gasped. "Olga! Altamira! What on Earth—"

"Don't stand there gasping," snapped Mrs. Chaim. "Get us clothes. Those frightful savages tore us to shreds."

Mrs. Chickering turned in confusion to Magnus Ridolph. "Just what has happened! Surely you can't have—"

Magnus Ridolph cleared his throat. "Mrs. Chickering, a word with you aside." He drew her out of earshot of the others. "Mrs. Chaim and Mrs. Borgage—are they friends of yours?"

Mrs. Chickering cast an anxious glance over her shoulder. "I can't understand the situation at all," she muttered feverishly. "Mrs. Chaim is the president of the Woman's League and Mrs. Borgage is treasurer. I can't understand them running around with their clothing in shreds. . . ."

Magnus Ridolph said candidly, "Well, Mrs. Chickering, in carrying out your instructions, I allowed scope to the natural combativeness of the natives, and perhaps they—"

"Martha," came Mrs. Chaim's grating voice close at hand, "what is your connection with this man? I have reason to suspect that he is mixed up in this terrible attack. Look at him!" Her voice rose furiously. "They haven't laid a finger on him! And the rest of us—"

Martha Chickering licked her lips. "Well, Olga, dear, this is Magnus Ridolph. In accordance with last month's resolution, we hired him to close down the gambling here at the inn."

Magnus Ridolph said in his suavest tones, "Following which, Mrs. Chaim and Mrs. Borgage naturally thought it best to come out and study the situation at first hand; am I right?"

Mrs. Chaim and Mrs. Borgage glared. Mrs. Chaim said, "If

you think, Martha Chickering, that the Woman's League will in any way recognize this rogue—''

"My dear Mrs. Chaim," protested Magnus Ridolph.

"But, Olga—I promised him a thousand munits a week!"

Magnus Ridolph waved his hand airily. "My dear Mrs. Chickering, I prefer that any sums due me be distributed among worthy charities. I have profited during my short stay here—''

"See!" came Captain Bussey's voice. "For God's sake, man, control yourself!"

Magnus Ridolph, turning, found See struggling in the grasp of Captain Bussey. "Try and collect!" See cried out to Magnus Ridolph. He angrily thrust Captain Bussey's arms aside, stood with hands clenching and unclenching. "Just try and collect!"

"My dear Mr. See, I have already collected.''

"You've done nothing of the sort—and if I catch you in my boat again, I'll break your scrawny little neck!"

Magnus Ridolph held up his hand. "The hundred thousand munits I wrote off immediately; however, there were six other bets which I placed by proxy; these were paid, and my share of the winnings came to well over three hundred thousand munits. Actually, I regard this sum as return of the capital which I placed with the Outer Empire Investment and Realty Society, plus a reasonable profit. Everything considered, it was a remunerative as well as instructive investment.''

"Ridolph," muttered See, "one of these days—''

Mrs. Chaim shouldered forward. "Did I hear you say 'Outer Empire Realty and Investment Society'?''

Magnus Ridolph nodded. "I believe that Mr. See and Mr. Holpers were responsible officials of the concern.''

Mrs. Chaim took two steps forward. See frowned uneasily; Bruce Holpers began to edge away. "Come back here!" cried Mrs. Chaim. "I have a few words to say before I have you arrested.''

Magnus Ridolph turned to Captain Bussey. "You return to Methedeon on schedule, I assume?''

"Yes," said Captain Bussey dryly.

Magnus Ridolph nodded. "I think I will go aboard at once, since there will be considerable demand for passage.''

"As you wish," said Captain Bussey.

"I believe No. 12 is your best cabin?''

"I believe so," said Captain Bussey.

"Then kindly regard Cabin No. 12 as booked."

"Very well, Mr. Ridolph."

Magnus Ridolph looked up the mountainside. "I noticed Mr. Pilby running along the ridge a few minutes ago. I think it would be a real kindness if he were notified that the war is over."

"I think so too," said Captain Bussey. They looked around the group. Mrs. Chaim was still engaged with Julius See and Bruce Holpers. Mrs. Borgage was displaying her bruises to Mrs. Chickering. No one seemed disposed to act on Magnus Ridolph's suggestion.

Magnus Ridolph shrugged, climbed the gangway into the *Archaeornyx*. "Well, no matter. In due course he will very likely come by himself."

FIESTA BRAVA

by Mack Reynolds

For once, Supervisor Sid Jakes of Section G., Bureau of Investigation, Department of Justice, Commissariat of Interplanetary Affairs, was flabbergasted. Gone as the snows of yesteryear was the easygoing, happy-go-lucky expression on his face.

He said blankly, "You mean Supervisor Li Chang Chu sent you people for this Falange assignment?"

The large one, who had named himself Dorn Horsten, nodded seriously. His facial muscles would perhaps have been hard put to register anything other than stolid sincerity. "That is correct, Citizen Jakes."

The Section G official looked at him in puzzlement. "Horsten . . . Horsten. Dorn Horsten. You're not Dr. Horsten, the algae specialist?"

"That is correct."

"But . . . but what are you doing in my office? In Section G? Li Chang was shaping up a small troupe for me to send to a far-out planet that's been giving us a hard time."

Horsten nodded. "I understand the size of your organization precludes you knowing all your agents, Supervisor Jakes. I was recruited by Ronny Bronston, after he had saved my life under somewhat remarkable circumstances. Although I embrace the purpose of Section G as ardently as any other agent, thus far I have been utilized on only two assignments.''

Sid Jakes shook his head and turned to the middle-aged couple seated sedately before his desk. The woman was small and demure, the man on the plumpish side. There was the feeling of servants; long years in service—he perhaps a butler, she a maid or cook.

''And you two also are Section G agents?''

''We three,'' the man said.

Sid Jakes stared at the little girl in her pink go-to-party dress, a blue ribbon in her neatly combed blond hair to match her baby-blue eyes.

He blurted, ''How in the world did you get past the Octagon guards with that child?''

The child tinkled a laugh.

The woman said, ''Helen is . . . is it twenty-five?''

''Twenty-six,'' Helen said. She made a childish face at Sid Jakes, who blinked.

The woman, who had been introduced as Martha Lorans, said, ''Helen isn't really our daughter, of course. It's camouflage. In putting the team together, Li Chang thought it would go far as protective coloring.''

''Especially,'' Helen said, ''since otherwise I'm so conspicuous.''

''But . . . then you're a midget,'' Sid Jakes blurted.

''Not exactly,'' the seeming child said, an element of irritation in her voice. ''There's a situation on our planet that thus far our research people haven't solved. For that matter, we are not so sure we wish to solve it. What is the basis of this belief that people should strive to be taller? Why was the Viking the ideal, rather than the Japanese?''

''For one thing,'' Dr. Dorn Horsten said, deadpanned, ''the Viking could clobber the Japanese.''

She looked over at him and snorted. ''Not always, you big lummox. It was the Jap who perfected judo and karate, remember. But even if it was true that in the old days of swords and spears the large man dominated the small, we don't use such weapons today.''

''What started all this jetsam?'' Sid Jakes said. The interview had a feeling of unreality so far as he was concerned. He had more than an averagely serious situation on his hands, and had requested a team of trained Section G operatives. His colleague, Li Chang Chu, had sent him what would appear an average middle-aged family, man, woman and eight-year-old, and a staid, though admittedly king-sized, scientist of interplanetary reputation.

Helen said, "I was just telling you that on my home planet, of Gandharvas, we are small in stature, as averages go, and we also are longlived and mature rather slowly, insofar as appearance is concerned. In my case, and under these circumstances, I also, of course, am relying upon children's clothes, a child's hairdo, and even a certain amount of cosmetic to put over the effect desired."

"The effect desired?" Sid Jakes said blankly. "What in the name of the Holy Ultimate did Li Chang think the effect desired was? I need a troupe of agents, tough agents, to lick the situation on Falange."

"How tough?" Helen said sweetly. She had allowed the childish lisp to return to her voice.

It was a matter of exasperation now. Sid Jakes glared at her. "Tougher than any seeming eight-year-old kid could handle," he snapped. "Listen, they're onto Section G on this planet Falange. We've lost three agents there in the past year and a half. In each case they were unmasked and brought to trial on trumped-up charges. One was accused of murder, one of subversion and the other disrespect of the Caudillo; all capital offenses. Their *Policía Secreta* is one of the most efficient in the some three thousand member worlds of United Planets. They ought to be, they've had enough practice. And now they're just sitting there, waiting for the next batch of Section G operatives to show up."

Sid Jakes came to his feet suddenly, paced around the desk and up and down the floor, in sheer disgust. "It's going to be a neat trick to even land there, not to speak of overthrowing the crackpot government."

"Overthrowing the government?" Pierre Lorans said interestedly. "Li Chang didn't tell us what the assignment involved."

The Section G supervisor turned on him. "I suppose that if you've made agent in this bureau, you must have something on the ball. What did you do before you were recruited?"

"I was, and am, a chef," Lorans said.

"A chef!" Jakes rolled his eyes upward in search of divine

guidance. Then he looked at the drab appearing woman. "And you?"

"I'm a housewife."

"A housewife. Holy Jumping Zen. Except for the training I *assume* Li Chang put you through before making you a full agent, did you have any earlier background that would . . ."

She shook her head. "No. Not exactly."

He rounded the desk again and plumped himself down in his swivel chair. He closed his eyes and said, "I give up. I surrender. Three of our best agents down the drain and to replace them I get a double-domed scientist, a pint-sized girl in a baby getup, a chef and a housewife."

Dr. Dorn Horsten lumbered to his feet. He was a big man, at least six-four and some two hundred and forty pounds. However, his conservative dress, his pince-nez glasses and his scholarly facial expression, tended to offset his size.

He said gently, "Helen, I suppose we should make some effort to indicate why Li Chang Chu chose us for the assignment."

The little girl looked up at him in wide-eyed innocence. "Allez oop!" she tinkled suddenly.

In a blur of motion, the hulking scientist reached down and grabbed her by the feet, swung her mightily, in a giant circle, launched her brutally at the far wall, head first.

Sid Jakes's eyes bugged. He came halfway to his feet, froze there momentarily, sank back again.

She turned in the air, her small arms tucked around her knees, hit the wall, feet first, bounced upward, hit the ceiling, feet first, ricocheted off to a set of steel files, bounced onto the desk of the Section G supervisor, seemed to go up into the air and spin around three times. She wound up sitting on his shoulder, his paperknife in her tiny, chubby hand. The point of the paperknife was behind his right ear.

Dr. Dorn Horsten nonchalantly picked up Sid Jakes's ultra-large steel desk, tucked it under his left arm and walked over to the wall where he leaned, on his right hand, still holding the desk.

Horsten said mildly, "The widely held prejudice that double-domes—I believe was your term—don't have muscles fails to stand up on my home world of Ftörsta, Citizen Jakes. You see, we have a 1.6 G planet. On top of that, the original colonists were, ah, nature boys, I believe is the usual term of contempt. At any rate, in the same manner that Helen's world possibly has the smallest average citizen in United Planets, surely Ftörsta has the strongest.''

Sid Jakes was still in a condition of shock.

He blatted, ''You can't pick that up!''

Dorn Horsten let his eyebrows rise.

''It must weight a ton!'' Jakes protested.

''I doubt it,'' Horsten said. ''It doesn't have the heft.''

Helen, with a skip and a jump, bounced from her superior's shoulder to the floor and in a graceful, flowing motion, back into the chair she had originally occupied.

The overgrown doctor returned the desk to its place, an apologetic air about him. ''It speeds things up, sometimes, to be a bit melodramatic,'' he said.

Sid Jakes closed his eyes and rubbed them with his right hand. He opened them again and looked accusingly at Mr. and Mrs. Pierre Lorans.

Pierre Lorans shifted in his chair slightly and said, ''I throw things.''

''I'll bet you do,'' Jakes muttered. And then, ''What do you mean, you throw things? Why?''

''Well, it's always been a hobby. Ever since childhood I've got a kick out of throwing things.'' He came to his feet and approached the Section G official's desk. ''For instance,'' he said and picked up the paperknife.

The office of Sid Jakes was done with a British Victorian revival motif. At the far end of the more than averagely large room was an antique calendar.

''For instance,'' Lorans repeated and suddenly flicked the paperknife. ''It is, June 23rd; old calendar, isn't it?''

Jakes's eyes went to the calendar. ''Hey,'' he said, ''that's a collector's item!''

The professional chef took up an ancient pen, a decorative antique on the supervisor's desk. That flicked suddenly too, and also buried itself in the tiny square devoted to June 23rd.

He turned back to his superior. ''Just about anything. Knives, spears, hatchets, meat cleavers . . .''

Jakes shuddered.

'' . . . Ball bearings . . .''

''Ball bearings?'' Jakes said.

"Hm-m-m," the plump man fished into his jerkin pocket and came forth with a shiny steel marble. "You'd be surprised what you can do with a ball bearing. See the right eye in that portrait down there?"

"Oh no, you don't . . ." Jakes said much too late.

The ball bearing instead of bouncing off, penetrated the eye completely and evidently imbedded itself in the wall.

" . . . Baseballs," Lorans was saying, "boomerangs, shovels, crowbars, wrenches—"

"Shovels!" Jakes said. "All right, all right. Sit down. Don't throw anything else. I accept your word." He bent his eye on Mrs. Lorans. "Do you throw things, too, or is it only a one-member-of-the-family vice?"

"Oh, no," she said primly. "Pierre and I met at the Special Talents class of Supervisor Li Chang . . ."

"Is *that* where she dug you all up?" he muttered. "I'm going to have to find the time to look into that pet project of Li Chang's."

"We attended at the same time. I'd never seen anyone throw things before. Not like Pierre does. You should see him throw a fork."

Sid Jakes looked pained and muttered something about inviting the other to dinner, but then he said, aloud, "And your, ah, Special Talent?"

"Well," she came to her feet and approached the antique bookshelves, pursed her lips and selected a volume of the "Encyclopedia Britannica."

"Holy Jumping Zen," Jakes snapped. "Easy with that. It's worth its weight in platinum. Don't throw it."

"I wasn't going to throw it," she said. She put it down on the desk, opened it at random, spent possibly one flat second scanning the page and then pushed the book in front of Jakes and returned to her chair.

He stared at her.

Her eyes went vague and she began to recite "*. . . which is shown a lion holding a sword. The whole has a border of yellow. This flag was first hoisted on the morning of February 4, 1948 and became . . .*"

She droned on and on.

Sid Jakes scowled, looked from one of the four to the other, finally looked down at the book. He blinked.

Mrs. Pierre Lorans was reciting, word for word, the "Encyclopedia's" article on flags—word for word and without a single mistake.

"All right," he interrupted finally. He looked at her accusingly. "You could do the whole page?"

"Yes."

"You could do the whole 'Encyclopedia'?" he said unbelievingly.

"If I scanned each page."

"Holy Ultimate, why don't you rent yourself out as a computer memory bank?"

"I have held somewhat equivalent positions," she said.

Sid Jakes sat there for a long moment, looking at them. Finally he said, "Forgive me, but frankly you four are the most unlikely set of freaks I've ever had in my office."

Dr. Dorn Horsten said stolidly, "Actually, we are not as far out as all that. It is just that you are seeing us all together. In truth, man has always been a freak among animals. Even right here on Earth, in the old days were men who trained themselves to the point where they could pick up four thousand pounds— two tons. There were others who could run down a wild horse and capture it. There were gymnasts who could put a monkey to shame. There were others with eidetic memories, such as Lord MacCauley; still others with freak brains who could do fantastic mathematical problems in their heads. I will not even mention various well authenticated psi phenomena, ranging from levitation to clairvoyance."

Sid Jakes pushed his hand back through his hair and said, "All right. But the thing is, what'd Li Chang have in mind when she sent you here?"

Helen looked at him mockingly, her childish eyes bright. "But you have already mentioned the reason. How did you put it? The *Policía Secreta* of the planet Falange is onto Section G and they're just sitting there waiting for the next batch of agents to show up."

He blinked at her.

She shrugged tiny shoulders. "Did you expect your next troupe to be able to land with Model H guns and all the gadgets of the Department of Dirty Tricks? They'd be detected before the ship ever set down."

Some of Sid Jakes's natural exuberance returned to him. "Holy Ultimate," he muttered. "At least they're going to have some surprises coming. But what's the excuse for you going to Falange? They don't welcome strangers. Tourists are not allowed. They're one of the most backward worlds in United Planets and want to keep it that way."

Horsten said, "All worlds settled by man owe their existence to the chlorophyll containing plants. All of them have problems involving algae. Citizen Jakes, I do not know of a world that has any science whatsoever that would not welcome a visit by Dorn Horsten. Excuse me, I speak in all modesty. The slightest drop of a hint to a colleague on Falange, and I would be overwhelmed with invitations."

"Hm-m-m," Sid Jakes said. "I suppose you're right." He looked at Pierre Lorans.

The plump man who loved to throw things, puffed out his cheeks. A certain Gallic quality seemed to come over him. He said pompously, "I am a *Nouveau Cordon Bleu* chef. One of my specialties is the dishes of the Iberian peninsula. I assure you, my *paella* is unsurpassed. At this time, however, many of the dishes once famed in Spain now continue only on the planet Falange where they were taken centuries ago when that world was colonized. Citizen Jakes, there are few, if any, worlds where a *Cordon Bleu* chef would be unwelcome. Haute cuisine is one of the gentler arts. I will arrive with the announced intention of studying the dishes of Falange, but I shall also give of my knowledge and skill to chefs residing there. I will, of course, be accompanied by my somewhat, ah, forgive me Martha, colorless wife, and my little girl. What could be more innocent?"

Sid Jakes took them all in again, one by one. He grinned. "It'll be a neat trick," he said. Then, "Let me brief you on the situation." He squirmed nervously in his chair, more his old self at last. He said, "You know, most people are in favor of progress. Of course, it's an elastic term. For instance, some centuries ago early nuclear physicists devised a method of splitting the atom. Their discoveries were turned over to the military which utilized them to blow up a couple of cities. It all came under the head of progress. Earlier still, missionaries landed on the islands of the South Pacific. Within a century, the populations had been decimated; however, they had been baptized before succumbing to tuberculosis, syphilis, measles and the wearing of Mother Hubbards in that climate, so the missionaries considered it progress.''

Martha Lorans laughed, displaying a desirable side of her that had thus far been hidden.

Sid Jakes said, "However, *all* people are not in favor of progress. And the ruling elite of Falange are among them. Have any of you ever heard of the Spanish Civil War?''

The three Lorans shook their heads but Dr. Horsten scowled seriously and said, "Slightly. Nineteenth or twentieth century, old calendar, wasn't it?''

Jakes said, "It was a strange war. Supposedly a civil war, it was actually a preliminary conflict preceding a global one. Spain was used as a proving ground for weapons and troops and tens of thousands of Europeans, Asiatics and Americans swarmed there to participate. It was a brutal war and devastated Spain. When the smoke cleared, the forces of *der Führer* and *Il Duce* had enabled the more reactionary elements to come to power under their own dictator, El Caudillo.

"However, no problem is ever settled until it is settled right, and the elements that had achieved power under the Caudillo were not those needed for the country to develop. The government and the socio-economic system were anachronisms and it began to show. While the rest of Europe snowballed into the Second Industrial Revolution, Spain remained stationary. Soon, the more intelligent and trained elements in the country realized the situation and began to take what action they could. The very things that El Caudillo had won on the battlefields, he lost in the day-by-day developments of civilian life. Uneducated peasants cannot be trusted to operate machinery. Schools had to go up. Underpaid workers are inefficient—they don't eat well enough. Pay began to go up. Tourists don't come to countries where there are terrifying secret police everywhere. The *Guardia Civil* was cut down numerically, and no longer paraded the roads and bridges openly armed with submachine guns. Slowly, the Caudillo's victory was eroding away.

"Most of the Spanish, of course, were profiting by this and most were pleased. Spain eventually boomed to the point where it entered Common Europe. However, there was a hard core element that objected. They lived in the past and wanted to stay there. They had won their reactionary war behind the Caudillo and demanded that what they had won be forever observed. When this became impossible, in Europe, they became one of the first groups to colonize another world—Falange.''

Little Helen was frowning. "I can see these stick-in-the-muds wanting to maintain their old privileges, their positions of power. I can see them deciding to migrate to a new planet where they could, uh, go to hell in their own way. But I can't imagine them getting any peasants, servants and so forth to go with them. And a ruling elite is no longer a ruling elite, unless it has somebody to rule."

Jakes chuckled. "Then you're wrong, my dear. In any given social system, the majority of the ruled *like* to be ruled in the manner in which they are being ruled. Otherwise, they'd do something about it. Under slavery, the majority liked being slaves, or they would have taken measures to end the situation. Under feudalism, the serfs, the artisans in the towns, the middle-class merchants all *liked* being ruled by the aristocracy. When they stopped liking it they stormed the palaces and some clever chap invented the guillotine to speed matters up."

Helen made a face. "I suppose you're right," she said, "but you'd have one damn rough time making a slave or serf of me."

Jakes chuckled again. He was beginning to like this pint-sized operative. "I am sure you would either become free or die in the attempt, and, of course, a dead slave is not a slave. At any rate, our malcontents were able to recruit all the elements they needed for their new colony. Several thousand strong, they migrated. Their new society was dedicated to the past and the prevention of change. And there it is today."

"And that's where we come in," Dr. Horsten said. "But why?"

Sid Jakes looked at him. "Surely you know that. You're a Section G agent."

Pierre Lorans said, "Obviously, we know the reason for the existence of this cloak-and-dagger department. It is to forward the progress of the worlds settled by man so that we will be as strong as possible, as a life form, when our inevitable confrontation with the intelligent aliens beyond takes place. But why the need to overthrow the government of Falange?"

The Section G supervisor nodded. "Whether they want to be forwarded or not, and most of them don't, our task is to push into progress our member planets. Nothing is clung to so assiduously as socio-economic systems, and nothing can become so detrimental to progress. The immediate factor that motivates us is that the most highly industrialized planets, for example Avalon and Catalina, are somewhat desperately in need of various rare metals that are present in ample supply on Falange. Mining methods are so primitive there that unless she is more highly industrialized and welcomes in engineers from more advanced worlds, these minerals will never be exploited.''

Dr. Horsten had taken his pince-nez glasses from his nose and was polishing them. "Very well, our task will be to overthrow this restrictive government and establish a new regime more conducive to progress.''

Sid Jakes looked at the four of them doubtfully. It was, of course, partly their clothing and deliberate effort to look harmless. But for the moment a more unlikely group of revolutionists could hardly be imagined.

Pierre Lorans said, ''Just what is their present governmental form?''

''An absolute dictator,'' Jakes said. ''The Caudillo, who rules for life.''

Lorans said, ''But the regime has been in power for centuries. When the Caudillo dies, how does a new one come in?''

Jakes looked around at them. ''The best matador is appointed.''

The four stared at him.

''The *what*?'' Helen demanded.

''The best bullfighter.''

II

It had been decided that there was no particular reason for them to avoid each other in the spaceship *Golden Hind*. The most natural thing for the noted Dr. Dorn Horsten, who was traveling alone, would be to strike up a companionship with Chef Pierre Lorans and his wife, since they were all headed for a common destination, the planet Falange and its capital city Nuevo Madrid.

So it was that early in the journey the doctor introduced himself and soon became the constant companion of the chef who specialized in Iberian dishes. They spent considerable time playing battle chess while Mrs. Lorans read through the ship's tapes, and little Helen played with the scant supply of toys she had been allowed to bring along.

The child was a good-natured, cheerful tike, the other passengers decided, usually with a slight smile on her face as though she was amused by some inner thoughts. She was obviously too young to have much understanding of the world of adults; and businessmen discussing deals, or diplomats en route from one world to another, paid no attention to her if she sat at their feet during some discussion.

On the third day out, Helen came to where Martha Lorans was rapidly flipping through some tapes. It looked, to an outsider, as though she was quickly scanning, searching for something she wished to read but failing to find anything. The two men, as usual, had their heads over a battlechess board.

Helen said to Martha, "What are you sopping up?"

Martha looked at her, her eyes at first blank, but then clearing as she came into the here and now. "How to run this spaceship," she said.

The little girl winced. "Let's hope it doesn't come to that."

Martha laughed. As always, on her it looked particularly good. "You never know," she said. "There is very little knowledge that is worthless."

"Well, I hope that'll remain so," Helen said. "Look, how about you going to the captain and sending a subspace cable to Avalon for me?"

Dr. Horsten looked up and scowled at her. "Avalon? Why?"

"I want to buy in on a development there."

They were all looking at her now. She looked down at her feet, shod in her little girl shoes, and looked like nothing so much as an eight-year-old asking for a privilege she suspected was going to be denied.

She added, "I have some savings banked in the exchange computers on Terra. I'd like to have them transferred to Avalon and invested with the Sky-High Development Corporation."

Lorans's eyes narrowed. "Why?"

"Oh, I just want to."

Dr. Horsten nodded sourly. "What is this corporation?"

"Oh, it's just in the process of being organized."

"Hm-m-m. And why is it you're so anxious to buy in?"

"Oh, there've been a few rumors around the ship."

Horsten shook his head. "You little sneak. I saw you playing with your doll under the table of those two sharpies from Avalon. Now look, if Martha did make such a purchase then those two businessmen would know there'd been a leak on this ship. The Lorans family would come under suspicion. And we don't want anybody to start wondering about the Lorans family, nor their friend, Dr. Horsten."

"Little sneak," she snorted. "Why, you big ox. I ought to clobber you."

Martha Lorans laughed. "That I'd like to see some day. But Dorn's right, Helen."

Little Helen snorted again, but jumped up into one of the lounge's chairs and spread her dress neatly, the way a precocious child spreads her skirt.

She snarled under her breath, "What the hell's the use of getting onto a good thing, if you're not allowed to profit by it? I could triple my exchange credits."

The others went back to their pursuits.

After a few minutes, Helen sighed and said, "I still don't believe it. Martha, how about reciting that about the bullfighting again."

Martha looked up with a sigh. "All of it?"

"Not all the details about the history of the bullfight. Imagine! That relic of the Roman arena coming down to the twentieth century and beyond."

"Twentieth century," Lorans grunted. "All the way down to the present. At least on Falange."

"It's unbelievable," Helen said. "Imagine those cloddies going to the trouble of freighting enough of these, what was the name of the breed of bull, Martha?"

"Bos taurus ibericus."

"Evidently useless for anything except the so-called fiesta brava. Shipping enough of them all the way from Earth, to stock bull farms."

"Fincas," Martha supplied. "They call bull ranches *fincas.*"

"Well," Horsten said, "it's still their national spectacle, their national fascination. Evidently, every Falangist on the planet is an aficionado, a bull fight buff."

"But using it as a method of picking a Chief of State! When the Caudillo dies, that matador pronounced *Número Uno* becomes the new Caudillo. Why, that's chaos! Nothing to do with education or intelligence quotient. Nothing to do with background in governing. Nothing to do with anything save bullfighting. Why, there's nothing so silly in the whole of United Planets.''

"I don't know," Pierre Lorans said. "There're some pretty silly methods of selecting those who govern." He looked thoughtful. "A top matador would have to be in physically fine shape. He'd have to be sharp, quick, or he would never have become *Número Uno*. He couldn't be stupid, either, because although a stupid person with good reflexes might survive in the ring for a time, the occasions would come up when he could save himself from disaster only by utilizing intelligence."

"Anything for an argument, eh?" Helen snorted. "Defending the silliest method of selecting a dictator that's ever come down the pike."

Dorn Horsten put down the piece he was holding and said thoughtfully, "What I can't understand is the danger the elite goes through of having one of the under-privileged classes win control. No power elite ever willingly gives up its position. Why, if the wrong man got in there—wrong from their view—he could upset their applecart for all time."

Martha said, or rather recited, "Our information on this aspect of Falange government is scanty. It would seem that one of the factors that keeps the average Falangist contented with the status quo is that every person on the planet, theoretically, has the chance to become Caudillo. When the old Caudillo dies, an enthusiasm sweeps the planet evidently beyond anything known elsewhere in the system in the way of fiestas, Mardi Gras, ferias, carnivals. For weeks, during which the fights are being held, contestants being eliminated, the planet Falange is in a state of euphoria difficult to conceive of on the part of anyone who has not witnessed it."

"That's a point," Horsten said. "If you condone the system, and even enjoy it, and especially if you take part yourself, or support a friend, relation or comrade in the fights, you can hardly protest the system later." He took up the chess piece again and muttered thoughtfully, "I still can't imagine the Falange powers that would be taking the chance of a peasant, or unskilled worker, becoming Caudillo."

Helen evidently grew suddenly bored and bounced down from her chair. "I think I'll go pester Ferd."

Dorn Horsten scowled at her. "Who?"

Martha looked at Helen. "You mean that brain surgeon?"

"Ferdinand Zogbaum," Helen said. "But he's not a brain surgeon, he's some sort of electronics wizard."

"Not necessarily mutually exclusive," Horsten said seriously. "What is the attraction of Citizen Zogbaum?"

Helen giggled. "Well, for one thing, he's the nearest thing to a man my size on board."

Pierre Lorans looked at her accusingly. "Pester him, is right. I saw you sitting on his lap yesterday, pulling at the poor cloddy's cravat and him trying to carry on a serious conversation with the second officer."

Helen said, "He's cute."

Martha snorted. "Cute! He looks like a half-sized Lincoln."

Helen started out the compartment entry. She said over her shoulder, "If he'd stop wearing those elevator heels, he'd be almost just right."

Pierre looked after her and said thoughtfully, "That little witch is going to make a mistake and bust up the whole act one of these days."

Horsten shrugged. "It must be difficult. She can't allow herself to be seen participating in any adult activity. How would you like to be in a spot where you couldn't even read? At least nothing but children's tapes."

The arrival at the Nuevo Madrid spaceport, the only entry point to Falange, was even less eventful than they had hoped for. Their coming, of course, was anticipated. Securing a visa at the Falange Embassy on Terra was no small matter. No one, but no one, arrived unannounced on Falange.

There was a delegation of biochemists from the University, breathless at meeting the celebrated Dr. Dorn Horsten. He was hustled off to a group of horse-drawn *carruajes*.

The Lorans family looked after him.

"Holy Ultimate," Helen said under her breath. "I never expected to see a landau pulled by a span of horses anywhere except in a Tri-Di-historical."

"Well, get ready to ride in one," Martha told her. "It seems to be the method of transportation locally."

They were being approached by what were obviously Customs and Immigration officials, done up in costumes seemingly out of the Iberia of the nineteenth century, but also by two civilians wearing clothing of the diplomats of the Victorian period.

"Here we go," Pierre Lorans said. He puffed his cheeks up and went into his Gallic facial expression.

Helen said to Martha, her voice still low. "Look. Evidently, Ferd Zogbaum has been snagged by the local fuzz-yoke."

Martha turned her eyes in the indicated direction. The young electronics engineer, or whatever he was, was being marched in the direction of some very military looking buildings at the far end of the field. The guards, in their *Guardia Civil* uniforms, complete with hard, black hats, were, however, carrying his bags.

Martha said, "Probably some minor technicality in his papers. He doesn't seem particularly worried."

Their own delegation was nearly to them. Martha's voice changed in caliber. "Now sweetie, be quiet for a while. Mummie and Daddy have to talk to these nice gentlemen."

"Curd," Helen said under her breath.

The uniformed men after well executed bows and murmured politenesses, took over passports, interplanetary health cards and the rest of the red-tape documents involved in aliens landing upon the planet Falange. The civilians, it turned out, were members of the cultural affairs department of the Caudillo's government.

While the papers were being perused and stamped, they made meaningless conversation and minor gushings of welcome. When the papers were obviously approved, the gushing became more pronounced.

Martha even got her hand kissed.

In a sudden childish burst of enthusiasm, Helen jumped up and put her arms around the neck of one of the Falangists, her sturdy little legs about his waist.

"Oh, isn't he a *nice* man!"

Martha said, "Helen!"

The cultural aide blinked, smiled in attempted acceptance, and put his hands under the little girl's bottom, as though to support her weight. The vaguest of incomprehensible expressions crossed his face momentarily.

Pierre Lorans grabbed Helen and pulled her away. "Don't be so impulsive, chocolate drop," he scolded.

Evidently, the Terran Embassy of Falange had forwarded full

information on the highly noted *Nouveau Cordon Bleu* chef, Pierre Lorans. It was a pleasure to welcome such an artist of haute cuisine to Falange. It was thought possible that he would be invited to an audience with El Caudillo himself.

El Caudillo was extremely fond of Basque cuisine. Perhaps Senor Lorans . . .

Senor Lorans puffed out his cheeks. "Gentlemen, I am perhaps the most proficient preparer of *bacalao a la vizcaina* and *angulas a la bilbaino* in all the United Planets."

The one who had introduced himself as Manola Camino, looked blank. "But Senor Lorans, we have neither codfish nor eels on Falange. These dishes we know of only through traditions and the writings brought with us from Earth."

Lorans glared at him in indignation. "No *bacalao*, no *angulas*! Are you barbarians? How can your . . . ah . . . Caudillo, or whatever you call him, be a connoisseur of Basque food if you have no *bacalao*, no *angulas*?" He sneered openly. "Next you will tell me you have no beans for *fabada*!

The Falangist winced, opened his mouth unhappily, closed it again.

The other cultural aide said hurriedly, "Perhaps we had better proceed to the Posada."

They led the way, the Lorans trailing after.

Martha said from the side of her mouth, "Listen, you show-off cloddy, aren't you overdoing it?"

"No," he said back. "it's all in character."

Helen skipped as they went, singing, in her tinkle of a child's voice, something about three little girls in blue.

Senor Manola Camino led the way to two of the horse-drawn carriages which seemed the local equivalent of taxis and they were shortly underway. There were comparitively few powered vehicles on the streets of Nuevo Madrid, and it came to them that these few must be imports and almost exclusively for police, military and, perhaps, the highest ranking authorities. The planet Falange lived in the day of the horse.

It came to them, also, that the Posada San Francisco was the only hotel in the city that catered to aliens. Either that, or it was the best hostelry in town and VIPs were automatically taken there. At any rate, they could see Dr. Horsten at the desk, still surrounded by his bevy of welcoming scientists. And while they went through their own routine of registering, they saw Ferdinand Zogbaum enter, still accompanied by his two police.

Their schedule didn't begin until the next day, when Lorans was to have a tour of the leading restaurants of Nuevo Madrid. As soon as they were delivered to their suite, and their guides had bowed their way out, they began to make the usual sounds of unpacking.

The rooms were monstrous in size. A living room, two bedrooms and a rather antiquated bath. The antiquated quality prevailed in general, giving the impression it was deliberately laid on. Even the furniture was Victorian in design. The ceilings were more than thrice as high as could have been expected in population packed Earth and there was a wood-burning fireplace.

While Martha and Helen did the unpacking, Pierre made a tour of the suite, jabbering along as he went.

"Now dear," Martha said shrilly, "please stay out of Mother's way."

Helen snarled softly at her.

Pierre said, "Did you hear that drivel? Do they think me a dunderhead? How can one cook in the fashion of the Basques without *bacalao*?"

"Now dear, you know perfectly well they were very pleasant. And it was nice to meet us out there on that terrible expanse of cement and all."

Helen shrilled, "Three little girls in blue, tra la. Three little girls in blue!"

Pierre spotted what he was looking for. At the very top of the chain from which the chandelier was suspended. Right at the ceiling, a good twenty feet above them. He pointed and they looked up.

There was no apparent way in which any of them could reach the bug. No combination of furniture piled atop each other. Martha nodded to Pierre.

Pierre Lorans took a ballbearing from his pocket. Seconds later, he said with satisfaction, "I doubt if there's any more."

Helen said, "Look, for a day or two, we're going to be safe. They won't get around to suspecting a thing, not even a broken bug. And until tomorrow, when you'll have your time monopolized, we're free. We better get busy tonight."

"At what?" Martha said. "They didn't give us a clue on how

we were to begin this big subversion fling, back on Earth. You'd think Jakes would have something for us to start with. Somebody to see.''

Helen snapped chubby fingers. ''That's it. We've got to find the local underground.''

Pierre Lorans looked at her. ''Wonderful. How do we go about that? What local underground?''

''There must be one. Given any government at all and there's some opposition. It might be large or it might be small, but somewhere on Falange there's an underground.''

Martha said slowly, ''You're probably right, but how to get in touch is another thing. If the *Policía Secreta* can't find them, how can we?''

Something came to Helen. ''Those former three agents from Section G. What was it Sid Jakes said happened to them?''

Martha's eyes took on their empty look. She recited, *''In each case they were unmasked, in one manner or the other, and brought to trial on trumped-up charges. One was accused of murder; one of subversion; and the other disrespect of the Caudillo; all capital offenses.''*

''O.K.,'' Helen said, an edge of excitement in her voice. ''That's it. One of them was charged with subversion. A man doesn't commit subversion on his own. He works with a group, a party, an underground organization of some sort or other.''

''So,'' Lorans scowled.

''So that Section G operative wasn't tried alone. There had to be others involved. Others captured at the same time. It's almost sure to be.''

''Perhaps,'' Martha said. ''But, if so, what of it? Surely they've all been executed by now.''

''Not necessarily,'' Helen insisted. ''They would execute the Section G agent quickly before United Planets took some measures to free him. But their own citizens they might keep alive in hopes of squeezing information out of them.''

''Hm-m-m,'' Lorans said.

Martha said, ''But what of it?''

''Don't you see? Somewhere there are trial records. If we can get hold of them, we can locate where these companions of our Section G agent are. What prison they're in.''

Martha and Pierre Lorans were both unhappy now. They thought about it.

"We don't even know where the court records might be—if any," Lorans objected. "For all we know, the trial was secret."

Helen said decisively, "That's for you to find out. This afternoon take a guided tour. Those culture department aides are just dying to show you the sights. Among them will be the Caudillo's palace, the post office, the museum and city hall. If you can, worm out of them just where the archives are. It shouldn't be too hard if you blather along like usual sightseers. And the Holy Ultimate knows, no two persons in United Planets can blather like you two."

Pierre Lorans aimed a backhanded swipe at her, knowing perfectly well it would never connect.

Helen bounced back, tinkling laughter.

Martha said, "How about you?"

"Tell them I'm tired and don't want to leave the hotel. You might even hint it's a relief to get away from me, after the long trip. Meanwhile, I'll see Dorn and tell him what's up."

Martha and Pierre Lorans looked at each other. "I can't think of anything else," he admitted.

Helen was already out of the room and on her way down to the lobby.

She met Ferdinand Zogbaum coming up the wide stairway, the two police and several bellhops with luggage trailing him.

She grabbed him about the waist. "Uncle Ferd, why are those nasty policemen always following you!"

Martha had been right. Ferdinand Zogbaum looked nothing so much as the youthful Lincoln, cut down almost half in stature. Now he was flushing. He looked apologetically over his shoulder at the two *Guardia Civil*. The whole party had ground to a halt under the child's assault.

He patted her on the head. "Now, now, Helen. I'm not being arrested. They're friends."

"They're policemen," Helen shrilled. "Mommy told me they were policemen. Why are they following you, Uncle Ferd?"

One of the guards was grinning his amusement, the other was only bored.

Ferd Zogbaum cleared his throat unhappily, and patted her head again. "They're guarding me, honey. Don't you worry. Your Uncle Ferd is a very important man brought all the way from Terra for a special job, so he had to have these big policemen guard him so he can't come to any harm."

"Is that straight?" she said under her breath into his ear.

He blinked. "What?" he said, unbelievingly.

"I love you, Uncle Ferd," she said, her voice high again. "You be sure you say good-bye to me before you go anywhere away from the hotel. Or I'll go run to the United Planets Embassy and tell everybody you've been kidnapped. I can lie real good."

The bored guard became animated enough to scowl.

Ferd said, "Don't worry. If I leave here, I'll say good-bye to you first."

She pressed her full, cupid bow lips to his cheek and released him and headed down the steps again. For a moment, he looked after her, a strange look on his face. But then he shook his head unbelievingly and resumed his way to his suite, followed by his entourage.

III

Helen skipped into the lobby and up to the desk of the concierge.

"Where's Uncle Dorn?" she trilled.

He looked over the desk and down at her. "Who, Senorita?"

"Uncle Dorn!"

An inconspicuous type who had been standing at a nearby pillar next to a potted fern, strolled over and murmured to the hotel employee.

"Ah, the Senor Doctor. He has retired to his room, little Senorita."

Helen cocked her blond head to one side and eyed him speculatively. Finally she said in her childish treble, "What's all this Senorita and Senor jetsam?"

He looked a bit startled. "Jetsam?"

She looked at him as unblinkingly as only a child can look.

The concierge cleared his throat. "Little girl, when our people came from Earth, long, long ago, EarthBasic was already the language all spoke. However, as a concession to our traditions we have maintained a few words of the old tongue. Do you understand?"

"No," Helen said flatly. "Where is Uncle Dorn?"

The concierge maintained his official aplomb. "He is in Suite

A, little Senorita, but I do not think he would wish to be disturbed.''

She snorted at that opinion. "He is my Uncle Dorn," she informed him and headed for the stairs. The concierge shrugged and looked at the inconspicuous representative of the *Policía Secreta* who shrugged as well and obviously forgot about it.

Helen located Suite A and pounded a tiny fist on the door. It was answered by one of the Falange scientists who had met the visiting celebrity at the spaceport. Helen slipped under his arm before he had actually seen her.

Dorn Horsten was seated in a Victorian style easy chair, evidently in the midst of earnest conversation with two of the other local biochemists.

"Ah, the little Princess. Are you also stopping at this hotel, my dear? How are your good parents?"

Helen bent a blue eye on him. Obviously, both questions were of too little importance to require answer. She said, "Uncle Dorn, I want a bedtime story."

"A bedtime story?" He looked at his colleagues in apology, and then out the window. "But, little Princess, it is still only afternoon."

"Mommy and Daddy have gone off to look at the buildings or something and left me all alone to take a nap and I want a story."

"But, Helen, I am busy with these gentlemen."

She began to pucker up.

Dorn Horsten cleared his throat and came to his feet. "Now . . . now . . ." he began.

"I don't like it here," she wailed. "I wanna go *home*!"

"Now, now, Helen. Your mother and father will . . ."

"I wanna *bed*time story!" she wailed.

Dorn Horsten looked apologetically at the Falangists. "Senores, if you will pardon me. In actuality, I am a bit weary myself. Perhaps we could postpone our discussion on the phylum *Thallophyta* until tomorrow."

They had all come to feet before his first three words were out. In moments they were gone.

Horsten glared down at the diminutive agent and began to say, "What in the . . ."

She had a finger to her lips.

" . . . World kind of bedtime story did you have in mind, little Princess?"

She sneered at him, held her peace for a moment while her baby blue eyes searched the room. Finally, she located the bug. It was in approximately the same position as the one in the Lorans suite which Pierre had broken with his ball bearing. She pointed it out to him with a chubby finger.

Horsten took off his pince-nez glasses and wiped them, his eyebrows up.

"Would you like the story about Allez oop?" he said in the tone one uses with an eight-year-old.

"No, no, Uncle Dorn. That's the one you always tell. I want a different one. You come to our place and tell me a different one."

He sighed deeply. "All right, all right, little Princess."

"I'm not so little, Uncle Dorn." As though to prove it, she went over to the table bearing the bottle of cognac, poured herself a hefty slug and knocked it back.

He followed her to the door and down the hall toward the Lorans suite.

"There was one in our place, too," she said lowly. "Pierre broke it. It would be too much of a good thing if we broke the one in your suite as well."

He grunted concern. "I don't like this. Rooms bugged already. You think they suspect us?"

She shrugged tiny shoulders. They were proceeding down the hall, hand in hand, a pretty picture of an oversized man and a trusting child. "They probably keep a twenty-four hour watch on every alien on Falange. They didn't particularly pick on us."

He growled, "That'll mean we'll have tails, too. Restrict our movements."

They reached the door of the Lorans suite and entered.

Helen told him where Pierre and Martha had gone and he thought about it a while and nodded acceptance. "It'll probably come to nothing, but I admit I can't think of anything else." He walked over to the window and stared out as though unseeing, and she joined him, standing at his side, her head barely high enough to see over the sill.

She said, "It's not an unattractive city, Dorn. It's like, well, a Tri-Di historical set."

He said, "It looks like prints I've seen of nineteenth century

Madrid. See that area down there? It's almost a replica of the Plaza Mayor.''

"It's beautiful," she said with unwonted softness.

"Yes, perhaps. The original Plaza Mayor is where the Inquisition held its famed *autos de fé*. I wonder what the equivalent is here?''

She looked up at him. "Does there have to be an equivalent?''

"I'm afraid yes. For centuries this culture hasn't moved an iota, either up or down. It's not a natural trait in civilized man. There's only one answer. When someone attempts to move it, he's clobbered. They've built up an efficient machine to do the clobbering. It was no mistake that the *Policía Secreta* detected our first three agents and eliminated them. Section G operatives are supposedly the most effective in United Planets but thus far it's been unable to make a dent in this throwback society.''

She sighed. "But still it's a beautiful city, something like a museum.''

Dorn Horsten grunted and his eyes went up to the sky. "Out there," he said, "are the Dawn Planets. Frighteningly near. Sooner or later, man will be face to face with that alien race. As things stand now, we know only that they are megayears in advance of us. The longer we can put off the confrontation, the better, but it is a matter of time.''

"I know, I know. And we can't afford anachronisms such as Falange. It is later than we think.''

He turned back to the room. "What did you have in mind, if and when we are able to locate the trial papers pertaining to our subversive colleague?''

Helen plopped herself into a chair and frowned prettily. "We didn't take it any further than that.''

At the dinner table in the hotel restaurant that evening, Pierre Lorans stared down at the soup plate the waiter had put before him.

"What," he demanded, "is that?''

The waiter said anxiously, "It is *gazpacho*, Senor Lorans. The chef is awaiting your verdict.''

"Then," Lorans said ominously, "he will wait until Mercury freezes over.''

Martha said, "Now, Pierre.''

Helen giggled.

Lorans ignored his family and held up his fingers to enumerate for the squirming waiter.

"*Gazpacho* is without doubt the most superlative cold soup ever devised. It is basically oil and vinegar, but it is not *gazpacho* until finely strained tomatoes, garlic, bread crumbs, chopped cucumber, green pepper and sometimes onions are added. I myself am not strongly opinionated on the matter of the onions; over the years I have vacillated. Immediately before serving the *gazpacho*, croutons are added."

The waiter squirmed, his eyes went around the dining room. Those at the nearer tables were listening. Lorans was making no attempt to keep his voice low.

"Yes, Senor Lorans," the waiter said. And he made the mistake of repeating, "The chef is anxious to have your opinion."

"My opinion is that he is an idiot," Lorans said flatly. "Where, in the name of the Holy Ultimate, are the cucumbers!"

"Cucumbers?"

The plump man glared at him.

The waiter closed his eyes in suffering and said, "I do not know what these cucumbers are."

Lorans took a deep breath, as though restraining himself. "I am sure you don't. Please, take this swill away. No eels on this forsaken planet, no dried cod, and now no cucumbers! Away with it. Away!"

The waiter took up the plate of chilled soup and began to return in the direction of the kitchen.

Lorans said imperiously, "And that for my wife and daughter as well. I refuse to allow them to eat swill."

"Now, Pierre," Martha said. "It isn't as bad as all that. I tasted it."

"Silence. I insist. No swill."

Helen giggled. "I don't like soup anyway," she tinkled. She evidently spotted Dr. Dorn Horsten for the first time. He was seated at a table on the other side of the room.

Helen waved at him. "Uncle Dorn! Uncle Dorn!"

It seemed to all but break his face, but he managed a stolid smile and a slight wave in return. He was evidently nearly through his meal.

The Lorans table maintained a chilly quiet while awaiting the next course. Even the exuberant Helen seemed frozen to silence by her father's irritation.

When the waiter returned he was accompanied by the head waiter, who hovered about while his underling served the new dish.

"And what is this?" Pierre Lorans demanded.

The headwaiter bowed. "The Posada's specialty, Senor Lorans. *Pastel de Pescado.*"

"Fish pie, eh? Then you do have fish on this forsaken world?"

"Yes, Senor Lorans. If I am not mistaken, the white fish utilized by the chef in *Pastel de Pescado* is remarkably similar to the sole of Earth."

Pierre Lorans touched the plate the waiter had put before him and seemed somewhat mollified when he found it so hot as to be almost untouchable.

He waited until the others had been served and then cautiously tasted. The headwaiter held his breath. Lorans tasted again.

Martha and Helen were eating rapidly, as though they had been through this before and knew what was coming.

Pierre Lorans, his face expressionless, put down his fork. He said to the headwaiter, "I am willing to give the chef the benefit of the doubt. Everybody has an off day. Undoubtedly it is an off day. Possibly he is seriously ill. On the verge of death. Martha! Helen!"

He came to his feet.

Martha and Helen, both with a sigh, put down their own utensils and stood also.

The headwaiter wrung his hands, his Iberian face in agony.

Lorans said, "We shall resort to our emergency supplies." He turned and stalked toward the door, followed by Martha, apology all over her face, with the rear brought up by Helen who had snagged a hard roll from the table before leaving.

All eyes followed the interplanetary celebrated chef. Half the guests looked down into their dishes, suspiciously, which was not missed by the headwaiter, who once again closed his eyes in agony.

Pierre Lorans hesitated at the table of Dr. Horsten. He stared down at the dessert the other was about to eat. "Is that supposed to be Spanish *flan*?" he said.

The doctor looked a bit startled. "Why, I believe so." He looked at the menu. "Yes, *flan*."

"My dear Doctor, it will poison you. I am convinced. Do me the honor to adjourn to our rooms with us. I have been through this before. We never travel without our emergency supplies. Among other items I have a few tins of Camembert. Real Camembert from Normandy. I have also a bottle or two of stoneage Martell cognac. You can finish your, ah, meal with us. Camembert, rather than pseudo-*flan*. While we make do as best we can.''

''Why . . . why—'' the doctor hesitated.

Behind her husband, Martha was nodding emphatically for the other to accept the invitation. On the face of it, she didn't want to be alone with her enraged spouse.

''Very well, very gracious of you, I am sure,'' Dorn Horsten said, putting down his napkin and coming to his feet. ''Very old Martell, eh? Imagine that. It's been years. Actually real cognac, not the synthetic?''

Pierre Lorans looked at him, his lips beginning to go pale.

The doctor cleared his throat. ''Hm-m-m, yes, of course. It wouldn't . . . ah, couldn't be anything else but genuine cognac.''

Lorans turned on his heel and marched out, followed now by Martha, then Dr. Horsten, with Helen bringing up the rear. She managed to snag another roll from the doctor's table as she passed. Obviously, Helen was an old hand at this emergency.

In the Lorans's suite, Pierre Lorans darted a look up at the bug he had smashed earlier. He looked at Helen, then Dorn Horsten, even as he was talking at full pitch about something involving eels, codfish and cucumbers.

Helen hissed, ''Allez oop!''

The hulking doctor grabbed her about the waist and tossed her aloft. Her head all but touched the ceiling, a chubby hand went out and, briefly, grasping the chain that held the chandelier, she seemed to be poised in the air.

She said, ''It hasn't been repaired,'' twisted her body and fell gracefully into the arms of the big man beneath.

Lorans, still mouthing his rage and dwelling now upon the allegedly inedible fish pie he had been served, darted a look at his watch.

''All right,'' he whispered. ''Fifteen minutes.'' Then he went back to his loud monologue which most certainly could have been heard through the suite's door to the hall.

Dr. Dorn Horsten went over to the window, flung it open and vaulted out.

Martha winced. "I'll never get used to seeing him do that," she said.

Helen jumped up on the windowsill and peered down. "It's only four floors," she said. "Besides, there's a lawn down there. After all, he comes from a high-gravity planet. Bye, bye."

She launched herself after Horsten.

And Martha winced again.

Down below, the doctor caught his diminutive partner neatly and they started hurrying their way through the small park that edged the Posada San Francisco on this side. He didn't bother to put her down. Her small legs weren't up to the pace.

He said, "How in the world did they locate this place? Sheer luck?"

"Evidently couldn't have been easier," Helen said. "They took a tour of the city, and one of the first things the guide pointed out was the *Policía Secreta* headquarters. Pierre and Martha were suitably impressed and the flunky blabbered out just about everything they wanted to know; they had no trouble guiding his conversation. They asked why it was necessary to have such a large police, and he told them all about the subversives who had recently been caught. Standing there in the street, he pointed out a window where interrogations were alleged to take place. Pointed out a window which was the only one, evidently, opening into the vaults where the police archives were kept. Oh, he was most helpful."

The doctor grunted. He was walking at a rapid pace now, the girl on his shoulder. A passer-by would probably have smiled at the pleasant picture they made. However, there were no other pedestrians at this hour. The Falangists supped late and went almost immediately to bed afterwards.

"I hope we find what we're looking for," he said. "But I doubt it. You brought that supposed toy of yours, didn't you? The rings that actually unfold into a set of knuckledusters?"

"You think I'm stupid, you big lummox?"

"No," Dorn Horsten sighed. "I don't think you're stupid. But I'm certainly glad you're the size you are."

"Why?" she said suspiciously.

"Because if you were my size, I might ask you to marry me, and the very thought changes my muscles to water."

"Why, you overgrown oaf!"

"That must be it, up ahead," he said. "No other building would be quite so large and quite so grim looking. Now, let me remember how Martha told me to locate that window."

They found the spot from which the Lorans had observed the building earlier.

Helen said, "You think there's a guard there?"

"Evidently. It's one of the few windows in the building with a light. This whole wing is dark except for it." He sized up the situation. "I hope they didn't repair the window as yet."

Helen was on the ground now, chubby fists on her hips. "Not in this country. One of the things they brought from Terra most enthusiastically was the do-it-mañana philosophy. I've already noticed that. How in the world did Pierre manage to break it, anyway?"

Horsten was still casing the situation. He said absently, "You know him. He simply waited until nobody else was around, and then, while Martha distracted the guide's attention, he reached down, picked up a half brick or some other stone, and heaved it. Evidently, a few minutes later a couple of *Guardia Civil* came dashing from the building, but didn't even bother to question the Lorans. The guide was mystified by them. When they pointed out the window, high above, the guide said reasonably that nobody could throw a brick that high, and anyway, they hadn't seen any young people, or criminal types loitering around."

He came to a decision. "I think I can make it up that wall, the gravity on this planet seems to be a mite less than even Earth and that brickwork will give hand- and toeholds. However, I can't go into that window and get down into the room beyond if there's an armed guard there. He'd zap me before I could get to him."

"Funker," Helen sneered. "Put all the strongarm stuff onto a little girl."

"All right, all right," he said, "Got any better ideas?"

"No," she said. And then, "Allez oop!"

He swung the miniature gymnast and acrobat around several times before releasing her. She sailed in an impossible flight to the iron bars that sheltered the small window. Tiny hands shot out and grasped them.

There was ample room to squeeze her childish body through. She paused a moment there, turned and made an age-old gesture to the man below, a circle with thumb and forefinger. He lumbered quickly to the wall and started scrambling up. He could see her tiny body swing through and cursed beneath his breath that she had gone on ahead before he arrived on the scene.

He reached the ten-story high window and, supporting himself with one hand, tore the iron bars off with the other. He knocked what was left of the glass out of the way and squeezed through. He dropped to the floor.

Helen stood there, absently shining the brass knucks on her chubby right hand with the palm of her left. She said, her voice at its most childish treble, "Where've you been so long, you slow-moving cloddy?"

He stared about the room. It was obviously devoted to special records. A sort of file-within-files arrangement. He looked down at the uniformed man who was stretched out on the floor.

"What did you do to him?" he said.

"Nothing much," Helen said modestly. "He was somewhat startled to see me dropping out of the heavens."

Horsten grunted. "What I wanted to know was, will he revive fairly soon?" He squatted next to the Falangist guard and slapped his face back and forth stingingly.

The other's eyes opened and at first expressed disbelief and then suddenly widened into terror. He reached clumsily for his side arm.

Horsten took it gently from his hand. It was a long barreled 9 mm military pistol of a period so remote that on Earth it would have taken its place in a museum. Horsten bent the barrel and made a knot in it and handed it back.

He said to the guard gently, "Where are the records of the subversion trial of the Earthling?"

The other was bug-eyeing the gun.

Horsten said, "Please, Senor, you would not want me to have to . . ." He let the sentence dribble away.

The guard said, "No. No, no. I do not know what you want. But it is impossible."

"What's impossible?"

"I do not have the combination."

Horsten took the gun back again and bent the barrel into a sort of pretzel shape, to the other's horrified fascination.

"I didn't ask you that, did I?"

The guard pointed weakly at a large, iron safe. "Those are

the top secret files pertaining to attempts to overthrow the government of El Caudillo.''

Horsten came to his feet, and looked down at the other contemplatively. Helen had been scouting the room, now she took her place beside him.

''We should crisp him,'' the scientist muttered.

She took a deep breath and held her elbows tightly against her sides, in feminine rejection.

He looked at her in disgust. ''All right, all right, I haven't got the guts either.'' He bent quickly and seemingly tapped the fallen man across the jawbone. Eyes rolled upward.

Horsten growled, ''Look around for some wire, or rope . . . anything to tie him with.''

''Telephone over here,'' she said.

He went over and ripped it out and returned to tie the guard.

Moments later, that worthy revived enough, once more, to see his assailants leaving. The man with the six hundred pound safe under one arm, the little girl seated on a shoulder.

She saw the eyes open and waved and lisped, ''Goo' bye, Mr. Policeman.''

He closed his eyes again and started in on several prayers he had not said since childhood.

IV

Colonel inspector Miguel Segura looked about the room unbelievingly. His eyes finally came back to the *Guardia Civil* private. He said, ''The story again?''

''Senor Colonel, I do not know how many of them there were, nor even where they came from. I was here, wide awake. Suddenly, they were upon me. There must have been at least six.''

One of the colonel's assistants said, ''I would think so, if they managed to get that safe out of here and all the way down and out of the building.''

The colonel growled, ''Quiet, Raul. Go on with the story.''

''I fought as best I could. There were too many. They beat me unconscious and tied me. When I awoke, the safe was gone.''

The colonel looked at the other unbelievingly and uncomprehendingly. He pointed to the broken window above. ''The bars are broken from that window. Why? How? Surely they couldn't have done that without you hearing. But even if they could have, why? The safe was too large to have been let out there.''

"Senor Colonel," the *Guardia Civil* told him. "I do not know. It is all as though the work of devils.''

The colonel sighed deeply. "If it was not for the fact that the safe has been found, the door torn off, in the park, I could hardly credit a word of this.''

Another aide came in. The colonel inspector looked at him. "Yes?''

"The clerks have been through the papers contained in the safe. There are only a very few missing.''

"Well?''

"They pertained to the recent trial of the suspected Section G agent and his accomplices.''

The colonel shook his head and stared at the guard. "Where did you say they came from? Supposedly the door was locked from inside, but you say they burst suddenly upon you.''

The subject of interrogation squirmed. "Senor Colonel, I do not know. The door *was* locked. Uhhh, it was as though they descended from the heavens.''

Colonel inspector Miguel Segura—chief inspector of the Nuevo Madrid *Policía Secreta* and rumored to be one of the handful of men who spent their evenings with El Caudillo in the Presidential Palace playing cards, sipping sherry and Fundador imported from Terra, and being entertained by flamenco dancers noted more for their pulchritude than their competence at the Iberian entertainment—had sent his card in formally.

He was in full uniform and accompanied only by his youthful aide, *Teniente* Raul Dobarganes, also in formal attire. Their manner was grave and, if anything, overly polite.

Dr. Horsten had been located and brought to the Lorans suite so that all could be addressed at once. They were seated, save Helen, who stood, toes pointed in, and staring up at *Teniente* Dobarganes, unblinkingly. It had to be admitted, the dress uniform of the *Policía Secreta* was not exactly drab.

The two police officers had hardly more than presented their stiff bows than Pierre Lorans shot to his feet dramatically. He crossed his arms over his chest. "I confess," he blurted. "I admit everything.''

Inspector Segura stared at him. "You do?''

"Yes! Everything! I should never have come to this barbarian planet. Police everywhere. No freedom for the artist. I should have known better. It is impossible for me to equivocate. Impossible. I am a *Nouveau Cordon Bleu* chef. I am willing to die."

He shut his mouth and stood there defiantly.

Martha began to cry.

Helen didn't even bother to turn. She continued to stare up at the lieutenant, stationed no more than three feet from him.

The doctor looked blank.

The inspector raised eyebrows to his assistant, who shrugged a shrug that would have done every Spaniard since the Phoenicians first came to trade for tin, full proud.

The inspector turned his eyes back to the defiant chef. "Ah, what do you confess?" he said cautiously.

"To insulting this benighted, probably starving planet! Its food, its chefs, its lack of even such simplicities as *bacalao*, eels, cucumbers. Its . . ."

The inspector held up a hand to stem the tide.

"Please, Senor Lorans, will you be seated? This is a very serious matter."

The lips of Senor Lorans began to go pale.

Martha said hurriedly, "Now, Pierre. Please sit down. You are not being insulted. We must at least hear what Sergeant What's-his-name wants. And nobody is arresting you, Pierre."

The inspector shot a look from the side of his eyes, but the face of Raul Dobarganes was without expression.

When Lorans had been urged back into his chair, the colonel inspector took up again, though not without misgivings. He began, "Dear guests of Falange . . ."

Helen said, "I think you're pretty." But she was talking to *Teniente* Dobarganes, not the inspector, not even the mother of whom would have possibly considered the description.

Raul Dobarganes could feel the pink ascending from his tight collar.

"Gosh, you even blush pretty," Helen told him with satisfaction.

Martha said, "Helen, you be quiet now. The gentlemen have something to say." She smiled sweetly at the inspector. "You go right ahead, Sergeant."

Inspector Segura opened his mouth, closed it again. Paused for a long moment, then started all over.

He said to Pierre Lorans, "There is complete freedom on Falange, Senor. You have not observed correctly. This is the most stable socio-economic system ever devised. All are happy. All are in their place. Those whom the Holy Ultimate meant to administrate, do. Those whom fate meant to serve, serve. Everybody is satisfied with their lot on the planet Falange. Of how many of our sister members of United Planets can you say the same, eh?"

"Why, it sounds very nice," Martha nodded encouragingly.

Helen piped up. "Then how come you got so many cops everywheres?"

Both the colonel and his aide looked at her blankly for a long frustrated moment.

"Ah," Dr. Horsten murmured, "an interesting point. Out of the mouth of babes, so to speak." His stolid face took on an absentminded quality. "It seems to me I can think of a, uh, parallel some few centuries back on Earth. A period during which the leading nations paraded about in great style loudly boasting of their degrees of freedom and how highly they valued peace and despised aggression. However, somehow, those who disclaimed loudest of their love of democracy, peace and freedom had the largest police forces, secret police, intelligence agencies, armies and navies. Such nations as Switzerland and the Scandinavian, who didn't need to talk about their internal freedoms, invariably had small police forces and military, even judged on a per capita basis."

The inspector said, his voice verging on the snappish now, "Forgive me. Somehow we seem to have gotten off on a tangent. I must get to the point. Last night a major crime was committed. One of such nature that only an alien could possibly be interested. You are some of the few aliens registered in this vicinity and, by coincidence, you arrived only yesterday, from Terra, the planet involved."

"Terra? Mother Earth!" Pierre Lorans blurted, unbelievingly.

The inspector said dryly, "Rumors are beginning to go through the member planets of United Planets that Mother Earth seems to have developed into a strange parent. However, the point is that you are within a quarter mile of the scene of the crime, and you have just arrived from Terra."

Dr. Horsten said vaguely, "Crime. When did this, uh, crime take place, my dear Inspector?"

Segura said, "At almost exactly eleven o'clock."

The heavy-set scientist scowled and tried to remember. "I am afraid I have no . . . ah, what do they say in the crime tapes on Tri-Di? Ah, yes. No alibi."

The inspector looked at Raul Dobarganes who had at long last escaped the fascinated stare of little Helen. His assistant brought forth a report.

"At eleven o'clock last night, Doctor, you were right here in this room. Senor Lorans had been dissatisfied with his evening meal."

"Ha!" Lorans blurted and began to come to his feet. His wife restrained him.

"You are right," Dr. Horsten exclaimed. "I was right here with the Lorans family. A perfect alibi. I couldn't possibly have committed this terrible crime." A fascinated gleam came to his eyes behind their pince-nez glasses. "I love Tri-Di crime shows," he confided. "What happened last night? Mass murder? An armed romp? Perhaps . . ."

"Romp?" the inspector said blankly.

"A caper. A job! Perhaps they knocked off the National Treasury, uh?" He came to his feet, portraying more excitement than anyone had ever expected this staid looking scientist to project. He held his hands as though cradling a twohanded weapon. "Muffle guns," he said. "Come driving up in fast hovercars. Leave a lookout outside. The rest go charging in, cutting down the guards . . ."

The inspector, stricken to silence, had closed his eyes in the Iberian expression of agony the Section G operatives were beginning to get used to.

It was Dobarganes who took over. He put a hand on the excited doctor's arm. "Please, Senor Horsten, it was not that at all. Please be seated." He got the good doctor into his chair and turned back to his superior. There was a strained element in his voice as well, by this time. "Senor Colonel?" he said.

The colonel had obviously decided to get it over with. He said, "The maids reported this morning that there was ash in your fireplace, as though papers had been burned there. It was, so far as we could analyze, paper of the type stolen last night. Undoubtedly, you have some explanation." He added, *sotto voce*, "Some weird explanation."

All except Helen looked blank. Helen was beginning to eye the colonel malevolently.

Martha said, "Why, why, I burned some papers last night. Heaven only knows why I ever brought them along when I packed."

"Senora, this paper was of the type stolen last night. Our laboratories . . ."

Dr. Horsten had recovered from his enthusiasm. He grunted deprecation. "My dear Inspector Sorghum . . ."

"Segura," Raul Dobarganes said quickly.

". . . I suspect your paper manufacturers produce many of the types originated by Earth. Undoubtedly, Mrs. Lorans, among her other effects, brought an identical, or at least similar, paper along with her."

The inspector was scowling.

The scientist went on, a certain impatience in his voice now. "Otherwise, you could always put the Senora under, ah, what is the term they use on the crime shows? Scop. Yes, Scop, truth serum, uh? Surely you will be able to, ah, dig out of her the method by which she sneaked from this fourth floor suite down through the hotel, captured these documents, or whatever, smuggled them back and then burnt them to hide the crime." He looked at Martha. "My dear Mrs. Lorans, you have not seen enough Tri-Di spy tapes. You must chew up and swallow such secret papers."

Martha's face revealed that she didn't understand what either of them were talking about.

The inspector gave up. He was wondering why he had bothered to come here when any of a hundred underlings could have checked the remote lead. He began making his preliminaries toward leaving. However, he reckoned without Helen.

She had evidently come to her decision and advanced on the quick to deal him a sharp kick on the shin. Startled, he bent to grab the leg assaulted.

She demanded in her childish treble, "What did you do to my Uncle Ferd? Did you go around arresting him, too? Don't you dare hurt my Uncle Ferd."

The inspector looked appealingly at his aide who came forward hurriedly to the rescue, however, Helen had already been snatched away by her mother.

"Don't you dare arrest my Uncle Ferd!" Helen shrilled.

For a moment, the inspector thought he might have something. He snarled, "Who's Uncle Ferd?"

His lieutenant cleared his throat. "Probably the technician for the *corridas*, Senor Colonel. He arrived on the same spaceship, you'll recall. Senor Zogbaum."

"Oh, yes." The colonel inspector straightened and did his gentlemanly best to smile at the child. "Your Uncle Ferd is very safe, little Senorita. He was in custody . . . ah, that is, he was guarded by friends all night, so he couldn't possibly be involved, uh, that is, couldn't be one of the gang of bad men. And now, Senora, Senores, little Senorita, forgive the *Teniente* and I for interrupting you. *Hasta luego.*"

He and his aide got out more speedily than protocol usually called for on Falange.

Back in the suite, Martha gestured upward at the bug.

Pierre Lorans took a pocketknife from his clothes and opened what would ordinarily have been the small blade, the end of which had been filed off to make a small screwdriver. He handed it to Helen.

Helen said, "Allez oop," and in a moment duplicated her performance of the day before, poising for a long moment, partially supported by a tiny hand grasping the chandelier chain. The other hand darted out with the improvised screwdriver, loosened a screw slightly, then she fell over gracefully and back down into the arms of her partner.

Horsten tossed her high again, she gave the screw another turn. On the third attempt, she pulled loose a wire before dropping away.

She muttered with satisfaction, "I'll bet whoever's in charge of bugging is going slowly drivel-happy."

Back in chairs, they looked around at each other.

Horsten looked at Martha. "You memorized the whole trial before burning it?"

"Of course I did," Martha said.

"Why didn't you flush away *all* the ashes?"

"Because to hide all signs of my burning some paper would have been practically impossible. By leaving a little ash, the fact of a considerable burning was hidden. My story held up."

"I suppose so," he said. "Some time today, Martha, it might be a good idea, while Pierre is busy with his colleague chefs, for you to go to a public library and memorize the Falange legal code. We might need it.''

Helen said thoughtfully, ''And while you're at it, all rules pertaining to the bullfights during this fantastic selection of their Caudillo.''

''I think you're right,'' Martha said. ''I'll do it.''

Horsten looked at the plumpish Lorans. ''At the rate you're going, they'll shoot you, or kick you off the planet, even before they find you're a Section G agent.''

Lorans grinned one of his rare grins, which gave him an impish quality. ''No. I'm impressing them more by the minute. They wouldn't dream of expelling such an obviously temperamental artist, until I have at least produced one complete repast. They recognize my type too well, not to understand it. At this point, they're in awe. The present El Caudillo evidently considers himself a gourmet. Heads would roll if anything happened to me before he could get his undoubtedly rounded belly under a table provided by my art.''

Helen said, '' The problem now is how do we get these two underground fellas out of the deep freeze?''

Martha looked at her. ''Deep freeze?''

''That Alcazar political prison.''

The doctor said unhappily, ''And what do we do with them once we get them out? We don't know where their friends may be, if they have friends. Very possibly they have no place to go to ground.''

Helen said, ''Why not here?''

And at their reception of that, snarled, ''I'm not as simple as all that. Today, Pierre goes out to buy some clothes suitable to Falange fashion. He buys several suits, including three that are semi-formal and very similar to the sort that the Posada waiters wear. Ready-made—he hasn't time for tailoring. One suit will be slightly too large, one just right, one for a slimmer man. Most of these Falangists seem of average size. O.K., we liberate the two former companions of our Section G agent who was shot as a subversive, bring them here and dress them in Pierre's suits. We should be able to get some sort of fit.

''We keep them around the suite. If the police come in, they walk out, with trays, or towels, or whatever. Who ever looks at a hotel waiter?''

Lorans said skeptically, ''Suppose a real waiter comes in?''

"There are four rooms, including the bath. We'll shuffle them around from room to room, in closets, under beds. Maybe we'll put over the idea that Martha doesn't like maids to make her bed, or even clear her room. She wants to do it herself. Hotels have more eccentric guests than that. We can keep our refugees hidden in her room when the maids come in."

Lorans wiped a hand over his brow. "Talk about the Purloined Letter!"

Horsten said, "It's a rather desperate expedient."

Helen snapped, "All right, double-dome, think up something better."

Lorans said, "How are we going to get out of here to raid the prison? And, if we do, how will we locate them? What were their names, Martha?"

Martha said, "Bartolomé Guerro and José Hoyos." She looked thoughtful. "I could probably find some sort of prison plan in the National Library."

"Hm-m-m," the doctor said. "I wonder if at the same time you could find a plan of the power plant serving Nuevo Madrid."

Helen looked at him speculatively. "I don't trust you," she said.

He beamed at her.

Colonel Segura, making his way with the use of an old-fashioned flashlight, covered the small room thoroughly. He was beginning to doubt, these days, the reports of his own senses. The place was a shambles.

Finally, Raul Dobarganes bringing up the rear, the colonel returned to where two of his plainclothesmen had the hotel electrician pinned to a chair.

The colonel inspector glowered down at that unfortunate. "You are under arrest," he snapped, "and will probably be shot for sabotage of government property. The Posada is government operated by the *Policía Secreta* to keep an eye on aliens and other suspects, as you well know."

The electrician groaned his misery and one of the plainclothesmen backhanded him across the mouth.

The colonel went on ominously. "You have one chance. Tell us the purpose of your crime and reveal all accomplices."

The technician shook his head in mute denial and hopeless appeal for mercy.

The colonel, directing the beam of the electric torch full into the other's face, said, "Every light in the building has been extinguished and every device dependent on electricity is disrupted. Why? What did you expect to accomplish?"

The other moaned his misery and the plainclothesman slapped him again.

The colonel sighed deeply. "Tell me your lie again . . . traitor."

"I am not a traitor. I am no traitor . . ."

He received another stinging slap across the mouth.

"Senor Colonel, I swear by the United Temple, by the Holy Ultimate, it is exactly as I have told you. A strange, whirling something came in through the door. Even as it whirled, it moved slowly and in . . . in a half circle around the room. I was spellbound, hypnotized. In all my life, Senor Colonel, I have never seen such a strange thing. I was paralyzed. It came in through the door, went down the room, whirling, whirling, and then came back and . . ."

"And hit you on the back of the head, you fool."

"Yes, Colonel," the other said in misery.

"And when you finally awoke what . . ."

"When I awoke, the control room was a mess. Everything capable of being smashed was smashed. It could have been but moments, but when I awoke there was damage of an extent I would have thought would have taken hours."

The colonel boiled inwardly in his frustration, directed the beam of his flashlight upward. "There. That device, up near the ceiling, whatever it is. You can hardly see it from here. A group of saboteurs desiring to smash that would have had to have a ladder. Are you suggesting they marched through the halls of this hotel carrying a ladder?"

"No, Senor Colonel," the electrician moaned. "I don't know . . ."

Another vicious slap.

The colonel snarled, "These whirling mysteries of yours are an attempt to hide the true facts. Something is going on here. You have accomplices. Several of them must have come here and joined with you to wreck your charge."

"No . . . no . . ."

Another *Policía Secreta* underling came hurrying into the
room. Raul Dobarganes met him and spoke briefly in a low
whisper. The *teniente* approached his superior. The colonel
looked up at him, impatiently.

Dobarganes said unhappily, "Senor Colonel, the electricity is
now off all over the city. It is in darkness. Only the palace of El
Caudillo, with its private power plant, has lights."

The colonel stared at him, as though his lieutenant was an
idiot. "A temporary power break."

"No, Senor Colonel. From what this man says, there has been
unprecedented sabotage of the power plant."

"Are you insane! There are a hundred guards!"

"Yes, Senor Colonel."

"Come along! *Madre de Dios!* the world goes mad!" The
colonel stormed for the door.

Behind him, the electrician sighed in relief and, as though in
reflex, the plainclothesman smashed him across the mouth again.

V

As they made their uncomfortable way across the open field,
Lorans growled, "I suppose we should count our blessings. El
Caudillo's government concentrates practically everything here
in Nuevo Madrid. Suppose this confounded political prison was
all the way on the other side of the planet?"

Helen said, "I still don't know how we're going to locate
them." She was perched up on Dorn Horsten's shoulder, as always when time had to be made.

Horsten said. "If we have this right, they keep their prime
state prisoners in the left wing. Martha memorized it at the library."

Helen said, "Great, but there might be a thousand of them."

The doctor half stumbled over an unseen obstacle, caught himself and said, "No. Contrary to belief, police states don't necessarily have their prisons chock full. The worst political
prisoners they shoot, the least dangerous they send off to slave
labor projects. Why feed them in prison? Put them to work.
Those in between are kept in jail until they decide if they belong
to the first category, or the second."

They had come to a wall. Pierre Lorans took a rope he had

been carrying and handed it to Helen. She wrapped it about her tiny waist and turned to Horsten and said, ''Allez oop!''

He caught her, whirled her, released her. She shot upward.

Lorans growled, ''I wish I hadn't lost my boomerang, back there at the power station. What'll they think when they find it?''

''They won't,'' Horsten grunted, peering upward after his diminutive partner. ''Until you showed me that confounded thing, I'd never even heard of a boomerang, and I still don't quite believe the things you can do with it. There's no reason to believe they've ever heard of them, either.''

Lorans complained. ''It was my favorite little tool. And one of the few we could take a chance on and bring along—in Helen's box of toys, of course. What's taking that girl so long?''

At that very moment, the end of the rope slithered down.

Without further word, Dr. Horsten gave it a sharp tug or two, to make sure Helen had it well anchored, shoved his glasses firmly back on his nose, and then started up, hand over hand, his feet braced against the prison wall.

A few minutes later, the end of the rope jerked up and down, in signal. Lorans took it and tied a loop in the end and put one foot inside. He gave a sharp double tug and was drawn upward to where the others awaited him on the wall top.

It was pitch dark.

Horsten whispered. ''All right, let's go. We've seen a few prison guards going about below with improvised lights. Evidently, the place is in a tizzy.''

Helen whispered, ''Down this way, according to that chart Martha drew for us. The left wing is down this way.''

They came to a barred door.

Horsten came to the front and inspected it. ''The best thing,'' he murmured, even as his big hands went out, ''is simply to break the''—he grasped two of the heavy bars near the lock and suddenly pulled them toward him—''lock.'' With a rip of tortured metal, the door came open toward him.

''How about alarms?''

''Don't be silly,'' Helen told him. ''What do you think we fouled up that power plant for? Now let me go ahead and scout this out.''

The two men pressed back against a wall while she reconnoitered. She took longer to return than they found reasonable, so when she did show, both felt relief. She was breathing deeply.

"What happened?" Lorans demanded.

"I ran into two guards and had to clobber them."

The doctor looked down at her tiny figure and shook his head. "I'll never get used to it," he muttered under his breath.

Helen said, "I found out where they are."

"Where who are?"

"Don't be dense. Our boys. Hoyos and Guerro."

The two men stared at her. "How'd you find that out?" Lorans said.

"Oh, one of the two guards," Helen said lightly. "Down this way."

"Just a minute. What did you do to the guard? I want to know what's behind me."

She tried to brush it off. "I just kind of twisted his arm a little."

For a brief moment, Dr. Horsten had before his eyes the picture of this seemingly sweet little girl putting strongarm methods to work on a tough, burly prison guard until the other divulged information.

He said, "You mean you let him see you, clearly?"

Helen shrugged it off. "So what? You think he's going to report to his chief that an eight-year-old girl put the slug on him?"

They followed her. From time to time, through windows overlooking the prison yard below they could see guards, or other prison employees, going this way and that with lanterns, flashlights or torches. Civilized institutions fall apart drastically without power.

Helen whispered, "This way, I think."

Back at the hotel, they returned to the Lorans suite by much the same manner as they had scaled the prison wall. But this time there were an extra two members in the party.

After Horsten had made it up the wall, he hauled the others after him, one, two, three. Helen, of course, had gone first, propelled by her hefty partner.

Martha was there, ready with a drink all around.

Pierre Lorans said to her, "Anything while we were gone?"

"No. Not so much as a knock on the door."

Lorans turned to the two newcomers. "If you'll come this way, we'll get some new clothes on you. Later, either the doctor or I will take those you're wearing and dispose of them." He led the continually surprised Falangist underground men to his bedroom.

Meanwhile, Dorn Horsten opened the door to the hall and bellowed out into the darkness. "Hollo! Confound it, how long is this fantastic situation going to last! We want lights, food, something to drink! Hollo!"

Eventually, a hotel servant bearing a heavy candle came scurrying and the scientist made a big to-do about sitting around in the dark for the past couple of hours, and that they demanded some service.

The servant scurried off again. He gave the impression of having been doing a lot of scurrying all evening.

The doctor gave a grunt of satisfaction and turned back to Martha and Helen. "It'll never occur to anybody that we haven't been here all evening," he said.

"We hope," Helen muttered.

Lorans returned with the two liberated prisoners and the next fifteen minutes were expended explaining to the revolutionaries the purpose of the Lorans-Horsten team and the scheme to keep the two safely hidden by their remaining out in the open, disguised as waiters.

The older of the two, Bartolomé Guerro, was quite tall, all but gaunt, dark of complexion, inclined to flare in his speech. He was obviously a leader of men. The other, to the surprise of the Section G operatives, was a youngster, certainly not beyond his early twenties. Of medium height, he moved with a litheness seldom found in men and he seemed incapable of making an awkward movement.

It came out in moments. José Hoyos, full matador at the age of eighteen, had been the last, despairing hope of the Lorca Party, an illegal underground organization dedicated to the overthrow of the entire El Caudillo system. Even before the coming of the Section G operative who had worked with them, they had sought out this potential champion from the ranks of the organization. José was a third-generation son of a family devoted to the building of a new world-government to supersede the present system on Falange. His reflexes were fast, his appearance strik-

ingly handsome, his grace, superlative. Helen could hardly keep
her eyes off him.

They had groomed him for the next series of national games,
when the old Caudillo had died and a new one was to be selected. The idea was to have him acclaimed El Caudillo and
then to make sweeping changes from within. They had gathered
funds to see him through the best of the planet's bullfighting
schools. They had gone to the expense of advancing his career
through the *novillero* years, when as an amateur it was so difficult for the usual torero to find fights, it often being necessary
that the young hopeful buy his own bull.

They had backed his career for years, waiting, waiting. And
step by step José Hoyos had reached prominence, until in the
opinion of most aficionados, he was *Numero Tres*, third man
from the top in the lists of matadors. The two above him were
gentlemen toreros, both at least ten years his senior and both the
epitome of the hero of the fiesta brava, national spectacle of
the planet Falange.

They had arrived at a position of having only to wait for the
demise of the present Caudillo, for José to have his chance.
Needless to say, El Caudillo was in no hurry.

The lean Bartolomé Guerro looked around at the Section G
operatives. "It was then your colleague, Phil Birdman, came to
Falange and stressed the importance of dispatch. He couldn't
wait for the Caudillo's natural death."

Martha said, "You mean he favored assassination?" There
was discomfort in her voice.

The Falangist looked at her. "Not necessarily. It would be
impossible to assassinate El Caudillo. His security is simply too
embracing. Birdman was trying to find some other method of
speeding things."

Horsten shook his head. They were talking now by the light
of a small fire Lorans had built in the fireplace.

"Any public figure can be assassinated, given a determined
enough group, with adequate resources."

The youthful Hoyos, usually silent, spoke up. "Not El Caudillo," he said. "His police are thick as soup."

The doctor grunted. "Of course, I don't advocate political
assassinations," he said, "but listen to this one. Some centuries
ago on Earth a desperate radical political group decided it was

necessary to kill a titled foreigner who was to have a parade in their city. Troops and police, they knew, would be present in literally tens of thousands. So twenty-five of their number gathered in a room and drew straws and the five who had the shortest were given bombs or pistols and were told where to spot themselves along the path of the parade. Then they left. Those twenty remaining drew straws. The five with the shortest were given pistols and instructed to place themselves behind the appointed assassins, in the crowd. If, when it came the turn of one of the assassins to make his try at the victim, he failed to try, then the man stationed behind him was to shoot him. Those five then left and the remaining men drew straws and the five with the shortest were given pistols and instructed to stand behind the second man. If the first man failed to make his try, and the second man failed to shoot the first man, then it was the task of the third to shoot the second. These five left and straws were chosen again. The five short ones were issued pistols and instructed to stand behind the third man in the crowd, if the first man failed to make his try and the second man failed to shoot him and the third man failed to shoot the second, then the fourth man's task was to shoot the third. The five remaining men need, of course, draw no straws. They issued themselves guns and left to assume their posts—behind the fourth man.''

The doctor let his eyes go around the group. ''Next day, the parade started on schedule. The automobile containing the titled victim and his wife reached the first assassin who attempted to throw his bomb but was caught. The police then reached the second assassin who tried to shoot them with his pistol, but was pulled down by the surrounding mob. They reached the third assassin—and got no further.''

Horsten held his peace for a moment, and then said, ''The assassins claimed their victim, but they didn't know what the cost was to be. His name was Archduke Ferdinand and his death precipitated the first of the World Wars.''

Bartolomé Guerro thought about it. Finally he said, ''Why do you tell us this?''

The scientist shrugged. ''Merely pointing out that dedicated men can do what must be done. Your problem here, of course, is different.''

''Yes, of course.'' The Falange revolutionist stirred in his chair. ''José and I must get out and reestablish our contacts, get in touch with the cells of our Nuevo Madrid organization. Our arrest caused considerable disruption of long-laid plans."

Horsten said, "One thing. Our central offices have decided that the government of El Caudillo stands in the way of progress, but there is no point in tearing down one socioeconomic system if a superior one is not available to take its place. What is your own philosophy of government, Senor Guerro?"

The gaunt man took his time. Finally, he said, "Government should be by the elite, nothing else makes sense. Who wishes to be led by someone competent only to bring up the rear? But each generation must find its own elite. They are not automatically the children of the last generation's, nor are they necessarily to be found among those with titles, great traditions behind them, nor accumulated wealth."

Both Horsten and Lorans were nodding basic agreement. The doctor said, "And your method of selecting your governing elite?"

The Falangist looked full into his eyes and said very slowly, "This is an internal problem of our world. We will solve it based on local conditions, needs, traditions—all the factors that make Falange unique." His voice went slower still. "We do not need the assistance of even friends from worlds beyond, where our institutions are not fully understood. We thank you for your assistance in destroying the corrupt government of El Caudillo, but we must insist on being the engineers of our future."

"Damn well put," Helen said.

"And now we must go," Guerro said.

Martha said worriedly, "You'll be safe? We planned to keep you here for the time."

Guerro and Hoyos came to their feet. "We'll be as safe as can be expected," Guerro said. "Your group will be here?"

"Yes," Horsten said. "Our cover is excellent. When your people have come to some plan of action, let us know. Meanwhile, we shall put our own minds to the situation."

José Hoyos was looking down at Helen speculatively. There was an element of apology in his voice when he said, "How old are you truly?"

Helen said snappishly, "That is a question no man should ever ask a woman."

He looked down at her again, taking in the little girl's dress, sprinkled with wild flowers, at the blond hair caught up in its ribbon. He shook his head.

"You want to Indian wrestle?" she snarled.

"I beg your pardon?" The good-looking torero was confused.

"Leave him alone, Helen," Martha said.

"I'll clobber him," Helen muttered under her breath. "How long am I supposed to go between dates in this damned Section G! I'm a normal young woman."

They saw the two Falangist citizens to the door, the doctor checking the hall up and down, before letting them go.

"Holy Jumping Zen," Helen said, "but he's beautiful. You should have seen his eyes pop when I wiggled through the bars of his cell."

Colonel inspector Segura did what little there was in his power to make his voice soothing. He was seated in the gray drabness of his office, his heavy Castilian style desk a litter of papers and reports, a heavy military revolver used as a paperweight to hold down a pile to his right.

He said now, "No loyal *ciudadano* need fear the officials of El Caudillo's government. They need only tell the truth and receive the acclaim of El Caudillo's faithful servants."

The man before him him squirmed. In his time, the other had run afoul of El Caudillo's so-called faithful servants before. Never seriously, though any contact at all with the *Policía Secreta* was serious enough. But he had never dreamed—save possibly in nightmare—that he would ever confront Miguel Segura himself. One heard stories of Miguel Segura.

"Now," the colonel inspector said in heavy gentleness, "just what was it you saw?"

"Senor Colonel, I was taking a walk through the park . . ."

"So I understand. At perhaps two o'clock in the morning."

The other squirmed again. "Senor Colonel, I can explain. My wife and I . . ."

Segura held up an impatient hand. "I am not at present interested in why a supposedly honest *ciudadano* might find fit to prowl the streets in the dead of night. Get to your story."

"Senor Colonel, it is unbelievable."

The colonel was beginning to lose patience. "There have been many unbelievable things happening in this city, recently. Quick now!"

"Senor Colonel, your excellency. I was not drunk."

"Your story!" the colonel roared.

The other faltered, took a deep breath. "Senor Colonel, I saw a man walk up the side of the Posada San Francisco."

"You saw *what!*"

"Senor Colonel, I was not drunk. I insist. When I told my wife, she told a neighbor. Soon it had spread throughout the block and the *Guardia Civil* came to question me, as they always come if there is the slightest deviation from everyday routine."

"All right. What do you mean, you saw a man walk up the side of the Posada? You mean he was climbing up the side of the hotel, do you not?"

"Senor Colonel, it was at a distance, one admits. It was none too clear. But it was a man, and he was not climbing. Not in the ordinary sense. He was *walking* up the wall. He got to the fourth, or perhaps the fifth floor and then disappeared."

"Disappeared? You mean he went into a window?"

"Perhaps. For me, he simply disappeared."

The colonel stared at the other for a long unprofitable minute. He said finally, "Could it have been that he had a rope suspended from the window and was climbing it, walking up the wall holding onto such a rope?"

"Perhaps, Colonel. It was at a distance, as one has said."

"Get out," the colonel said. "Leave your complete story with the secretary outside. And now get out."

After his informant had left, the colonel inspector sat for a long time, staring unseeingly into a far corner of the office. A light flashed on his desk. He pressed a button.

Teniente Raul Dobarganes entered, a curved piece of wood in hand. The thing might have been a yard in length in all, it might have been a club, but, if so, an unlikely looking one.

Segura growled a sour welcome, then, "Well?"

"It is a boomerang."

The colonel looked at him.

Raul Dobarganes cleared his throat. "A weapon of the Australian Aborigines."

"What in the name of the Holy Ultimate is an Australian whatever-you-said?"

"A very primitive people of Earth. Evidently, according to my historical informant, the device also showed up on other parts of Terra. They were found in Egyptian tombs. One form of the boomerang was more a toy than anything else. You threw it and it made a large circle out into the air and then returned to you.''

The colonel looked at the instrument again as though unbelieving but kept his peace.

His lieutenant went on. ''The hunting and war boomerangs were different. They were meant to strike the game, or enemy, at a distance and with great accuracy and force.''

''You mean you simply threw the thing? Why should it be any more accurate than any other . . . well . . . club?''

''It twirls in the air.'' The young aide demonstrated. ''Going around and around like this. The way it's twisted, the wood . . . it evidently acts as some sort of airfoil.''

''Let me see that damned thing,'' the colonel snapped.

He stared down at it.

Finally he snapped, ''Get me the customs report on the possessions brought in by Pierre Lorans and his family and by Dr. Horsten. Check back to make double sure that the inspection was as thorough as usual. I want to know if as much as a single toothpick could have gotten past undetected.''

''Yes, Colonel Segura.''

When the reports came, the colonel pored over them with a feeling of frustration. He didn't know what he was looking for. Nevertheless, eventually he found it.

He stabbed with his finger, accusingly. ''A box of toys.''

Raul Dobarganes looked blank.

''*What* toys?'' the colonel rasped.

''Why . . . why, a girl's toys, I suppose,'' his aide said. ''Toys for that little girl, dolls and so forth.''

''Ha!'' the colonel said. ''Put a man in the Lorans's suite at the first opportunity. When they are at dinner, or something. I want to know what's in the box of supposed toys. Also check thoroughly on that confounded microphone that is continually breaking. And another thing, Raul. That electrician from the Posada. Have him in here. And that guard of the archives who had the fanciful story of a half dozen or more men descending upon him from the skies. Bring him here. And those hysterical guards from the Alcazar Prison. I want them, too. One the double, Raul!''

His assistant was interrupted for one last order. ''And Raul.

You might get in touch with that Temple monk assigned to the task of exorcising the poltergeists at the city power plant. You can tell him it won't be necessary.''

''Yes, Colonel Segura,'' Raul Dobarganes said, bewildered.

Colonel Inspector Miguel Segura bent a baleful eye on the night guard of the archives of the *Policía Secreta*. He said, infinite cold in his voice, ''This time I want the real story of what happened that night the safe was robbed.''

''Senor Colonel . . .'' There were blisters of cold sweat on the man's forehead. If anything, he seemed more distraught than he had been the night of the crime. Evidently, he'd had time to think it over in detail and the thinking hadn't reassured him. Which was interesting, the colonel decided.

The colonel said, ''Your life is at stake. I want the truth.''

''Senor Colonel, I told the truth. Most of it is a mystery to me. They descended upon me from I know not where. Seemingly from the air. I was helpless, immediately.''

''How many of them did you say there were?''

The guard's eyes darted, but there was no escape. ''I . . . I don't know, Senor Colonel.''

The colonel leaned forward. ''Were there only two . . . or three?''

The blisters of sweat were such now that the man had to wipe them away desperately.

The colonel's eyes shot suddenly to his lieutenant. ''Put him to the question!'' he rasped.

''No . . . no . . . !'' the guard squealed.

''Torture him. I want every tiny detail of what really happened in that archives room.''

''Yes, Colonel,'' Raul Dobarganes said unhappily. He didn't like this phase of his work. He put his head out the office door and summoned four plainclothesmen.

''No . . . no . . .'' the victim was still squealing as they hauled him off.

The colonel's mouth worked. ''Now those prison wardens who allowed the subversives to escape. Bring them in. I want a rehash on that story, too.''

Martha Lorans looked out the window and said, ''Oh, oh.''

''What's the matter?'' Helen said.

"Come here, quick. That line of men, crossing the park."

Helen took one look, said, "Get Pierre," and darted for the hall and the suite of Dorn Horsten.

She made it only halfway. Suddenly, from around a corner of the hotel corridor, two brawny *Policía Secreta*, both carrying pistols, grabbed her up.

Kicking and squealing, she was carried unceremoniously off.

Back in the Lorans apartment, Pierre entered from an inner room. "What's the matter?"

Martha said hurriedly, "Pierre, armed men are closing in from all sides. It must be for us. Is there any last thing we can do? Are there any papers to burn or . . ."

"No, of course not. All our papers are in your head. Where's Helen, Dorn . . ."

"She's gone to get him. You think we can get out of here?"

"No. But we can try. Come on, Martha!"

He headed for the door, she immediately behind him.

It opened and they were confronted by Colonel Inspector Miguel Segura. Behind him were at least a dozen armed men.

"Ah," the colonel said politely, "the *Cordon Bleu* chef who doesn't appreciate the cuisine of Falange, eh? We shall see what you think of the food we serve the inmates of Alcazar Prison, especially those sentenced to be shot for illegal activities against the government of El Caudillo."

There were sounds of a battle royal going on down the hall; great shouts, breaking of furniture, cries of agony.

The colonel turned coldly to one of his minions. "Take four more men with stun guns. A freak who can carry a six hundred pound safe down ten flights of stairs and then tear the door off, evidently with his bare hands, can take a lot of subduing. Be sure not to kill him."

He turned back to the Lorans. "You will accompany me to the *Policía Secreta* headquarters for interrogation."

Pierre Lorans said, "This is an outrage. I wish to inform the United Planets Embassy of my arrest, so that I can arrange for an attorney for my defense."

Some police underling in the background chuckled at that.

The colonel said formally, "Pierre Lorans, you are unfamiliar with Falange legal procedure. The court will appoint an attorney to handle your defense."

"A Falange attorney?" Lorans snorted, drawing himself up in his Gallic stance. "I want a United Planets lawyer!"

Martha said lowly, "That's their law, Pierre. The court appoints defense attorneys in cases involving subversion and espionage."

They were marched into the hall where they were met by another delegation of *Policía Secreta*, these carrying a trussed up Helen. Still further along the hall came two more *Guardia Civil*, looking the worse for wear. They carried a stretcher and upon it, unconscious and breathing deeply, Dr. Dorn Horsten.

A service elevator took them down to street level, and they emerged into an alley behind the hotel. Police limousines awaited them there and they were whisked to the large gray, dominating *Policía Secreta* building which Helen and Horsten had penetrated so short a time ago, looking for the court records of the trial of the Section G agent.

They were hurried through passages, into a large gloomy interrogation room.

The others were pushed into chairs. The colonel eyed the now stirring Dr. Horsten. He said to his bully-boys, "Two of you station yourselves across the room with your guns trained on him. If he shows any belligerence at all, stun him again."

The doctor, groaning from the aftermath of the blast he had received earlier, revived rather quickly, once the process had started. His bones felt as though he had suffered rheumatism and arthritis for a decade and more. He rubbed them painfully, even as he looked up.

He managed to get out, in indignation: "What is the meaning of this? You have a warrant for this outrage?"

"A technicality we dispense with on Falange, and as temporary residents, you come under our legal code. All our laws apply to you," the colonel told him smoothly. "And now, just so as not to waste time, let me inform you that your trial will take place within the hour, and you will be shot this afternoon, at latest. Between then and now, you will be placed on Scop, truth serum, to reveal any accomplices you may have had in your vicious schemes."

"Some trial that's going to be, if you already know we're going to be shot," Helen said bitterly. She made no effort to maintain her childish treble.

The colonel looked at her and made a mocking bow. "I have

not forgotten the kick you gave me, Senorita Lorans." He afforded a light laugh. "Our investigations tell us that there is a whole planet of people such as yourself, though evidently you are one of the top gymnasts. A champion acrobat on a world that loves gymnastics. It explains a great deal of what would have seemed unexplainable." He turned to the doctor. "And you, Dorn Horsten. We have a bit of information on your own home planet, ah, Ftörsta. It must be a strange world, indeed."

The doctor said, "I'd like to get just two fingers around your neck."

"I am sure you would. But time presses. The court is being set up for your brief trial. Immediately, we will resort to our Scop . . ."

Teniente Raul Dobarganes burst open the door and came in, his face ghost-pale.

"What in the name of the Holy Ultimate is wrong?" his superior growled.

Raul Dobarganes shook his head, as though to achieve clarity. "El Caudillo," he whispered. "El Caudillo has been shot."

VI

"Shot!" the colonel rasped.

"Dead. Shot dead. The parade in Almeria. The parade in honor of the glorious matadors who have fallen in the arena. The assassins were stationed all along the route of the parade. There must have been at least five of them in all. The fourth gunman got him. El Caudillo is dead."

Horsten winced. He muttered, "I didn't expect them to be so susceptible, when I told them that story."

Helen looked at him, speculatively. "Are you sure?"

"I don't know," he said defensively. "I suppose it doesn't make much difference now."

The colonel had sped from the room, roaring orders right and left.

Pierre Lorans found the courage to laugh. "Well, at least it will probably give us a respite for an hour or so."

Martha said, "More than that." Her eyes seemed to go empty and she recited, *"Falange Legal Code, Article Three, Section Three. During the National Fiesta Brava and until the new Cau-*

dillo is confirmed, there are no criminals on the planet Falange. Each resident must be free to compete as a torero if such is his desire."

Horsten looked his astonishment. "You mean to say they open the prisons?"

"Evidently. It must be a madhouse."

Helen growled, "Let's get out of here and back to the hotel. Evidently, there's nothing to stop us." She looked over at Raul Dobarganes. "Is there, cutey?"

He had been taking in their conversation, blankly. In actuality, the last National Fiesta Brava had been held while he was still so young that few of the details remained with him. All he could recall was the great excitement. Now, he was almost as confused as the Section G operatives by the sudden change in the situation.

However, he knew the law. He shook his head. "No. There is nothing to stop you. There are no criminals on Falange. But as soon as the new Caudillo has been selected, you will again be apprehended and your trial will take place."

Helen winked at him. "Let's go, folks."

They stood on the balcony of the Lorans's suite at the Posada San Francisco and looked glumly down at the merrymaking crowds.

"Look at those costumes," Martha said. "You would have thought that it would take weeks to make some of them."

Horsten grunted. "They were out on the streets within half an hour of the flashing of the news of El Caudillo's death."

Bartolomé Guerro was with them, his expression sour. "For some of them, it is the one real excitement of their lives. The world turns upside down. The peon is free to leave the *finca* and journey into town for the local corridas. If he has the wherewithal, he can even make the trip here to Nuevo Madrid for the finals. The poorest laborer, in costume in the fiestas, rubs shoulders with the wealthiest hidalgo; may steal a kiss, if he's handsome enough, from a titled lady."

Helen said, staring down at the mobs of dancing, running, laughing, drinking, milling Falangists, "This going on all over the planet?"

Guerro nodded. "Everywhere. There are few towns so small as not to have a bullring. It is the Falange equivalent of the

Roman circus, and serves the same purpose. So long as the people are completely caught up in the fiesta brava, they have little time to realize the inadequacies of the life they lead. And this is the fiesta of all fiestas. The National Fiesta Brava, seldom witnessed more than once or twice in a single man's lifetime."

Horsten said, "And the elimination fights are taking place throughout the planet?"

"That is correct. Local toreros fight in their local arenas. The best is then sent to the county seat, where he competes with those others who have survived the local corridas. From hence, he goes to the nearest large city, and eventually here to Nuevo Madrid for the finals. Thousands of corridas are being held all over Falange at this very moment."

Pierre Lorans said, "How is it decided who wins? It would seem to me that it could be rigged by the judges."

The Falangist shook his head. "No, that is not where the rigging comes in. It is the crowd that decides, by popular acclaim, and no judge would dare go against it. If a torero fights well, he is awarded an ear, if he fights superlatively he will get two ears. If he triumphs, he gets two ears and a tail. On the rarest of occasions, he is awarded a hoof on top of all the rest."

Horsten was looking at him. "Where does the rigging come in?" he said. "I've wondered about this before. How can the ruling class take the chance that some peon, or other lower caste member, might win and upset the applecart?"

The other grunted deprecation. "Theoretically, it's all fair. However, the sons of the elite *finca* owners begin playing with fighting bulls when they are two or three years old—and the bulls one or two days old. By the time they're ten, instructed by the most competent veterans of the arena, they fight calves. By the time they're twelve, they are fighting small bulls at *tientas*, the testing of the young bulls. At about the same time they are allowed to kill steers at the ranch slaughterhouse, literally by the hundreds, learning every trick of the game. Ah, believe me, my friends, by the time our young hidalgo is sixteen he knows just about everything there is to know about the *Bos taurus ibericus* and the fiesta brava."

The Section G agents had been interested. Lorans said, "Any other way they have of getting an advantage?"

Guerro made his very Iberian shrug. "Well, the matador's *cuadrillas*; his assistants: picadors, *banderilleros*, and peons.

They have a double purpose: one, to come to his rescue when he's in trouble; and, two, to make him look good in there. If a man can afford the most expensive *cuadrilla* that it is possible to hire, then he has a big advantage. On the face of it, one of Falange's ruling elite can so afford, and some youngster up from the slums hasn't got a chance of acquiring top assistants.''

Helen said suddenly, "How's José Hoyos doing?''

Guerro pulled a great gust of air down into his lungs. "He is doing . . . adequately. The crowds call him Joseíto and he is still *Numero Tres*. Number One and Number Two, hidalgos named Perico and Carlitos by their fans, have been shifting back and forth as favorites, but Joseíto has consistently remained third in popularity. None of these top three has had a serious goring yet, they've all been lucky.''

"Third place, eh? How about his, what did you call it, his assistants?'' Horsten said.

"His *cuadrilla*? Top men. All members of the Lorca Party, all professional toreros. They're nearly as good as those of either *Numero Uno*, or *Numero Dos*.'' There was a shine in the gaunt man's eyes. "For once, we have possibly an even chance. For once, one of ours will at least participate in the finals. If he could only make it! El Caudillo! One of our party!''

The sounds of the mob dancing in the streets wafted up to them.

Helen said, "Is it going to be possible for us to watch the final fights?''

"Why not? It is simply a matter of being willing to pay enough for tickets. People have been known to sell their homes, beggar themselves, to buy a ticket for the final corrida. The arena sits but fifty thousand, and all Falange would like to attend. However, I imagine with United Planets resources behind you . . .''

Martha said grimly, "We have to be there to cheer on Joseíto. If he wins, we've got it made, mission accomplished and everything. If he loses, Colonel Segura will have us back in the Alcazar before we can blink.''

Guerro looked at her, frowning. "Couldn't you make a run for it now?'' He looked round at the others.

Horsten grunted. "Run to where? They certainly aren't going to let us get aboard a spaceship, even if there were one available, and there isn't.''

Whatever the moral implications of the fiesta brava, either in the old days in Spain and Mexico, or on the planet Falange, a colorful spectacle beyond compare it most certainly is.

Fifty thousand persons packed the seats, and another ten, perhaps, stood in the rear and in the aisles. All dressed in their most colorful best. All brimming with excitement. The bands blared out the "Diana," hawkers took beer, soft drinks, nuts and other edibles through the crowd, friends screamed greetings at each other over the heads of intervening hundreds. Fans and handkerchiefs fluttered. Masculine aficionados cheered each time a youthful senorita found it necessary to hike full skirts a fraction in order to climb over stone seats, seeking her own reserved space.

The Section G operatives, still accompanied by Bartolomé Guerro, had superlative seats right on the *barrera*, immediately above the *callejon*, the passage which circles the arena proper and behind which the toreros, not immediately in action, shelter themselves during the corrida. It would have been impossible to have been any closer to the action without joining it. Immediately to their left was the gate of the bull, which led back from the arena to the *toril*, the bull's enclosure.

None of them, save Guerro, had ever seen a corrida, with the exception of portions in a Tri-Di historical tape on Earth, or one of the other advanced planets.

He explained procedure to them as the afternoon wore on. There were three matadors, Carlitos, Perico and Joseíto, who had wound up in the finals, *Numbers Uno*, *Dos* and *Tres*. Joseito, the Lorca Party champion, was *Numero Tres*, as he had been consistently through the preliminary fights.

Carlitos, a tall, beautifully graceful man of possibly thirty, was to have the first bull. Scion of one of the planet's wealthiest rancher families, he had for years been one of Falange's most popular matadors and was by far and gone the favorite of the crowd.

Perico, a smaller, dark complected man, was not nearly the physical specimen of his opponent, but evidently, from what Guerro said, was noted for the impossible chances he took, the *desplantes* he indulged in so arrogantly, the *adornos*. He was famous for taking the tip of a dominated bull's horn in his mouth, to the horror of the crowd. A sudden flip upward of the horn and his brain would have been pierced. He, too, was of one of the very best families.

The preliminary parade, each matador followed by his *cuadrilla*, brought the audience cheering to its feet, each shouting the name of his champion.

To the swinging strains of "La Golondrina," that song of the torero come down through the centuries, they marched to the judge's stand and made their salute, in dim, dim memory of the gladiators who once stood and shouted, *"We who are about to die . . ."*

The *cuadrillas* dispersed, most to take their places in the *callejón* until it was time for their own performances. The peons of Carlitos remained in the ring waiting for the first bull.

He came exploding into the ring, half a ton and more of deliberately bred trouble. Deliberately bred for thousands of years to meet death in the afternoon, in the arena.

Carlitos stood alone in the ring center, cape in hands. The bull spotted him and again exploded.

Helen sucked in her breath.

Guerro explained. "He is noted for his Veronicas. Some say he is the greatest master of the Veronica since the legendary Manolete of Spain. It is the most graceful of cape passes and the basic of them all."

Carlitos made no preliminary passes to gauge the bull's mettle. The first pass was taken inches from the bull's horns and the second, and the third. The crowd screamed its *olés*.

Guerro wiped his brow with a handkerchief. "He is unbelievable," he said. "Joseíto could never present such Veronicas."

Helen looked at him. "So far we're losing, eh?"

"Nobody on Falange could perform such Veronicas, save Carlitos," Guerro said unhappily.

Lorans growled, "Why does the confounded bull charge so straight? The slightest deviation and our torero would have a horn in the guts."

"It is a perfect bull," Guerro admitted. "They are bred to run straight. When a matador has such a bull, he is assured of a triumph. Carlitos is fortunate. His bull is perfect. We can only pray that Joseíto has similar fortune."

The matador passed the animal eight times before finally bringing it to a frustrated standstill and stalking arrogantly away, not bothering to look over his shoulder to see if the animal was making one last charge.

The fight proceeded through the quarter of the picadors, through the quarter of the *banderilleros*.

Guerro wiped his forehead again. "Perfect," he said. "Everything perfect. It is possibly the most superlative corrida I have ever seen."

"We're losing, eh?" Helen said lowly. "And our boy hasn't even been to bat yet."

For the moment, the bull stood immediately below them, breathing deeply from his exertions, waiting while Carlitos selected his sword and *muleta*. Waiting while Carlitos dedicated the animal to the three judges of the National Fiesta Brava finals. The matador wound it up by tossing his hat back over his shoulder into the stands and advanced toward the animal.

Pierre Lorans pursed plump lips. "Those are strange looking horns," he muttered.

Guerro looked at him. "Beef animals no longer have such horns, it is true. But they are especially bred fighting bulls, these, and the wide horn spread and length are necessary for a proper corrida."

"It is not that," Lorans grumbled. "As an apprentice at the *Cordon Bleu*, I had to become a butcher. One cannot cook if one does not know what he cooks. Each *Cordon Bleu* chef is a butcher as well as many other things. And I say . . ."

He lost the attention of his listeners as Carlitos went into his *faena*, the final series of passes that culminated in the moment of truth, the bull's death.

The kill was perfect, the bull dropped as though he had been poleaxed. Carlitos paraded the ring, the crowd cheering. He and his assistants held up his award, two ears, the tail and a hoof.

"The highest possible award," Guerro told them, wiping his mouth in despair with his handkerchief.

Perico had the next bull, a *cárdeno*, Guerro explained, an animal with a black and white coat.

The dark complected matador lived up to his reputation for foolhardy chances by beginning the fight on his knees, his cape spread before him, his arms spread wide, as though in supplication to the bull. Immediately upon entering the ring, it spotted him and banged in his direction.

Helen closed her eyes; seemingly, there was no chance of the avoiding of destruction. At the last split second, the matador grabbed up the cape and fluttered it to one side, and the animal exploded past. The crowed screamed itself hoarse.

Perico was awarded two ears and a tail. Not quite as much as Carlito had taken, but each had one more bull to fight.

It was the turn of Joseíto. Elements in the crowd yelled, "Lorca! Lorca!"

Dorn Horsten looked at Guerro, who shook his head. "They take their chances, but the rumor has been deliberately spread. They know Joseíto is the champion of the Lorca Party and what it means if he is proclaimed El Caudillo."

Martha was looking about the stands, in this short period between fights. She said to Helen, "I wonder where your boyfriend is, the brain surgeon."

Something came to Helen out of the blue.

She muttered, "Brain surgeon, electronics technician." She turned to Martha quickly. "When Colonel Segura and his stooge were interrogating us about the ash in the fireplace, what was it that aide said about Ferd Zogbaum?"

Martha scowled momentarily, but then her eyes went empty and she recited, "The assistant said, *'Probably the technician for the corridas, Senor Colonel. He arrived on the same spaceship, you'll recall. Senor Zogbaum.'*"

"Technician for the corridas," Helen snarled. "What kind of technician? A brain surgeon!"

Lorans hadn't been listening. He was scowling at the new bull, Joseíto's bull, that had just come dashing into the ring in a great swirl of dust. "As a butcher," he muttered, "They are the strangest horns I have ever seen. They are not . . ."

"They're not horns, they're radios!" Helen snapped suddenly. "Come on, Pierre! Those animals are being controlled, the deck's stacked! Come on Dorn! Martha, you stay here and keep your eyes open." With no more than that, the diminutive acrobat vaulted over the *barrera* wall into the *callejón* below, the two masculine Section G operatives only split seconds behind her.

Startled ring attendants reacted too slowly to halt the progress of the unlikely three. The little girl, the hulking six and a half footer wearing pince-nez glasses, the puffing, heavy-set, servant type bringing up the rear. They ducked, dodged and elbowed their way around the wooden shelter.

Horsten, who had immediately accepted her words, as had
Lorans, called, "What are we looking for?"

"It must be somewhere right on the ring, where the fight can
be watched. Some kind of a control room. What's *that*?" She
skidded to a halt.

"One of the infirmaries," Lorans puffed. "Guerro pointed it
out. For emergency gorings. Behind this one is the chapel of the
United Temple."

"Those opaque windows," Helen snapped. "Polarized glass.
Infirmary, my foot. Come on!"

Two *Guardia Civil* attempted to stop them, and nearly had their
chests caved in by the sweeping arm of Dorn Horsten. The door
was heavy, closed and evidently barred from within.

"Dorn!" Helen said.

His heavy shoulder crashed into the wooden barrier.

Behind them, the crowd had gone hysterical, shouting over
and over, *"Olé! Olé! Olé!"* at whatever it was Joseíta was doing
with his bull.

The door caved in, even as *Guardia Civil* and *Policía Secreta*
approached at the double, guns drawn.

Inside, Ferd Zogbaum looked up and blinked. He was seated
at a control board, a headset over his ears, a dozen dials and an
equal number of switches, before him.

At one of the windows, binoculars to eyes, stood a uniformed
comandante of the *Policía Secreta*. As the trio burst unceremoniously in, he was saying, "The right horn, a quick toss!"

Ferd Zogbaum's small hands were dancing over the control
switches.

Helen snapped, "Pierre!"

The ballbearings came so fast that seemingly there were a
score of them in the air at once. Tubes crashed, dials shattered,
Ferd Zogbaum's headset was torn magically from his head. In
split seconds, the room was an electronic shambles.

Helen stood there, hands on hips and glared at Zogbaum.
"Aren't you ashamed of yourself!"

He blinked. He blurted, "To tell the truth, yes. But there was
nothing I could do. I wasn't quite clear on what this job was
when they hired me, but the pay was fantastic. The old technician died. He was from Earth, too. They hire you for life, they

don't have men here capable of operating this equipment, and they use it at every major fight in this arena."

Horsten was staring around the room. He looked out the one-way window, after brushing the startled *Policía Secreta comandante* to one side.

"I knew it!" he growled. "It had to be something like this. The big corridas rigged. Electrodes attached to the brain of the animal. Radio impulses from this control booth, causing the bull to dash straight ahead, without veering, or to toss right or left, as electronically ordered."

Martha and Guerro entered from behind them. Her face was gray. "Whatever you've found, it's too late," she said.

"What do you mean!" Helen said.

"Joseíto," Guerro said emptily. "He has taken a *cornada*."

"A what?"

"He has been gored. Seriously. He is out of the running."

"Then . . . then we can't possibly win."

A new voice came from the door. It was Colonel Inspector Segura, military revolver in hand. "No," he said. "You can't possibly win, you of the Lorca Party, you of Section G. You have lost. Within fifteen minutes, the fight will be decided. Either Carlitos or Perico will be declared the new El Caudillo and all of you will be brought to trial on subversion charges."

Helen glared at him. "Not quite yet, you funker. Come on Dorn, Pierre, Martha. To the judges' stand!"

"Why?" Lorans said, hope gone from his voice.

"Because I just remembered something Martha recited to us from the Tauromachy Code."

Dorn led the way again, pushing through police and ring attendants, finding an exit that led upward into the stands. They pushed and wedged themselves through packed aisles on the way to the box of the presiding judges of the National Fiesta Brava.

A bevy of *Guardia Civil* was the ultimate obstacle to their getting through. Dorn Horsten brushed them aside. Helen, chubby hands on hips, confronted the three aged judges.

She said shrilly, "I declare myself a contestant and demand the right to fight!"

There was only astonishment in the faces of the three Falangists. Colonel Segura had scurried to the box. He bent over the judges and whispered to them.

One went to the trouble of saying, "Please, Senorita, this is a most serious event. It is no time for jest. Joseíto has been eliminated from the corridas, but two bulls remain to be fought."

"I'm not joking," Helen bit out. "I demand the right to participate."

"Hey," Horsten said. "What about me?"

"You lumbering ox," Helen growled under her breath. "Support me. I've got an idea." She turned back to the judges. "We quote from the Tauromachy Code. Martha! That section on discovery of fraud in the National Fiesta Brava."

Martha's eyes went lackluster. She said, *"Tauromachy Code. Article Eight, Section Two. If a participant can prove fraud in the National Fiesta Brava, he may demand to enter the eliminations of the level the fraud was revealed—even though already eliminated."*

"That's it!" Helen said. "I declare myself a participant. The evidence of fraud is there to be seen in the supposed infirmary. The bulls were being directed by radio, through electrodes embedded in their skulls."

The judges stared at each other. Colonel Inspector Segura bowed over them again and whispered.

One said snappishly, "You're a woman!"

"Martha!"

"There is nothing in the Tauromachy Code preventing a woman from fighting in the National Fiesta Brava. Women matadors are not unknown. I quote from the Juno 335, of the year of Falange, issue of *El Toro* magazine. *The Senorita Octoviana Gonzales participated as a rejoneadore and cut two ears at the Plaza de Toros in the town of Nuevo Murcia today. The occasion was . . ."*

One of the judges leaned forward angrily. A deep hush had fallen over the arena, as though the sixty-thousand spectators were attempting to hear what was being said—an impossibility.

The judge said, "Admittedly, women have on rare occasion, and usually on their own *fincas*, very informally, participated in corridas . . ."

"There is nothing in Falange law preventing a woman from participating in the National Fiesta Brava," Martha said stubbornly.

"You are a criminal alien!" the third of the judges barked, breaking his silence for the first time.

"There is nothing in Falange law to prevent a criminal from participating, nor need I be a citizen. I am a temporary resident of Falange and eligible to participate."

"Why, you're not even a woman," the first judge bleated indignantly.

Helen flushed her anger. "I am a normal woman and citizen of the planet Gandharvas where my size is ordinary," she flared. "But now I am a resident of Falange and demand my right to participate in the eliminations."

The third judge turned sly. "Very well, Senorita. However, you must realize that there are certain requirements, instituted to eliminate some of the early would-be contestants so as to speed up the National Fiesta Brava. Our national spectacle is highly stylized. Each participant must fight in a given school. What school do you choose?"

"School?" Helen said blankly.

The judge was triumphant. "We do not let the fiesta brava become a comic farce. Do you fight La Ronda style, Seville style, or Madrid style? If you chose one, then you must stick to that school of bullfighting."

Helen's eyes darted around desperately. Her face pleaded at Dorn Horsten, then Pierre Lorans. Both shook their heads, blankly.

The judge whinnied amusement. "Come. What style, Senorita?"

She snapped, "I fight Cretan style!"

They gaped at her.

Helen said, "Surely anybody claiming a knowledge of the history of bullfighting realizes that the earliest style of all is that once practiced at the Minoan palace of Knossos on the island of Crete, two thousand and more years before the fiesta brava was ever dreamed of in Spain."

Deep rumblings were going through the crowd, even as Martha and Helen improvised a Cretan kilt for her costume. Rumors were evidently flying, and Guerro's underground adherents of the Lorca Party were doing their best to make hay.

Dorn Horsten was to act as her *sobresaliente*, her sole assistant in the ring. There was no time for costume for him. He peeled down to trousers and shirt, which he left open at the neck, and kicked off his shoes, the better to operate in the sand of the arena.

She dashed out into the ring, followed by the lumbering Dorn Horsten, even as the *Bos taurus ibericus* came charging in from the other side.

Diminutive she still was, fearfully so in view of the size of the rampaging animal, but child she was no longer. That was obvious to all.

She sped toward the beast. He spotted her. Changed slightly his line of charge, and with the speed of a locomotive came storming down.

The shouts from the crowd were of horror.

The bull was scant feet away, animal and tiny human still heading full toward each other. It lowered its head to toss, and for a moment they seemed to blend.

Small chubby hands went out, seized horn tips. The bull tossed, she spun over his head in a somersault, landed on her feet on his back, facing toward his hind quarters. She somersaulted again, off his back and to the sands beyond. Dorn Horsten caught and steadied her.

The mob in the arena stands screamed in disbelief, thrill and applause.

The bull was heading back. The performance was repeated. And again and again.

At long last, the bewildered animal was exhausted, run to a standstill. It stood there, head lowered, tongue hanging out, breathing deeply, confused, utterly dominated.

The stands were a madhouse. The stands were screaming confusion. The stands were bedlam.

There was nothing more that could be done with the exhausted animal. Helen began a tour of the ring, in somewhat the fashion the matadors had done earlier when they had been awarded the ears, tails and hoofs of their fallen victims.

But she did it with a difference. She toured the ring like a pinwheel, a top, a bouncing, spinning, cartwheeling demonstration of acrobatics such as had never been seen on the staid old planet of Falange before.

And behind her, running as the assistants of the matadors had run behind their principals earlier, came the lumbering Dr. Dorn Horsten.

Only with a difference. He did not carry the awarded ears,

tail and hoofs as had the assistants of Carlitos and Perico, to hold up to the view of the crowd.

Slung over his shoulders he carried the bewildered bull.

The stands were now screaming laughter.

Afterward

They were rehashing the details in the suite of the Posada San Francisco. The Section G operatives were present, Bartolomé Guerro, a highly bandaged José Hoyos and a dozen of the upper echelons of the once underground organization of the Lorca Party.

Dorn Horsten was summing it up. "No government can stand in the face of the onset of farce, of ridicule. No government can stand without dignity. Any government that becomes farcical, falls. Nero with all his power, with all the traditions of the defied Caesars behind him, fell when he allowed himself to appear the clown."

Guerro was nodding agreement. "How quickly the institution of El Caudillo became a laughingstock when a tiny girl took over the title after first revealing the games rigged and then making a mockery of the national spectacle."

Helen entered the room, dressed now not as an eight-year-old, but in the latest of Falange style, including flamenco style high heels and a touch of lipstick.

Horsten looked at her, somewhat taken aback. "Where are you going?"

She said snappishly, "What business is it of yours, you overgrown lummox? But if you must know, I have a date with Ferd Zogbaum. First, I'm going to give the cloddy a knockdown, drag-out dressing down. Then I'm going to relent. After all, he is the nearest thing to a man my size for a couple of hundred light-years." She added, a devilish glint in her eyes, "And I suspect he has new opinions about little Helen since seeing me in that Cretan costume."

ARENA

by Fredric Brown

Carson opened his eyes, and found himself looking upward into a flickering blue dimness.

It was hot, and he was lying on sand, and a sharp rock embedded in the sand was hurting his back. He rolled over to his side, off the rock, and then pushed himself up to a sitting position.

"I'm crazy," he thought. "Crazy—or dead—or something." The sand was blue, bright blue. And there wasn't any such thing as bright blue sand on Earth or any of the planets.

Blue sand.

Blue sand under a blue dome that wasn't the sky nor yet a room, but a circumscribed area—somehow he knew it was circumscribed and finite even though he couldn't see to the top of it.

He picked up some of the sand in his hand and let it run through his fingers. It trickled down onto his bare leg. *Bare?*

Naked. He was stark naked, and already his body was dripping perspiration from the enervating heat, coated blue with sand wherever sand had touched it.

But elsewhere his body was white.

He thought: Then this sand is really blue. If it seemed blue

167

only because of the blue light, then I'd be blue also. But I'm white, so the sand *is* blue. *Blue sand.* There isn't any blue sand. There isn't any place like this place I'm in.

Sweat was running down in his eyes.

It was hot, hotter than hell. Only hell—the hell of the ancients—was supposed to be red and not blue.

But if this place wasn't hell, what was it? Only Mercury, among the planets, had heat like this and this wasn't Mercury. And Mercury was some four billion miles from—

It came back to him then, where he'd been. In the little one-man scouter, outside the orbit of Pluto, scouting a scant million miles to one side of the Earth Armada drawn up in battle array there to intercept the Outsiders.

That sudden strident nerve-shattering ringing of the alarm bell when the rival scouter—the Outsider ship—had come within range of his detectors—

No one knew who the Outsiders were, what they looked like, from what far galaxy they came, other than that it was in the general direction of the Pleiades.

First, sporadic raids on Earth colonies and outposts. Isolated battles between Earth patrols and small groups of Outsider spaceships; battles sometimes won and sometimes lost, but never to date resulting in the capture of an alien vessel. Nor had any member of a raided colony ever survived to describe the Outsiders who had left the ships, if indeed they had left them.

Not a too-serious menace, at first, for the raids had not been too numerous or destructive. And individually, the ships had proved slightly inferior in armament to the best of Earth's fighters, although somewhat superior in speed and maneuverability. A sufficient edge in speed, in fact, to give the Outsiders their choice of running or fighting, unless surrounded.

Nevertheless, Earth had prepared for serious trouble, for a showdown, building the mightiest armada of all time. It had been waiting now, that armada, for a long time. But now the showdown was coming.

Scouts twenty billion miles out had detected the approach of a mighty fleet—a showdown fleet—of the Outsiders. Those scouts had never come back, but their radiotronic messages had. And now Earth's armada, all ten thousand ships and half-million fighting spacemen, was out there, outside Pluto's orbit, waiting to intercept and battle to the death.

And an even battle it was going to be, judging by the advance reports of the men of the far picket line who had given their lives to report—before they had died—on the size and strength of the alien fleet.

Anybody's battle, with the mastery of the solar system hanging in the balance, on an even chance. A last and *only* chance, for Earth and all her colonies lay at the utter mercy of the Outsiders if they ran that gauntlet—

Oh yes. Bob Carson remembered now.

Not that it explained blue sand and flickering blueness. But that strident alarming of the bell and his leap for the control panel. His frenzied fumbling as he strapped himself into the seat. The dot in the visiplate that grew larger.

The dryness of his mouth. The awful knowledge that this was *it*. For him, at least, although the main fleets were still out of range of one another.

This, his first taste of battle. Within three seconds or less he'd be victorious, or a charred cinder. Dead.

Three seconds—that's how long a space-battle lasted. Time enough to count to three, slowly, and then you'd won or you were dead. One hit completely took care of a lightly armed and armored little one-man craft like a scouter.

Frantically—as, unconsciously, his dry lips shaped the word "One"—he worked at the controls to keep that growing dot centered on the crossed spiderwebs of the visiplate. His hands doing that, while his right foot hovered over the pedal that would fire the bolt. The single bolt of concentrated hell that had to hit—or else. There wouldn't be time for any second shot.

"Two." He didn't know he'd said that, either. The dot in the visiplate wasn't a dot now. Only a few thousand miles away, it showed up in the magnification of the plate as though it were only a few hundred yards off. It was a sleek, fast little scouter, about the size of his.

And an alien ship, all right.

"Thr—" His foot touched the bolt-release pedal—

And then the Outsider had swerved suddenly and was off the crosshairs. Carson punched keys frantically, to follow.

For a tenth of a second, it was out of the visiplate entirely,

and then as the nose of his scouter swung after it, he saw it
again, diving straight toward the ground.

The ground?

It was an optical illusion of some sort. It *had* to be, that
planet—or whatever it was—that now covered the visiplate.
Whatever it was, it couldn't be there. Couldn't possibly. There
wasn't any planet nearer than Neptune three billion miles away—
with Pluto around on the opposite side of the distant pinpoint
sun.

His *detectors! They* hadn't shown any object of planetary dimensions, even of asteroid dimensions. They still didn't.

So it couldn't be there, that whatever-it-was he was diving
into, only a few hundred miles below him.

And in his sudden anxiety to keep from crashing, he forgot
even the Outsider ship. He fired the front braking rockets, and
even as the sudden change of speed slammed him forward against
the seat straps, he fired full right for an emergency turn. Pushed
them down and *held* them down, knowing that he needed everything the ship had to keep from crashing and that a turn that
sudden would black him out for a moment.

It did black him out.

And that was all. Now he was sitting in hot blue sand, stark
naked but otherwise unhurt. No sign of his spaceship and—for
that matter—no sign of *space*. That curve overhead wasn't a sky,
whatever else it was.

He scrambled to his feet.

Gravity seemed a little more than Earth-normal. Not much
more.

Flat sand stretching away, a few scrawny bushes in clumps
here and there. The bushes were blue, too, but in varying shades,
some lighter than the blue of the sand, some darker.

Out from under the nearest bush ran a little thing that was like
a lizard, except that it had more than four legs. It was blue, too.
Bright blue. It saw him and ran back again under the bush.

He looked up again, trying to decide what was overhead. It
wasn't exactly a roof, but it was dome-shaped. It flickered and
was hard to look at. But definitely, it curved down to the ground,
to the blue sand, all around him.

He wasn't far from being under the center of the dome. At a
guess, it was a hundred yards to the nearest wall, if it was a
wall. It was as though a blue hemisphere of *something*, about

two hundred and fifty yards in circumference, was inverted over the flat expanse of the sand.

And everything blue, except one object. Over near a far curving wall there was a red object. Roughly spherical, it seemed to be about a yard in diameter. Too far for him to see clearly through the flickering blueness. But, unaccountably, he shuddered.

He wiped sweat from his forehead, or tried to, with the back of his hand.

Was this a dream, a nightmare? This heat, this sand, that vague feeling of horror he felt when he looked toward the red thing?

A dream? No, one didn't go to sleep and dream in the midst of a battle in space.

Death? No, never. If there were immortality, it wouldn't be a senseless thing like this, a thing of blue heat and blue sand and a red horror.

Then he heard the voice—

Inside his head he heard it, not with his ears. It came from nowhere or everywhere.

"Through spaces and dimensions wandering," rang the words in his mind, *"and in this space and this time I find two people about to wage a war that would exterminate one and so weaken the other that it would retrogress and never fulfill its destiny, but decay and return to mindless dust whence it came. And I say this must not happen."*

"Who . . . what are you?" Carson didn't say it aloud, but the question formed itself in his brain.

"You would not understand completely. I am—" There was a pause as though the voice sought—in Carson's brain—for a word that wasn't there, a word he didn't know. *"I am the end of evolution of a race so old the time can not be expressed in words that have meaning to your mind. A race fused into a single entity, eternal—*

"An entity such as your primitive race might become"—again the groping for a word—*"time from now. So might the race you call, in your mind, the Outsiders. So I intervene in the battle to come, the battle between fleets so evenly matched that destruction of both races will result. One must survive. One must progress and evolve."*

"One?" thought Carson. "Mine, or—?"

"It is in my power to stop the war, to send the Outsiders back

to their galaxy. But they would return, or your race would sooner or later follow them there. Only by remaining in this space and time to intervene constantly could I prevent them from destroying one another, and I cannot remain.

"So I shall intervene now. I shall destroy one fleet completely without loss to the other. One civilization shall thus survive."

Nightmare. This had to be a nightmare, Carson thought. But he knew it wasn't.

It was too mad, too impossible, to be anything but real.

He didn't dare ask *the* question—*which?* But his thoughts asked it for him.

"The stronger shall survive," said the voice. "That I can not—and would not—change. I merely intervene to make it a complete victory, not"—groping again—"not Pyrrhic victory to a broken race.

"From the outskirts of the not-yet battle I plucked two individuals, you and an Outsider. I see from your mind that in your early history of nationalisms battles between champions, to decide issues between races, were not unknown.

"You and your opponent are here pitted against one another, naked and unarmed, under conditions equally unfamiliar to you both, equally unpleasant to you both. There is no time limit, for here there is no time. The survivor is the champion of his race. That race survives."

"But—" Carson's protest was too inarticulate for expression, but the voice answered it.

"It is fair. The conditions are such that the accident of physical strength will not completely decide the issue. There is a barrier. You will understand. Brain-power and courage will be more important than strength. Most especially courage, which is the will to survive."

"But while this goes on, the fleets will—"

"No, you are in another space, another time. For as long as you are here, time stands still in the universe you know. I see you wonder whether this place is real. It is, and it is not. As I— to your limited understanding—am and am not real. My existence is mental and not physical. You saw me as a planet; it could have been as a dustmote or a sun.

"But to you this place is now real. What you suffer here will be real. And if you die here, your death will be real. If you die,

*your failure will be the end of your race. That is enough for you
to know.''*

And then the voice was gone.

And he was alone, but not alone. For as Carson looked up,
he saw that the red thing, the red sphere of horror which he now
knew was the Outsider, was rolling toward him.

Rolling.

It seemed to have no legs or arms that he could see, no features. It rolled across the blue sand with the fluid quickness of
a drop of mercury. And before it, in some manner, he could not
understand, came a paralyzing wave of nauseating, retching,
horrid hatred.

Carson looked about him frantically. A stone, lying in the
sand a few feet away, was the nearest thing to a weapon. It
wasn't large, but it had sharp edges, like a slab of flint. It looked
a bit like blue flint.

He picked it up, and crouched to receive the attack. It was
coming faster, faster than he could run.

No time to think out how he was going to fight it, and how
anyway could he plan to battle a creature whose strength, whose
characteristics, whose method of fighting he did not know? Rolling so fast, it looked more than ever like a perfect sphere.

Ten yards away. Five. And then it stopped.

Rather, it *was stopped*. Abruptly the near side of it flattened
as though it had run up against an invisible wall. It bounced,
actually bounced back.

Then it rolled forward again, but more slowly, more cautiously. It stopped again, at the same place. It tried again, a few
yards to one side.

There was a barrier there of some sort. It clicked, then, in
Carson's mind. That thought projected into his mind by the Entity who had brought them there: ''—accident of physical strength
will not completely decide the issue. There is a barrier.''

A force-field, of course. Not the Netzian Field, known to Earth
science, for that glowed and emitted a crackling sound. This one
was invisible, silent.

It was a wall that ran from side to side of the inverted hemisphere; Carson didn't have to verify that himself. The Roller
was doing that; rolling sideways along the barrier, seeking a
break in it that wasn't there.

Carson took half a dozen steps forward, his left hand groping out before him, and then his hand touched the barrier. It felt smooth, yielding, like a sheet of rubber rather than like glass. Warm to his touch, but no warmer than the sand underfoot. And it was completely invisible, even at close range.

He dropped the stone and put both hands against it, pushing. It seemed to yield, just a trifle. But no farther than that trifle, even when he pushed with all his weight. It felt like a sheet of rubber backed up by steel. Limited resiliency, and then firm strength.

He stood on tiptoe and reached as high as he could and the barrier was still there.

He saw the Roller coming back, having reached one side of the arena. That feeling of nausea hit Carson again, and he stepped back from the barrier as it went by. It didn't stop.

But did the barrier stop at ground level? Carson knelt down and burrowed in the sand. It was soft, light, easy to dig in. At two feet down the barrier was still there.

The Roller was coming back again. Obviously, it couldn't find a way through at either side.

There must be a way through, Carson thought. *Some* way we can get at each other, else this duel is meaningless.

But no hurry now, in finding that out. There was something to try first. The Roller was back now, and it stopped just across the barrier, only six feet away. It seemed to be studying him, although for the life of him, Carson couldn't find external evidence of sense organs on the thing. Nothing that looked like eyes or ears, or even a mouth. There was though, he saw now, a series of grooves—perhaps a dozen of them altogether, and he saw two tentacles suddenly push out from two of the grooves and dip into the sand as though testing its consistency. Tentacles about an inch in diameter and perhaps a foot and a half long.

But the tentacles were retractable into the grooves and were kept there except when in use. They were retracted when the thing rolled and seemd to have nothing to do with its method of locomotion. That, as far as Carson could judge, seemed to be accomplished by some shifting—just *how* he couldn't even imagine—of its center of gravity.

He shuddered as he looked at the thing. It was alien, utterly alien, horribly different from anything on Earth or any of the life forms found on the other solar planets. Instinctively, somehow, he knew its mind was as alien as its body.

But he had to try. If it had no telepathic powers at all, the attempt was foredoomed to failure, yet he thought it had such powers. There had, at any rate, been a projection of something that was not physical at the time a few minutes ago when it had first started for him. An almost tangible wave of hatred.

If it could project that, perhaps it could read his mind as well, sufficiently for his purpose.

Deliberately, Carson picked up the rock that had been his only weapon, then tossed it down again in a gesture of relinquishment and raised his empty hands, palms up, before him.

He spoke aloud, knowing that although the words would be meaningless to the creature before him, speaking them would focus his own thoughts more completely upon the message.

"Can we not have peace between us?" he said, his voice sounding strange in the utter stillness. "The Entity who brought us here has told us what must happen if our races fight—extinction of one and weakening and retrogression of the other. The battle between them, said the Entity, depends on what we do here. Why can not we agree to an external peace—your race to its galaxy, we to ours?"

Carson blanked out his mind to receive a reply.

It came, and it staggered him back, physically. He actually recoiled several steps in sheer horror at the depth and intensity of the hatred and lust-to-kill of the red images that had been projected at him. Not as articulate words—as had come to him the thoughts of the Entity—but as wave upon wave of fierce emotion.

For a moment that seemed an eternity he had to struggle against the mental impact of that hatred, fight to clear his mind of it and drive out the alien thoughts to which he had given admittance by blanking out his own thoughts. He wanted to retch.

Slowly his mind cleared as, slowly, the mind of a man wakening from nightmare clears away the fear-fabric of which the dream was woven. He was breathing hard and he felt weaker, but he could think.

He stood studying the Roller. It had been motionless during the mental duel it had so nearly won. Now it rolled a few feet to one side, to the nearest of the blue bushes. Three tentacles whipped out of their grooves and began to investigate the bush.

"O.K.," Carson said, "so it's war then." He managed a wry

grin. "If I got your answer straight, peace doesn't appeal to you." And, because he was, after all, a quiet young man and couldn't resist the impulse to be dramatic, he added, "To the death!"

But his voice, in that utter silence, sounded very silly, even to himself. It came to him, then, that this *was* to the death. Not only his own death or that of the red spherical thing which he now thought of as the Roller, but death to the entire race of one or the other of them. The end of the human race, if he failed.

It made him suddenly very humble and very afraid to think that. More than to think it, to *know* it. Somehow, with a knowledge that was above even faith, he knew that the Entity who had arranged this duel had told the truth about its intentions and its powers. It wasn't kidding.

The future of humanity depended upon *him*. It was an awful thing to realize, and he wrenched his mind away from it. He had to concentrate on the situation at hand.

There had to be some way of getting through the barrier, or of killing through the barrier.

Mentally? He hoped that wasn't all, for the Roller, obviously had stronger telepathic powers than the primitive, undeveloped ones of the human race. Or did it?

He had been able to drive the thoughts of the Roller out of his own mind; could it drive out his? If its ability to project were stronger, might not its receptivity mechanism be more vulnerable?

He stared at it and endeavored to concentrate and focus all his thoughts upon it.

"Die," he thought. *"You are going to die. You are dying. You are—"*

He tried variations on it, and mental pictures. Sweat stood out on his forehead and he found himself trembling with the intensity of the effort. But the Roller went ahead with its investigation of the bush, as utterly unaffected as though Carson had been reciting the multiplication table.

So *that* was no good.

He felt a bit weak and dizzy from the heat and his strenuous effort at concentration. He sat down on the blue sand to rest and gave his full attention to watching and studying the Roller. By close study, perhaps, he could judge its strength and detect its weaknesses, learn things that would be valuable to know when and if they should come to grips.

It was breaking off twigs. Carson watched carefully, trying to judge just how hard it worked to do that. Later, he thought, he could find a similar bush on his own side, break off twigs of equal thickness himself, and gain a comparison of physical strength between his own arms and hands and those tentacles.

The twigs broke off hard; the Roller was having to struggle with each one, he saw. Each tentacle, he saw, bifurcated at the tip into two fingers, each tipped by a nail or claw. The claws didn't seem to be particularly long or dangerous. No more so than his own fingernails, if they were let to grow a bit.

No, on the whole, it didn't look too tough to handle physically. Unless, of course, that bush was made of pretty tough stuff. Carson looked around him and, yes, right within reach was another bush of identical type.

He reached over and snapped off a twig. It was brittle, easy to break. Of course, the Roller might have been faking deliberately but he didn't think so.

On the other hand, where was it vulnerable? Just how would he go about killing it, if he got the chance? He went back to studying it. The outer hide looked pretty tough. He'd need a sharp weapon of some sort. He picked up the piece of rock again. It was about twelve inches long, narrow, and fairly sharp on one end. If it chipped like flint, he could make a serviceable knife out of it.

The Roller was continuing its investigation of the bushes. It rolled again, to the nearest one of another type. A little blue lizard, many-legged like the one Carson had seen on his side of the barrier, darted out from under the bush.

A tentacle of the Roller lashed out and caught it, picked it up. Another tentacle whipped over and began to pull legs off the lizard, as coldly and calmly as it had pulled twigs off the bush. The creature struggled frantically and emitted a shrill squealing sound that was the first sound Carson had heard here other than the sound of his own voice.

Carson shuddered and wanted to turn his eyes away. But he made himself continue to watch; anything he could learn about his opponent might prove valuable. Even this knowledge of its unnecessary cruelty. Particularly, he thought with a sudden vicious surge of emotion, this knowledge of its unnecessary cruelty. It would make it a pleasure to kill the thing, if and when the chance came.

He steeled himself to watch the dismembering of the lizard, for that very reason.

But he felt glad when, with half its legs gone, the lizard quit squealing and struggling and lay limp and dead in the Roller's grasp.

It didn't continue with the rest of the legs. Contemptuously it tossed the dead lizard away from it, in Carson's direction. It arced through the air between them and landed at his feet.

It had come through the barrier! The barrier wasn't there any more!

Carson was on his feet in a flash, the knife gripped tightly in his hand, and leaped forward. He'd settle this thing here and now! With the barrier gone—

But it wasn't gone. He found that out the hard way, running head on into it and nearly knocking himself silly. He bounced back, and fell.

And as he sat up, shaking his head to clear it, he saw something coming through the air toward him, and to duck it, he threw himself flat again on the sand, and to one side. He got his body out of the way, but there was a sudden sharp pain in the calf of his left leg.

He rolled backward, ignoring the pain, and scrambled to his feet. It was a rock, he saw now, that had struck him. And the Roller was picking up another one now, swinging it back gripped between two tentacles, getting ready to throw it again.

It sailed through the air toward him, but he was easily able to step out of its way. The Roller, apparently, could throw straight, but not hard nor far. The first rock had struck him only because he had been sitting down and had not seen it coming until it was almost upon him.

Even as he stepped aside from that weak second throw, Carson drew back his right arm and let fly with the rock that was still in his hand. If missiles, he thought with sudden elation, can cross the barrier, then two can play at the game of throwing them. And the good right arm of an Earthman—

He couldn't miss a three-foot sphere at only four-yard range, and he didn't miss. The rock whizzed straight, and with a speed several times that of the missiles the Roller had thrown. It hit dead center, but it hit flat, unfortunately, instead of point first.

But it hit with a resounding thump, and obviously it hurt. The Roller had been reaching for another rock, but it changed its mind and got out of there instead. By the time Carson could pick up and throw another rock, the Roller was forty yards back from the barrier and going strong.

His second throw missed by feet, and his third throw was short. The Roller was back out of range—at least out of range of a missile heavy enough to be damaging.

Carson grinned. That round had been his. Except—

He quit grinning as he bent over to examine the calf of his leg. A jagged edge of the stone had made a pretty deep cut, several inches long. It was bleeding pretty freely, but he didn't think it had gone deep enough to hit an artery. If it stopped bleeding of its own accord, well and good. If not, he was in for trouble.

Finding out one thing, though, took precedence over that cut. The nature of the barrier.

He went forward to it again, this time groping with his hands before him. He found it; then holding one hand against it, he tossed a handful of sand at it with the other hand. The sand went right through. His hand didn't.

Organic matter versus inorganic? No, because the dead lizard had gone through it, and a lizard, alive or dead, was certainly organic. Plant life? He broke off a twig and poked it at the barrier. The twig went through, with no resistance, but when his fingers gripping the twig came to the barrier, they were stopped.

He couldn't get through it, nor could the Roller. But rocks and sand and a dead lizard—

How about a live lizard? He went hunting, under bushes, until he found one, and caught it. He tossed it gently against the barrier and it bounced back and scurried away across the blue sand.

That gave him the answer, in so far as he could determine it now. The screen was a barrier to living things. Dead or inorganic matter could cross it.

That off his mind, Carson looked at his injured leg again. The bleeding was lessening, which meant he wouldn't need to worry about making a tourniquet. But he should find some water, if any was available, to clean the wound.

Water—the thought of it made him realize that he was getting awfully thirsty. He'd *have* to find water, in case this contest turned out to be a protracted one.

Limping slightly now, he started off to make a full circuit of his half of the arena. Guiding himself with one hand along the barrier, he walked to his right until he came to the curving sidewall. It was visible, a dull blue-gray at close range, and the surface of it felt just like the central barrier.

He experimented by tossing a handful of sand at it, and the sand reached the wall and disappeared as it went through. The hemispherical shell was a force-field, too. But an opaque one, instead of transparent like the barrier.

He followed it around until he came back to the barrier, and walked back along the barrier to the point from which he'd started.

No sign of water.

Worried now, he started a series of zigzags back and forth between the barrier and the wall, covering the intervening space thoroughly.

No water. Blue sand, blue bushes, and intolerable heat. Nothing else.

It must be his imagination, he told himself angrily, that he was suffering *that* much from thirst. How long had he been here? Of course, no time at all, according to his own spacetime frame. The Entity had told him time stood still out there, while he was here. But his body processes went on here, just the same. And according to his body's reckoning, how long had he been here? Three or four hours, perhaps. Certainly not long enough to be suffering seriously from thirst.

But he was suffering from it; his throat dry and parched. Probably the intense heat was the cause. It was *hot*! A hundred and thirty Fahrenheit, at a guess. A dry, still heat without the slightest movement of air.

He was limping rather badly, and utterly fagged out when he'd finished the futile exploration of his domain.

He stared across at the motionless Roller and hoped it was as miserable as he was. And quite possibly it wasn't enjoying this, either. The Entity had said the conditions here were equally unfamiliar and equally uncomfortable for both of them. Maybe the Roller came from a planet where two-hundred degree heat was the norm. Maybe it was freezing while he was roasting.

Maybe the air was as much too thick for it as it was too thin for him. For the exertion of his explorations had left him panting. The atmosphere here, he realized now, was not much thicker than that on Mars.

No water.

That meant a deadline, for him at any rate. Unless he could find a way to cross that barrier or to kill his enemy from this side of it, thirst would kill him, eventually.

It gave him a feeling of desperate urgency. He *must* hurry.

But he made himself sit down a moment to rest, to think.

What was there to do? Nothing, and yet so many things. The several varieties of bushes, for example. They didn't look promising, but he'd have to examine them for possibilities. And his leg—he'd have to do something about that, even without water to clean it. Gather ammunition in the form of rocks. Find a rock that would make a good knife.

His leg hurt rather badly now, and he decided that came first. One type of bush had leaves—or things rather similar to leaves. He pulled off a handful of them and decided, after examination, to take a chance on them. He used them to clean off the sand and dirt and caked blood, then made a pad of fresh leaves and tied it over the wound with tendrils from the same bush.

The tendrils proved unexpectedly tough and strong. They were slender, and soft and pliable, yet he couldn't break them at all. He had to saw them off the bush with the sharp edge of a piece of the blue flint. Some of the thicker ones were over a foot long, and he filed away in his memory, for future reference, the fact that a bunch of the thick ones, tied together, would make a pretty serviceable rope. Maybe he'd be able to think of a use for rope.

Next he made himself a knife. The blue flint *did* chip. From a foot-long splinter of it, he fashioned himself a crude but lethal weapon. And of tendrils from the bush, he made himself a rope-belt through which he could thrust the flint knife, to keep it with him all the time and yet have his hands free.

He went back to studying the bushes. There were three other types. One was leafless, dry, brittle, rather like a dried tumbleweed. Another was of soft, crumbly wood, almost like punk. It looked and felt as though it would make excellent tinder for a fire. The third type was the most nearly woodlike. It had fragile leaves that wilted at a touch, but the stalks, although short, were straight and strong.

It was horribly, unbearably hot.

He limped up to the barrier, felt to make sure that it was still there. It was.

He stood watching the Roller for a while. It was keeping a safe distance back from the barrier, out of effective stonethrowing range. It was moving around back there, doing something. He couldn't tell what it was doing.

Once it stopped moving, came a little closer, and seemed to concentrate its attention on him. Again Carson had to fight off a wave of nausea. He threw a stone at it and the Roller retreated and went back to whatever it had been doing before.

At least he could make it keep its distance.

And, he thought bitterly, a devil of a lot of good *that* did him. Just the same, he spent the next hour or two gathering stones of suitable size for throwing, and making several neat piles of them, near his side of the barrier.

His throat burned now. It was difficult for him to think about anything except water.

But he *had* to think about other things. About getting through that barrier, under or over it, getting *at* that red sphere and killing it before this place of heat and thirst killed him first.

The barrier went to the wall upon either side, but how high and how far under the sand?

For just a moment, Carson's mind was too fuzzy to think out how he could find out either of those things. Idly, sitting there in the hot sand—and he didn't remember sitting down—he watched a blue lizard crawl from the shelter of one bush to the shelter of another.

From under the second bush, it looked out at him.

Carson grinned at it. Maybe he was getting a bit punchdrunk, because he remembered suddenly the old story of the desert-colonists on Mars, taken from an older desert story of Earth—"Pretty soon you get so lonesome you find yourself talking to the lizards, and then not so long after that you find the lizards talking back to you—"

He should have been concentrating, of course, on how to kill the Roller, but instead he grinned at the lizard and said, "Hello, there."

The lizard took a few steps toward him. "Hello," it said.

Carson was stunned for a moment, and then he put back his head and roared with laughter. It didn't hurt his throat to do so, either; he hadn't been *that* thirsty.

Why not? Why should the Entity who thought up this nightmare of a place not have a sense of humor, along with the other powers he had? Talking lizards, equipped to talk back in my own language, if I talk to them—It's a nice touch.

He grinned at the lizard and said, "Come on over." But the lizard turned and ran away, scurrying from bush to bush until it was out of sight.

He was thirsty again.

And he had to *do* something. He couldn't win this contest by sitting here sweating and feeling miserable. He had to *do* something. But what?

Get through the barrier. But he couldn't get through it, or over it. But was he certain he couldn't get under it? And come to think of it, didn't one sometimes find water by digging? Two birds with one stone—

Painfully now, Carson limped up to the barrier and started digging, scooping up sand a double handful at a time. It was slow, hard work because the sand ran in at the edges and the deeper he got the bigger in diameter the hole had to be. How many hours it took him, he didn't know, but he hit bedrock four feet down. Dry bedrock; no sign of water.

And the force-field of the barrier went down clear to the bedrock. No dice. No water. Nothing.

He crawled out of the hole and lay there panting, and then raised his head to look across and see what the Roller was doing. It must be doing something back there.

It was. It was making something out of wood from the bushes, tied together with tendrils. A queerly shaped framework about four feet high and roughly square. To see it better, Carson climbed up onto the mound of sand he had excavated from the hole, and stood there staring.

There were two long levers sticking out of the back of it, one with a cup-shaped affair on the end of it. Seemed to be some sort of a catapult, Carson thought.

Sure enough, the Roller was lifting a sizable rock into the cup-shaped outfit. One of his tentacles moved the other lever up and down for awhile, and then he turned the machine slightly as though aiming it and the lever with the stone flew up and forward.

The stone raced several yards over Carson's head, so far away that he didn't have to duck, but he judged the distance it had traveled, and whistled softly. He couldn't throw a rock that weight more than half that distance. And even retreating to the rear of his domain wouldn't put him out of range of that machine, if the Roller shoved it forward almost to the barrier.

Another rock whizzed over. Not quite so far away this time.

That thing could be dangerous, he decided. Maybe he'd better do something about it.

Moving from side to side along the barrier, so the catapult couldn't bracket him, he whaled a dozen rocks at it. But that wasn't going to be any good, he saw. They had to be light rocks, or he couldn't throw them that far. If they hit the framework, the bounced off harmlessly. And the Roller had no difficulty, at that distance, in moving aside from those that came near it.

Besides, his arm was tiring badly. He ached all over from sheer weariness. If he could only rest awhile without having to duck rocks from that catapult at regular intervals of maybe thirty seconds each—

He stumbled back to the rear of the arena. Then he saw even that wasn't any good. The rocks reached back there, too, only there were longer intervals between them, as though it took longer to wind up the mechanism, whatever it was, of the catapult.

Wearily he dragged himself back to the barrier again. Several times he fell and could barely rise to his feet to go on. He was, he knew, near the limit of his endurance. Yet he didn't dare stop moving now, until and unless he could put that catapult out of action. If he fell asleep, he'd never wake up.

One of the stones from it gave him the first glimmer of an idea. It struck upon one of the piles of stones he'd gathered together near the barrier to use as ammunition, and it struck sparks.

Sparks. Fire. Primitive man had made fire by striking sparks, and with some of those dry crumbly bushes as tinder—

Luckily, a bush of that type was near him. He broke it off, took it over to a pile of stones, then patiently hit one stone against another until a spark touched the punklike wood of the bush. It went up in flames so fast that it singed his eyebrows and was burned to an ash within seconds.

But he had the idea now, and within minutes he had a little fire going in the lee of the mound of sand he'd made digging the hole an hour or two ago. Tinder bushes had started it, and other bushes which burned, but more slowly, kept it a steady flame.

The tough wirelike tendrils didn't burn readily; that made the fire-bombs easy to make and throw. A bundle of faggots tied about a small stone to give it weight and a loop of the tendril to swing it by.

He made half a dozen of them before he lighted and threw the first. It went wide, and the Roller started a quick retreat, pulling the catapult after him. But Carson had the others ready and threw them in rapid succession. The fourth wedged in the catapult's framework, and did the trick. The Roller tried desperately to put out the spreading blaze by throwing sand, but its clawed tentacles would take only a spoonful at a time and his efforts were ineffectual. The catapult burned.

The Roller moved safely away from the fire and seemed to concentrate its attention on Carson and again he felt that wave of hatred and nausea. But more weakly; either the Roller itself was weakening or Carson had learned how to protect himself against the mental attack.

He thumbed his nose at it and then sent it scuttling back to safety by throwing a stone. The Roller went clear to the back of its half of the arena and started pulling up bushes again. Probably it was going to make another catapult.

Carson verified—for the hundredth time—that the barrier was still operating, and then found himself sitting in the sand beside it because he was suddenly too weak to stand up.

His leg throbbed steadily now and the pangs of thirst were severe. But those things paled beside the utter physical exhaustion that gripped his entire body.

And the heat.

Hell must be like this, he thought. The hell that the ancients had believed in. He fought to stay awake, and yet staying awake seemed futile, for there was nothing he could do. Nothing, while the barrier remained impregnable and the Roller stayed back out of range.

But there must be *something*. He tried to remember things he had read in books of archaeology about the methods of fighting used back in the days before metal and plastic. The stone missile, that had come first, he thought. Well, that he already had.

The only improvement on it would be a catapult, such as the Roller had made. But he'd never be able to make one, with the tiny bits of wood available from the bushes—no single piece longer than a foot or so. Certainly he could figure out a mechanism for one, but he didn't have the endurance left for a task that would take days.

Days? But the Roller had made one. Had they been here days already? Then he remembered that the Roller had many tentacles to work with and undoubtedly could do such work faster than he.

And besides, a catapult wouldn't decide the issue. He had to do better than that.

Bow and arrow? No; he had tried archery once and knew his own ineptness with a bow. Even with a modern sportsman's durasteel weapon, made for accuracy. With such a crude, pieced-together outfit as he could make here, he doubted if he could shoot as far as he could throw a rock, and knew he couldn't shoot as straight.

Spear? Well, he *could* make that. It would be useless as a throwing weapon at any distance, but would be a handy thing at close range, if he ever got to close range.

And making one would give him something to do. Help keep his mind from wandering, as it was beginning to do. Sometimes now, he had to concentrate awhile before he could remember why he was here, why he had to kill the Roller.

Luckily he was still beside one of the piles of stones. He sorted through it until he found one shaped roughly like a spearhead. With a smaller stone he began to chip it into shape, fashioning sharp shoulders on the sides so that if it penetrated it would not pull out again.

Like a harpoon? There was something in that idea, he thought. A harpoon was better than a spear, maybe, for this crazy contest. If he could once get it into the Roller, and had a rope on it, he could pull the Roller up against the barrier and the stone blade of his knife would reach through that barrier, even if his hands wouldn't.

The shaft was harder to make than the head. But by splitting and joining the main stems of four of the bushes, and wrapping the joints with the tough but thin tendrils, he got a strong shaft about four feet long, and tied the stone head in a notch cut in the end.

It was crude, but strong.

And the rope. With the thin tough tendrils he made himself

twenty feet of line. It was light and didn't look strong, but he knew it would hold his weight and to spare. He tied one end of it to the shaft of the harpoon and the other end about his right wrist. At least, if he threw his harpoon across the barrier, he'd be able to pull it back if he missed.

Then when he had tied the last knot and there was nothing more he could do, the heat and the weariness and the pain in his leg and the dreadful thirst were suddenly a thousand times worse than they had been before.

He tried to stand up, to see what the Roller was doing now, and found he couldn't get to his feet. On the third try, he got as far as his knees and then fell flat again.

"I've got to sleep," he thought. "If a showdown came now, I'd be helpless. He could come up here and kill me, if he knew. I've got to regain some strength."

Slowly, painfully, he crawled back away from the barrier. Ten yards, twenty—

The jar of something thudding against the sand near him waked him from a confused and horrible dream to a more confused and more horrible reality, and he opened his eyes again to blue radiance over blue sand.

How long had he slept? A minute? A day?

Another stone thudded nearer and threw sand on him. He got his arms under him and sat up. He turned around and saw the Roller twenty yards away, at the barrier.

It rolled away hastily as he sat up, not stopping until it was as far away as it could get.

He'd fallen asleep too soon, he realized, while he was still in range of the Roller's throwing ability. Seeing him lying motionless, it had dared come up to the barrier to throw at him. Luckily, it didn't realize how weak he was, or it could have stayed there and kept on throwing stones.

Had he slept long? He didn't think so, because he felt just as he had before. Not rested at all, no thirstier, no different. Probably he'd been there only a few minutes.

He started crawling again, this time forcing himself to keep going until he was as far as he could go, until the colorless, opaque wall of the arena's outer shell was only a yard away.

Then things slipped away again—

When he awoke, nothing about him was changed, but this time he knew that he had slept a long time.

The first thing he became aware of was the inside of his mouth; it was dry, caked. His tongue was swollen.

Something was wrong, he knew, as he returned slowly to full awareness. He felt less tired, the stage of utter exhaustion had passed. The sleep had taken care of that.

But there was pain, agonizing pain. It wasn't until he tried to move that he knew that it came from his leg.

He raised his head and looked down at it. It was swollen terribly below the knee and the swelling showed even halfway up his thigh. The plant tendrils he had used to tie on the protective pad of leaves now cut deeply into the swollen flesh.

To get his knife under that imbedded lashing would have been impossible. Fortunately, the final knot was over the shin bone, in front, where the vine cut in less deeply than elsewhere. He was able, after an agonizing effort, to untie the knot.

A look under the pad of leaves told him the worst. Infection and blood poisoning, both pretty bad and getting worse.

And without drugs, without cloth, without even *water*, there wasn't a thing he could do about it.

Not a thing, except *die*, when the poison had spread through his system.

He knew it was hopeless, then, and that he'd lost.

And with him, humanity. When he died here, out there in the universe he knew, all his friends, everybody, would die too. And Earth and the colonized planets would be the home of the red, rolling, alien Outsiders. Creatures out of nightmare, things without a human attribute, who picked lizards apart for the fun of it.

It was the thought of that which gave him courage to start crawling, almost blindly in pain, toward the barrier again. Not crawling on hands and knees this time, but pulling himself along only by his arms and hands.

A chance in a million, that maybe he'd have strength left, when he got there, to throw his harpoon-spear just *once*, and with deadly effect, if—on another chance in a million—the Roller would come up to the barrier. Or if the barrier was gone, now.

It took him years, it seemed, to get there.

The barrier wasn't gone. It was as impassable as when he'd first felt it.

And the Roller wasn't at the barrier. By raising up on his

elbows, he could see it at the back of its part of the arena, working on a wooden framework that was a half-completed duplicate of the catapult he'd destroyed.

It was moving slowly now. Undoubtedly it had weakened, too.

But Carson doubted that it would ever need that second catapult. He'd be dead, he thought, before it was finished.

If he could attract it to the barrier, now, while he was still alive—He waved an arm and tried to shout, but his parched throat would make no sound.

Or if he could get through the barrier—

His mind must have slipped for a moment, for he found himself beating his fists against the barrier in futile rage, and made himself stop.

He closed his eyes, tried to make himself calm.

"Hello," said the voice.

It was a small, thin voice. It sounded like—

He opened his eyes and turned his head. It *was* the lizard.

"Go away," Carson wanted to say. "Go away, you're not really there, or you're there but not really talking. I'm imagining things again."

But he couldn't talk; his throat and tongue were past all speech with the dryness. He closed his eyes again.

"Hurt," said the voice. "Kill. Hurt—kill. Come."

He opened his eyes again. The blue ten-legged lizard was still there. It ran a little way along the barrier, came back, started off again, and came back.

"Hurt," it said. "Kill. Come."

Again it started off, and came back. Obviously it wanted Carson to follow it along the barrier.

He closed his eyes again. The voice kept on. The same three meaningless words. Each time he opened his eyes, it ran off and came back.

"Hurt. Kill. Come."

Carson groaned. There would be no peace unless he followed the blasted thing. Like it wanted him to.

He followed it, crawling. Another sound, a high-pitched squealing, came to his ears and grew louder.

There was something lying in the sand, writhing, squealing. Something small, blue, that looked like a lizard and yet didn't—

Then he saw what it was—the lizard whose legs the Roller had pulled off, so long ago. But it wasn't dead; it had come back to life and was wriggling and screaming in agony.

"Hurt," said the other lizard. "Hurt. Kill. Kill."

Carson understood. He took the flint knife from his belt and killed the tortured creature. The live lizard scurried off quickly.

Carson turned back to the barrier. He leaned his hands and head against it and watched the Roller, far back, working on the new catapult.

"I could get that far," he thought, "if I could get through. If I could get through, I might win yet. It looks weak, too. I might—"

And then there was another reaction of black hopelessness, when pain snapped his will and he wished that he were dead. He envied the lizard he'd just killed. It didn't have to live on and suffer. And he did. It would be hours, it might be days, before the blood poisoning killed him.

If only he could use that knife on himself—

But he knew he wouldn't. As long as he was alive, there was the millionth chance—

He was straining, pushing on the barrier with the flat of his hands, and he noticed his arms, how thin and scrawny they were now. He must really have been here a long time, for days, to get as thin as that.

How much longer now, before he died? How much more heat and thirst and pain could flesh stand?

For a little while he was almost hysterical again, and then came a time of deep calm, and a thought that was startling.

The lizard he had just killed. *It had crossed the barrier, still alive.* It had come from the Roller's side; the Roller had pulled off its legs and then tossed it contemptuously at him and it had come through the barrier. He'd thought, because the lizard was dead.

But it hadn't been dead; it had been unconscious.

A live lizard couldn't go through the barrier, but an unconscious one could. The barrier was not a barrier, then, to living flesh, but to conscious flesh. It was a *mental* projection, a *mental* hazard.

And with that thought, Carson started crawling along the barrier to make his last desperate gamble. A hope so forlorn that only a dying man would have dared try it.

No use weighing the odds of success. Not when, if he didn't try it, those odds were infinitely to zero.

He crawled along the barrier to the dune of sand, about four feet high, which he'd scooped out in trying—how many days ago?—to dig under the barrier or to reach water.

That mound was right at the barrier, its farther slope half on one side of the barrier, half on the other.

Taking with him a rock from the pile nearby, he climbed up to the top of the dune and over the top, and lay there against the barrier, his weight leaning against it so that if the barrier were taken away he'd roll on down the short slope, into the enemy territory.

He checked to be sure that the knife was safely in his rope belt, that the harpoon was in the crook of his left arm and that the twenty-foot rope was fastened to it and to his wrist.

Then with his right hand he raised the rock with which he would hit himself on the head. Luck would have to be with him on that blow; it would have to be hard enough to knock him out, but not hard enough to knock him out for long.

He had a hunch that the Roller was watching him, and would see him roll down through the barrier, and come to investigate. It would think he was dead, he hoped—he thought it had probably drawn the same deduction about the nature of the barrier that he had drawn. But it would come cautiously. He would have a little time—

He struck.

Pain brought him back to consciousness. A sudden, sharp pain in his hip that was different from the throbbing pain in his head and the throbbing pain in his leg.

But he had, thinking things out before he had struck himself, anticipated that very pain, even hoped for it, and had steeled himself against awakening with a sudden movement.

He lay still, but opened his eyes just a slit, and saw that he had guessed rightly. The Roller was coming closer. It was twenty feet away and the pain that had awakened him was the stone it had tossed to see whether he was alive or dead.

He lay still. It came closer, fifteen feet away, and stopped again. Carson scarcely breathed.

As nearly as possible, he was keeping his mind a blank, lest its telepathic ability detect consciousness in him. And with his mind blanked out that way, the impact of its thought upon his mind was nearly soul-shattering.

He felt sheer horror at the utter *alienness*, the *differentness* of those thoughts. Things that he felt but could not understand and could never express, because no terrestrial language had words, no terrestrial mind had images to fit them. The mind of a spider, he thought, or the mind of a praying mantis or a Martian sand-serpent, raised to intelligence and put in telepathic rapport with human minds, would be a homely familiar thing, compared to this.

He understood now that the Entity had been right: Man or Roller, and the universe was not a place that could hold them both. Farther apart than god and devil, there could never be even a balance between them.

Closer. Carson waited until it was only feet away, until its clawed tentacles reached out—

Oblivious to agony now, he sat up, raised and flung the harpoon with all the strength that remained to him. Or he thought it was all; sudden final strength flooded through him, along with a sudden forgetfulness of pain as definite as a nerve block.

As the Roller, deeply stabbed by the harpoon, rolled away, Carson tried to get to his feet to run after it. He couldn't do that; he fell, but kept crawling.

It reached the end of the rope, and he was jerked forward by the pull of his wrist. It dragged him a few feet and then stopped. Carson kept on going, pulling himself toward it hand over hand along the rope.

It stopped there, writhing tentacles trying in vain to pull out the harpoon. It seemed to shudder and quiver, and then it must have realized that it couldn't get away, for it rolled back toward him, clawed tentacles reaching out.

Stone knife in hand, he met it. He stabbed, again and again, while those horrid claws ripped skin and flesh and muscle from his body.

He stabbed and slashed, and at last it was still.

A bell was ringing, and it took him a while after he'd opened his eyes to tell where he was and what it was. He was strapped into the seat of his scouter, and the visiplate before him showed only empty space. No Outsider ship and no impossible planet.

The bell was the communications plate signal; someone

wanted him to switch power into the receiver. Purely reflex action enabled him to reach forward and throw the lever.

The face of Brander, captain of the *Magellan*, mothership of his group of scouters, flashed into the screen. His face was pale and his black eyes glowed with excitement.

"*Magellan* to Carson," he snapped. "Come on in. The fight's over. We've won!"

The screen went blank; Brander would be signaling the other scouters of his command.

Slowly, Carson set the controls for the return. Slowly, unbelievingly, he unstrapped himself from the seat and went back to get a drink at the cold-water tank. For some reason, he was unbelievably thirsty. He drank six glasses.

He leaned there against the wall, trying to think.

Had it happened? He was in good health, sound, uninjured. His thirst had been mental rather than physical; his throat hadn't been dry. His leg—

He pulled up his trouser leg and looked at the calf. There was a long white scar there, but a perfectly healed scar. It hadn't been there before. He zipped open the front of his shirt and saw that his chest and abdomen was criss-crossed with tiny, almost unnoticeable, perfectly healed scars.

It *had* happened.

The scouter, under automatic control, was already entering the hatch of the mother-ship. The grapples pulled it into its individual lock, and a moment later a buzzer indicated that the lock was air-filled. Carson opened the hatch and stepped outside, went through the double door of the lock.

He went right to Brander's office, went in, and saluted.

Brander still looked dizzily dazed. "Hi, Carson," he said. "What you missed! What a show!"

"What happened, sir?"

"Don't know, exactly. We fired one salvo, and their whole fleet went up in dust! Whatever it was jumped from ship to ship in a flash, even the ones we hadn't aimed at and that were out of range! The whole fleet disintegrated before our eyes, and we didn't get the paint of a single ship scratched!

"We can't even claim credit for it. Must have been some unstable component in the metal they used, and our sighting shot just set it off. Man, oh man, too bad you missed all the excitement."

Carson managed to grin. It was a sickly ghost of a grin, for it would be days before he'd be over the mental impact of his experience, but the captain wasn't watching, and didn't notice.

"Yes, sir," he said. Common sense, more than modesty, told him he'd be branded forever as the worst liar in space if he ever said any more than that. "Yes, sir, too bad I missed all the excitement."

BROOD WORLD BARBARIAN

by Perry A. Chapdelaine

Sand, fear, blood and gawkers—the trivia of a thousand arenas on a thousand planets in a thousand ages. I am an athlete of great proportions, strength and skill—one who kills by order of the gawkers or my master, whichever calls first—and I am one soon to be killed.

She came yesterday on the day of the games after I had neatly decapitated the former champion of the Sabre worlds by means of wrist pressors only. Declared the season's Grand Champion, head garlanded with red-brandy vines, chest proudly extended against chest band, I swaggered away from the game's space on wrist pressors only, as if to say, *Look at me, you weaklings. I have bested your best. Now who is master and who is slave?*

Their sun of a thousand yellow rays beat down on my back as I pushed my way across the game's space into the lower ramp to my cage, expecting there to relax with wine, song and the caress of the opposite sex as, I suppose, has been done by my kind for ages past.

Then she came. The lights burned brightly as the crowd surged past our flux cages. The public was not satisfied with the death, pain and sadism of the arena, but demanded that my cage—all our cages—be kept open to public gathering. Like my cell-mates

I was a freakish one-G animal, trained by means of gravity-like pressor and tractor beams to tear and hew at others.

She walked with her father. He, merely a seven-tenths-G animal, was human and shaped like myself. He had a strong smile, cropped gray hair and rugged features set-off by sunken eyes, a bulbous nose and bright, straight teeth. Oh God! How I hated that animal—that all-powerful, all-great leader of the Sabre planets. Trevic Strenger and his family walked in public gathering to view *me*, this season's Grand Champion, in my "natural" habitat!

First came the retinue of sycophants and guards. Cloaked in tight plastic of weblon to nullify pressor and tractor rays, they stationed themselves to one side of my cage, holding the crowded path open for the dictator Strenger and his family.

I threw my wine outward to vent my disgust and anger, helplessly watching as it struck the surrounding magnetic field, to be sucked inward and downward instantaneously as the powerful field latched onto minute iron particles in the liquid.

They didn't yield an inch nor did they acknowledge my act by even a twitch of the mouth—except Trevic Strenger. He passed his hand back to his beautiful wife and gently tugged her forward so as not to miss the show, just as he did the night I was taken, five years ago, on my rocky planet.

I came from an unusual brood and, had I known then what I now know, even their fleetest hunters would have gone back to the ship empty. My brood cell—brothers, sisters, mother and father—had left me for the day. I tossed rocks at the passing pack animals below our cave, not aware of the hunters swooping over me, preparing to entangle me in their rays and beams. I spat at Trevic with the thought, and he pulled his head back to laugh, just as he had the day I was brought, bound and struggling before him.

Oh, I was more than a barbarian from the Planet of Rocks. I was an educated barbarian, for their pleasure would not be enough unless they knew that inside of each gladiator lay a trapped, cunning and scheming modern mind—a mind equal perhaps even to their own in knowledge, yet trapped by their science and their orders to fight on a barbaric level of their choice. I spat again when I thought of their educators and how facts were poured into my animal brain day and night, indiscriminate facts. Did you know that a man named Plato once said, "Know thyself?"

I spat again in honor of such useless information.

His wife's face strained at her husband's sadistic laughter and I imagined that she disapproved. Then I vowed some day to kill Trevic Strenger with my own bare hands. I watched the daughter.

She pushed through the crowd and I saw perfection. I had known many other women, slave women thrown to us along with victory wines and victory songs. I had seen none with the grace, the litheness, the color, the shadows of this one. Daughter of a mad king and a radiant slave-queen, she was—and her eyes seemed to glow with a kind of empathy for me I had never before known outside of the brood chamber.

I opened my gnarled fists, dropping my cups, and sprang to the field's side. My chest band pulsed with heat as its magnetic field fought against the lines of force. I strained my body mightily to bring it closer to her side until only inches separated us and my metal chest-belt glowed cherry red from hysteresis.

Across those billions of lines of flux sprang the stronger invisible rays of my love. Her blue eyes met my gray ones and mine clung while the world dissolved around us. Though worlds of differing customs and a powerful kingdom lay between us, I vowed to reach her as deeply and strongly as I had just vowed to kill her father.

Would Patricia Strenger respond to me? Could a barbaric brood-world creature reach her more refined heart? Though doubt assailed my thoughts, I clung to my twin emotions of hate for her father and my new-born love for her.

"Barbarian," he said, "You must come to terms with your simple emotions. In you lie only the pure emotions—hate, love, anger—not any refined, civilized, subtle and complex ones."

Snarling, I threw my drinking vessel at him, only to see it stop in mid-air, then retreat backward from the invisible wall. He did not even laugh at my anger.

"Our people crave heroes," he continued evenly. "You may be a great one. With gladiator success come civilized opportunities which would normally be denied one of your kind. You may soon see complete freedom, then complete citizenship with all the rights and privileges of a Sabre citizen. Shall we drop this silly feud now?''

Hate boiled in me like a hidden volcano and I did not answer.

Trevic Strenger paused silently to watch my heaving chest, then added: ''After all, barbarian, had it not been you who was captured, another from your brood world would now be standing where you are—another would now be offered full education, citizenship and opportunity for world-wide adulation.''

I could not control my emotions. So complete was my hatred for this man who had torn me from brood-home that my whole muscular body convulsed as I spat directly at his face.

Without change of tone in his voice he said, ''Tomorrow I will introduce you to Urut of Ewit, a two-point-five-G champion.''

I sneered, as I had yet to learn of either Ewit or Urut of Ewit and therefore lacked comprehension of his plans for the morrow.

Trevic narrowed his browless eyes to watch as he bored in with his varied rapier-like pieces of knowledge, ''Urut can crush rocks on your planet between his two hands. On his world a day lasts seven of yours. A day's work to him means seven times twenty-four or one hundred and sixty-eight of your hours. Can you fight him even one of his days, Grand Champion?''

I knew the answer. Urut's skin would be as tough as rock, his stamina far beyond any normal one-G human's bounds, and his strength would be like ordinary muscle taut against the pressure of invariant hydraulic presses. I would most surely die tomorrow. I knew it and Trevic Strenger knew it. But I spat again in barbaric defiance.

II

I awoke in the morning to the sounds of tractor and pressor duels around me and knew I had overslept on this, my last day. According to my educated brain, thousands of years before a certain B. Franklin had said, *Early to bed and early to rise will make a man healthy, wealthy and wise.*

I paused briefly in disgust at giving thought to such revolting associations. Why had not my mind been permitted to remain that of a normal brood-world barbarian?

I bound my two pressor beams to my wrists and my two tractor beams to my ankles and gyrated my body through the endless contortions of tension and counter-tension so necessary to the modern gladiator.

I pulled my leg muscles to their limit of endurance, slowly but surely overcoming the tractor-versus-tractor configuration. Then, and so rapidly that the eye would be unable to follow, I twisted my body muscles to push pressor against pressor until, biceps bulging, I heard the faint clink of wrist plate against wrist plate, signifying I had once again overcome the hidden power of my death machinery.

Only then did I eat lightly, my good nature returning slowly as I felt a sense of well-being.

Again I passed my body through every one of the hard-learned exercises designed to test to the utmost one muscle against another, passing through the last just as the aurora at the side of my cage indicated that I was to move out into the arena.

To avoid death from chest-band pressure, as my cell slowly contracted around me, I moved forward, following the energy glow. There, under the beat of their merciless sun, was the open arena, its sand, its hate-driven gawkers, its blood of the past and psychic blood yet to flow.

Pushing my way toward the ellipsoid's nearest focus, I then squinted to see the squat hulk of Urut of Ewit at the far end.

The crowd of blood-mongers surrounding our large cage, except at floor level, howled on my entry. Knowing I was the handicapped, they screamed for Urut's blood which, could I but arrange it, would be most happily furnished them—for it was his blood or mine.

Almost I felt sorry for that hulk—short, broad of torso, leg and arm; flat-headed with parrot-like lips; humanoid of form and lizard-hided of skin.

My survival was at stake and my mind swiveled back to life and death calculations. He had the sun. Trevic Strenger would have seen to that. He had more. As strong as I was, my muscles were but one-G trained. As quick as I was, he would act faster. Very probably I would not find any weak spot in his natural armor, whereas to him I was but an anthropomorphic jellyfish.

In a gladiator's daze I calculated my survival paths overlong— already he was swimming toward me with tractors and pressors working together.

No sooner had I tensed to meet his first attack than he was beyond me, already rebounding from the magnetic wall.

I pushed both tractors outward at the widest angle of my legs, unconsciously reaching for the bedrock which I knew to exist there. Both arms were folded against my chest band to place pressors in their firmest position. He struck like a ten-ton boulder rolling down the mountainside. My muscle-banded legs vibrated with the pressure and my reserves soon evaporated.

His right tractor could reach around to the side of my head to hold while his left reached to my right side and I knew scant instants stood between me and decapitation.

More in instinctive desperation than for any reason I switched pressors down low and slipped my body under his. He rocketed overhead to slam mightily against the far side of the arena's shield, chest band glowing red, while I twisted around from back to belly on the sand floor.

Still no strategy came to my mind. Can a pygmy subdue the elephant? Can the ant topple the pedestrian? Can a simple one-G human resist for long the heavy-planet man under one-G conditions?

I concentrated every bit of thought and will on my survival. Brute force against inhuman force was my only strategy.

He sliced through the air again and I dodged. He brought both legs into play to cut me in two and I again dodged. He tried the ploy of alternating leg tractors and arm pressors and I eluded him. Not until he sat above me in the overhead tractor-lock position did my strategy bloom. Though only tiny moments of time were involved, my thoughts ran as follows,

Why can I dodge this lightning-like man so easily? How is it he misuses his speed so much? Could it be that he is unused to fighting in a one-G environment—that this is his first experience on such a light world? If so, his timing must be too fast and I am not really eluding him. He misses me and then I dodge.

Using tractors, pressors, fingers and toes, I crawled excruciatingly slowly across the bottom until his tractors caught bedrock below and I could slide out from under.

He jabbed down with pressors but this time I was ready. I kicked my tractors into his squat belly and followed behind his moving arms with my own pressors. He somersaulted then and pinwheeled before catching himself.

Now I had the trick. Every time he moved I swung either tractor or pressor, catching his motion from behind and enforcing it. I used his own strength and speed against him until finally, during one complex maneuver where his tractors reinforced his pressor movement, I doubly reinforced his action with my pressors and tractors and his two arms snapped.

The gawkers screamed and howled for blood but I had other ideas. Already exhausted, I doubted my ability to penetrate his thick hide, though he lay helpless. More important to me than his destruction were the death of another and the love of a third.

Urut floated around and around on tractors, frantically twisting his body to redirect his dangling arms and their pressors. I shot forward and spoke for the first time.

"Urut. Cooperate with me and live to fight another day."

In a high, squeaking voice he warily asked, "What is it you want?"

"I want out of this cage and you can help. What they do to me outside and where I go should be of no concern to anyone but me—and no one will suspect your help in what will follow."

"What do I do?"

"I am going to use both pressors and tractors to propel myself through the cage. Only if I go very quickly will my chest band remain sufficiently cool for me to survive. I am going to place myself within range of your tractors and with their help, and the quickness of your legs, I can crash through. Will you do this Urut?"

"But you will die if we are not quick enough. Why should you place yourself within my control when you have already won?"

"Urut, my friend, you and I have no quarrel. We have never had. We fight only to survive—now let us help each other live. I want freedom and revenge. You want your life. Why should we not bargain?"

The crowd began the death chant.

"Blood—blood! Kill the hulk! Kill the hulk—"

I could tell from their frenzy that soon something must be done or their passion would be on all of us. Urut could also sense it. The idea of mutual help was not yet fully integrated in his mind but he nodded.

"May your mud-nest be pleasing!"

I swung to the other side of the arena to begin my plan.

From hundreds of previous fights I knew every inch of the arena bedrock and I used the knowledge to advantage. I flung wrist pressors at each point behind me and ankle tractors ahead of me, accelerating swiftly in line with Urut. The crowd hushed and Urut patiently moved his hulk into position for the throw.

I swung past his body swiftly. More swiftly still he lashed onto me with both tractors webbed together. I felt the fringe of their beams pass my arms, then my head and thick neck absorbed the pull and I was flung up to and against the magnetic shield surrounding us.

My chest band glowed and part of my body tried to wrench itself backward—but still onward and through I passed. I flew over the heads of those in the first tiers, then plowed into the next ranks.

Heads popped; chest, arm and leg bones snapped. I arose amidst the gore of dead and dying gawkers. Their hush changed to screams. Pandemonium reigned.

A small number in the crowd rushed to the exits but the majority stood shouting, "Champion! Champion! Champion!"

Over and over again their acknowledgement echoed—like the beating of surf on the rocky shores—until my very bones vibrated with the chant. Never before had one escaped the magnetic arena and the crowd was wild with enthusiasm.

I should have trusted to my judgment of their emotion. My next move was utterly foolish. I swung out to reach for Trevic Strenger, hoping to crush his thin neck between my pressors. Above and below and all around me flew his weblon-encased protectors.

High over me were the platforms of heavy rays, while on each side were the smaller hand weapons—but I had agility, speed and coordination far beyond those of any group of Strenger guards. I had one tactic which would catch them by surprise. My muscles were trained to use beams but my mind was trained to use muscles. With those I bowled over the first group, tumbling weapon and guard onto the tiers below.

III

Fighting one-G animals in an open environment and with full knowledge of their beams and rays, I was more than a match for them all. But no matter how I hacked and hewed, how cleverly I spilled their heavy weapons, I still could not reach Strenger. I can see him yet in my memory, sitting back, watching with faint amusement as I tossed his guards here and there like feathers—only to find more guards taking their places.

The gawkers shrieked with pleasure over this new form of entertainment and I turned and ran, dashing up beyond the seat rims, finding space between the roof and two structural pressor beams to squeeze my bulky body through.

Outside the arena I fell several hundred feet before my rays caught bedrock below and I could twist myself across the pylons and roadways of this ungodly civilization to search for the city's end and silent peace.

Behind me, perhaps a mile away, the guards boiled out from the arena area and I swept down low below their sight level. Another mile and another and another—when would the city end?

Then little by little trees, parks and farms replaced city blocks, until only farm land and tall mountains lay ahead. That first night I slept in peace among the wild foothills of this strange world, free for the first time since being taken from my brood world. In my dreams lived the face of Strenger—but also in my dreams was the sad, melancholy face of Patricia and my body longed for both in their proper place.

The morning sun no longer seemed so hot and sultry. The air seemed fresher and the planet, even with its strange flora and fauna, appeared friendly. I speared a small carnivore with a tractor beam, drank fresh water and ate the raw meat, then washed and rested while I thought.

Were I to go back to the city my large bulk would easily identify me as the Champion. My muscles would be impossible to hide in this civilization.

Farmers I knew about because of my helter-skelter education—I knew, for example, that some Sabre planet genius had called farmers stewards of the state. Could I trust the farmer not to turn me in for one of Strenger's high rewards? I thought not.

Though I searched my brain for other informative tidbits on

this society, I concluded that only the mountains and hills would hide me.

I removed my tractors and pressors, fastening them to my chest band by means of twisted fibers, then unhesitatingly I strode off toward the snow-capped mountains ahead.

Day followed day and night followed night. I easily speared game with tractor or pressor while I followed the animal trails from elevation to elevation. My body stayed in trim and my hate gradually oozed outward as my path came closer to the appearance of rocky plateaus similar to my brood world—all, that is, except the tiny, reserved corner of my emotions which repeated my need over and over.

Kill Strenger.

The rock path wound upward and I trod closer to the snowy peaks, my body now covered with animal skins for warmth. Slowly the rock turned to snow, then snow to mixed snow and ice, glazing white while I moved onward and upward, never hurrying, never slowing.

Miles of ice were crossed and only once did I have to pull myself from a deep crevice by means of a tractor beam. Finally the downslope snow line was reached on the mountain's other side. I stepped with relief into familiar rocky plateaus, fully expecting a similar leisurely pace downward. Then it happened.

It was Strenger again. I was caught. His men dropped the cage neatly over my body and turned the field on high. He came from behind the rocks with his bold smile and just looked, hands folded against his chest.

"The gawkers now love you, barbarian, and we can still make a truce. Come, I invite you to bury your hatred. You are one of the greatest of our world's champions—over all time—and it saddens me, your waste. By popular demand I can now release you from gladiator status to become a free citizen. But how can I permit a hate-driven barbarian to roam free among us?"

I showed my feeling by emitting a low growl. I clenched my fists, imagining his thick neck in my hands.

Trevic beckoned his retainers to lower the cage. He found a convenient rock upon which to sit while he pleaded his case again with me.

"Know this, barbarian. Your use of tractor and pressor beams can be traced wherever you go on the Sabre planets. Even so, you have no further need for them, no matter what your decision."

He motioned with his finger and my cage began to tighten until my chest band squeezed me from all directions. Weblon-encased tools drove through my shield and skillfully cut my beams from my chest band, after which the cage was restored in size.

"Your chest band is made of the world's strongest metal. It cannot be removed without special scientific tools. Wherever you wear it, you are subject to immediate seizure and capture. Do you still wish these marks of the gladiator?"

My tongue finally loosed.

I spoke in an angry voice, "You tore me from my brood-world without my permission, mad king, and I shall one day kill you!"

Unable to reason with me further, he beckoned his men forward. My cage was lifted by weblon devices and I continued my trans-mountain flight as his captive.

IV

They towed me farther into the mountains, disregarding any inconvenience inertia might make to my caged body. My chest band glowed again and again as my body bounced off the cage's sides.

Perhaps fifty miles inward, we followed another rocky path down to the valley of our destination. Below us, laid out in neat geometrical array, were the energy cages of thousands of humans.

Walking like tiny bugs between each cage were the weblon-protected guards who passed out either food or water or else the whip—whichever seemed most appropriate for the moment.

A scrap of random information forced its way into my conscious mind—forced, I suppose, by the association of the antlike men far below. Only a century ago someone named G. Harcel had said, "Men are tiny bugs once they have seen their souls."

Could any information be more useless at a time like this?

High on one side were the mine tailings, glistening red from the evening sun. Immediately behind those tailings stood the factory, puffing out streamers of noxious gases which, I eventually learned, represented part of the physical and chemical wastes resulting from separating weblon metal from the ores found deep in the planet's crust.

My cage was tugged next to a larger one. The aurora along the side, signifying an opening in my cage, burned brightly and I hurried across into the larger. Trevic Strenger paid his last respects then.

"Enjoy your new lessons, barbarian. When you have learned more, find a way to contact me. Perhaps we may yet be friends."

He walked away and I flung myself furiously at my magnetic shield.

My routine was simple. Each day, every day, I was chained to a row of ten other prisoners who walked two miles along the valley floor and three miles downward on sloping shafts to our work area. Here alternating tractor-pressor beams were given to us, each a model considered too large for a single human to support.

Two of us would hold the mining tool, aiming it at the green streak of weblon metal running throughout the enormous, partly natural and partly man-made caverns. The alternating tractor-pressor forces acted swiftly on the cavern walls, grinding all but the impervious weblon metal to thin mono-molecular layers.

Follow-up crews sucked up the dust-mixed metal and transported it back to the surface, where further chemical and physical processes separated the pure weblon metal from the mono-molecular dust layers. Large ships transported the purified weblon to other industrial locations for treatment into forms and shapes for use wherever beam neutrality was required.

It was obvious from the beginning that I was different from the others. Most were political prisoners with only puny muscles. Most were gregarious creatures, friendly with one another, some counting days until their release while others were hopelessly resigned to making the best of a lifetime under lock and chain.

Though I was as sociable as anyone on my brood world, here I snarled and spat until, like one with a great scabrous disease, I was avoided by all.

Enemies were easy to make. The chip on my shoulder was as big as a sturdy oak, balanced precariously and waiting patiently for anyone to tip its trunk toward the ground.

It took only one or two short tussles for my strength, agility and training to show.

We were fed in line and normally the distance between my chained figure and others in my line was the maximum length of chain between us. One day a particularly fast, aggressive person bumped against my broad body in his eagerness to get nourishment. I swung around snarling, grabbed his neck between my giant paws and began to squeeze the life from him.

Only the whips of the guards and the combined pulls of other prisoners dragged me from his body while life still throbbed in him.

Another day my reflexes were sufficiently quick to grab the whip from a guard as he swung its tip toward me. I turned the whip around and nearly lacerated the guard to death before others could stop me.

That was the day all of them, prisoners and guards alike, combined positive efforts against me. That I was not only asocial but beyond the restraints of any ordinary prison had now become obvious.

In the first attempt at my life one of the heavy tractor-pressor beam generators was tipped on me from a height of about fifteen feet. Fortunately my gladiator-honed senses caught the movement and I easily side-stepped and safely evaded what seemed to me was the generator's slow fall. I didn't catch on then.

The next time a small, wiry prisoner pushed his body against mine in such a way that I tumbled backward into the yawning black chasm below us. I twisted and caught the edge of the chasm's rim and quickly drew myself upward.

Already the guards had moved my attacker beyond reach, passing him quickly to the surface to become part of a different and unreachable work crew. It was then I began to suspect.

One day the guards left our work crew. All became quiet and I looked up from my work to see every eye staring at me. Some had grasped rocks and stones while others grabbed the neck chains lying nearby. Slowly the group closed in on me, eyes glazed and muscles taut.

I moved swiftly to my gladiator's stance and waited quietly. Every sense on the alert, I could place every one of the nine around me. How little they knew of my training. None had access to gladiator power-beams and I was now faced with a purely two-dimensional problem.

The rocks came first and I easily dodged them. Then, in quick resolve, all nine swooped in toward me. I rushed through the circle, grabbing the nearest one holding the chain. Lifting him from the ground I flailed the group, though the chain was still held by two others. Those poor misguided point-seven-G fools had no concept of a gladiator's training and strength.

I flailed until it seemed that none survived. But two had climbed above me during the melee to redirect the mining beam at my body.

I am quick and well coordinated but even I could not move as fast as their fingers on the machine's switch.

Quite probably the alternating tractor-pressor beam had never been used on human flesh around these prisoners before. They certainly had no knowledge of the effect of the beams when used this way. I stood my ground and let the waves of current ripple through my body, neither resisting nor helping the flow of alternate tugs and pulls, and my gladiator-trained body as well as my water-based tissue withstood the strains well. Every piece of metal I wore—including my hated chest band and the newly attached neck band—disintegrated into mono-molecular powder as fine as any created in the weblon mines. I was truly free of their hated instruments of capture now.

I leaped to the machine's top and from there crushed my attackers' heads like eggshells. Now only I, the mining machine and the solitude of the caverns remained in this branch of the tunnel, I wondered how long I had before the guards returned?

Behind me lay certain capture. Directly ahead of me lay granitic rock, but to my side lay the deep, perhaps more dangerous chasm. What choice did I have?

I picked up the mining tool and chain, using the latter to tie the tool to my back. Then slowly, using trained fingers and toes, I picked my way down the steep crevice's side, using the slightest of indentations along the wall to support my own two hundred pounds and the additional two hundred on my back.

Down I crawled. Down until my fingers and toes were sore beyond description—down until I reached the first ledge. Here I rested, conserving my strength for the next lap downward. Again and yet again I traveled downward, resting from ledge to ledge, sometimes finding one only when it seemed that my last reserves of strength had been reached. Would I never reach the bottom?

• • •

I dropped pebbles down the long, dark, silent tube, hearing only the sibilance of air sweeping around its path—never hearing splash or bounce of its final strike. It was then I paused to consider.

It was highly doubtful that I could go up again and going farther down seemed useless. Now was the time to unlimber my mining instrument.

Then I pointed the alternating tractor-pressor inward against the chasm's wall and powdered my way forward. The first layer powdered at my feet and swept outward into the chasm below. Soon I was scrabbling with hands and knees to force the dust backward behind me. Fortunately the mono-molecular layers filled less space than their more complex forms and air from the chasm swept in behind me as the stone ahead powdered to the floor.

Mile after mile I bored ahead. When tired, I rested. Then I bored again for miles. Days passed. Even my gladiator's physique suffered from lack of nourishment. My body became sluggish, my mind tormented by memories of the sneering laughter and red-spurting throat of Trevic Strenger and by the graceful body and full lips of his daughter. The latter vision filled my mind to overflowing until my muscles responded.

I pressed on, even forgetting which was was up and which down and distrusting my fatigued senses for knowledge of either direction.

Dust filled my mouth, my eyes, my ears and, it seemed, even my mind, until I could go no farther. With one last effort at survival I shoved my poundage and my machine against the wall, lurched forward. Under sudden acceleration both the machine and my body fell outward and down as the thin wall between my tunnel and the opening broke through.

My body revolved around and around. Centrifugal force flung my arms and legs outward as I plunged through a narrow fissure.

I strained my back, neck and belly muscles to bring my turning to a stop but did not succeed. Light glimmered several hundred feet below and my frustrated mind focused on it until my spinning made it appear a whole galaxy of light particles swinging around me in tighter and tighter circles. My mind let go.

My back and head hit the water first. To this day, I am unaware of the extent of the true damage done to me in the fall.

V

How long did I lie there? Weeks? Days? Minutes? No one will ever know. I do know that hundreds of thousands of scraps of their educative process passed through my mind, only one of which I remembered on regaining consciousness.

" 'The time has come,' the Walrus said, 'to talk of many things: Of shoes—and ships—and sealing wax—Of cabbages—and kings—' "

Could any thought have been more out of place and foolish or less useful?

On returning to consciousness, I found my body to be whole and undamaged but bruised terribly. Water was washing over me. Some trickled into my open mouth and some laved my nose and ears, trailing my hair downstream like fine wires extended.

My right arm lay under me, touching the rocky stream bed below. My left arm lay partially submerged, the hand resting on a shallow bank.

My legs were upstream, resting on rock. My eyes were pasted shut by the dust around their rims. Soon I became aware of the mining tool's soft hum and the gentle tugging and pulling of my flesh under its influence.

I waved my right hand around in a circle and felt the broken chain with which I had attached the mining tool to my chest. I scraped mud from my swollen eyes, opened them and found I could see. Phosphorescent particles emitted sufficient photons for me to view my surroundings dimly. The mining instrument was on and pointed steadily in my direction.

I drank until my shrunken belly was fully distended, then lay back to rest and to sleep peacefully under the gentle vibration and hum of the tractor-pressor beam. Probably never before in history had a human being been subjected so long to the rapid alternate pull and push of the tractor-pressor beam. Would its effect be harmful? I didn't know.

When I awoke I crawled again to the stream, taking my fill. Below me I could see the shining shapes of water creatures, among them the unmistakably welcome shape of a fish. I struck with my right hand and grabbed the unwary creature tightly. Its cold flesh furnished my first nourishment in what seemed like months but may have been only days.

Again I slept, then ate and slept again. Later I walked over to my mining instrument and turned it off.

I felt light-headed, but oddly healthy and not in the least tired. I attributed this to the effect of poisons manufactured by my own system under unusual stress and at the time had no idea of the damage done to my body. I could have acted no differently under the conditions. Suffice it to say that I felt unusually alert and full of a sense of well-being, though attributing all of these characteristics to normal results of excessive stress.

I began my long walk along the stream hopefully toward light, air and freedom, packing the mining instrument on my back once more. The walls of the stream bed became narrower. Soon they reached a point where my broad shoulders could no longer squeeze through. My way forward was finally halted by granite blocks.

With almost a swagger of confidence, certainly more than the moment warranted, I unlimbered the tractor-pressor and blasted my way out.

The ship waited for me at my exit point. Of course—use of tractor or pressor beams anywhere on the planet could be easily followed by Strenger and his men.

I turned too late to reenter my cavern retreat. A rock bounded from my head and I fell forward to lie unconscious once again.

When I gained consciousness, my feet were trussed together, my arms tied behind my back and my head ached. I was in a cabin. Two gnarled men sat in front of me, alternately eating and gawking. Was I back in the arena? Were these my new keepers?

I strained at the bonds on my hands and feet but the ties were stronger than I. I humped my body to a sitting position and looked at my two captors, hatred washing through me in waves.

"Pretty, ain't he?" the one on my left said to the other.

"Needs a bath though. Think we could oblige him?"

Both stopped eating. One tied a drag rope to my legs and hauled me outside the cabin to a nearby spring. My flesh was torn and bleeding from the sharp rocks and sticks over which I was dragged and my head was still dizzy from the blow on my head but I uttered no complaint.

They pulled the rope end over an overhanging rock until I was dangling upside down over the water, my head scant inches from its surface. I took a deep breath, expecting the worst. It came. I was dunked under water seven or eight times, probably saved from drowning only by my one-G physique and high lung capacity.

I was dragged back into the cabin, trussed up against the post and forgotten for the time being.

They finished their dinner, checked various instruments lying around the cabin, then turned back to me. The older one—grayhaired and with a stubble-covered chin—was the first to speak directly to me.

"You might as well tell us why you were snooping around our private weblon mine. It's your only chance of saving your life."

My mind, now quite confused, failed to function as quickly as it might have under gladiator conditions. I said nothing.

The one with black hair and coal-black eyes bent his bulk over me and said, "If you are a government agent we will let you go free on another planet. It's to your advantage to tell us the truth."

I coughed some water from my burning lungs and said, "I am a gladiator. I have no name."

"All gladiators have names," the first one said. "Besides, what would a gladiator be doing using pressor-tractor equipment in these mountains? Come on, fellow—if you value your life— tell us the truth."

I strained every muscle of my body to burst the bonds. At last my body sagged. I knew a spasm of futility before I lost consciousness again.

I came to inside their ship. The interior was pure luxury and there I learned how the gawkers had searched for me in vain. I was one of the most popular heroes of all Sabre history—my life was public property and not even Trevic Strenger, dictator over all, would dare to violate it openly.

But no trace of me was found until my mining equipment had been sensed by these law-violating miners near their illegal mine.

I was kept bound inside their ship while they checked and double-checked my now clean-shaven features with pictures taken during my gladiator days.

Convinced I was truly the escaped Grand Champion, they struck my bonds, not knowing how close they were to true death at the moment.

I soon learned that everywhere I was loved by the people. But

I felt certain that I would still be unsafe anywhere on a planet ruled by Trevic Strenger and his type.

I stayed with the mining ship, hoping to get back to my brood world one day. But how could I flee when my two goals of hate and love were here? Not only would deserting them be unnatural to my brood training—it was unnatural to the unusual state of my biology, still deeply hidden from my conscious processes.

Still, in violation of every instinct, I left civilization behind to flee toward the Planet of Rocks of my birth. Seven long light-years lay ahead, meaning months of travel. Hundreds of thousands of strange worlds would be silently, unknowingly passed as we sped onward. How many contained brood worlds? How many had produced two-and-a-half-G monstrosities like Urut of Ewit? How many contained Patricia Strengers or Trevic Strengers? How many had educated barbarian champions and how many even held the humanoid form?

The days passed slowly. I became acquainted with the two outlaws. An objective study of their patterns of behavior gave me a certain recognition of their finer shadings of emotions. All three of us were outside the law but these two still subscribed to certain ethics and species-assisting patterns of behavior—much as each of the brood helps another for the sake of survival of the whole.

Unlike the brood, they had days when their minds were dominated by mixtures of pure emotions. They certainly exhibited pure forms of overt anger and calm complacency but they also showed fine shadings of moroseness and languor. I began to recognize emotional subtleties and, for the first time, began to question my pure hatred response to Trevic Strenger. Was he really as bad as I had projected or did he, too, have comprehensible feelings and behavior-motives mixed into his treatment of me?

One day I noted the outlaws' deep concern for one dial on the ship's panel. Daily the dial's indicator swung upward and daily other instruments were checked and rechecked against it. Presently I read their concern—patrols were on our path. A whole fleet crawled toward us, closing in slowly.

There are no maneuvers that can deceive a determined fleet. Our only hope lay in an act of some god who, out of the goodness of his being and the emptiness of space, would reach outward and hand us some device or means by which to escape.

To make matters worse, I had no place to stand and make the fight mine, using my gladiator's training. I felt trapped like an animal and could almost feel civilization's magnetic cages crush through my bones again. My chest, where I had worn the metal band of servitude, had healed and was covered with keloids. I wanted no more slavery.

One slim hope remained to me. My captors searched the directory for any kind of planet with breathable air. Then they began long-range perturbation analysis of surrounding stars, hoping to spot planets within range.

One bright yellow sun on our pathway seemed to offer hope and they quickly adjusted our route slightly to pass near its planets. We swung inward in a giant cycloidal loop, and an automatic analysis assured us that one planet, fourth from center, had breathable, oxidizing air.

But now our range was within the patrol's striking power and their beams reached out for hundreds of thousands of miles to vibrate our craft ceaselessly.

Though weakened structurally, we recklessly approached the planet's atmosphere, dropping swiftly into its density to skip and skip again as the craft was buffeted by the force of its own passage. Now weakened further and red from heat, it plunged at even sharper angles until its tail section broke off and our front portion spun uncontrolled toward the water below.

VI

The miners must surely have been killed in the plunge. At the time I attributed my survival to my gladiator's training and my powerful physique. I had bunched my muscles together and dived out the ship an instant before it splashed.

I hit hard, maybe as hard as Urut had hit me. Maybe a little harder—I don't know. In any case my body sustained the shock and I swam to the surface, spotting land perhaps ten miles away. Toward this I swam and just before sundown reached the sandy beach where I lay in exhausted stupor.

The jungle ahead of me was unrecognizable. Whether fern or animal, flora or fauna, I could not tell. Only experience would show.

Food was my immediate concern. Next came shelter and water. I rose, rather unnaturally recovered, and strode confidently into the strange organic configurations ahead.

Suddenly my emotional complex dropped from open elation and overwhelming optimism to complete apathy. Death would have seemed a pleasant release. Striving always with my gladiator's training and the stubbornness born of brood world, I consciously searched everywhere without success—no recognizable cause was creating my emotional void.

Down the scales of emotions my feelings plummeted—and slowly and silently the fibrous matting of the jungle undulated toward me. It was white with streaks of gray running through it and gave the appearance of some broad-patterned, supine foliage which moved like a leech. Who could tell what it really was? I wanted to back away but my apathy was too deep. I stood in an abandonment of despair, even squatting so the slimy thing could more easily flow up my body.

My apathy was dense—as dense as thick glue—and the thing nearly covered my back. I squatted lower to let it cover more of me, then felt its acid trickle over my skin. Apathy prevailed—nonetheless, under the stimulus of pain, my gladiator's instinct snapped my body erect and my hands and feet flung the horrible thing from me.

Acid had etched the skin all over my back, neck, arms and shoulders. Just as suddenly as the skin had been destroyed my body began its preconditoned, rapid repairs, though at the time I was too busy to give the phenomenon thought.

I was not yet safe, however. The thing flowed toward me as before and my apathy was as leaden as before. Why should I move when all of life seemed so useless, so hopeless? W. Shakespeare did not quite say it, but my mind, sunken in depths beyond conscious control and mired in the facts of the educators, paraphrased it as: "O mighty barbarian—dost thou lie low? Are all thy conquests, glories, triumphs, spoils, shrunk to this little measure?"

I will say this about the paraphrase—at least there was some relation between its semantics and my condition of the moment, though there was little else to recommend it.

Yet my fighting instinct had been aroused and at another level of my being I exploringly fought back. First I strove for excitement and the adrenalin lift which accompanies it. Then I strove

to force enthusiasm into the cellular portions of my body—to no
avail. Whatever force the thing had, my manufactured enthusiasm was not the answer.

I let my body freely wage swift endocrine war as my emotions
tore from cheerfulness through antagonism, overt anger, covert
anger, resentment, fear, grief and apathy. Nothing manufactured
by my body for my body helped.

As the thing crawled closer I switched my endocrine war outward against the whole world of loops and snakelike whorls
around me, raging within my soul but nonetheless subtly spout-
ing torrents of emotion outward through some unseen orifice of
my stilled body.

It was when I again hit the apathy band that the thing stilled.
Each time my body broadcast apathy, it retreated a little farther.
My body had instinctively found the key to survival on this
planet. The thing's emotional load lifted from my body. Again
I felt lighthearted and full of a sense of health, though I still
poured tons of black apathy at the crawling thing now scurrying
away so rapidly.

I turned back to the tangle of organic misshapes and little by
little ferreted out its secrets. The ropy black serpent-like form
dangling from above responded to fear. The flapping fan-like
objects responded to overt anger and the other dangers responded to other emotions either singly or in combination.

No single entity could easily be identified as food, but now that
I was learning to walk though the jungle by casting my emotions
externally here and there, I followed the first stream upward with
hopes of learning what was edible and what was not. Clearly the
acid and base-forming entities were inedible. Time after time I
succumbed to all their emotional complexities, learning only
after their acidic or basic sting to fling them off and redirect my
emotions outward. Time after time, my skin rapidly healed itself.

Order began to appear from the chaos surrounding me. I
watched the slinker root, a slob of jellylike flesh that looked like
a weathered tree-root from my Planet of the Rocks, as it flushed
out its quarry, a small blob of milksac covered with horny pro-
jections.

Using almost pure fear, its emotion swept outward to cover
growths of pink and purple velvety layers of some vertical ma-

terials. From the bottom of this growth the milksac animals—if that's what they were—rushed directly toward the jellylike growth.

There they were easily held until the chemical base dissolved their vital layers, after which they were absorbed into the attacker's system.

For lack of better hunch, I followed the next jellylike sack. It captured a victim. I tore it away from its grasp, using my hands for the act of tearing and my emotions for the act of neutralizing the strange beast.

I placed the juices of the injured beast on my tongue and found them sweet—but some poisons are sweet. I didn't know the difference but my body did—or so I thought at the time.

I chewed and swallowed and stayed healthy. Looking back on the experience now, I wonder. Did my body adapt to the alien food or did my instinct determine what was food and what was not?

I ate my way across thousands of miles of outrageous growths and forms as I traveled from coast to coast across one great continent. Occasionally I hid from search ships—the Patrol would not rest until our bodies were discovered, I reasoned. I left no daily trail by use of tractor or pressor beam and my human body could hide among the fibrous, gelatinous, oozing, slinking, stinking mess around me.

I crossed two mountain ranges, walking high above the life-plateau, living for weeks on air, water, fat and determination. Lonely pools of water were to be found at these higher levels.

The longer I survived in that emotional jungle the more grip I had on my own emotions—until I could instantly turn up the emotion of hate against Trevic Strenger or the passion and hunger of love for his daughter.

I soon was aware of his ships less often and rightly assumed their surveillance of the planet to be more or less precautionary and automatic.

Now I wanted the ships down, but only under my own terms. The problem was to attract their attention in order to make them a bit suspicious—but not overly so—and to trap the trappers.

Fire is common to most planets—but during a year's survival on this one, I had never seen a conflagration. I assumed that the patrol would also have observed this obvious fact. Could I make the unnatural happen by natural means?

The unnatural did happen but in a different way. I found a large piece of metal with fused pieces and burned spots. Either our ship or another had caused this piece to be flung across the continent where it had burned and fused on entry into the atmosphere; but whatever the true case, I had the part I needed to attract Strenger's persistent watchers.

Above the organic line, which is also above the rain line, are mountains, thin dry air and pools of water resting in bowls of rock lined with streaks of nearly pure lead. No weather or natural disturbance occurs at these heights or does so only occasionally. The pools are remnants of another era in the planet's ecology.

Before placing my plan into action, I had much work ahead and hoped my body was equal to its task. First, I found the pool nearest to the organic growth line. The pool I chose featured rocks jutting overhead. From one of these overhangs I tossed in more stones until the pile below the water's level was nearly to its surface.

I then lowered a large organic membrane to this new rock level under the surface, folding it into a kind of loosely formed bag with its corners and sides above water. I tied the corners together loosely and tied the other end to a rock overhead.

Within the newly separated layer of water I slowly lowered the spaceship's metal part, keeping one end high above the rock projection and lowering the other end to the bottom of the water-filled bag.

I tied another piece of organic rope to the top of the metal structure and looped its end to a rock some seven feet back from the water's edge. Then, carefully, I pulled on the metal, bending it farther and farther until it just touched a streak of partially oxidized lead jutting from the banks of the pool. Again and again I pulled the metal until I was in absolute control of its motion and could touch the lead streak with the ease of long practice.

The next day I drove hundreds of organic entities ahead of me, using only the apathy band, for I had learned that this emotion was associated with acid-bearing life. Up the rocks they tumbled and rolled, gyrated, squirmed and crawled until the pool was reached.

When the pool was made sufficiently acid by these monsters, I went after the base-bearing kind, using covert hostility for the drive, and I also drove them into the pool without qualms. There the bases partially neutralized the acids, forming a serviceable electrolyte.

How many beasts of which kind should I drive to create the huge battery I wanted? I did not know. Neither did I know about the permeability of the membrane sectioning off some liquid from the rest, nor the difference in electrolytic potential between the streaks of partially oxidized lead crawling along the pond's basin and the unknown metal now jutting above the pond's surface. With so many unknowns I could only try—perhaps to fail and try again.

After rest I pulled the metal down to the lead streak by means of the attached rope and was rewarded by observing a weak spark as the gap nearly closed. I returned to the herding of more creatures. Night came and the following day and I still herded creatures to the pond, testing the spark size with every new batch.

I hoped that the spark of light could be seen from a spaceship at night—or at least that the electro-magnetic waves radiating from the source would alert the patrolling monitors. I had not figured on the quick response which actually occurred.

I was driving my last batch of creatures ahead when the ship came. I crouched behind the rocks to watch when the rays hit and I was stuck rigid to the spot.

Through instruments of science or intellect, possibly both, they had outwitted me again. I was incapable of moving a muscle.

The ship I had seen was the decoy. Another one had landed somewhat earlier to trap me.

VII

There were two of them, one on either side of me, and they held me fast with heavy portable pressors. I strained with every bit of muscle tissue to no useful end.

All around me the life I had driven from the jungle below

boiled in confusion and from that movement came my idea. I summoned my energy and emoted apathy, driving the group toward one of the men. He faltered, then fell under the onslaught. The other also slumped. The pressors slipped from me and I ran to each man in turn. One pressor I threw into the acid pond. The second I focused on the ship, wedging it between two rocks.

I turned to the fallen men. One was encrusted with an acid which had eaten deeply. Almost dead, he would be of no help to me. The other was visibly shaken. I ran my own emotional output back up and down the scale several times until I could key into his basic confusion, then brought him up to a comfortable emotional level.

"How many are in the ship?" I quietly asked.

"Three. But who are you? What are you doing alone on this surrealistic planet?"

Now it's strange, but up to that point I had not thought of myself as a name. On the planet of my birth I was just one of the brood and could easily be identified by smell or appearance. On the Sabre planet I was known as barbarian or Champion or Grand Champion. Here on an alien planet, under an alien sun, I was again being asked a most fundamental question whose answer I could not give.

"Are you on regular patrol around this planet?" I asked.

"Yes."

"What are your duties?"

"We are to observe and report any slightest irregularity in shape or phenomenon or behavior over the whole planet's surface."

"How long has your patrol had the planet under surveillance?"

"Better than a year. Ever since outlaws were seen to approach the planet."

I moved the patrolman closer to the pressor beam so that I could more quickly reach its controls if I needed to.

"What did you expect to find here?" I asked.

"None of us knows. We merely take orders. We sighted the pond's heat activity by auto-infrared surveillance and watched you at work. It was then we laid our trap to capture you and find out what was happening."

"Are you a follower of the gladiators?" I asked.

"Who isn't?" he replied. He looked up expectantly.

"Then you are familiar with the disappearance of your Grand Champion over a year and a half ago?"

He looked me over from top to bottom before answering, then said excitedly, "Why, I believe you are he. Yes—you must be—"

His emotions bounced from my artificially maintained level to his interest and sincerity.

"If you are indeed the Grand Champion of a year ago—you should know that your status is that of a free man. After your successful fight with Urut of Ewit and your escape from the arena you were declared free by the enthusiasm and will of all the people. How did you get here?"

At one time I might have snarled and growled at this representative of their civilization. Now my mind froze as my conscious portion became aware of my own lack of emotional response to him. I listened politely and rationally to his talk. My mind, though, buzzed with consternation. Was I wrong to hate Trevic Strenger so? Was their world really all bad? Would I have been better off on the Planet of the Rocks, chasing rock wolves and fighting with others of the brood?

Then, against all the instincts which make up a brood world barbarian, I freed the man and docilely followed him to his ship.

The way back to Sabre planet was filled with wining and dining in the best of the patrol tradition. Word went out that the Grand Champion had survived shipwreck on a horribly inimical planet, and space for parsecs around was charged with the news.

My fame had spread—and my prowess increased. I had been the Greatest of Grand Champions and had so been declared on official gladiator roles. And only Trevic Strenger knew my true status but even he was not certain how I had come to be found on the forlorn Planet of Emotion.

VIII

We were like two giant computers battling one another. Trevic Strenger knew that every move I made might lead inevitably to his death—for I still meant to keep my vow. I knew that anything he did might cause my destruction directly or indirectly. He held the power, the education and the experience.

I was the Great Grand Champion, beloved of the people and not entirely unused to facing the thought of daily danger. Urut of Ewit was now champion, for no ordinary one-G humanoid had been able to withstand his stamina, strength and speed once he had grown experienced in one-G conditions. Between Urut and myself the people gawked as only gawkers can.

When I entered the gladiator stands, the gawkers stood and cheered for fifteen minutes. On the other side, far away from my grasping hands, Trevic Strenger sat surrounded by his sycophants and guards. Did I still wish him ill? I genuinely did not know. I knew only that I meant to kill him.

Urut entered and the crowd applauded with enthusiasm. Today was his show as well as mine. Then Trevic began his clever move against me. He arose, stilled the crowd, announced that it was only fitting that the newest and best of champions, Urut of Ewit, be challenged by the world's Great Grand Champion.

As he knew it would, the idea caught the gawkers' imagination and they howled their approval. I was committed before my barbaric wits could form a defensive reply.

Only by sustaining the people's good will could I be safe from Trevic and he had cleverly made use of the situation. I had to fight. I flung off my civilized accouterments and leaped into the arena, no longer bound by chest band, free to enter and leave whenever I wished.

I caught the tractor and pressor beams, tying them quickly to my ankles and wrists, and waited for Urut to move. He looked at me sadly from his heavy-lidded eyes and parrot-shaped mouth and I knew he had no desire for what he felt was sure to come.

His first blow, with pressor, was light and I knew he was pulling his attack. As any other one-G gladiator would be, I was clumsy, slow and weak compared to Urut. I was also out of training. At any time he could have decapitated me or ripped my body to shreds, for his timing was perfect.

For purpose of show, I'm sure, he let me cartwheel him several times and the gawkers thought my response would soon build in duration and quality. I knew and he knew that we were mismatched and that he had the advantage. Survival on the Planet of Emotion had taught me that emotion, too, can be a club if only one knows how to generate it. I had much practice and while Urut had his will with me—now under tractor lock, then under pressor throw—I sought the key to the emotions in his humanoid bulk.

My endocrine system worked rapidly, generating pure emotions from apathy to grief, resentment to fear, boredom to happiness. None worked. I then tried combinations as I had learned to do on the Planet of Emotions. Once I saw Urut falter briefly and pause to stare from glazed eyes. I thought then I had the key but lost the combination.

My powerful physique was tiring fast. Urut had pressors on opposite sides of my body and tractors at right angles, on opposite sides. I was being simultaneously squeezed and pulled on different body sections. I could almost feel cartilage tear and muscle tissues pop.

The gawkers were yelling for blood as I continued my search.

I caught the emotional combination to his alien form and Urut paused again briefly. I drove my emotional wedge in and he faltered. He stumbled and fell to his chest as I slowly rose from the sand, giving every appearance of pushing back on pressors and pulling back from tractors still clinging to me.

The gawkers screamed.

As my body strengthened, my emotional output rose and Urut twitched in agony. I have not idea what the emotional content meant to his way of life; but it was a powerful antidote to his physical superiority.

By the time I reached his side, my body was fully recovered and, using every ounce of my two hundred pounds of muscle, I might have been able to decapitate him. I looked to the crowd and asked their pleasure and I thanked the great brood-God that nearly all screamed for his release.

The gawkers yelled, stamped their feet and clapped their hands together. For them the solution had the appeal of a well-laid plot. How else could they have both their Great Grand Champion and the newest Champion to carry on with their future entertainment?

The day of Strenger's trap ended and I rested in my public-donated apartment that was lined with trophies of my earlier slave-status wins. Now, I thought, it was my turn against Strenger. My plan took form.

During my planning stages and the impasse to follow the faulty educative process to which I had been subjected caused A. Zlinsky's phrase to repeat though my mind. It ran: "To the wise go words!" A meaningless utterance. I tried to suppress it. It wouldn't go away, so I found myself trying to rationalize it. I did need a true and honest education to compete with Stenger—maybe that was what Zlinsky's silly quotation meant. I don't know. But eventually it led me directly to more efficient and better organized educators.

The habit pattern my mind had developed of tracing all knowledge through quotations or simulated quotations whenever possible was disturbing. My new educators explained that I would slowly lose the habit with time if I made a conscious effort to do so and that it arose from faulty use of the educator when I was a gladiator trainee.

Time passed. I became more acclimated to civilized behavior patterns. My emotional control was nearly perfect and I could more easily read the emotional patterns of others. Were it not for my vow against Strenger's life, I might have learned to enjoy my new free status.

When I was invited to attend the annual fealty procession and to serve as one of many state showpieces for public consumption, I could not help but suspect that Trevic Strenger's next trap was ready. My own plan was shelved and I prepared myself to look for any opening, regardless of cost to myself.

Since our procession was to approach Trevic Strenger's seat within a matter of feet, I knew our day of confrontation had come and that I was being baited. He couldn't know of my new ability to manipulate emotion, with which I would trap trapper.

I took his challenge. On each leg and arm I attached secret pressor and tractor beams and joined the grand procession. Behind the others, I slowly approached his position to give my symbol of fealty to the state. I could sense Trevic's muscles tighten as I approached him. His emotions became snarled and bent by covert hostility.

I grabbed his emotions by means of my new talents and twisted them down through grief and apathy. Downward they went until his face became placid, his arms and neck muscles relaxed and his whole stance presented a hopelessness.

Only one person stood between Trevic and me and that one

quickly left, urged on by another emotional impulse from my hulking body.

I faced Strenger as if he and I were alone in the world. His eyes seemed to plead and I scorned him, for what power could this emotional invalid have over me?

And then I knew that my hate for him was over and I dropped my long vow of hate and vengeance.

Suddenly the floor dropped from under me. Instantly my reflexes snapped on tractors and pressors and I curved my body into the best stance to slow my fall.

Slow it would not! Somewhere above me automatics caught and sheared off my powers. No matter how I scrambled and twisted my body, the machinery kept up with my efforts, seeming to anticipate every one of my merely human emotions.

The fall was not far. I landed catlike on all fours and bounded up to my feet again. Automatic machinery continued to nullify my pressors and tractors and steel bars surrounded me. Light came from the walls outside my new steel cage.

I heard a door open in the outside wall and then Trevic Strenger's careful tread. He did not smile; neither did he frown. I reached forward with my emotions to engulf him in apathy again but he spoke quickly.

"Turn off your machinery, barbarian. Throw out your tractor and pressor beams, too. I expected you to try for my life again and, as you can see, your attempt has not and cannot succeed. Face up to the fact that your machine-built education is only veneer-deep, your emotional control is uncivilized and your continuous attempts to kill me are more barbaric than our gladiator's arena. At least, there you know the rules."

I threw the pressor and tractors outward but remained silent. "That's better," he said. "At least you are intelligent enough to know when you are captured. That's more than I could say for you when I first caught you on your Planet of the Rocks. You fought until exhaustion then. Why not now?"

I remained quiet but watchful. I read less emotional hatred in his voice and actions than before, perhaps because I projected less of my own thoughts into the situation.

"I don't know what mutational talent you used to control my emotions to such a deep apathy before I triggered your fall into this chamber," he continued, "but I can assure you, you are here to stay until this senseless hatred of me is gone or—as is most likely from your stubborn character—you die of old age. Which shall it be?"

Unbidden to my mind came Farragut's thought, "Damn the torpedoes! Go ahead!" I pushed it below my conscious level and spoke to Trevic for the first time since his capture of me.

"I thought to kill you upstairs but then realized its futility just before your trap door opened. My hate has burned itself out."

He smiled and I noted how pleasant the smile was—not at all malevolent as I had believed for so long.

"How can I believe your statement mow?" he asked.

"You have urged me to accept the civilization you represent. What guarantee do I have that it consists of the advantages you have told me about?"

"Try it," he said instantly.

"Then try me," I also said instantly.

He laughed at my answer and seemed to consider my request quite seriously. He reflected only minutes, however, then bravely motioned to his retainers.

"Free him."

The bars around me rose and I faced Trevic Strenger, separated by only feet. I could easily have killed him at that moment.

IX

Years had passed since Trevic's momentous decision to free me. Sitting at the helm of this tiny empire known as the Sabre planets I looked back with nostalgia at my innocent entrance into its society.

Man had gone to the stars and returned, gone again. And those remaining at home had formed a weakened gene reservoir. Noting this state of affairs, man had returned the gladiator games to his home planet and then had forcibly invited back the barbaric and the humanoid—any mutational sports or freaks bearing new and untested genes were brought to Earth as gladiators.

Here in the arena of strength, agility, intelligence and courage the long screening took place—its purpose to find new blood for the human race. Those freed, like myself, were the backbone of humanity's new drive outward and inward. Slowly man returned his genetic protoplasm to an honored, aggressive, survival status.

I'll not forget the day of my final release from both the steel cell and my own inward-driven emotions. Trevic Strenger stood before me, bravely waiting for me to call his bluff—to kill him suddenly or to accept his offer for civilized peace. He waited. Then suddenly he tore off his shirt and I could see the thickened keloids around his chest where his gladiator band had once burned into him.

Patricia Strenger, hair now grayed, skin wrinkled, figure long gone, sat by my side. She crushed my hand in thoughtful empathy as I looked down on the newcomer from far beyond the Sabre planets. His hatred of me was volatile and could have exploded at any moment, were it a gaseous compound.

I could have dulled the edge of his emotions with my own freakish control over external emotions, of course, but this would also crush his spirit. Who knew? Perhaps the young barbarian below me would be my replacement. I smiled at the thought, all the time knowing that he would interpret my brief flicker as a sneering grin of hatred.

To my mind came unbidden phrases from quotes of our ancient past and I had finally learned to reconcile my thoughts to their contents. J. Christ had said, "And ye shall know the truth, and the truth shall make you free."

I signaled to have the snarling barbarian thrown into our ship and prepared myself for our long trek home.

THE DUELING MACHINE

by Ben Bova

Dulaq rode the slide to the upper pedestrian level, stepped off and walked over to the railing. The city stretched out all around him—broad avenues thronged with busy people, pedestrian walks, vehicle thoroughfares, aircars gliding between the gleaming, towering buildings.

And somewhere in this vast city was the man he must kill. The man who would kill him, perhaps.

It all seemed so real! The noise of the streets, the odors of the perfumed trees lining the walks, even the warmth of the reddish sun on his back as he scanned the scene before him.

It is an illusion, Dulaq reminded himself, *a clever manmade hallucination. A figment of my own imagination, amplified by a machine.*

But it seemed so very real.

Real or not, he had to find Odal before the sun set. Find him and kill him. Those were the terms of the duel. He fingered the stubby cylindrical stat-wand in his tunic pocket. That was the weapon he had chosen, his weapon, his own invention. And this was the environment he had picked: his city, busy, noisy, crowded, the metropolis Dulaq had known and loved since childhood.

Dulaq turned and glanced at the sun. It was halfway down toward the horizon, he judged. He had about three hours to find Odal. When he did—kill or be killed.

Of course no one is actually hurt. That is the beauty of the machine. It allows one to settle a score, to work out aggressive feelings, without either mental or physical harm.

Dulaq shrugged. He was a roundish figure, moonfaced, slightly stooped shoulders. He had work to do. Unpleasant work for a civilized man, but the future of the Acquataine Cluster and the entire alliance of neighboring star systems could well depend on the outcome of this electronically synthesized dream.

He turned and walked down the elevated avenue, marveling at the sharp sensation of hardness that met each footstep on the paving. Children dashed by and rushed up to a toyshop window. Men of commerce strode along purposefully, but without missing a chance to eye the girls sauntering by.

I must have a marvelous imagination, Dulaq thought smiling to himself.

Then he thought of Odal, the blond, icy professional he was pitted against. Odal was an expert at all the weapons, a man of strength and cool precision, an emotionless tool in the hands of a ruthless politician. But how expert could he be with a statwand, when the first time he saw one was the moment before the duel began? And how well acquainted could he be with the metropolis, when he had spent most of his life in the military camps on the dreary planets of Kerak, sixty light-years from Acquatainia?

No, Odal would be lost and helpless in this situation. He would attempt to hide among the throngs of people. All Dulaq had to do was to find him.

The terms of the duel restricted both men to the pedestrian walks of the commercial quarter of the city. Dulaq knew the area intimately, and he began a methodical hunt through the crowds for the tall, fair-haired, blue-eyed Odal.

And he saw him! After only a few minutes of walking down the major thoroughfare, he spotted his opponent, strolling calmly along a crosswalk, at the level below.

Dulaq hurried down the next ramp, worked his way through the crowd, and saw the man again. Tall and blond, unmistakable. Dulaq edged along behind him quietly, easily. No disturbance. No pushing. Plenty of time. They walked along the street for a quarter hour while the distance between them slowly shrank from fifty feet to five.

Finally Dulaq was directly behind him, within arm's reach. He grasped the stat-wand and pulled it from his tunic. With one quick motion he touched it to the base of the man's skull and started to thumb the button that would release the killing of energy . . .

The man turned suddenly. It wasn't Odal!

Dulaq jerked back in surprise. It couldn't be. He had seen his face. It was Odal—and yet this man was definitely a stranger.

He stared at Dulaq as the duelist backed away a few steps, then turned and walked quickly from the place.

A mistake, Dulaq told himself. *You were overanxious. A good thing this is an hallucination, or else the autopolice would be taking you in by now.*

And yet . . . he had been so certain that it was Odal. A chill shuddered through him. He looked up, and there was his antagonist, on the thoroughfare above, at the precise spot where he himself had been a few minutes earlier. Their eyes met, and Odal's lips parted in a cold smile.

Dulaq hurried up the ramp. Odal was gone by the time he reached the upper level. *He could not have gotten far,* Dulaq reasoned. Slowly, but very surely, Dulaq's hallucination turned into a nightmare. He spotted Odal in the crowd, only to have him melt away. He saw him again, lolling in a small park, but when he got closer, the man turned out to be another stranger. He felt a chill of the duelist's ice-blue eyes on him again and again, but when he turned to find his antagonist, no one was there but the impersonal crowd.

Odal's face appeared again and again. Dulaq struggled through the throngs to find his opponent, only to have him vanish. The crowd seemed to be filled with tall, blond men crisscrossing before Dulaq's dismayed eyes.

The shadows lengthened. The sun was setting. Dulaq could feel his heart pounding within him and perspiration pouring from every square inch of his skin.

There he is! Definitely, positively him! Dulaq pushed through the homeward-bound crowds toward the figure of a tall, blond man leaning against the safety railing of the city's main thoroughfare. It was Odal, the damned smiling confident Odal.

Dulaq pulled the wand from his tunic and battled across the

surging crowd to the spot where Odal stood motionless, hands in pockets, watching him.

Dulaq came within arm's reach . . .

"TIME, GENTLEMEN. TIME IS UP, THE DUEL IS ENDED."

High above the floor of the antiseptic-white chamber that housed the dueling machine was a narrow gallery. Before the machine had been installed, the chamber had been a lecture hall in Acquatainia's largest university. Now the rows of students' seats, the lecturer's dais and rostrum were gone. The chamber held only the machine, the grotesque collection of consoles, control desks, power units, association circuits, and booths where the two antagonists sat.

In the gallery—empty during ordinary duels—sat a privileged handful of newsmen.

"Time limit is up," one of them said. "Dulaq didn't get him."

"Yes, but he didn't get Dulaq, either."

The first one shrugged. "The important thing is that now Dulaq has to fight Odal on *his* terms. Dulaq couldn't win with his own choice of weapons and situation, so—"

"Wait, they're coming out."

Down on the floor below, Dulaq and his opponent emerged from their enclosed booths.

One of the newsmen whistled softly. "Look at Dulaq's face . . . it's positively gray."

"I've never seen the Prime Minister so shaken."

"And take a look at Kanus' hired assassin." The newsmen turned toward Odal, who stood before his booth, quietly chatting with his seconds.

"Hm-m-m. There's a bucket of frozen ammonia for you."

"He's enjoying this."

One of the newsmen stood up. "I've got a deadline to meet. Save my seat."

He made his way past the guarded door, down the rampway circling the outer walls of the building, to the portable tri-di transmitting unit that the Acquatainian government had permitted for the newsmen on the campus grounds outside the former lecture hall.

The newsman huddled with his technicians for a few minutes, then stepped before the transmitter.

"Emile Dulaq, Prime Minister of the Acquataine Cluster and acknowledged leader of the coalition against Chancellor Kanus of the Kerak Worlds, has failed in the first part of his psychonic duel against Major Par Odal of Kerak. The two antagonists are now undergoing the routine medical and psychological checks before renewing their duel."

By the time the newsman returned to his gallery seat, the duel was almost ready to begin again.

Dulaq stood in the midst of the group of advisors before the looming impersonality of the machine.

"You need not go through with the next phase of the duel immediately," his Minister of Defense was saying. "Wait until tomorrow. Rest and calm yourself."

Dulaq's round face puckered into a frown. He cocked an eye at the chief meditech, hovering at the edge of the little group.

Meditch, one of the staff that ran the dueling machine, pointed out, "The Prime Minister has passed the examinations. He is capable, within the agreed-upon rules of the contest, of resuming."

"But he has the option of retiring for the day, does he not?"

"If Major Odal agrees."

Dulaq shook his head impatiently. "No, I shall go through with it. Now."

"But—"

The prime minister's face suddenly hardened; his advisors lapsed into a respectful silence. The chief meditech ushered Dulaq back into his booth. On the other side of the room, Odal glanced at the Acquatainians, grinned humorlessly, and strode to his own booth.

Dulaq sat and tried to blank out his mind while the meditechs adjusted the neurocontacts to his head and torso. They finished at last and withdrew. He was alone in the booth now, looking at the deadwhite walls, completely bare except for the viewscreen before his eyes. The screen finally began to glow slightly, then brightened into a series of shifting colors. The colors merged and changed, swirled across his field of view. Dulaq felt himself being drawn into them gradually, compellingly, completely immersed in them.

The mists slowly vanished, and Dulaq found himself standing on an immense and totally barren plain. Not a tree, not a blade of grass; nothing but bare, rocky ground stretching in all directions to the horizon and disturbingly harsh yellow sky. He looked down and at his feet saw the weapon that Odal had chosen.

A primitive club.

With a sense of dread, Dulaq picked up the club and hefted it in his hand. He scanned the plain. Nothing. No hills or trees or bushes to hide him. No place to run to.

And off on the horizon he could see a tall, lithe figure holding a similar club walking slowly and deliberately toward him.

The press gallery was practically empty. The duel had more than an hour to run, and most of the newsmen were outside, broadcasting their hastily-drawn guesses about Dulaq's failure to win with his own choice of weapon and environment.

Then a curious thing happened.

On the master control panel of the dueling machine, a single light flashed red. The meditech blinked at it in surprise, then pressed a series of buttons on his board. More red lights appeared. The chief meditech rushed to the board and flipped a single switch.

One of the newsmen turned to his partner. "What's going on down there?"

"I think it's all over . . . Yes, look, they're opening up the booths. Somebody must've scored a victory."

They watched intently while the other newsmen quickly filed back into the gallery.

"There's Odal. He looks happy."

"Guess that means—"

"Good Lord! Look at Dulaq!"

II

Dr. Leoh was lecturing at the Carinae Regional University when the news of Dulaq's duel reached him. An assistant professor perpetrated the unthinkable breach of interrupting the lecture to whisper the news in his ear.

Leoh nodded grimly, hurriedly finished his lecture, and then accompanied the assistant professor to the university president's office. They stood in silence as the slideway whisked them through the strolling students and blossoming greenery of the quietly-busy campus.

Leoh remained wrapped in his thoughts as they entered the administration building and rode the lift tube. Finally, as they stepped through the president's doorway, Leoh asked the assistant professor:

"You say he was in a state of catatonic shock when they removed him from the machine?"

"He still is," the president answered from his desk. "Completely withdrawn from the real world. Cannot speak, hear, or even see—a living vegetable."

Leoh plopped down in the nearest chair and ran a hand across his fleshy face. He was balding and jowly, but his face was creased from a smile that was almost habitual, and his eyes were active and alert.

"I don't understand it," he admitted. "Nothing like this has ever happened in a dueling machine before."

The university president shrugged. "I don't understand it either. But, this is your business." He put a slight emphasis on the last word, unconsciously perhaps.

"Well, at least this will not reflect on the university. That is why I formed Psychonics as a separate business enterprise." Then he added, with a grin, "The money was, of course, only a secondary consideration."

The president managed a smile. "Of course."

"I suppose the Acquatainians want to see me?" Leoh asked academically.

"They're on the tri-di now, waiting for you."

"They're holding a transmission frequency open over eight hundred parsecs?" Leoh looked impressed. "I must be an important man."

"You're the inventor of the dueling machine and the head of Psychonics, Inc. You're the only man who can tell them what went wrong."

"Well, I suppose I shouldn't keep them waiting."

"You can take the call here," the president said, starting to get up from his chair.

"No, no, stay there at your desk," Leoh insisted. "There's no reason for you to leave. Or you either," he said to the assistant professor.

The president touched a button on his desk communicator. The far wall of the office glowed momentarily, then seemed to dissolve. They were looking into another office, this one on Acquatainia. It was crowded with nervous-looking men in business clothes and military uniforms.

"Gentlemen," Dr. Leoh said.

Several of the Acquatainians tried to answer him at once. After a few seconds of talking together, they all looked toward one of their members—a tall, purposeful, shrewd-faced civilian who bore a neatly-trimmed black beard. "I am Fernd Massan, the Acting Prime Minister of Acquatainia. You realize, of course, the crisis that has been precipitated in my Government because of this duel?"

Leoh blinked. "I realize that apparently there has been some difficulty with the dueling machine installed on the governing planet of your star cluster. Political crises are not in my field."

"But your dueling machine has incapacitated the Prime Minister," one of the generals bellowed.

"And at this particular moment," the defense minister added, "in the midst of our difficulties with Kerak Worlds."

"If the Prime Minister is not—"

"Gentlemen!" Leoh objected. "I cannot make sense of your story if you all speak at once."

Massan gestured them to silence.

"The dueling machine," Leoh said, adopting a slightly professorial tone, is "nothing more than a psychonic device for alleviating human aggressions and hostilities. It allows two men to share a dream world created by one of them. There is nearly-complete feedback between the two. Within certain limits, the two men can do anything they wish within their dream world. This allows men to settle grievances with violence—in the safety of their own imaginations. If the machine is operated properly, no physical or mental harm can be done to the participants. They can alleviate their tensions safely—without damage of any sort to anyone, and without hurting society.

"Your own Government tested one of the machines and approved its use on Acquatainia more than three years ago. I see several of you who were among those to whom I personally demonstrated the device. Dueling machines are in use through wide portions of the galaxy, and I am certain that many of you have used the machine. You have, general, I'm sure."

The general blustered. "That has nothing to do with the matter at hand!"

"Admittedly," Leoh conceded. "But I do not understand how

a therapeutic machine can possibly become entangled in a political crisis."

Massan said, "Allow me to explain. Our Government has been conducting extremely delicate negotiations with the stellar governments of our neighboring territories. These negotiations concern the rearmament of the Kerak Worlds. You have heard of Kanus of Kerak?"

"I recall the name vaguely," Leoh said. "He's a political leader of some sort."

"Of the worst sort. He has acquired complete dictatorship of the Kerak Worlds, and is now attempting to rearm them for war. This is in direct countervention of the Treaty of Acquatainia, signed only thirty Terran years ago."

"I see. The treaty was signed at the end of the Acquataine-Kerak war, wasn't it?"

"A war that we won," the general pointed out.

"And now the Kerak Worlds want to rearm and try again," Leoh said.

"Precisely."

Leoh shrugged. "Why not call in the Star Watch? This is their type of police activity. And what has all this to do with the dueling machine?"

Massan explained patiently, "The Acquataine Cluster has never become a full-fledged member of the Terran Commonwealth. Our neighboring territories are likewise unaffiliated. Therefore the Star Watch can intervene only if all parties concerned agree to intervention. Unless of course, there is an actual military emergency. The Kerak Worlds, of course, are completely isolationist—unbound by any laws except those of force."

Leoh shook his head.

"As for the dueling machine," Massan went on, "Kanus of Kerak has turned it into a political weapon—"

"But that's impossible. Your government passed strict laws concerning the use of the machine; I recommended them and I was in your Council chambers when the laws were passed. The machine may be used only for personal grievances. It is strictly outside the realm of politics."

Massan shook his head sadly. "Sir, laws are one thing—people are another. And politics consists of people, not words on paper."

"I don't understand," Leoh said.

Massan explained, "A little more than one Terran year ago, Kanus picked a quarrel with a neighboring star-group—the Safad Federation. He wanted an especially favorable trade agreement with them. Their minister of trade objected most strenuously. One of the Kerak negotiators—a certain Major Odal—got into a personal argument with the minister. Before anyone knew what had happened, they had challenged each other to a duel. Odal won the duel, and the minister resigned his post. He said that he could no longer effectively fight against the will of Odal and his group . . . he was psychologically incapable of it. Two weeks later he was dead—apparently a suicide, although I have doubts."

"That's . . . extremely interesting," Leoh said.

"Three days ago," Massan continued, "the same Major Odal engaged Prime Minister Dulaq in a bitter personal argument. Odal is now a military attaché of the Kerak Embassy here. He accused the Prime Minister of cowardice, before a large group at an Embassy party. The Prime Minister had no alternative but to challenge him. And now—"

"And now Dulaq is in a state of shock, and your government is tottering."

Massan's back stiffened. "Our Government shall not fall, nor shall the Acquataine Cluster acquiesce to the rearmament of the Kerak Worlds. But"—and his voice lowered—"without Dulaq, I fear that our neighboring governments will give in to Kanus' demands and allow him to rearm. Alone, we are powerless to stop him."

"Rearmament itself might not be so bad," Leoh mused, "if you can keep the Kerak Worlds from using their weapons. Perhaps the Star Watch might—"

"Kanus could strike a blow and conquer a star system before the Star Watch could be summoned and arrive to stop him. Once Kerak is armed, this entire area of the galaxy is in peril. In fact, the entire galaxy is endangered."

"And he's using the dueling machine to further his ambitions," Leoh said. "Well, gentlemen, it seems I have no alternative but to travel to the Acquataine Cluster. The dueling machine is my responsibility, and if there is something wrong with it, or with the use of it, I will do my best to correct the situation."

"That is all we ask," Massan said. "Thank you."

The Acquatainian scene faded away, and the three men in the university president's office found themselves looking at a solid wall once again.

"Well," Dr. Leoh said, turning to the president, "it seems that I must request an indefinite leave of absence."

The president frowned. "And it seems that I must grant your request—even though the year is only half-finished."

"I regret the necessity," Leoh said; then, with a broad grin, he added, "My assistant professor, here, can handle my courses for the remainder of the year very easily. Perhaps he will even be able to deliver his lectures without being interrupted."

The assistant professor turned red.

"Now then," Leoh muttered, mostly to himself, "who is this Kanus, and why is he trying to turn the Kerak Worlds into an arsenal?"

III

Chancellor Kanus, the supreme leader of the Kerak Worlds, stood at the edge of the balcony and looked across the wild, tumbling gorge to the rugged mountains beyond.

"These are the forces that mold men's actions," he said to his small audience of officials and advisors, "the howling winds, the mighty mountains, the open sky and the dark powers of the clouds."

The men nodded and made murmurs of agreement.

"Just as the mountains thrust up from the pettiness of the lands below, so shall we rise above the common walk of men," Kanus said. "Just as a thunderstorm terrifies them, we will make them bend to our will!"

"We will destroy the past," said one of the ministers.

"And avenge the memory of defeat," Kanus added. He turned and looked at the little group of men. Kanus was the smallest man on the balcony: short, spare, sallow-faced; but he possessed piercing dark eyes and a strong voice that commanded attention.

He walked through the knot of men and stopped before a tall, lean, blond youth in light-blue military uniform. "And you, Major Odal, will be a primary instrument in the first steps of conquest."

Odal bowed stiffly. "I only hope to serve my leader and my worlds."

"You shall. And you already have," Kanus said, beaming. "Already the Acquatainians are thrashing about like a snake whose head has been cut off. Without Dulaq, they have no head, no brain to direct them. For your part in this triumph"—Kanus snapped his fingers, and one of his advisors quickly stepped to his side and handed him a small ebony box—"I present you with this token of the esteem of the Kerak Worlds, and of my personal high regard."

He handed the box to Odal, who opened it and took out a small jeweled pin.

"The Star of Kerak," Kanus announced. "This is the first time it has been awarded to anyone except a warrior on the battlefield. But then, we have turned their so-called civilized machine into our own battlefield, eh?"

Odal grinned. "Yes, sir, we have. Thank you very much sir. This is the supreme moment of my life."

"To date, major. Only to date. There will be other moments, even higher ones. Come, let's go inside. We have many plans to discuss . . . more duels . . . more triumphs."

They all filed in to Kanus' huge, elaborate office. The leader walked across the plushly ornate room and sat at the elevated desk, while his followers arranged themselves in the chairs and couches placed about the floor. Odal remained standing, near the doorway.

Kanus let his fingers flick across a small control board set into his desktop, and a tri-dimensional star map glowed into existence on the far wall. At its center were the eleven stars that harbored the Kerak Worlds. Around them stood neighboring stars, color-coded to show their political groupings. Off to one side of the map was the Acquataine Cluster, a rich mass of stars—wealthy, powerful, the most important political and economic power in the section of the galaxy. Until yesterday's duel.

Kanus began one of his inevitable harangues. Objectives, political and military. Already the Kerak Worlds were unified under his dominant will. The people would follow wherever he led. Already the political alliance built up by Acquatainian diplomacy since the last war were tottering, now that Dulaq was out of the picture. Now was the time to strike. A political blow *here*, at the Szarno Confederacy, to bring them and their armaments

industries into line with Kerak. Then, finally, the military blow—
against the Acquatainians.

"A sudden strike, a quick, decisive series of blows, and the
Acquatainians will collapse like a house of paper. Before the
Star Watch can interfere, we will be masters of the Cluster.
Then, with the resources of Acquatainia to draw on, we can
challenge any force in the galaxy—even the Terran Common-
wealth itself!"

The men in the room nodded their assent.

They've heard this story many, many times, Odal thought to
himself. This was the first time he had been privileged to listen
to it. If you closed your eyes, or looked only at the star map,
the plan sounded bizarre, extreme, even impossible. But, if you
watched Kanus, and let those piercing, almost hypnotic eyes
fasten on yours then the leader's wildest dreams sounded not
only exciting, but inevitable.

Odal leaned a shoulder against the paneled wall and scanned
the other men in the room.

There was fat Greber, the vice chancellor, fighting desperately
to stay awake after drinking too much wine during the luncheon
and afterward. And Modal, sitting on the couch next to him,
was bright-eyed and alert, thinking only of how much money
and power would come to him as Chief of Industries once the
rearmament program began in earnest.

Sitting alone on another couch was Kor, the quiet one, the
head of Intelligence, and—technically—Odal's superior. Silent
Kor, whose few words were usually charged with terror for those
whom he spoke against.

Marshal Lugal looked bored when Kanus spoke of politics,
but his face changed when military matters came up. The marshal lived for only one purpose; to avenge his army's humiliating
defeat in the war against the Acquatainians, thirty Terran years
ago. What he didn't realize, Odal thought, smiling to himself,
was that as soon as he had reorganized the army and re-equipped
it, Kanus planned to retire him and place younger men in charge.
Men whose only loyalty was not to the army, nor even to the
Kerak Worlds and their people, but to the chancellor himself.

Eagerly following every syllable, every gesture of the leader
was little Tinth. Born to the nobility, trained in the arts, a student of philosophy, Tinth had deserted his heritage and joined

the forces of Kanus. His reward had been the Ministry of Education; many teachers had suffered under him.

And finally there was Romis, the Minister of Intergovernmental Affairs. A professional diplomat, and one of the few men in government before Kanus' sweep to power to survive this long. It was clear that Romis hated the chancellor. But he served the Kerak Worlds well. The diplomatic corps was flawless in their handling of intergovernmental affairs. It was only a matter of time, Odal knew, before one of them—Romis or Kanus—killed the other.

The rest of Kanus' audience consisted of political hacks, roughnecks-turned-bodyguards, and a few other hangers-on who had been with Kanus since the days when he held his political monologues in cellars, and haunted the alleys to avoid the police. Kanus had come a long way: from the blackness of oblivion to the dazzling heights of the chancellor's rural estate.

Money, power, glory, revenge, patriotism: each man in the room, listening to Kanus, had his reasons for following the chancellor.

And my reasons? Odal asked himself. *Why do I follow him? Can I see into my own mind as easily as I see into theirs?*

There was duty, of course. Odal was a soldier, and Kanus was the duly-elected leader of the government. Once elected, though, he had dissolved the government and solidified his powers as absolute dictator of the Kerak Worlds.

There was gain to be had by performing well under Kanus. Regardless of his political ambitions and personal tyrannies, Kanus rewarded well when he was pleased. The medal—the Star of Kerak—carried with it an annual pension that would nicely accommodate a family. *If I had one,* Odal thought, sardonically.

There was power, of sorts, also. Working the dueling machine in his special way, hammering a man into nothingness, finding the weaknesses in his personality and exploiting them, pitting his mind against others, turning sneering towers of pride like Dulaq into helpless whipped dogs—that was power. And it was a power that did not go unnoticed in the cities of the Kerak Worlds. Already Odal was easily recognized on the streets; women especially seemed to be attracted to him now.

"The most important factor," Kanus was saying, "and I cannot stress it overmuch, is to build up an aura of invincibility."

This is why your work is so important, Major Odal. You must be invincible! Because today you represent the collective will of the Kerak Worlds. Today you are the instrument of my own will—and you must triumph at every turn. The fate of your people, of your government, of your chancellor rests squarely on your shoulders each time you step into a dueling machine. You have borne that responsibility well, major. Can you carry it even further?''

"I can, sir," Odal answered crisply, "and I will."

Kanus beamed at him. "Good! Because your next duel—and those that follow it—will be to the death."

IV

It took the starship two weeks to make the journey from Carinae to the Acquataine Cluster. Dr. Leoh spent the time checking over the Acquatainian dueling machine, by direct tri-di beam; the Acquatainian government gave him all the technicians, time and money he needed for the task.

Leoh spent as much of his spare time as possible with the other passengers of the ship. He was gregarious, a fine conversationalist, and had a nicely-balanced sense of humor. Particularly, he was a favorite of the younger women, since he had reached the age where he could flatter them with his attention without making them feel endangered.

But still, there were long hours when he was alone in his stateroom with nothing but his memories. At times like these, it was impossible not to think back over the road he had been following.

Albert Robertus Leoh, Ph.D., Professor of Physics, Professor of Electronics, master of computer technology, inventor of the interstellar tri-di communications system; and more recently, student of psychology, Professor of Psycholphysiology, founder of Psychonics, Inc., inventor of the dueling machine.

During his earlier years, when the supreme confidence of youth was still with him, Leoh had envisioned himself as helping mankind to spread his colonies and civilizations throughout the galaxy. The bitter years of galactic war had ended in his childhood, and now human societies throughout the Milky Way were linked together—in greater or lesser degree of union—into a more-or-less peaceful coalition of star groups.

There were two great motivating forces at work on those human societies spread across the stars, and these forces worked toward opposite goals. On the one hand was the urge to explore, to reach new stars, new planets, to expand the frontiers of man's civilizations and found new colonies, new nations. Pitted against this drive to expand was an equally-powerful force: the realization that technology had finally put an end to physical labor and almost to poverty itself on all the civilized worlds of man. The urge to move off to the frontier was penned in and buried alive under the enervating comforts of civilization.

The result was inescapable. The civilized worlds became constantly more crowded as time wore on. They became jampacked islands of humanity sprinkled thinly across the sea of space that was still full of unpopulated islands.

The expense and difficulty of interstellar travel was often cited as an excuse. The starships *were* expensive: their power demands were frightful. Only the most determined—and the best financed—groups of colonists could afford them. The rest of mankind accepted the ease and safety of civilization, lived in the bulging cities of the teeming planets. Their lives were circumscribed by their neighbors, and by their governments. Constantly more people crowding into a fixed living space meant constantly less freedom. The freedom to dream, to run free, to procreate, all became state-owned, state-controlled monopolies.

And Leoh had contributed to this situation.

He had contributed his thoughts and his work. He had contributed often and regularly—the interstellar communications systems was only the one outstanding achievement in a long career of achievements.

Leoh had been nearly at the voluntary retirement age for scientists when he realized what he, and his fellow scientists, had done. Their efforts to make life richer and more rewarding for mankind had made life only less strenuous and more rigid.

And with every increase in comfort, Leoh discovered, came a corresponding increase in neuroses, in crimes of violence, in mental aberrations. Senseless wars of pride broke out between star-groups for the first time in generations. Outwardly, the peace of the galaxy was assured; but beneath the glossy surface of the Terran Commonwealth there smoldered the beginnings of a volcano. Police actions fought by the Star Watch were increasing ominously. Petty wars between once-stable people were flaring up steadily.

Once Leoh realized the part he had played in this increasingly-tragic drama, he was confronted with two emotions—a deep sense of guilt, both personal and professional; and, countering this, a determination to do something, anything, to restore at least some balance to man's collective mentality.

Leoh stepped out of physics and electronics, and entered the field of psychology. Instead of retiring, he applied for a beginner's status in his new profession. It had taken considerable bending and straining of the Commonwealth's rules—but for a man of Leoh's stature, the rules could be flexed somewhat. Leoh became a student once again, then a researcher, and finally a Professor of Psychophysiology.

Out of this came the dueling machine. A combination of electroencephalograph and autocomputer. A dream machine, that amplified a man's imagination until he could engulf himself into a world of his own making.

Leoh envisioned it as a device to enable men to rid themselves of hostility and tension safely. Through his efforts, and those of his colleagues, dueling machines were quickly becoming accepted as devices for settling disputes.

When two men had a severe difference of opinion—deep enough to warrant legal action—they could go to the dueling machine instead of the courts. Instead of sitting helplessly and watching the machinations of the law grind impersonally through their differences, the two antagonists could allow their imaginations free rein in the dueling machine. They could settle their differences personally, as violently as they wished, without hurting themselves or anyone else. On most civilized worlds, the results of properly-monitored duels were accepted as legally binding.

The tensions of civilized life could be escaped—albeit temporarily—in the dueling machine. This was a powerful tool, much too powerful to allow it to be used indiscriminately. Therefore Leoh safeguarded his invention by forming a private company—Psychonics, Inc.—and securing an exclusive license from the Terran Commonwealth to manufacture, sell, install and maintain the machines. His customers were government health and legal agencies; his responsibilities were: legally, to the

Commonwealth; morally, to all mankind; and, finally, to his own restless conscience.

The dueling machines succeeded. They worked as well, and often better, than Leoh had anticipated. But he knew that they were only a stopgap, only a temporary shoring of a constantly-eroding dam. What was needed, really needed, was some method of exploding the status quo, some means of convincing people to reach out for those unoccupied, unexplored stars that filled the galaxy, some way of convincing men that they should leave the comforts of civilization for the excitement of colonization.

Leoh had been searching for that method when the news of Dulaq's duel against Odal reached him.

Now he was speeding across parsecs of space, praying to himself that the dueling machine had not failed.

The two-week flight ended. The starship took up a parking orbit around the capital planet of the Acquataine Cluster. The passengers transhipped to the surface.

Dr. Leoh was met at the landing disk by an official delegation, headed by Massan, the acting prime minister. They exchanged formal greetings there at the base of the ship, while the other passengers hurried by.

As Leoh and Massan, surrounded by the other members of the delegation, rode the slideway to the port's administration building, Leoh commented:

"As you probably know, I have checked through your dueling machine quite thoroughly via tri-di for the past two weeks. I can find nothing wrong with it."

Massan shrugged. "Perhaps you should have checked then, the machine on Szarno."

"The Szarno Confederation? Their dueling machine?"

"Yes. This morning Kanus' hired assassin killed a man in it."

"He won another duel," Leoh said.

"You do not understand," Massan said grimly. "Major Odal's opponent—an industrialist who had spoken out against Kanus— was actually killed in the dueling machine. The man is dead!"

V

One of the advantages of being Commander-in-Chief of the Star Watch, the old man thought to himself, is that you can visit any planet in the Commonwealth.

He stood at the top of the hill and looked out over the green tableland of Kenya. This was the land of his birth, Earth was his homeworld. The Star Watch's official headquarters may be in the heart of a globular cluster of stars near the center of the galaxy, but Earth was the place the commander wanted most to see as he grew older and wearier.

An aide, who had been following the commander at a respectful distance, suddenly intruded himself in the old man's reverie.

"Sir, a message for you."

The commander scowled at the young officer. "I gave orders that I was not to be disturbed."

The officer, slim and stiff in his black-and-silver uniform, replied, "Your chief of staff has passed the message on to you, sir. It's from Dr. Leoh, of Carinae University. Personal and urgent, sir."

The old man grumbled to himself, but nodded. The aide placed a small crystalline sphere on the grass before him. The air above the sphere started to vibrate and glow.

"Sir Harold Spencer here," the commander said.

The bubbling air seemed to draw in on itself and take solid form. Dr. Leoh sat at a desk chair and looked up at the standing commander.

"Harold, it's a pleasure to see you once again."

Spencer's stern eyes softened, and his beefy face broke into a well-creased smile. "Albert, you ancient scoundrel. What do you mean by interrupting my first visit home in fifteen years?"

"It won't be a long interruption," Leoh said.

"You told my chief of staff that it was urgent," Sir Harold groused.

"It is. But it's not the sort of problem that requires much action on your part. Yet. You are familiar with recent political developments on the Kerak Worlds?"

Spencer snorted. "I know that a barbarian named Kanus has established himself as a dictator. He's a troublemaker. I've been talking to the Commonwealth Council about the advisability of quashing him before he causes grief, but you know the

Council . . . first wait until the flames have sprung up, then thrash about and demand that the Star Watch do something!"

Leoh grinned. "You're as irascible as ever."

"My personality is not the subject of this rather expensive discussion. What about Kanus? And what are you doing, getting yourself involved in politics? About to change your profession again?"

"No, not at all," Leoh answered, laughing. Then, more seriously, "It seems as though Kanus has discovered some method of using the dueling machines to achieve political advantages over his neighbors."

"What?"

Leoh explained the circumstances of Odal's duels with the Acquatainian prime minister and Szarno industrialist.

"Dulaq is completely incapacitated and the other poor fellow is dead?" Spencer's face darkened into a thundercloud. "You were right to call me. This is a situation that could easily become intolerable."

"I agree," Leoh said. "But evidently Kanus has not broken any laws or interstellar agreements. All that meets the eye is a disturbing pair of accidents, both of them accruing to Kanus' benefit."

"Do *you* believe that they were accidents?"

"Certainly not. The dueling machine cannot cause physical or mental harm . . . unless someone has tampered with it in some way."

"That is my thought, too." Spencer was silent for a moment, weighing the matter in his mind. "Very well. The Star Watch cannot act officially, but there is nothing to prevent me from dispatching an officer to the Acquataine Cluster, on detached duty, to serve as liaison between us."

"Good. I think that will be the most effective method of handling the situation, at present."

"It will be done," Sir Harold pronounced. His aide made a mental note of it.

"Thank you very much," Leoh said. "Now, go back to enjoying your vacation."

"Vacation? This is no vacation," Spencer rumbled. "I happen to be celebrating my birthday."

"So? Well, congratulations. I try not to remember mine," Leoh said.

"Then you must be older than I," Spencer replied, allowing only the faintest hint of a smile to appear.

"I suppose it's possible."

"But not very likely, eh?"

They laughed together and said good-by. The Star Watch commander tramped through the hills until sunset, enjoying the sight of the grasslands and distant purple mountains he had known in his childhood. As dusk closed in, he told his aide he was ready to leave.

The aide pressed a stud on his belt and a two-place aircar skimmed silently from the far side of the hills and hovered beside them. Spencer climbed in laboriously while the aide remained discreetly at his side. While the commander settled his bulk into his seat the aide hurried around the car and hopped into his place. The car glided off toward Spencer's personal planetship, waiting for him at a nearby field.

"Don't forget to assign an officer to Dr. Leoh," the commander muttered to his aide. Then he turned and watched the unmatchable beauty of an Earthly sunset.

The aide did not forget the assignment. That night, as Sir Harold's ship spiraled out to a rendezvous with a starship, the aide dictated the necessary order into an autodispatcher that immediately beamed it to the Star Watch's nearest communications center, on Mars.

The order was scanned and routed automatically and finally beamed to the Star Watch unit commandant in charge of the area closest to the Acquataine Cluster, on the sixth planet circling the star Perseus Alpha. Here again, the order was processed automatically and routed through the local headquarters to the personnel files. The automated files selected three microcard dossiers that matched the requirements of the order.

The three microcards and the order itself appeared simultaneously on the desktop viewer of the Star Watch personnel officer. He looked at the order, then read the dossiers. He flicked a button that gave him an updated status report on each of the three men in question. One was due for leave after an extensive period of duty. The second was the son of a personal friend of the local commandant. The third had just arrived a few weeks ago, fresh from the Star Watch Academy on Mars.

The personnel officer selected the third man, routed his dossier and Sir Harold's order back into the automatic processing system, and returned to the film of primitive dancing girls he had been watching before this matter of decision had arrived at his desk.

VI

The space station orbiting around Acquatainia—the capital planet of the Acquataine Cluster—served simultaneously as a transfer point from starships to planet-ships, a tourist resort, meteorological station, communications center, scientific laboratory, astronomical observatory, medical haven for allergy and cardiac patients, and military base. It was, in reality, a good-sized city with its own markets, its own local government, and its own way of life.

Dr. Leoh had just stepped off the debarking ramp of the starship from Szarno. The trip there had been pointless and fruitless. But he had gone anyway, in the slim hope that he might find something wrong with the dueling machine that had been used to murder a man.

A shudder went through him as he edged along the automated customs scanners and paper-checkers. What kind of people could these men of Kerak be? To actually kill a human being in cold blood; to plot and plan the death of a fellow man. Worse than barbaric. Savage.

He felt tired as he left customs and took the slideway to the planetary shuttle ships. Halfway there, he decided to check at the communications desk for messages. That Star Watch officer that Sir Harold had promised him a week ago should have arrived by now.

The communications desk consisted of a small booth that contained the output printer of a communications computer and an attractive young dark-haired girl. Automation or not, Leoh thought smilingly, there were certain human values that transcended mere efficiency.

A lanky, thin-faced youth was half-leaning on the booth's counter, trying to talk to the girl. He had curly blond hair and crystal blue eyes; his clothes consisted of an ill-fitting pair of slacks and tunic. A small traveler's kit rested on the floor at his feet.

"So, I was sort of, well thinking . . . maybe somebody might, uh, show me around . . . a little," he was stammering to the girl. "I've never been, uh, here . . ."

"It's the most beautiful planet in the galaxy," the girl was saying. "Its cities are the finest."

"Yes . . . well, I was sort of thinking . . . that is, I know we just uh, met a few minutes ago . . . but, well, maybe . . . if you have a free day or so coming up . . . maybe we could, uh, sort of—"

She smiled coolly. "I have two days off at the end of the week, but I'll be staying here at the station. There's so much to see and do here, I very seldom leave."

"Oh—"

"You're making a mistake," Leoh interjected dogmatically. "If you have such a beautiful planet for your homeworld, why in the name of the gods of intellect don't you go down there and enjoy it? I'll wager you haven't been out in the natural beauty and fine cities you spoke of since you started working here on the station."

"Why, you're right," she said, surprised.

"You see? You youngsters are all alike. You never think further than the ends of your noses. You should return to the planet, young lady, and see the sunshine again. Why don't you visit the university at the capital city? Plenty of open space and greenery, lots of sunshine and available young men!"

Leoh was grinning broadly, and the girl smiled back at him. "Perhaps I will," she said.

"Ask for me when you get to the university. I'm Dr. Leoh. I'll see to it that you're introduced to some of the girls and gentlemen of your own age."

"Why . . . thank you, doctor. I'll do it this week end."

"Good. Now then, any messages for me? Anyone aboard the station looking for me?"

The girl turned and tapped a few keys on the computer's control console. A row of lights flicked briefly across the console's face. She turned back to Leoh:

"No, sir, I'm sorry. No messages and no one has asked for you."

"Hm-m-m. That's strange. Well, thank you . . . and I'll expect to see you at the end of this week."

The girl smiled a farewell. Leoh started to walk away from

the booth, back toward the slideway. The young man took a step toward him, stumbled on his own traveling kit, and staggered across the floor for a half-dozen steps before regaining his balance. Leoh turned and saw that the youth's face bore a somewhat ridiculous expression of mixed indecision and curiosity.

"Can I help you?" Leoh asked, stopping at the edge of the moving slideway.

"How . . . how did you do that, sir?"

"Do what?"

"Get that girl to agree to visit the university. I've been talking to her for half an hour, and, well, she wouldn't even look straight at me."

Leoh broke into a chuckle. "Well, young man, to begin with, you were much too flustered. It made you appear overanxious. On the other hand, I am at an age where I can be strictly platonic. She was on guard against you, but she knows she has very little to fear from me."

"I see . . . I think."

"Well," Leoh said, gesturing toward the slideway, "I suppose this is where we go our separate ways,"

"Oh, no, sir. I'm going with you. That is, I mean, you *are* Dr. Leoh, aren't you?"

"Yes, I am. And you must be—" Leoh hesitated. *Can this be a Star Watch officer?* he wondered.

The youth stiffened to attention and for an absurd flash of a second, Leoh thought he was going to salute. "I am Junior Lieutenant Hector, sir; on special detached duty from the cruiser SW4-J188, home base Perseus Alpha VI."

"I see," Leoh replied. "Um-m-m . . . is Hector your first name or your last?"

"Both, sir."

I should have guessed, Leoh told himself. Aloud, he said, "Well, lieutenant, we'd better get to the shuttle before it leaves without us."

They took to the slideway. Half a second later, Hector jumped off and dashed back to the communications deck for his traveling kit. He hurried back to Leoh, bumping into seven bewildered citizens of various descriptions and nearly breaking both his legs when he tripped as he ran back onto the moving slideway. He went down on his face, sprawled across two lanes moving at different speeds, and needed the assistance of several persons before he was again on his feet and standing beside Leoh.

"I . . . I'm sorry to cause all that, uh, commotion, sir."

"That's all right. You weren't hurt, were you?"

"Uh, no . . . I don't think so. Just embarrassed."

Leoh said nothing. They rode the slideway in silence through the busy station and out to the enclosed berths where the planetary shuttles were docked. They boarded one of the ships and found a pair of seats.

"Just how long have you been with the Star Watch, lieutenant?"

"Six weeks, sir. Three weeks aboard a starship bringing me out ot Perseus Alpha VI, a week at the planetary base there, and two weeks aboard the cruiser SW4-J188. That is, it's been six weeks since I received my commission. I've been at the Academy . . . the Star Watch Academy on Mars . . . for four years."

"You got through the Academy in four years?"

"That's the regulation time, sir."

"Yes, I know."

The ship eased out of its berth. There was a moment of free-fall, then the drive engine came on and the grayfield equilibrated.

"Tell me, lieutenant, how did you get picked for this assignment?"

"I wish I knew, sir." Hector said, his lean face twisting into a puzzled frown. "I was working out a program for the navigation officer . . . aboard the cruiser. I'm pretty good at that . . . I can work out computer programs in my head, mostly. Mathematics was my best subject at the Academy—"

"Interesting."

"Yes, well, anyway, I was working out this program when the captain himself came on deck and started shaking my hand and telling me that I was being sent on special duty on Acquatainia by direct orders of the Commander-in-Chief. He seemed very happy . . . the captain, that is."

"He was no doubt pleased to see you get such an unusual assignment," Leoh said tactfully.

"I'm not so sure," Hector said truthfully. "I think he regarded me as some sort of a problem, sir. He had me on a different duty-berth practically every day I was on board the ship."

"Well now," Leoh changed the subject, "what do you know about psychonics?"

"About what, sir?"

"Eh . . . electroencephalography?"

Hector looked blank.

"Psychology, perhaps?" Leoh suggested, hopefully. "Physiology? Computer molectronics?"

"I'm pretty good at mathematics!"

"Yes, I know. Did you, by any chance, receive any training in diplomatic affairs?"

"At the Star Watch Academy? No, sir."

Leoh ran a hand through his thinning hair. "Then why did the Star Watch select you for this job? I must confess, lieutenant, that I can't understand the workings of a military organization."

Hector shook his head ruefully, "Neither do I, sir."

VII

The next week was an enervatingly slow one for Leoh, evenly divided between tedious checking of each component of the dueling machine, and shameless ruses to keep Hector as far away from the machine as possible.

The Star Watchman certainly wanted to help, and he actually *was* little short of brilliant in doing intricate mathematics completely in his head. But he was, Leoh found, a clumsy, chattering, whistling, scatter-brained, inexperienced bundle of noise and nerves. It was impossible to do constructive work with him nearby.

Perhaps you're judging him too harshly, Leoh warned himself. *You just might be letting your frustrations with the dueling machine get the better of your sense of balance.*

The professor was sitting in the office that the Acquatainians had given him in one end of the former lecture hall that held the dueling machine. Leoh could see its impassive metal hulk through the open office door.

The room he was sitting in had been one of a suite of offices used by the permanent staff of the machine. But they had moved out of the building completely, in deference to Leoh, and the Acquatainian government had turned the other cubbyhole offices into sleeping rooms for the professor and the Star Watchman, and an autokitchen. A combination cook-valet-handyman appeared twice each day—morning and evening—to handle any special chores that the cleaning machines and autokitchen might miss.

Leoh slouched back in his desk chair and cast a weary eye on the stack of papers that recorded the latest performances of the machine. Earlier that day he had taken the electroencephalographic records of clinical cases of catatonia and run them through the machine's input unit. The machine immediately rejected them, refused to process them through the amplification units and association circuits.

In other words, the machine had recognized the EEG traces as something harmful to a human being.

Then how did it happen to Dulaq? Leoh asked himself for the thousandth time. It couldn't have been the machine's fault; it must have been something in Odal's mind that simply overpowered Dulaq's.

"Overpowered?" That's a terribly unscientific term, Leoh argued against himself.

Before he could carry the debate any further, he heard the main door of the big chamber slide open and then bang shut, and Hector's off-key whistle shrilled and echoed through the high-vaulted room.

Leoh sighed and put his self-contained argument off to the back of his mind. Trying to think logically near Hector was a hopeless prospect.

"Are you in, doctor?" Hector's voice rang out.

"In here."

Hector ducked in through the doorway and plopped his rangy frame on the office's couch.

"Everything going well, sir?"

Leoh shrugged. "Not very well, I'm afraid. I can't find anything wrong with the dueling machine. I can't even *force* it to malfunction."

"Well, that's good, isn't it?" Hector chirped happily.

"In a sense," Leoh admitted, feeing slightly nettled at the youth's boundless, pointless optimisn. "But, you see, it means that Kanus' people can do things with the machine that I can't."

Hector frowned, considering the problem. "Hm-m-m . . . yes, I guess that's right, too, isn't it?"

"Did you see the girl back to her ship safely?" Leoh asked.

"Yes, sir," Hector replied, bobbing his head vigorously. "She's on her way back to the communications booth at the space station. She said to tell you she enjoyed her visit very much."

"Good. It was, eh, very good of you to escort her about the campus. It kept her out of my hair . . . what's left of it, that is."

Hector grinned. "Oh, I liked showing her around, and all that—And, well, it sort of kept *me* out of your hair, too, didn't it?"

Leoh's eyebrows shot up in surprise.

Hector laughed. "Doctor, I may be clumsy, and I'm certainly no scientist . . . but I'm not completely brainless."

"I'm sorry if I gave you that impression—"

"Oh no . . . don't be sorry. I didn't mean that to sound so . . . well, the way it sounded . . . that is, I know I'm just in your way—" He started to get up.

Leoh waved him back to the couch. "Relax, my boy, relax. You know I've been sitting here all afternoon wondering what to do next. Somehow, just now, I came to a conclusion."

"Yes?"

"I'm going to leave the Acquataine Cluster and return to Carinae."

"What? But you can't! I mean—"

"Why not? I'm not accomplishing anything here. Whatever it is that this Odal and Kanus have been doing, it's basically a political problem, and not a scientific one. The professional staff of the machine here will catch up to their tricks sooner or later."

"But sir, if you can't find the answer, how can they?"

"Frankly, I don't know. But, as I said, this is a political problem more than a scientific one. I'm tired and frustrated and I'm feeling my years. I want to return to Carinae and spend the next few months considering beautifully abstract problems about instantaneous transportation devices. Let Massan and the Star Watch worry about Kanus."

"Oh! That's what I came to tell you. Massan has been challenged to a duel by Odal!"

"What?"

"This afternoon, Odal went to the Council building. Picked an argument with Massan right in the main corridor and challenged him."

"Massan accepted?" Leoh asked.

Hector nodded.

Leoh leaned across his desk and reached for the phone unit. It took a few minutes and a few levels of secretaries and assistants, but finally Massan's dark, bearded face appeared on the screen above the desk.

"You have accepted Odal's challenge?" Leoh asked, without preliminaries.

"We meet next week," Massan replied gravely.

"You should have refused."

"On what pretext?"

"No pretext. A flat refusal, based on the certainty that Odal or someone else from Kerak is tampering with the dueling machine."

Massan shook his head sadly. "My dear learned sir, you still do not comprehend the political situation. The Government of the Acquaine Cluster is much closer to dissolution than I dare to admit openly. The coalition of star groups that Dulaq had constructed to keep the Kerak Worlds neutralized has broken apart completely. This morning, Kanus announced that he would annex Szarno. This afternoon, Odal challenges me."

"I think I see—"

"Of course. The Acquatainian Government is paralyzed now, until the outcome of the duel is known. We cannot effectively intervene in the Szarno crisis until we know who will be heading the Government next week. And, frankly, more than a few members of our Council are now openly favoring Kanus and urging that we establish friendly relations with him before it is too late."

"But, that's all the more reason for refusing the duel," Leoh insisted.

"And be accused of cowardice in my own Council meetings?" Massan smiled grimly. "In politics, my dear sir, the *appearance* of a man means much more than his substance. As a coward, I could soon be out of office. But, perhaps, as the winner of a duel against the invincible Odal . . . or even as a martyr . . . I may accomplish something useful."

Leoh said nothing.

Massan continued, "I put off the duel for a week, hoping that in that time you might discover Odal's secret. I dare not postpone the duel any longer; as it is the political situation may collapse about our heads at any moment."

"I'll take this machine apart and rebuild it again, molecule by molecule," Leoh promised.

As Massan's image faded from the screen, Leoh turned to Hector. "We have one week to save his life."

"And avert a war, maybe," Hector added.

"Yes." Leoh leaned back in his chair and stared off into infinity.

Hector shuffled his feet, rubbed his nose, whistled a few bars of off-key tunes, and finally blurted, "How can you take apart the dueling machine?"

"Hm-m-m?" Leoh snapped out of his reverie.

"How can you take apart the dueling machine?" Hector repeated. "Looks like a big job to do in a week."

"Yes, it is. But, my boy, perhaps we . . . the two of us . . . can do it."

Hector scratched his head. "Well, uh, sir . . . I'm not very . . . that is, my mechanical aptitude scores at the Academy—"

Leoh smiled at him. "No need for mechanical aptitude, my boy. You were trained to fight, weren't you? We can do the job mentally."

VIII

It was the strangest week of their lives.

Leoh's plan was straightforward: to test the dueling machine, push it to the limits of its performance, by actually operating it—by fighting duels.

They started off easily enough, tentatively probing and flexing their mental muscles. Leoh had used the dueling machines himself many times in the past, but only in tests of the machines' routine performance. Never in actual combat against another human being. To Hector, of course, the machine was a totally new and different experience.

The Acquatainian staff plunged into the project without question, providing Leoh with invaluable help in monitoring and analyzing the duels.

At first, Leoh and Hector did nothing more than play hide-and-seek, with one of them picking an environment and the other trying to find his opponent in it. They wandered through jungles and cities, over glaciers and interplanetary voids, seeking each other—without ever leaving the booths of the dueling machine.

Then, when Leoh was satisfied that the machine could reproduce and amplify thought patterns with strict fidelity, they began to fight light duels. They fenced with blunted foils—Hector won, of course, because of his much faster reflexes. Then they tried other weapons—pistols, sonic beams, grenades—but always with the precaution of imagining themselves to be wearing protective equipment. Strangely, even though Hector was trained in the use of these weapons, Leoh won almost all the bouts. He was neither faster nor more accurate, when they were target-shooting. But when the two of them faced each other, somehow Leoh almost always won.

The machine projects more than thoughts, Leoh told himself. *It projects personality.*

They worked in the dueling machine day and night now, enclosed in the booths for twelve or more hours a day, driving themselves and the machine's regular staff to near-exhaustion. When they gulped their meals, between duels, they were physically ragged and sharp-tempered. They usually fell asleep in Leoh's office, while discussing the results of the day's work.

The duels grew slowly more serious. Leoh was pushing the machine to its limits now, carefully extending the rigors of each bout. And yet, even though he knew exactly what and how much he intended to do in each fight, it often took a conscious effort of will to remind himself that the battles he was fighting were actually imaginary.

As the duels became more dangerous, and the artificially-amplified hallucinations began to end in blood and death, Leoh found himself winning more and more frequently. With one part of his mind he was driving to analyze the cause of his consistent success. But another part of him was beginning to really enjoy his prowess.

The strain was telling on Hector. The physical exertion of constant work and practically no relief was considerable in itself. But the emotional effects of being "hurt" and "killed" repeatedly were infinitely worse.

"Perhaps we should stop for a while," Leoh suggested after the fourth day of tests.

"No. I'm all right."

Leoh looked at him. Hector's face was haggard, his eyes bleary.

"You've had enough," Leoh said quietly.

"Please don't make me stop," Hector begged. "I . . . I can't stop now. Please give me a chance to do better. I'm improving . . . I lasted twice as long in this afternoon's two duels as I did in the ones this morning. Please, don't end it now . . . not while I'm completely lost—"

Leoh stared at him. "You want to go on?"

"Yes, sir."

"And if I say no?"

Hector hesitated. Leoh sensed he was struggling with himself. "If you say no," he answered dully, "then it will be no. I can't argue against you any more."

Leoh was silent for a long moment. Finally he opened a desk drawer and took a small bottle from it. "Here, take a sleep capsule. When you wake up we'll try again."

It was dawn when they began again. Leoh entered the dueling machine determined to allow Hector to win. He gave the youthful Star Watchman his choice of weapon and environment. Hector picked one-man scoutships, in planetary orbits. Their weapons were conventional force beams.

But despite his own conscious desire, Leoh found himself winning! The ships spiraled about an unnamed planet, their paths intersecting at least once in every orbit. The problem was to estimate your opponent's orbital position, and then program your own ship so that you arrived at that position either behind or to one side of him. Then you could train your guns on him before he could turn on you.

The problem should have been an easy one for Hector, with his knack for intuitive mental calculation. But Leoh scored the first hit—Hector had piloted his ship into an excellent firing position, but his shot went wide; Leoh maneuvered around clumsily, but managed to register an inconsequential hit on the side of Hector's ship.

In the next three passes, Leoh scored two more hits. Hector's ship was badly damaged now. In return, the Star Watchman had landed one glancing shot on Leoh's ship.

They came around again, and once more Leoh had outguessed

his younger opponent. He trained his guns on Hector's ship, then hesitated with his hand poised above the firing button.

Don't kill him again, he warned himself. *His mind can't accept another defeat.*

But Leoh's hand, almost of its own will reached the button and touched it lightly. Another gram of pressure and the guns would fire.

In that instant's hesitation, Hector pulled his crippled ship around and aimed at Leoh. The Watchman fired a searing blast that jarred Leoh's ship from end to end. Leoh's hand slammed down on the firing button, whether he intended to do it or not, he did not know.

Leoh's shot raked Hector's ship but did not stop it. The two vehicles were hurling directly at each other. Leoh tried desperately to avert a collision, but Hector bored in grimly, matching Leoh's maneuvers with his own.

The two ships smashed together and exploded.

Abruptly, Leoh found himself in the cramped booth of the dueling machine, his body cold and damp with perspiration, his hands trembling.

He squeezed out of the booth and took a deep breath. Warm sunlight was streaming into the high-vaulted room. The white walls glared brilliantly. Through the tall windows he could see trees and people and clouds in the sky.

Hector walked up to him. For the first time in several days, the Watchman was smiling. Not much, but smiling. "Well, we broke even on that one."

Leoh smiled back, somewhat shakily, "Yes. It was . . . quite an experience. I've never died before."

Hector fidgeted. "It's, uh, not so bad, I guess—it does sort of, well, shatter you, you know."

"Yes. I can see that now."

"Another duel?" Hector asked, nodding his head toward the machine.

"Let's get out of this place for a few hours. Are you hungry?"

"Starved."

They fought seven more duels over the next day and a half. Hector won three of them. It was late afternoon when Leoh called a halt to the tests.

"We can still get in another one or two," the Watchman pointed out.

"No need," Leoh said. "I have all the data I require. To-morrow Massan meets Odal, unless we can put a stop to it. We have much to do before tomorrow morning."

Hector sagged into the couch. "Just as well. I think I've aged seven years in the past seven days."

"No, my boy," Leoh said gently. "You haven't aged. You've matured."

IX

It was deep twilight when the groundcar slid to a halt on its cushion of compressed air before the Kerak Embassy.

"I still think it's a mistake to go in there," Hector said. "I mean, you could've called him on the tri-di just as well, couldn't you?"

Leoh shook his head. "Never give an agency of any government the opportunity to say 'hold the line a moment' and then huddle together to consider what to do with you. Nineteen times out of twenty, they'll end by passing your request up to the next higher echelon, and you'll be left waiting for weeks."

"Still," Hector insisted, "you're simply stepping into enemy territory. It's a chance you shouldn't take."

"They wouldn't dare touch us."

Hector did not reply, but he looked unconvinced.

"Look," Leoh said, "there are only two men alive who can shed light on this matter. One of them is Dulaq, and his mind is closed to us for an indefinite time. Odal is the only other one who knows what happened."

Hector shook his head skeptically. Leoh shrugged, and opened the door of the groundcar. Hector had no choice but to get out and follow him as he walked up the pathway to the main entrance of the Embassy. The building stood gaunt and gray in the dusk, surrounded by a precisely-clipped hedge. The entrance was flanked by a pair of tall evergreen trees.

Leoh and Hector were met just inside the entrance by a female receptionist. She looked just a trifle disheveled—as though she had been rushed to the desk at a moment's notice. They asked for Odal, were ushered into a sitting room, and within a few minutes—to Hector's surprise—were informed by the girl that Major Odal would be with them shortly.

"You see," Leoh pointed out jovially, "when you come in person they haven't as much of a chance to consider how to get rid of you."

Hector glanced around the windowless room and contemplated the thick, solidly closed door. "There's a lot of scurrying going on on the other side of that door, I'll bet. I mean . . . they may be considering how to, uh, get rid of us . . . permanently."

Leoh shook his head, smiling wryly. "Undoubtedly the approach closest to their hearts—but highly improbable in the present situation. They have been making most efficient and effective use of the dueling machine to gain their ends."

Odal picked this moment to open the door.

"Dr. Leoh . . . Lt. Hector . . . you asked to see me?"

"Thank you, Major Odal; I hope you will be able to help me," said Leoh. "You are the only man living who may be able to give us some clues to the failure of the Dueling Machine."

Odal's answering smile reminded Leoh of the best efforts of the robot-puppet designers to make a machine that smiled like a man. "I am afraid I can be of no assistance, Dr. Leoh. My experiences in the machine are . . . private."

"Perhaps you don't fully understand the situation," Leoh said. "In the past week, we have tested the dueling machine here on Acquatainia exhaustively. We have learned that its performance can be greatly influenced by a man's personality, and by training. You have fought many duels in the machines. Your background of experience, both as a professional soldier and in the machines, gives you a decided advantage over your opponents.

"However, even with all this considered, I am convinced that you cannot kill a man in the machine—under normal circumstances. We have demonstrated that fact in our tests. An unsabotaged machine cannot cause actual physical harm.

"Yet you have already killed one man and incapacitated another. Where will it stop?"

Odal's face remained calm, except for the faintest glitter of fire deep in his eyes. His voice was quiet, but had the edge of a well-honed blade in it: "I cannot be blamed for my background and experience. And I have not tampered with your machines."

The door to the room opened, and a short, thick-set, bullet-headed man entered. He was dressed in a dark street suit, so that it was impossible to guess his station at the Embassy.

"Would the gentlemen care for refreshments?" he asked in a low-pitched voice.

"No, thank you," Leoh said.

"Some Kerak wine, perhaps?"

"Well—"

"I don't, uh, think we'd better, sir," Hector said. "Thanks all the same."

The man shrugged and sat on a chair next to the door.

Odal turned back to Leoh. "Sir, I have my duty. Massan and I duel tomorrow. There is no possibility of postponing it."

"Very well," Leoh said. "Will you at least allow us to place some special instrumentation into the booth with you, so that we can monitor the duel more fully? We can do the same with Massan. I know that duels are normally private and you would be within your legal rights to refuse the request. But, morally—"

The smile returned to Odal's face. "You wish to monitor my thoughts. To record them and see how I perform during the duel. Interesting. Very interesting—"

The man at the door rose and said, "If you have no desire for refreshments, gentlemen—"

Odal turned to him. "Thank you for your attention."

Their eyes met and locked for an instant. The man gave a barely perceptible shake of his head, then left.

Odal returned his attention to Leoh. "I am sorry, professor, but I cannot allow you to monitor my thoughts during the duel."

"But—"

"I regret having to refuse you. But, as you yourself pointed out, there is no legal requirement for such a course of action. I must refuse. I hope you understand."

Leoh rose from the couch, and Hector popped up beside him. "I'm afraid I do understand. And I, too, regret your decision."

Odal escorted them out to their car. They drove away, and the Kerak major walked slowly back into the Embassy building. He was met in the hallway by the darksuited man who had sat in on the conversation.

"I could have let them monitor my thoughts and still crush Massan," Odal said. "It would have been a good joke on them."

The man grunted. "I have just spoken to the Chancellor on the tri-di, and obtained permission to make a slight adjustment in our plans."

"An adjustment, Minister Kor?"

"After your duel tomorrow, your next opponent will be the eminent Dr. Leoh," Kor said.

X

The mists swirled deep and impenetrable about Fernd Massan. He stared blindly through the useless viewplate in his helmet, then reached up slowly and carefully to place the infrared detector before his eyes.

I never realized an hallucination could seem so real, Massan thought.

Since the challenge by Odal, he realized, the actual world had seemed quite unreal. For a week, he had gone through the motions of life, but felt as though he were standing aside, a spectator mind watching its own body from a distance. The gathering of his friends and associates last night, the night before the duel— that silent, funereal group of people—it had all seemed completely unreal to him.

But now, in this manufactured dream, he seemed vibrantly alive. Every sensation was solid, stimulating. He could feel his pulse throbbing through him. Somewhere out in those mists, he knew, was Odal. And the thought of coming to grips with the assassin filled him with a strange satisfaction.

Massan had spent a good many years serving his government on the rich but inhospitable high-gravity planets of the Acquataine Cluster. This was the environment he had chosen: crushing gravity; killing pressure; atmosphere of ammonia and hydrogen, laced with free radicals of sulphur and other valuable but deadly chemicals; oceans of liquid methane and ammonia; "solid ground" consisting of quickly crumbling, eroding ice; howling superpowerful winds that could pick up a mountain of ice and hurl it halfway around the planet; darkness; danger; death.

He was encased in a one-man protective outfit that was half armored suit, half vehicle. There was an internal grayfield to keep him comfortable in 3.7 gees, but still the suit was cumbersome, and a man could move only very slowly in it, even with the aid of servomotors.

The weapon he had chosen was simplicity itself—a handsized capsule of oxygen. But in a hydyrogen/ammonia atmosphere, oxygen could be a deadly explosive. Massan carried several of these "bombs"; so did Odal. *But the trick,* Massan thought to himself, *is to know how to throw them under these conditions; the proper range, the proper trajectory. Not an easy thing to learn, without years of experience.*

The terms of the duel were simple: Massan and Odal were situated on a rough-topped iceberg that was being swirled along one of the methane/ammonia ocean's vicious currents. The ice was rapidly crumbling; the duel would end when the iceberg was completely broken up.

Massan edged along the ragged terrain. His suit's grippers and rollers automatically adjusted to the roughness of the topography. He concentrated his attention on the infrared detector that hung before his viewplate.

A chunk of ice the size of a man's head sailed through the murky atmosphere in a steep glide peculiar to heavy gravity and banged into the shoulder of Massan's suit. The force was enough to rock him slightly off-balance before the servos readjusted. Massan withdrew his arm from the sleeve and felt the inside of the shoulder seam. *Dented, but not penetrated.* A leak would have been disastrous, possibly fatal. Then he remembered: *Of course—I cannot be killed except by direct action of my antagonist. That is one of the rules of the game.*

Still, he carefully fingered the dented shoulder to make certain it was not leaking. The dueling machine and its rules seemed so very remote and unsubstantial, compared to this freezing, howling inferno.

He diligently set about combing the iceberg, determined to find Odal and kill him before their floating island disintegrated. He thoroughly explored every projection, every crevice, every slope, working his way slowly from one end of the 'berg toward the other. Back and forth, cross and re-cross, with the infrared sensors scanning three hundred-sixty degrees around him.

It was time-consuming. Even with the suit's servomotors and propulsion units, motion across the ice, against the buffeting wind, was a cumbersome business. But Massan continued to work his way across the iceberg, fighting down a gnawing, growing fear that Odal was not there at all.

And then he caught just the barest flicker of a shadow on his detector. Something, or someone, had darted behind a jutting rise of the ice, off by the edge of the iceberg.

• • •

Slowly and carefully, Massan made his way toward the base of the rise. He picked one of the oxy-bombs from his belt and held it in his right-hand claw.

Massan edged around the base of the ice cliff, and stood on a narrow ledge between the cliff and the churning sea. He saw no one. He extended the detector's range to maximum, and worked the scanners up the sheer face of the cliff toward the top.

There he was! The shadowy outline of a man etched itself on the detector screen. And at the same time, Massan heard a muffled roar, then a rumbling toward him. *That devil set off a bomb at the top of the cliff!*

Massan tried to back out of the way, but it was too late. The first chunk of ice bounced harmlessly off his helmet, but the others knocked him off-balance so repeatedly that the servos had no chance to recover. He staggered blindly for a few moments, as more and more ice cascaded down on him, and then toppled off the ledge into the boiling sea.

Relax! he ordered himself. *Do not panic! The suit will float you. The servos will keep you right-side-up. You cannot be killed accidentally; Odal must perform the* coup-de-grace *himself.*

Then he remembered the emergency rocket units in the back of the suit. If he could orient himself properly, a touch of a control stud on his belt set him off, and he would be boosted back onto the iceberg. He turned slightly inside the suit and tried to judge the iceberg's distance through the infrared detector. It was difficult, especially since he was bobbing madly in the churning currents.

Finally he decided to fire the rocket and make final adjustments of distance and landing site after he was safely out of the sea.

But he could not move his hand.

He tried, but his entire right arm was locked fast. He could not budge it an inch. And the same for the left. Something, or someone, was clamping his arms tight. He could not even pull them out of their sleeves.

Massan thrashed about, trying to shake off whatever it was. No use.

Then his detector screen was lifted slowly from the viewplate.

He felt something vibrating on his helmet. The oxygen tubes! They were being disconnected.

He screamed and tried to fight free. No use. With a hiss, the oxygen tubes pulled free of his helmet. Massan could feel the blood pounding through his veins as he fought desperately to free himself.

Now he was being pushed down into the sea. He screamed again and tried to wrench his body away. The frothing sea filled his viewplate. He was under. He as being held under. And now . . . now the viewplate itself was being loosened.

No! Don't! The scalding cold methane ammonia sea seeped in through the opening viewplate.

"It's only a dream!" Massan shouted to himself. "Only a dream. A dream. A—"

XI

Dr. Leoh stared at the dinner table without really seeing it. Coming to this restaurant had been Hector's idea. Three hours earlier, Massan had been removed from the dueling machine—dead.

Leoh sat stolidly, hands in lap, his mind racing in many different directions at once. Hector was off at the phone, getting the latest information from the meditechs. Odal had expressed his regret perfunctorily, and then left for the Kerak Embassy, under a heavy escort of his own plainclothes guards. The government of the Acquataine Cluster was quite literally falling apart, with no man willing to assume responsibility . . . and thereby expose himself. One hour after the duel, 'Kanus' troops had landed on all the major planets of the Szarno Confederacy; the annexation was *fait accompli*.

And what have I done since I arrived on Acquatainia? Leoh demanded of himself. *Nothing. Absolutely nothing. I have sat back like a doddering old professor and played academic games with the machine, while younger, more vigorous men have USED the machine to suit their purposes.*

Used the machine. There was a fragment of an idea in that phrase. Something nebulous, that must be approached carefully or it will fade away. Used the machine . . . used it . . . Leoh toyed with the phrase for a few moments, then gave it up with a sigh of resignation. *Lord, I'm too tired even to think.*

Leoh focused his attention on his surroundings and scanned the busy dining room. It was a beautiful place, really; decorated with crystal and genuine woods and fabric draperies. Not a synthetic in sight. The waiters and cooks and busboys were humans, not the autocookers and servers that most restaurants employed. Leoh suddenly felt touched at Hector's attempt to restore his spirits—even if it *was* being done at Star Watch expense.

He saw the young Watchman approaching the table, coming back from the phone. Hector bumped two waiters and stumbled over a chair before reaching the relative safety of his own seat.

"What's the verdict?" Leoh asked.

Hector's lean face was bleak. "Couldn't revive him. Cerebral hemorrhage, the meditechs said—induced by shock."

"Shock?"

"That's what they said. Something must've, uh, overloaded his nervous system . . . I guess."

Leoh shook his head. "I just don't understand any of this. I might as well admit it. I'm no closer to an answer now than I was when I arrived here. Perhaps I should have retired years ago, before the dueling machine was invented."

"Nonsense."

"No, I mean it." Leoh said. "This is the first real intellectual puzzle I've had to contend with in years. Tinkering with machinery . . . that's easy. You know what you want, all you need is to make the machinery perform properly. But this . . . I'm afraid I'm too old to handle a real problem like this."

Hector scratched his nose thoughtfully, then answered. "If you can't handle the problem, sir, then we're going to have a war on our hands in a matter of weeks. I mean, Kanus won't be satisfied with swallowing the Szarno group . . . the Acquataine Cluster is next . . . and he'll have to fight to get it."

"Then the Star Watch can step in," Leoh said, resignedly.

"Maybe . . . but it'll take time to mobilize the Star Watch . . . Kanus can move a lot faster than we can. Sure, we could throw in a task force . . . a token group, that is. But Kanus' gang will chew them up pretty quick. I . . . I'm no politician, sir, but I think I can see what will happen. Kerak will gobble up the Acquataine Cluster . . . a Star Watch task force will be wiped out in the battle . . . and we'll end up with Kerak at war with the Terran Commonwealth. And it'll be a real war . . . a big one.''

Leoh began to answer, then stopped. HIs eyes were fixed on the far entrance of the dining room. Suddenly every murmur in the busy room stopped dead. Waiters stood still between tables. Eating, drinking, conversation hung suspended.

Hector turned in his chair and saw at the far entrance the slim, stiff, blue-uniformed figure of Odal.

The moment of silence passed. Everyone turned to his own business and avoided looking at the Kerak major. Odal, with a faint smile on his thin face, made his way slowly to the table where Hector and Leoh were sitting.

They rose to greet him and exchanged perfunctory salutations. Odal pulled up a chair and sat with them.

"I assume that you've been looking for me," Leoh said. "What do you wish to say?"

Before Odal could answer the waiter assigned to the table walked up, took a position where his back would be to the Kerak major, and asked firmly, "You dinner is ready, gentlemen. Shall I serve it now?"

Leoh hesitated a moment, then asked Odal, "Will you join us?"

"I'm afraid not."

"Serve it now," Hector said. "The major will be leaving shortly."

Again the tight grin broke across Odal's face. The waiter bowed and left.

"I have been thinking about our conversation of last night," Odal said to Leoh.

"Yes?"

"You accused me of cheating in my duels."

Leoh's eyebrows arched. "I said someone was cheating, yes—"

"An accusation is an accusation."

Leoh said nothing.

"Do you withdraw your words, or do you still accuse me of deliberate murder? I am willing to allow you to apologize and leave Acquatainia in peace."

Hector cleared his throat noisily. "This is no place to have an argument . . . besides, here comes our dinner."

Odal ignored the Watchman. "You heard me, professor. Will

you leave? Or do you accuse me of murdering Massan this afternoon?''

"I—"

Hector banged his fist on the table and jerked up out of his chair—just as the waiter arrived with a large tray of food. There was a loud crash. A tureen of soup, two bowls of salad, glasses, assorted rolls, vegetables, cheeses and other delicacies cascaded over Odal.

The Kerak major leaped to his feet, swearing violently in his native tongue. He sputtered back into basic Terran: "You clumsy, stupid oaf! You maggot-brained misbegotten peasant-faced—"

Hector calmly picked a salad leaf from the sleeve of his tunic. Odal abruptly stopped his tirade.

"I am clumsy," Hector said, grinning. "As for being stupid, and the rest of it, I resent that. I am highly insulted."

A flash of recognition lighted Odal's eyes. "I see. Of course. My quarrel here is not with you. I apologize." He turned back to Leoh, who was also standing now.

"Not good enough," Hector said. "I don't, uh, like the . . . tone of your apology."

Leoh raised a hand, as if to silence the younger man.

"I apologized; that is sufficient," Odal warned.

Hector took a step toward Odal. "I guess I could insult your glorious leader, or something like that . . . but this seems more direct." He took the water pitcher from the table and poured it calmly and carefully over Odal's head.

A wave of laughter swept the room. Odal went white. "You are determined to die." He wiped the dripping water from his eyes. "I will meet you before the week is out. And you have saved no one." He turned on his heel and stalked out.

"Do you realize what you've done?" Leoh asked, aghast.

Hector shrugged. "He was going to challenge you—"

"He will still challenge me, after you're dead."

"Un-m-m, yes, well, amybe so, I guess you're right— Well, anyway, we've gained a little more time."

"Four days." Leoh shook his head. "Four days to the end of the week. All right, come on, we have work to do."

Hector was grinning broadly as they left the restaurant. He began to whistle.

"What are you so happy about?" Leoh grumbled.

"About you, sir. When we came in here, you were, uh, well
. . . almost beaten. Now you're right back in the game again."

Leoh glanced at the Star Watchman. "In your own odd way,
Hector, you're quite a boy . . . I think."

XII

Their groundcar glided from the parking building to the restaurant's entrance ramp, at the radio call of the doorman. Within
minutes, Hector and Leoh were cruising through the city, in the
deepening shadows of night.

"There's only one man," Leoh said, "who has faced Odal
and lived through it."

"Dulaq," Hector agreed. "But . . . for all the information
the medical people have been able to get from him, he might as
well be, uh, dead."

"He's still completely withdrawn?"

Hector nodded. "The medicos think that . . . well, maybe in
a few months, with drugs and psychotherapy and all that . . .
they might be able to bring him back."

"It won't be soon enough. We've only got four days."

"I know."

Leoh was silent for several minutes. Then: "Who is Dulaq's
closest living relative? Does he have a wife?"

"I think his wife is, uh, dead. Has a daughter though. Pretty
girl. Bumped into her in the hospital once or twice—"

Leoh smiled in the darkness. Hector's term, "bumped into,"
was probably completely literal.

"Why are you asking about Dulaq's next-of-kin?"

"Because," Leoh replied, "I think there might be a way to
make Dulaq tell us what happened during his duel. But it is a
very dangerous way. Perhaps a fatal way."

"Oh."

They leaped into silence again. Finally he blurted, "Come
on, my boy, let's find the daughter and talk to her."

"Tonight?"

"Now."

She certainly is a pretty girl, Leoh thought as he explained very
carefully to Geri Dulaq what he proposed to do. She sat quietly

and politely in the spacious living room of the Dulaq residence. The glittering chandelier cast touches of fire on her chestnut hair. Her slim body was slightly rigid with tension, her hands were clasped in her lap. Her face—which looked as though it could be very expressive—was completely serious now.

"And that is the sum of it." Leoh concluded. "I believe that it will be possible to use the dueling machine itself to examine your father's thoughts and determine exactly what took place during his duel against Major Odal."

She asked softly. "But you are afraid that the shock might be repeated, and this could be fatal to my father?"

Leoh nodded wordlessly.

"Then I am very sorry, sir, but I must say no." Firmly.

"I understand your feelings," Leoh replied, "but I hope you realize that unless we can stop Odal and Kanus immediately, we may very well be faced with war."

She nodded. "I know. But you must remember that we are speaking of my father, of his very life. Kanus will have his war in any event, no matter what I do."

"Perhaps," Leoh admitted, "Perhaps."

Hector and Leoh drove back to the University campus and their quarters in the dueling machine chamber. Neither of them slept well that night.

The next morning, after an unenthusiastic breakfast, they found themselves standing in the antiseptic-white chamber, before the looming, impersonal intricacy of the machine.

"Would you like to practice with it?" Leoh asked.

Hector shook his head. "Maybe later."

The phone chimed in Leoh's office. They both went in. Geri Dulaq's faced showed on the tri-di screen.

"I have just heard the news, I did not know that Lieutenant Hector has challenged Odal." Her face was a mixture of concern and reluctance.

"He challenged Odal," Leoh answered, "to prevent the assassin from challenging me."

"Oh—You are a very brave man, Lieutenant."

Hector's face went through various contortions and slowly turned a definite red, but no words issued from his mouth.

"Have you reconsidered your decision?" Leoh asked.

The girl closed her eyes briefly, then said flatly "I am afraid

I cannot change my decision. My father's safety is my first responsibility. I am sorry."

They exchanged a few meaningless trivialities—with Hector
still thoroughly tongue-tied—and ended the conversation on a
polite but strained note.

Leoh rubbed his thumb across the phone switch for amoment,
then turned to Hector. "My boy, I think it would be a good idea
for you to go straight to the hospital and check on Dulaq's condition."

"But . . . why—"

"Don't argue, son. This could be vitally important."

Hector shrugged and left the office. Leoh sat down at his desk
and drummed his fingers on the top of it. Then he burst out of
the office and began pacing the big chamber. Finally, even that
was too confining. He left the building and started stalking
through the campus. He walked past a dozen buildings, turned
and strode as far as the decorative fence that marked the end of
the main campus, ignoring students and faculty alike.

Campuses are all alike, he muttered to himself, *on every human planet, for all the centuries there have been universities.
There must be some fundamental reason for it.*

Leoh was halfway back to the dueling machine facility when
he spotted Hector walking dazedly toward the same building.
For once, the Watchman was not whistling. Leoh cut across
some lawn and pulled up beside the youth.

"Well?" he asked.

Hector shook his head, as if to clear away an inner fog. "How
did you know she'd be at the hospital?"

"The wisdom of age. What happened?"

"She kissed me. Right there in the hallway of the—"

"Spare me the geography," Leoh cut in. "What did she say?"

"I bumped into her in the hallway. We, uh, started talking
. . . sort of. She seemed, well . . . worried about me. She got
upset. Emotional. You know? I guess I looked pretty forlorn and
frightened. I am . . . I guess. When you get right down to it, I
mean."

"You aroused her maternal instinct."

"I . . . I don't think it was that . . . exactly. Well, anyway,
she said that if I was willing to risk my life to save yours, she
couldn't protect her father any more. Said she was doing it out

of selfishness, really, since he's her only living relative. I don't believe she meant that, but she said it anyway.''

They had reached the building by now. Leoh grabbed Hector's arm and steered him clear of a collision with the half-open door.

"She's agreed to let us put Dulaq in the dueling machine?"

"Sort of."

"Eh?"

"The medical staff doesn't want him to be moved from the hospital . . . especially not back to here. She agrees with them.''

Leoh snorted. "All right. In fact, so much the better. I'd rather not have the Kerak people see us bring Dulaq to the dueling machine. So instead, we shall smuggle the dueling machine to Dulaq!''

XIII

They plunged to work immediately. Leoh preferred not to inform the regular staff of the dueling machine about their plan, so he and Hector had to work through the night and most of the next morning. Hector barely understood what he was doing, but with Leoh's supervision, he managed to dismantle part of the dueling machine's central network, insert a few additional black boxes that the professor had conjured up from the spare parts bins in the basement, and then reconstruct the machine so that it looked exactly the same as before they had started.

In between his frequent trips to oversee Hector's work, Leoh had jury-rigged a rather bulky headset and a handsized override control circuit.

The late morning sun was streaming through the tall windows when Leoh finally explained it all to Hector.

"A simple matter of technological improvisation," he told the bewildered Watchman. "You have installed a short-range transceiver into the machine, and this headset is a portable transceiver for Dulaq. Now he can sit in his hospital bed and still be 'in' the dueling machine.''

Only the three most trusted members of the hospital staff were taken into Leoh's confidence, and they were hardly enthusiastic about Leoh's plan.

"It is a waste of time," said the chief psychophysician, shaking his white-maned head vigorously. "You cannot expect a patient who has shown no positive response to drugs and therapy to respond to your machine.''

Leoh argued, Geri Dulaq coaxed. Finally the doctors agreed. With only two days remaining before Hector's duel with Odal, they began to probe Dulaq's mind. Geri remained by her father's bedside while the three doctors fitted the cumbersome transceiver to Dulaq's head and attached the electrodes for the automatic hospital equipment that monitored his physical condition. Hector and Leoh remained at the dueling machine, communicating with the hospital by phone.

Leoh made a final check of the controls and circuitry, then put in the last call to the tense little group in Dulaq's room. All was ready.

He walked out to the machine, with Hector beside him. Their footsteps echoed hollowly in the sepulchral chamber. Leoh stopped at the nearer booth.

''Now remember,'' he said, carefully, ''I will be holding the emergency control unit in my hand. It will stop the duel the instant I set it off. However, if something should go wrong, you must be prepared to act quickly. Keep a close watch on my physical condition; I've shown you which instruments to check on the control board—''

''Yes, sir.''

Leoh nodded and took a deep breath. ''Very well then.''

He stepped into the booth and sat down. The emergency control unit rested on a shelf at his side; he took it in his hand. He leaned back and waited for the semihypnotic effect to take hold. Dulaq's choice of this very city and the stat-wand were known. But beyond that, everything was locked and sealed in Dulaq's subconscious mind. Could the machine reach into that subconscious, probe past the lock and seal of catatonia, and stimulate Dulaq's mind into repeating the duel?

Slowly, lullingly, the dueling machine's imaginary yet very real mists enveloped Leoh. When the mists cleared, he was standing on the upper pedestrian level of the main commerical street of the city. For a long moment, everything was still.

Have I made contact? Whose eyes am I seeing with, my own or Dulaq's?

And then he sensed it—an amused, somewhat astonished marveling at the reality of the illusion. Dulaq's thoughts!

Make your mind a blank. Leoh told himself. *Watch. Listen. Be passive.*

He became a spectator, seeing and hearing the world through Dulaq's eyes and ears as the Acquatainian Prime Minister advanced through his nightmarish ordeal. He felt the confusion, frustration, apprehension and growing terror as, time and again, Odal appeared in the crowd—only to melt into someone else and escape.

The first part of the duel ended, and Leoh was suddenly buffeted by a jumble of thoughts and impressions. Then the thoughts slowly cleared and steadied.

Leoh saw an immense and totally barren plain. Not a tree, not a blade of grass; nothing but bare, rocky ground stretching in all directions to the horizon and a disturbingly harsh yellow sky. At his feet was the weapon Odal had chosen. A primitive club.

He shared Dulaq's sense of dread as he picked up the club and hefted it. Off on the horizon he could see a tall, lithe figure holding a similar club walking toward him

Despite himself, Leoh could feel his own excitement. He had broken through the shock-created armor that Dulaq's mind had erected! Dulaq was reliving the part of the duel that had caused the shock.

Reluctantly, he advanced to meet Odal. But as they drew closer together, the one figure of his opponent seemed to split apart. Now there were two, four, six of them. Six Odals, six mirror images, all armed with massive, evil clubs, advancing steadily on him.

Six tall, lean, blond assassins, with six cold smiles on their intent faces.

Horrified, completely panicked, he scrambled away, trying to evade the six opponents with the half-dozen clubs raised and poised to strike.

Their young legs and lungs easily outdistanced him. A smash in his back sent him sprawling. One of them kicked his weapon away.

They stood over him for a malevolent, gloating second. Then six strong arms flashed down, again and again, mercilessly. Pain and blood, screaming agony, punctured by the awful thudding of solid clubs hitting fragile flesh and bone, over and over again, endlessly.

Everything went blank.

•　•　•

Leoh opened his eyes and saw Hector bending over him.

"Are you all right, sir?"

"I . . . I think so."

"The controls all hit the danger mark at once. You were . . . well, sir, you were screaming."

"I don't doubt it," Leoh said.

They walked, with Leoh leaning on Hector's arm, from the dueling machine booth to the office.

"That was . . . an experience," Leoh said, easing himself onto the couch.

"What happened? What did Odal do? What made Dulaq go into shock? How does—"

The old man silenced Hector with a wave of his hand. "One question at a time, please."

Leoh leaned back on the deep couch and told Hector every detail of both parts of the duel.

"Six Odals," Hector muttered soberly, leaning back against the doorframe, "Six against one."

"That's what he did. It's easy to see how a man expecting a polite, formal duel can be completely shattered by the viciousness of such an attack. And the machine amplifies every impulse, every sensation."

"But how does he do it?" Hector asked, his voice suddenly loud and demanding.

"I've been asking myself the same question. We've checked over the dueling machine time and again. There is no possible way for Odal to plug in five helpers . . . unless—"

"Unless?"

Leoh hesitated, seemingly debating with himself. Finally he nodded his head sharply, and answered, "Unless Odal is telepath."

"Telepath? But—"

"I know it sounds farfetched. But there have been well-documented cases of telepathy for centuries throughout the Commonwealth."

Hector frowned. "Sure, everybody's heard about it . . . natural telepaths . . . but they're so unpredictable . . . I don't see how—"

Leoh leaned forward on the couch and clasped his hands in front of his chin. "The Terran races have never developed telepathy, or any of the extrasensory talents. They never had to, not with tri-di communication and superlight starships. But perhaps the Kerak people are different—''

Hector shook his head. ''If they had, uh, telepathic abilities, they would be using them everywhere. Don't you think?''

''Probably so. But only Odal has shown such an ability, and only . . . *of course*!''

''What?''

''Odal has shown telepathic ability only in the dueling machine.''

''As far as we know.''

''Certainly. But look, suppose he's a natural telepath . . . the same as a Terran. He has an erratic, difficult-to-control talent. Then he gets into a dueling machine. The machine amplifies his thoughts. And it also amplifies his talent!''

''Ohhh.''

''You see . . . outside the machine, he's no better than any wandering fortuneteller. But the dueling machine gives his natural abilities the amplification and reproducibility that they could never have unaided.''

Hector nodded.

''So it's a fairly straightforward matter for him to have five associates in the Kerak Embassy sit in on the duel, so to speak. Possibly they are natural telepaths also, but they needn't be.''

''They just, uh, pool their minds with his, hm-m-m? Six men show up in the duel . . . pretty nasty.'' Hector dropped into the desk chair.

''So what do we do now?''

''Now?'' Leoh blinked at his young friend. ''Why . . . I suppose the first thing we should do is call the hospital and see how Dulaq came through.''

Leoh put the call through. Geri Dulaq's face appeared on the screen.

''How's your father?'' Hector blurted.

''The duel was too much for him,'' she said blankly. ''He is dead.''

''No,'' Leoh groaned.

''I . . . I'm sorry,'' Hector said. ''I'll be right down there. Stay where you are.''

The young Star Watchman dashed out of the office as Geri broke the phone connection. Leoh stared at the blank screen for a few moments, then leaned far back in the couch and closed his eyes. He was suddenly exhausted, physically and emotionally. He fell asleep, and dreamed of men dead and dying.

Hector's nerve-shattering whistling woke him up. It was full night outside.

"What are you so happy about?" Leoh groused as Hector popped into the office.

"Happy? Me?"

"You were whistling."

Hector shrugged. "I always whistle, sir. Doesn't mean I'm happy."

"All right, " Leoh said, rubbing his eyes. "How did the girl take her father's death?"

"Pretty hard. Cried a lot."

Leoh looked at the younger man. "Does she blame . . . me?"

"You? Why, no, sir. Why should she? Odal . . . Kanus . . . the Kerak Worlds, But not you."

The old professor sighed, relieved. "Very well. Now then, we have much work to do, and little more than a day in which to finish it."

"What do you want me to do?" Hector asked.

"Phone the Star Watch Commander—"

"My commanding officer, all the way back at Alpha Perseus VI? That's a hundred light-years from here."

"No, no, no." Leoh shook his head. "The Commander-in-Chief, Sir Harold Spencer. At Star Watch Central Headquarters. That's several hundred parsecs from here. But get through to him as quickly as possible."

With a low whistle of astonishment, Hector began punching buttons on the phone switch.

XIV

The morning of the duel arrived, and precisely at the agreed-upon hour, Odal and a small retinue of Kerak representatives stepped through the double doors of the dueling machine changer.

Hector and Leoh were already there, waiting. With them stood another man, dressed in the black-and-silver of the Star Watch. He was a stocky, broad-faced veteran with iron-gray hair and hard, unsmiling eyes.

The two little groups of men knotted together in the center of the room, before the machine's control board. The white-uniformed staff meditechs emerged from a far doorway and stood off to one side.

Odal went through the formality of shaking hands with Hector. The Kerak major nodded toward the other Watchman. "Your replacement?"; he asked mischievously.

The chief meditech stepped between them. "Since you are the challenged party, Major Odal, you have the first choice of weapon and environment. Are there any instructions or comments necessary before the duel begins?"

"I think not," Odal replied. "The situation will be self-explanatory. I assume, of course, that Star Watchmen are trained to be warriors and not merely technicians. The situation I have chosen is one in which many warriors have won glory."

Hector said nothing.

"I intend," Leoh said firmly, "to assist the staff in monitoring this duel. Your aides may, of course, sit at the control board with me."

Odal nodded.

"If you are ready to begin, gentlemen," the chief meditech said.

Hector and Odal went to their booths. Leoh sat at the control console, and one of the Kerak men sat down next to him.

Hector felt every nerve and muscle tense as he sat in the booth, despite his efforts to relax. Slowly the tension eased, and he began to feel slightly drowsy. The booth seemed to melt away . . .

He was standing on a grassy meadow. Off in the distance were wooded hills. A cool breeze was hustling puffy white clouds across a calm blue sky.

Hector heard a snuffling noise behind him, and wheeled around. He blinked, then stared.

It had four legs, and was evidently a beast of burden. At least, it carried a saddle on its back. Piled atop the saddle was a conglomeration of what looked to Hector—at first glance—like a pile of junk. He went over to the animal and examined it carefully. The "junk" turned out to be a long spear, various pieces of armor, a helmet, sword, shield, battle-ax and dagger.

The situation I have chosen is one in which many warriors

have won glory. Hector puzzled over the assortment of weapons. They came straight out of Kerak's Dark Ages. No doubt Odal had been practicing with them for months, even years. He may not need five helpers.

Warily, Hector put on the armor. The breastplate seemed too big, and he was somehow unable to tighten the greaves on his shins properly. The helmet fit over his head like an ancient oil can, flattening his ears and nose and forcing him to squint to see through the narrow eye-slit.

Finally, he buckled on the sword and found attachments on the saddle for the other weapons. The shield was almost too heavy to lift, and he barely struggled into the saddle with all the weight he was carrying.

And then he just sat. He began to feel a little ridiculous. *Suppose it rains?* He wondered. But of course it wouldn't.

After an interminable wait, Odal appeared, on a powerful trotting charger. His armor was black as space, and so was his animal. *Naturally*, Hector thought.

Odal saluted gravely with his great spear from across the meadow. Hector returned the salute, nearly dropping his spear in the process.

Then, Odal lowered his spear and aimed it—so it seemed to Hector—directly at the Watchman's ribs. He pricked his mount into a canter. Hector did the same, and his steed jogged into a bumping, jolting gallop. The two warriors hurtled toward each other from opposite ends of the meadow.

And suddenly there were six black figures roaring down on Hector!

The Watchmen's stomach wrenched within him. Automatically he tried to turn his mount aside. But the beast had no intention of going anywhere except straight ahead. The Kerak warriors bore in, six abreast, with six spears aimed menacingly.

Abruptly, Hector heard the pounding of other hoofbeats right beside him. Through a corner of his helmet-slit he glimpsed at least two other warriors charging with him into Odal's crew.

Leoh's gamble had worked. The transceiver that had allowed Dulaq to make contact with the dueling machine from his hospital bed was now allowing five Star Watch officers to join Hector, even though they were physically sitting in a starship orbiting high above the planet.

The odds were even now. The five additional Watchmen were

the roughest, hardiest, most aggressive man-to-man fighters that
the Star Watch could provide on a one-day notice.

Twelve powerful chargers met head on, and twelve strong men
smashed together with an ear-splitting CLANG! Shattered spears
showered splinters everywhere. Men and animals went down.

Hector was rocked back in his saddle, but somehow managed
to avoid falling off.

On the other hand, he could not really regain his balance,
either. Dust and weapons filled the air. A sword hissed near his
head and rattled off his shield.

With a supreme effort, Hector pulled out his own sword and
thrashed at the nearest rider. It turned out to be a fellow Watchman, but the stoke bounced harmlessly off his helmet.

It was so confusing. The wheeling, snorting animals. Clouds
of dust. Screaming, raging men. A black-armored rider charged
into Hector, waving a battle-ax over his head. He chopped savagely, and the Watchman's shield split apart. Another frighten-
ing swing—Hector tried to duck and slid completely out of the
saddle, thumping painfully on the ground, while the ax cleaved
the air where his head had been a split-second earlier.

Somehow his helmet had been turned around. Hector tried to
decide whether to thrash around blindly or lay down his sword
and straighten out the helmet. The problem was solved for him
by the *crang!* of a sword against the back of his helmet. The
blow flipped him into a somersault, but also knocked the helmet
completely off his head.

Hector climbed painfully to his feet, his head spinning. It took
him several moments to realize that the battle had stopped. The
dust drifted away, and he saw that all the Kerak fighters were
down—except one. The black-armored warrior took off his helmet and tossed it aside. It was Odal. Or was it? They all looked
alike. *What difference does it make?* Hector wondered. *Odal's
mind is the dominant one.*

Odal stood, legs braced apart, sword in hand, and looked
uncertainly at the other Star Watchmen. Three of them were
afoot and two still mounted. The Kerak assassin seemed as confused as Hector felt. The shock of facing equal numbers had
sapped much of his confidence.

Cautiously, he advanced toward Hector, holding his sword out before him. The other Watchmen stood aside while Hector slowly backpedaled, stumbling slightly on the uneven ground.

Odal feinted and cut at Hector's arm. The Watchman barely parried in time. Another feint, at the head, and a slash in the chest; Hector missed the parry but his armor saved him. Grimly, Odal kept advancing. Feint, feint, crack! and Hector's sword went flying from his hand.

For the barest instant everyone froze. Then Hector leaped desperately straight at Odal, caught him completely by surprise, and wrestled him to the ground. The Watchman pulled the sword from his opponent's hand and tossed it away. But with his free hand, Odal clouted Hector on the side of the head and knocked him on his back. Both men scrambled up and ran for the nearest weapons.

Odal picked up a wicked-looking double-bladed ax. One of the mounted Star Watchmen handed Hector a huge broadsword. He gripped it with both hands, but still staggered off-balance as he swung it up over his shoulder.

Holding the broadsword aloft, Hector charged toward Odal, who stood dogged, short-breathed, sweat-streaked, waiting for him. The broadsword was quite heavy, even for a two-handed grip. And Hector did not notice his own battered helmet laying on the gound between them.

Odal, for his part, had Hector's charge and swing timed perfectly in his own mind. He would duck under the swing and bury his ax in the Watchman's chest. Then he would face the others. Probably with their leader gone, the duel would automatically end. But, of course, Hector would not really be dead; the best Odal could hope for now was to win the duel.

Hector charged directly into Odal's plan, but the Watchman's timing was much poorer than anticipated. Just as he began the downswing of a mighty broadsword stroke, he stumbled on the helmet. Odal started to duck, then saw that the Watchman was diving facefirst into the ground, legs flailing, and that heavy broadsword was cleaving through the air with a will of its own.

Odal pulled back in confusion, only to have the wildswinging broadsword strike him just above the wrist. The ax dropped out of his hand, and Odal involuntarily grasped the wounded forearm with his left hand. Blood seeped through his fingers.

He shook his head in bitter resignation, turned his back on the prostrate Hector, and began walking away.

Slowly, the scene faded, and Hector found himself sitting in the booth of the dueling machine.

XV

The door opened and Leoh squeezed into the booth. "You're all right?"

Hector blinked and refocused his eyes on reality. "Think so—"

"Everything went well? The Watchmen got through to you?"

"Good thing they did. I was nearly killed anyway."

"But you survived."

"So far."

Across the room, Odal stood massaging his forehead while Kor demanded: "How could they possibly have discovered the secret? Where was the leak?"

"That is not important now," Odal said quietly. "The primary fact is that they have not only discovered our secret, but they have found a way of duplicating it."

"The sanctimonious hypocrites," Kor snarled, "accusing us of cheating, and then they do the same thing."

"Regardless of the moral values of our mutual behavior," Odal said dryly, "it is evident that there is no longer any use in calling on telepathically-guided assistants. I shall face the Watchman alone during the second half of the duel."

"Can you trust them to do the same?"

"Yes. They easily defeated my aides a few minutes ago, then stood aside and allowed the two of us to fight by ourselves."

"And you failed to defeat him?"

Odal frowned. "I was wounded by a fluke. He is a very . . . unusual opponent. I cannot decide whether he is actually as clumsy as he appears to be, or whether he is shamming and trying to make me overconfident. Either way, it is impossible to predict his behavior. Perhaps he is also telepathic."

Kor's gray eyes became flat and emotionless. "You know, of course, how the Chancellor will react if you fail to kill this Watchman. Not merely defeat him. He must be killed. The aura of invincibility must be maintained."

"I will do my best," Odal said.

"He must be killed."

The chime that marked the end of the rest period sounded. Odal and Hector returned to their booths. Now it was Hector's choice of environment and weapons.

Odal found himself enveloped in darkness. Only gradually did his eyes adjust. He saw that he was in a spacesuit. For several minutes he stood motionless, peering into the darkness, every sense alert, every muscle coiled for immediate action.

Dimly he could see the outlines of jagged rock against a background of innumerable stars. Experimentally, he lifted one foot. It stuck, tackily, to the surface. *Magnetized boots*, Odal thought. *This must be a planetoid.*

As his eyes grew accustomed to the dimness, he saw that he was right. It was a small planetoid, perhaps a mile or so in diameter. Almost zero gravity. Airless.

Odal swiveled his head inside the fishbowl helmet of his spacesuit and saw, over his right shoulder, the figure of Hector—lank and ungainly even with the bulky suit. For a moment, Odal puzzled over the weapon to be used. Then Hector bent down, picked up a loose stone, straightened, and tossed it softly past Odal's head. The Kerak major watched it sail by and off into the darkness of space, never to return to the tiny planetoid.

A warning shot, Odal thought to himself. He wondered how much damage one could do with a nearly weightless stone, then remembered that inertial mass was unaffected by gravitational fields, or lack of them. A fifty-pound rock might be easier to lift, but it would be just as hard to throw—and it would do just as much damage when it hit, regardless of its gravitational "weight."

Odal crouched down and selected a stone the size of his fist. He rose carefully, sighted Hector standing a hundred yards or so away, and threw as hard as he could.

The effort of his throw sent him tumbling off-balance, and the stone was far off-target. He fell to his hands and knees, bounced lightly and skidded to a stop. Immediately he drew his feet up under his body and planted the magnetized soles of his boots firmly on the iron-rich surface.

But before he could stand again, a small stone *pinged* slightly off his oxygen tank. The Star Watchman had his range already!

Odal scrambled to the nearest upjutting rocks and crouched behind them. *Lucky I didn't rip open the spacesuit*, he told himself. Three stones, evidently hurled in salvo, ticked off the top of the rocks he was hunched behind. One of the stones bounced into his fishbowl helmet.

Odal scooped up a handful of pebbles and tossed them in Hector's general direction. That should make him duck. Perhaps he'll stumble and crack his helmet open.

Then he grinned to himself. That's it. Kor wants him dead, and that is the way to do it. Pin him under a big rock, then bury him alive under more rocks. A few at a time, stretched out nicely. While his oxygen supply gives out. That should put enough stress on his nervous system to hospitalize him, at least. Then he can be assassinated by more conventional means. Perhaps he will even be as obliging as Massan, and have a fatal stroke.

A large rock. One that is light enough to lift and throw, yet also big enough to pin him for a few moments. Once he is down, it will be easy enough to bury him under more rocks.

The Kerak major spotted a boulder of the proper size, a few yards away. He backed toward it, throwing small stones in Hector's direction to keep the Watchman busy. In return, a barrage of stones began striking all around him. Several hit him, one hard enough to knock him slightly off-balance.

Slowly, patiently, Odal reached his chosen weapon—an oblong boulder, about the size of a small chair. He crouched behind it and tugged at it experimentally. It moved slightly. Another stone *zinged* off his arm, hard enough to hurt. Odal could see Hector clearly now, standing atop a small rise, calmly firing pellets at him. He smiled as he coiled, catlike, and tensed himself. He gripped the boulder with his arms and hands.

Then in one vicious uncoiling motion he snatched it up, whirled around, and hurled it at Hector. The violence of his action sent him tottering awkwardly as he released the boulder. He fell to the ground, but kept his eyes fixed on the boulder as it tumbled end over end, directly at the Watchman.

For an eternally-long instant Hector stood motionless, seemingly entranced. Then he leaped sideways, floating dreamlike in the low gravity, as the stone hurtled inexorably past him.

Odal pounded his fist on the ground in fury. He started up, only to have a good-sized stone slam against his shoulder, and knock him flat again. He looked up in time to see Hector fire another. The stone puffed into the ground inches from Odal's helmet. The Kerak major flattened himself. Several more stones clattered on his helmet and oxygen tank. Then silence.

Odal looked up and saw Hector squatting down, reaching for more ammunition. The Kerak warrior stood up quickly, his own fists filled with throwing stones. He cocked his arm to throw—

But something made him turn to look behind him. The boulder looked before his eyes, still tumbling slowly, as it had when he had thrown it. It was too close and too big to avoid. It smashed into Odal, picked him off his feet and slammed him against the upjutting rocks a few yards away.

Even before he started to feel the pain in his midsection, Odal began trying to push the boulder off. But he could not get enough leverage. Then he saw the Star Watchman's form standing over him.

"I didn't really think you'd fall for it," Odal heard Hector's voice in his earphones. "I mean . . . didn't you realize that the boulder was too massive to escape completely after it had missed me? You could've calculated its orbit . . . you just threw it into a, uh, six-minute orbit around the planetoid. It *had* to come back to perigee . . . right where you were standing when you threw it, you know.'

Odal said nothing, but strained every cell in his painwracked body to get free of the boulder. Hector reached over his shoulder and began fumbling with the valves that were pressed against the rocks.

"Sorry to do this . . . but I'm not, uh, killing you, at least . . . just defeating you. Let's see . . . one of these is the oxygen valve, and the other, I think, is the emergency rocket pack . . . now, which is which?" Odal felt the Watchman's hands searching for the proper valve. "I should've dreamed up suits without the rocket pack . . . confuses things . . . there, that's it."

Hector's hand tightened on a valve and turned it sharply. The rocket roared to life and Odal was hurtled free of the boulder, shot uncontrolled completely off the planetoid. Hector was bowled over by the blast and rolled halfway around the tiny chink of rock and metal.

Odal tried to reach around to throttle down the rocket, but the pain in his body was too great. He was slipping into unconsciousness. He fought against it. He knew he must return to the planetoid and somehow kill the opponent. But gradually the pain overpowered him. His eyes were closing, closing—

And quite abruptly, he found himself sitting in the booth of the dueling machine. It took a moment for him to realize that he was back in the real world. Then his thoughts cleared. He had failed to kill Hector.

And at the door of the booth stood Kor, his face a grim mask of anger.

XVI

The office was that of the new prime minister of the Acquataine Cluster. It had been loaned to Leoh for his conversation with Sir Harold Spencer. For the moment, it seemed like a great double room: half of it was dark, warm woods, rich draperies, floor-to-ceiling bookcases. The other half, from the tri-di screen onward, was the austere, metallic utility of a starship compartment.

Spencer was saying, "So this hired assassin, after killing four men and nearly wrecking a government, has returned to his native worlds."

Leoh nodded. "He returned under guard. I suppose he is in disgrace, or perhaps even under arrest."

"Servants of a dictator never know when they will be the ones who are served—on a platter." Spencer chuckled. "And the Watchman who assisted you, this Junior Lieutenant Hector, what of him?"

"He's not here just now. The Dulaq girl had him in tow, somewhere. Evidently it's the first time he's been a hero—"

Spencer shifted his weight in his chair. "I have long prided myself on the conviction that any Star Watch officer can handle almost any kind of emergency anywhere in the galaxy. From your description of the past few weeks, I was beginning to have my doubts. However, Junior Lieutenant Hector seems to have won the day . . . almost in spite of himself."

"Don't underestimate him," Leoh said, smiling. "He turned out to be an extremely valuable man. I think he will make a fine officer."

Spencer grunted an affirmative.

"Well," Leoh said, "That's the complete story, to date. I believe that Odal is finished. But the Kerak Worlds have made good their annexation of the Szarno Confederacy, and the Acquataine Cluster is still very wobbly, politically. We haven't heard the last of Kanus—not by a long shot.''

Spencer lifted a shaggy eyebrow. ''Neither,'' he rumbled, ''has *he* heard the last from *us*.''

KILLER

by Karl Edward Wagner and David Drake

Rain was again trickling from the grayness overhead, and the damp reek of the animals hung on the misty droplets. A hyena wailed miserably, longing for the dry plains it would never see again. Lycon listened without pity. Let it bark its lungs out here in Brundisium, or die later in the amphitheater at Rome. He remembered the Ethiopian girl who had lived three days after a hyena had dragged her down. It would have been far better had the beast not been driven off before it had finished disemboweling her.

'Wish the rain would stop,' complained Vonones. The Armenian dealer's plump face was gloomy. 'A lot of these are going to die otherwise, and I'll be caught in the middle. In Rome they only pay me for live delivery, but I have to pay you regardless.'

Which is why I'm a hunter and you're a dealer, mused Lycon without overmuch sympathy. 'Well, it won't ruin you,' he reassured the dealer. 'Not at the prices you pay. You can replace the entire lot for a fifth of what they'll bring in Rome.'

The tiger whose angry cough had been cutting through the general racket thundered forth a full-throated roar. Lycon and the Armenian heard his heavy body crash against the bars of his cage. Vonones nodded toward the sound. 'There's one I can't replace.'

'What? The tiger?' Lycon's tone was surprised. 'I'll grant you he's the biggest I've ever captured, but I brought you back two others with him that are near as fine.'

'No, not the tiger,' Vonones grunted. 'I mean the thing he's snarling at. Come on, I'll show you. Maybe you'll know what it is.'

The Armenian put on his broad felt hat and snuggled up his cloak against the drizzle. Lycon followed, not really noticing the rain that beaded his close-cut black hair. He had been a mercenary scout in his youth, before he had sickened of butchering Rome's barbarian enemies and turned instead to hunting animals for her arenas. A score of years in the field left him calloused to the weather as to all else.

For the beasts themselves he felt only professional concern, no more. As they passed a wooden cage with a dozen maned baboons, he scowled and halted the dealer. 'I'd get them into a metal cage, if I were you. They'll chew through the lashings of that one, and you'll have hell catching them again.'

'Overflow,' the Armenian told him vexedly. 'Had to put them there. It's all I've got with your load and this mixed shipment from the Danube getting here at the same time. Don't worry, they move tomorrow when we sort things out for the haul to Rome.'

Beasts snarled and lunged as the men threaded through the maze of cages. Most of the animals were smeared with filth, their coats worn and dull where they showed through the muck. A leopard pining in a corner of its cage reminded Lycon of a cat he once had force fed—a magnificent mottled brown beast that he had purchased half-starved from a village of gap-toothed savages in the uplands of India. He needed four of his men to pin it down while he rammed chunks of raw flesh down its throat with a stake. That lithe killer was now the empress' plaything, and her slavegirls fed it tit-bits from silver plates.

'There it is,' Vonones announced, pointing to a squat cage of iron.

The creature stared back, ignoring the furious efforts of the tiger alongside to slash his paw through the space that separated their cages.

'You've got some sort of wild man!' Lycon blurted with first glance.

'Nonsense!' Vonones snorted. 'Look at the tiny scales, those talons! There may be a race somewhere with blue skin, but this thing's no more human than a mandrill.'

After that first startled impression, Lycon had to agree. The thing seemed far less human than any mandrill, which it somewhat resembled. Probably those hairless limbs made him think it was a man—that and the aura of evil intelligence its stare conveyed. But the collector had never seen anything like it, not in twenty years of professional hunting along the fringes of the known world. Lycon could not even decide whether it was mammal or reptile. It was scaled and exuded an acrid reptilian scent, but its movements and poise were feline. Apelike, it could walk erect and would be about man height if it straightened. Its face was cat-like, low browed and without much jaw. A flat, earless skull thrust forward on a snaky neck. Its eyes looked straight forward with human intensity, but were slit-pupiled with a swift nictating membrane.

'This came from the Danube?' Lycon questioned wonderingly.

'It did. There was a big lot of bears and aurochs that one of my agents jobbed from the Sarmatians. This thing came with them, and all I know about it is what Dama wrote me with the shipment—that a band of Sarmatians saw a hilltop explode and found this when they went to see what had happened.'

'A hilltop exploded!'

The dealer shrugged. 'That's all he wrote.'

Lycon studied the cage in silence.

'Why did you weld the cage shut instead of putting a chain and lock on it?'

'That's the way it came,' Vonones explained. 'I'll have to knock the door loose and put a proper lock on it before sending it off tomorrow, or those idiots at Rome will wreck a good cage trying to smash it open and never a denarius for the damage. I guess the Sarmatians just didn't have a lock—I'm a little surprised they even had an iron cage.'

Lycon frowned, uncomfortable at the way the beast stared back at him. 'It's its eyes,' he reflected. 'I wish all my crew looked that bright.'

'Or mine,' Vonones agreed readily. 'Oh, I make no doubt it's more cunning than any brute should be, but it's scarcely human.

Can you see those claws? They're curled back in its palms now, but—there!'

The creature made a stretching motion, opening its paws—or were they hands? Bones stood out, slim but like the limbs themselves hinting at adamantine hardness. The crystalline claws extended maybe a couple of inches, so sharp that their points seemed to fade into the air. No wild creature should have claws so delicately kept. The beast's lips twitched a needle-toothed grin.

'Hermes!' Lycon muttered, looking away. There was a glint of bloodlust in those eyes, something beyond natural savagery. Lycon remembered a centurion whose eyes held that look, an unassuming little man who once had killed over a hundred women and children during a raid on a German village.

'What are they going to pit this thing against?' he asked suddenly.

Vonones shrugged. 'Can't be sure. The buyer didn't say much except that he didn't like the thing's looks.'

'Can you blame him?'

'So? He's supposed to be running a beast show, not a beauty contest. If he wants pretty things, I should bring him gazelles. For the arena, I told him, this thing is perfect—a real novelty. But the ass says he doesn't like the idea of keeping it around until the show, and I have to cut my price to nothing to get him to take it. Think of it!'

'What's the matter?' Lycon gibed sardonically. 'Do you also like its looks so little you'll unload it at a sacrifice?'

'Hardly!' the dealer scoffed. 'Animals are animals, and business is business. But I've got a hundred other animals here right now, and *they* don't like the thing. Look at this tiger. All day, all night he's trying to get at it—even broke a tooth on the bars! Must be its scent, because all the animals hate it. No, I have to get this thing out of my compound.'

Lycon considered the enraged tiger. The huge cat had killed one of his men and maimed another for life before they had him safely caged. But even the tiger's rage at capture paled at the determined fury he showed toward Vonones' strange find.

'Well, I'll leave you to him, then,' the hunter said, giving up on the mystery. 'Tomorrow I'll be by to pick up my money, so try to stay out of reach of that thing's claws until then.'

• • •

'You could have gone on with it,' Vulpes told him. 'You could have made a fortune in the arena.'

Lycon tore off a hunk of bread and sopped it with greasy gravy. 'I could have gotten killed—or crippled for life.'

He immediately regretted his choice of words, but his host only laughed. The tavern owner's left arm was a stump, and that he walked at all was a testament to the man's fortitude. Lycon had seen him after they dragged him from the wreckage of his chariot. The surgeons doubted Vulpes would last the night, but that was a twenty-five years ago.

'No, it was stupidity that brought me down,' Vuples said. 'Or greed. I knew my chances of forcing through on that turn, but it was that or the race. Well, I was lucky. I lived through it and had enough of my winnings saved to open a wine shop. I get by.

'But you,' and he stabbed a thick finger in Lycon's grey-stubbled face. 'You were too good, too smart. You could have been rich. A few years was all you needed. You were as good with a sword as any man who'd ever set foot in the arena—fast, and you knew how to handle yourself. All those years you spent against the barbarians seasoned you. Not like these swaggering bullies the crowds dote on these days—gutless slaves and flashy thugs who learned their trade in dark alleys! Pit a combat-hardened veteran against this sort of trash and see whose lauded favorite gets dragged off by his heels!'

Vulpes downed a cup of his wares and glared about the tavern truculently. None of his few customers was paying attention.

Lycon ruefully watched his host refill their cups with wine and water. He wished his friend would let old memories lie. Vulpes, he noted, was getting red-faced and paunchy as the wineskins he sold here. Nor, Lycon mused, running a hand over his close cropped skull, was he himself as young as back then. At least he stayed fit, he told himself—but then, Vulpes could hardly be faulted for inaction.

Tall for a Greek, Lycon had only grown leaner and harder with the years. His face still scowled in hawk-like intensity; his features resembled seasoned leather stretched tightly over sharp angles. Spirit and sinew had lost nothing in toughness as Lycon drew closer to fifty, and his men still talked of the voyage of a few years past when he nursed an injured polar bear on deck while waves broke over the bow and left a film of ice as they slipped back.

Vulpes rumbled on. 'But you, my philosophic Greek, found the arena a bore. Just walked away and left it all. Been skulking around the most foresaken corners of the world for—what is it, more than twenty years now? Risking your life to haul back savage beasts that barely make your expenses when you sell them. And you could be living easy in a villa near Rome!'

'Maybe this is what I wanted,' Lycon protested. He tried to push away memories of sand and sweat and the smell of blood and the sound of death and an ocean's roar of voices howling to watch men die for their amusement.

Vulpes was scarcely troubling to add water to their wine. 'What you wanted!' he scoffed. 'Well, what *do* you want, my moody Greek?'

'I'm my own master. Maybe I'm not rich, but I've journeyed to lands Odysseus never dreamed of, and I've captured stranger beasts than the Huntress ever loosed arrow after.'

'Oh, here's to adventure!' mocked Vulpes good-humoredly, thumping his wine cup loudly.

Lycon, reminded of the blue-scaled creature in Vonones' cage, smiled absently.

'I, too, am a philosopher,' Vulpes announced loftily. 'Wine and sitting on your butt all day makes a good Roman as philosophic as any wander-witted Greek beast collector.' He raised his cup to Lycon.

'And you, my friend, you have a fascination with the deadly, for the killer trait. Deny it as you will, but it's there. You could have farmed olives, or studied sculpture. But no, it's the army for you, then the arena, and what next? Are you sick of killing? No, just bored with easy prey. So now you spend your days outwitting and ensnaring the most savage beasts of all lands!

'You can't get away from your fascination for the killer, friend Lycon. And shall I tell you why? It's because, no matter how earnestly you deny it, you've got the killer streak in your own soul too.'

'Here's to philosophy,' toasted Lycon sardonically.

Lycon had done business with Vonones for many years, and the fat Armenian was one of the handful that the hunter more or less considered as friends. Reasonably honest albeit shrewd,

Vonones paid with coins of full weight and had been known to add a bonus to the tally when a collector brought him something exceptional. Still, after a long night of drinking with Vulpes, Lycon was not pleased when the dealer burst in upon him well before noon in the room he shared with five other transients.

'What in the name of the buggering Twins do you mean getting me up at this hour!' Lycon snarled, surprised to see daylight. 'I said I'd come by later for my money.'

'No—it's not that!' Vonones moaned, shaking his arm. 'Come on, Lycon! You've got to help me!'

Lycon freed his arm and rolled to his feet. Someone cursed and threw a sandal in their direction. 'All right, all right,' the hunter yawned. 'Let's get out of here and let other people sleep.'

The stairs of the apartment block reeked of garbage and refuse. It reminded Lycon of the stench at Vonones' animal compound—the sour foulness of too many people living within cramped walls. Beggars clogged the stairs, living there for want of other shelter. Now and again the manager of the block would pay a squad of the watch to pummel them out into the street. Those who could pay for a portion of a room were little cleaner themselves.

'Damn it, Vonones! What is it!' Lycon protested, as the frantic Armenian took hold of his arm again.

'Outside—I can't. . . . That animal escaped. The blue one.'

'Well,' Lycon said reasonably, 'you said you didn't get much for the thing, so it can't be all that great a loss. Anyway, what has it to do with me?'

But Vonones set his lips and tugged the hunter down the stairs and out onto the cobbled street where eight bearers waited with his litter. He pushed Lycon inside and closed the curtains before speaking in a low, agitated voice. 'I don't dare let this get out! Lycon, the beast escaped only a few miles out of town. It's loose in an estate now—hundreds of little peasant grainplots, each worked by a tenant family.'

'So?'

'The estate is owned by the emperor, and that blue beast killed one of his tenants within minutes of escaping! You've got to help me recapture it before worse happens!'

'Hermes!' swore Lycon softly, understanding why the loss of the animal had made a trembling wreck of the dealer, 'How did it get loose?'

'That's the worst of it,' Vonones whimpered. 'It must have unlocked the cage somehow—I checked the fastenings myself before the caravan left. But nobody will believe that—they'll think I was careless and didn't have the cage locked properly in the first place. And if the emperor learns that one of his estates is being ravaged . . .'

'Domitian shows his displeasure in interesting ways,' Lycon finished sombrely. 'Are you sure it isn't already too late to hush the business up?'

Vonones struggled for composure. 'For now it's all right. The steward is no more interested in letting this get out than I am, knowing the emperor's temper. But there's a limit to what he can cover up, and . . . it won't take very much of what happened to that farmer to exceed that limit. You've got to catch the thing for me, Lycon!'

'All right,' Lycon decided. He knew he was plunging into a mess that might call down Domitian's wrath on all concerned, but his voice was edged with excitement. 'Let's get out to where the thing escaped.'

The caravan was still strung out along the road when they arrived in Vonones' mud-spattered carriage. There were thirty carts, most loaded with only a single cage to avoid fights between the bars. Despite wind, rain and jostling, the beasts seemed less restive than in the compound. Perhaps there was a reason. The third cage from the end stood open.

Lycon stepped between the pair of carts—then ducked quickly as a taloned paw ripped through the bars at him. Disappointed, the huge tiger snarled as he hunched back in his cage.

The hunter glanced to be certain his arm was still in place. 'There's one to watch out for,' he cautioned Vonones. 'That one was a man-killer when we captured him—and out of preference, not just because he was lame or too old to take other prey. When they turn him loose in the arena, he'll take on anything in sight.'

'Maybe,' muttered the Armenian. 'But he'd like to start with that blue thing. I never saw anything drive every animal around it to a killing rage the way it does. Maybe it's its scent, but at times I could swear it was somehow taunting them.'

Lycon grunted noncommittally.

'Suppose I should let the rest of the caravan go on?' Vonones suggested. 'They're just causing comment stopped here like this.'

Lycon considered. 'Why not get them off the road as much as you can and spread out. Don't let them get too far away though, because I'll need some men for this. Say, there aren't any hunting dogs here, are there?'

Vonones shook his balding head. 'No, I don't often handle dogs. There is a small pack in Brundisium for the local arena though. I know the trainer, and I think I can have them here by noon.'

'Better do it, then,' Lycon advised. 'It's going to be easiest just to run the thing down and let the dogs have it. If we can pull them off in time, maybe there'll be enough left for your buyer in Rome.'

'Forget the sale,' Vonones urged him. 'Just *get* that damned thing!'

But Lycon was studying the lock of the cage. It clearly had not been forced. There were only a few fine scratches on the wards.

'Any of your men mess with this?'

'Are you serious? They don't like it any better than the animals do.'

'Vonones, I think it had to have opened the lock with its claws.'

The Armenian looked sick.

Twenty feet from the cart were the first footprints of the beast, sunk deeply into the mud of the wheat field beside the road. In the black earth their stamp was as undefinable as the beast itself. More lizard than birdlike, Lycon decided. Long toes leading a narrow, arched foot, with a thick spurred heel.

'First I knew anything was wrong,' explained the armwaving driver of the next cart back, 'was when this thing all of a sudden swings out of its cage and jumps into the field. Why, it could just as easy have jumped back on me—and then where would I have been, I ask you?'

Lycon did not bother to tell him. 'Vonones, you've got a couple archers in your caravan, haven't you?'

'Yes, but they weren't any use—it was too sudden. The one in the rear of the column shot where he could see the wheat waving, but he didn't really have a target. If only the thing *had* turned back on the rest of the caravan instead of diving through the hedges! My archers would have skewered it for sure then,

and I wouldn't be in this fix. Lycon, this creature is a killer! If
it gets away . . .'

'All right, steady,' the hunter growled. 'Going to pieces isn't
going to help.' He rose from where he knelt in the wheat.

'You won't be so self-assured once you see the farmer,' Vonones warned.

The tenant's hut was a windowless beehive of wattle and daub,
stuck up on the edge of his holdings. Huddled in the doorway,
three of his children watched the strangers apathetically, numbed
by the cold drizzle and their father's death.

The farmer lay about thirty yards into the field. A scythe, its
rough iron blade unstained, had fallen near the body. Blank
amazement still showed in his glazed eyes. A sudden, tearing
thrust of the creature's taloned hands had eviscerated the man—
totally, violently. He lay on his back in a welter of gore and
entrails, naked ribs jagged through his ripped open chest cavity.

Lycon studied the fragments of flesh strewn over the furrows.
'What did you feed it in the compound?'

'The same as the other carnivores,' Vonones replied shakily.
'Scrap beef and parts of any animals that happened to die. It
wasn't fussy.'

'Well, if you manage to get it back alive, you'll know what it
really likes,' Lycon said grimly. 'Do you see any sign of his
liver?'

Vonones swallowed and stared at the corpse in dread. The
archers held arrows to their bows and looked about nervously.

Lycon, who had been following the tracks with his eye as they
crossed the gullied field, suddenly frowned. 'How is your bow
strung? he asked sharply of the nearest archer.

'With gut,' he answered, blinking.

Lycon swore in disgust. 'In this rain a gut string is going to
stretch like a judge's honor! Vonones, we've got to have spears
and bows strung with waxed horsehair before we do anything. I
don't want to be found turned inside out with a silly expression
like this poor bastard!'

Lycon chose a dozen of Vonones' men to follow the dogs with
him. After that nothing happened for hours, while Vonones
fumed and paced beside the wagons. At the prospect of extri-
cating himself from his dilemma, the Armenian's sick fear gave
way to impatience.

About mid-afternoon a battered farm cart creaked into view behind a pair of spavined mules. The driver was a stocky North Italian, whose short whip and leather armlets proclaimed him the trainer of the six huge dogs that almost filled the wagon bed. Following was a much sharper carriage packed with hunting equipment, nets as well as bows and spears.

'What took you so long, Galerius!' Vonones demanded. 'I sent for you hours ago—told you to spare no expense in hiring a wagon! Damn it, man—the whole business could have been taken care of by now if you hadn't come in this wreck!'

'Thought you'd be glad I saved you the money,' Galerius scowled with dull puzzlement. 'My father-in-law lets me use this rig at a special rate.'

'It doesn't matter,' Lycon headed off the quarrel. 'We had to wait for the weapons anyway. How about the dogs? Can they track in this drizzle?'

'Sure, they're real hunting dogs—genuine Molossians,' the trainer asserted proudly. 'They weren't bred for the arena. I bought them from an old boy who used to run deer on his estate before he offended Domitian.'

Vonones began to chew his ragged nails.

At least the pack looked fully capable of holding up its end of things, Lycon thought approvingly. The huge, brindle-coated dogs milled about the wagon bed, stifflegged and hackles lifted at the babel of sounds and scents from Vonones' caravan. Their flanks were lean and scarred, and their massive shoulders bespoke driving strength. Their trainer might be a slovenly yokel himself, but his hounds were excellent hunting stock and well cared for. With professional interest, Lycon wondered whether he could talk Galerius into selling the pack.

'Don't you have horses?' the trainer asked. 'Going to be tough keeping up with these on foot.'

'We'll have to do it,' Lycon snorted. The trainer's idea of hunting was probably limited to the arena. Well, this wasn't some confused animal at bay in the center of an open arena. 'Look at the terrain. Horses would be worse than useless!'

Beneath gray clouds, the land about them was broken with rocky gullies, shadowy ravines, and stunted groves of trees. Gateless hedgerows divided the tenant plots at short intervals, forming dark, thorny barriers in a maze-like pattern throughout the estate. There were a few low sections where a good horse might hurdle the hedge, but the rain had turned plowed fields into quagmires, and the furrows were treacherous footing.

Lycon frowned at the sky. The rain was now only a dismal mist, but the overcast was thick and the sun well down on the horizon. Objects at a hundred yards blurred indistinctly into the haze.

'We've got one, maybe two hours left if we're going to catch the thing today,' he judged. 'Well, let's see what they can do.'

Galerius threw open the back gate of the wagon, and the pack bounded onto the road. They milled and snarled uncertainly while their trainer whipped them into line and led them past the remaining wagons. As soon as they neared the open cage, the hounds began to show intense excitement. One of the bitches gave a throaty bay and swung off into the wheat field. The other five poured after her, and no more need be done.

They hate it too, mused Lycon, as the excited pack bounded across the field in full cry. 'Come on!' he shouted. 'And keep your eyes open!'

Taking a boar spear, the hunter plunged after the baying pack. Vonones' men strung out behind him, while the dogs raced far ahead in the wheat. Too heavy for a long run, Vonones held back with the others on the road. Fingering a bow nervously, he stood atop a wagon and watched the hunt disappear into the mist. He looked jumpy enough to loose arrow at the first thing to come out of the woods, and Lycon reminded himself to shout when they returned to the road.

Already the dogs had vanished in the wheat, so that the men heard only their distant cries. Trailing them was no problem— the huge hounds had torn through the grainfield like a chariot's rush—but keeping up with them was impossible. The soft earth pulled at their legs, and sandals were constantly mired with clay and straw.

'Can't you slow them up?' Lycon demanded of the trainer who panted at his side.

'Not on a scent like this!' Galerius gasped back. 'They're wild, plain wild! No way we can keep up without horses!'

Lycon grunted and lengthened his stride. The trainer quickly fell back, and when Lycon glanced back he saw the other had paused to clean his sandals. Of the others he saw only vague forms farther behind still. Lycon wasted a breath to curse them and ran on.

The dogs had plunged through a narrow gap in the first hedge. Lycon followed, pushing his boar spear ahead of him. Had the gap been there, or had their quarry broken it through in passing? Clearly the thing was powerful beyond proportion to its slight bulk.

The new field was already harvested, and stubble spiked up out of the cold mud to jab Lycon's toes. His side began to ache. Hermes, he thought, the beast could be clear to Tarantum by now if it wanted to be. If it did get away, there was no help for Vonones. Lycon himself might find it expedient to spend a few years beyond the limits of the empire. That's what happens when you get involved in things that really aren't your business . . .

Another farmhouse squatted near the next hedgerow. 'Hoi!' the hunter shouted. 'Did a pack of dogs cross your hedge?'

There was no sound within. Lycon stopped in sudden concern and peered through the open doorway.

A half-kneaded cake of bread was turning black on the fire in the center of the hut. The rest of the hut was wottled throughout with russet splashes of blood that dried in the westering sun. There were at least six bodies scattered about the tiny room. The beast had taken its time here.

Lycon turned away, shaken for the first time in long years. He looked back the way he had come. None of the others had crawled through the last hedgerow yet. This time he felt thankful for their flabby uselessness.

He used a stick of kindling to scatter coals into the straw bedding, and tossed the flaming brand after. With luck no one would ever know what had happened here. As Vonones had said, there was a limit. They had better finish the beast fast.

The pack began to bay fiercely not far away. From the savage eagerness of their voices, Lycon knew they had overtaken the creature. Whatever the thing was, its string had run out, Lycon thought with relief.

Recklessly he ducked into the hedge and wormed through, not pausing to look for an opening. Thorns shredded his tunic and gouged his limbs as he pulled himself clear and began running toward the sounds.

No chance of recapturing the beast alive now. Any one of the six Molossians was nearly the size of the blue creature, and the arena would have taught the pack to kill rather than to hold. By the time Vonones' men arrived with the nets, it would be finished. Lycon half regretted that—the beast fascinated him. But quite obviously the thing was too murderously powerful to be loose and far too clever to be safely caged. It was luck the beast had kept close to its kill instead of running farther. The pack was just beyond the next hedgerow now.

With an enormous bawl of pain, one of the hounds suddenly arched into view, flailing in the air above the hedge. A terrified clamor abruptly broke through the ferocious baying of the pack. Beyond the hedge a fight was raging—and by the sound of it, the pack was in trouble.

Lycon swore and made for the far hedge, ignoring the cramp in his side. His knuckles clamped white on the boar spear.

He could see three of the dogs ahead of him, snarling and milling uncertainly on the near side of the hedge. The other three were not to be seen. They were beyond the hedge, Lycon surmised—and from their silence, dead. The beast was cunning; it had lain in wait for the pack as it squirmed through the hedge. But surely it was no match for three huge Molossians!

Lycon was less than a hundred yards from the hedge, when the blue-scaled killer vaulted over the thorny barrier with an acrobat's grace. It writhed through the air, and one needle-clawed hand slashed out—tearing the throat from the nearest Molossian before the dog was fully aware of its presence. The creature bounced to the earth like a cat, as the last two snarling hounds sprang for it together. Spinning and slashing as it ducked under and away, the thing was literally a blur of motion. Deadly motion. Neither hound completed its leap, as lethal talons tore and gutted—slew with nightmarish precision.

Lycon skidded to a stop on the muddy field. He did not need to glance behind him to know he was alone with the beast. Its eyes glowed in the sunset as it turned from the butchered dogs and stared at its pursuer.

The hunter advanced his spear, making no attempt to throw. As fast as it moved, the thing would easily dodge his cast. And Lycon knew that if the beast leaped, he was dead, dead as Pentheus. His only chance was that he might drive his spear home, might take his slayer with him—and he thought the beast recognized that.

It crouched, its lips drawn in a savage grin—then vaulted back over the hedge again.

Lycon tried to make his dry mouth shape a prayer of thanks.

Eyes intent on the hedge, he held his spear at ready. Then he heard feet splatting at a clumsy run behind him.

Galerius puffed toward him, accompanied by several of the others in a straggling clot. 'That hut back there caught fire!' he blurted. 'Didn't you see it? Just a ball of flame by the time we could get to it. Don't know if anyone was there, or if they got out or . . .'

He caught sight of the torn bodies and trailed off. His voice drawled in wonder. 'What happened here!'

Lycon finally let his breath out. 'Well, I found the animal we were supposed to be hunting—while you fools were back there gawking at your fire! Now I think Vonones owes you for a pack of dogs.'

Lycon waited long enough to make certain the beast no longer lay in wait beyond the hedge. After seeing the hounds, no one had wanted to be first to wriggle through to the other side. Thinking of those murderous claws, the hunter had no intention of doing so either. There was a gap in the hedge some distance away, and he sent half the men to circle around. There was no sign of the beast other than three more mutilated hounds. In disgust Lycon hiked back to the caravan, letting the others follow as they would.

As he reached the road a shrill voice demanded, 'Who's there!'

Lycon swore and yelled before nervous fingers released an arrow. 'Don't shoot, damn you! Hermes, that's all it would take!'

Vonones thumped heavily on to the roadbed from his perch on the wagon. His face was anxious. 'How did it go? Did you get the thing? Where are the others?'

'Drag-assing back,' Lycon grunted wearily. 'Vonones, there isn't one of your men I'd trust to walk a dog.'

'They're wagon drivers, not hunters,' the dealer protested. 'But what about the beast?'

'We didn't get it.'

And while the others slowly drifted back, Lycon told the dealer what had happened. The damp stillness of the dusk settled around the wagons as he finished. Vonones slumped in stunned silence.

Lycon's weathered face was thoughtful. 'You got ahold of something from an arena, Vonones. I don't know where or whose—maybe the Sarmatians raided it from the Chinese. But the way it moves, the way its claws are groomed—the way it kills for pleasure . . . Somebody lost a fighting cock, and you bought it!'

The Armenian stared at him without comprehension. Licking his lips, Lycon continued. 'I can't say who could have owned it, or what the beast is—but I know the arena, and I tell you that thing is a superbly trained killer. The way it ambushed the dogs, slaughtered them without a wasted motion! And that thing moves fast! I'm fast enough that I've jumped back from a pit trap I didn't know was there until my feet started to go through. I knew a gladiator in Rome who moved faster than any man I've seen. He'd let archers shoot at him from sixty yards, then dodge the arrow, and I never could believe I saw it happen. But that thing out there in the fields is so much faster there's no comparison.'

'How did the Sarmatians capture it then!' Vonones demanded.

'Capture? They took its surrender!' Lycon exploded. 'A band of mounted archers on a thousand miles of empty plains—they could have run it down and killed it easily, and that damned thing knew it! Then they welded it into an iron cage, and strong as it is, the beast can't snap iron bars.'

'But it can pick locks.'

'Yeah.'

The dealer took a deep breath, shrugging all over and seeming to fill his garments even more fully. 'How do we recapture it, then?'

'I don't know.'

Lycon chewed his lips, looking at the ground rather than the Armenian. 'If the beast sleeps, maybe we could sneak up and get a shot. Maybe with a thousand men we could spread out through the hedgerows and gullies, encircle it somehow.'

'We don't have a thousand men,' Vonones stated implacably.

'I know.'

Smoky clouds were sliding past the full moon. With dusk the drizzle at last had lifted; the overcast was clearing. A few stars began to spike through the cobwebby sky. Across the twilit fields, shadows crept out from hedgerows and trees, flowed over the rocky gullies.

'I can lay my hands on a certain amount of money at short notice,' Vonones thought aloud. 'There will be ships leaving Brundisium in the morning . . .'

But Lycon was staring at the nearest cage.

'Vonones,' the hunter asked pensively. 'Have you ever seen a tiger track a man down?'

'What? No, but I've heard plenty of grisly reports about man-killers who will . . .'

'No, I don't mean hunt down as prey. I mean track down for, well, revenge.'

'No, it doesn't happen,' the dealer replied. 'A wolf maybe, but not one of the big cats. They don't go out of their way for anything, not even revenge.'

'I saw it happen once,' Lycon said. 'It was a female, and one of my men had cleaned out her litter while she was off hunting. We figured later she must have followed him fifty miles before she caught up to him.'

'She followed her cubs, not the man.'

The hunter shook his head. 'He'd given me the cubs. The man was three villages away when she got him. Her left forepaw had an extra toe; there was no mistake.'

'So what?'

'Vonones, I'm going to let that tiger out.'

The Armenian choked in disbelief. 'Lycon, are you mad? This isn't the same at all! You can't . . .'

'Have you got a better idea? You know how all the animals hate this thing . . . that tiger even broke a tooth trying to chew his way to the beast. Well, I'm going to give him his chance.'

'I can't let you turn yet another savage killer loose here!'

'Look, we can't get that blue-scaled thing any other way. Once it runs wild through a few more tenant holdings, Domitian isn't going to care if you turn the whole damn caravan loose!'

'So the tiger kills the beast. Then I'm responsible for turning a tiger loose on his estate! Lycon . . .'

'I caught this tiger once. I know about tigers. This thing, Vonones . . .'

The dealer's hand shook as he turned over the key.

Muttering, the drivers made an armed cluster in the middle of the road, watching Lycon as he unlocked the cage and vaulted to the roof as the door swung down. The tiger bounded onto the road almost before the door touched gravel. Tail lashing, he paused in a half-crouch to growl at the nervous onlookers. Several bows arched tautly.

Lady Artemis, breathed Lycon, let him scent that beast and follow it.

Turning from the men, the cat moved toward the other cage. He rumbled a challenge into the empty interior, then swung toward where the tracks stabbed into the damp earth. Without a backward glance, the tiger headed off across the field.

Lycon jumped down, boar spear in hand, and stepped across the ditch.

'Where are you going?' Vonones called after him.

'I want to see this,' he shouted back, and loped off along the track he earlier had followed with the hounds.

'Lycon, you're crazy!' Vonones shouted into the night.

Even after the earlier run, Lycon had no trouble keeping up with the tiger. Cats have speed but are not pacers like dogs, like men. The tiger was moving at a graceless quickstep, midway between his normal arrogant saunter and the awesome rush that launched him to his kill. Loose skin behind his neck wobbled awkwardly as his shoulder blades pumped up and down. Moonlight washed all the orange from between the black stripes, and it seemed to be a ghost cat that jolted through the swaying wheat. He ignored Lycon, ignored even the blood soaked earth where the first victim's corpse had lain—intent only on the strange, hated scent of its blue-scaled enemy.

Following at a cautious distance, Lycon marvelled that his desperate stratagem had worked. It seemed impossible that the great cat was actually stalking the other killer. It was pure hatred, the same unnatural fury that had maddened the dogs, that had turned the compound into a raging chaos as long as the creature had been among them.

And the men? None of the men had liked the blue-scaled devil either. Uncertain fear had made Vonones' crew useless in the hunt. And Vonones had unloaded the thing for a trivial sum, because neither he nor the buyer from Rome had wanted the beast around. Why then did he feel such fascination for the creature?

The tiger changed stride to clear the first hedgerow. Lycon warily climbed through after him, trotting toward the pall of reeking smoke that still hovered over the ruined hut. Vonones would see to things here, the hunter thought, praying that there would not be more such charnel scenes across the maze-like estate.

A dozen men passing and repassing had hacked a fair gap through the second hedge, and Lycon was glad he did not have to worm blindly through again. The tiger leaped it effortlessly and was speeding across the empty field at a swifter pace by the time he stepped through. Lycon lengthened his stride to stay within fifty yards.

More stars broke coldly through the clearing sky. The cat looked as deadly as Nemesis rippling through the moonlight. Lycon grimly recalled that he had thought much the same about the pack. The tiger was every bit as deadly as the blue killer, and probably was five times its weight. Speed and cunning could only count for so much.

The third hedge had not been trampled, and Lycon's belly tightened painfully as he dived through the goresplashed gap where the killer had awaited the dogs. But the tiger had already leapt over the brushy wall, and Lycon deigned to lose time by detouring to the opening farther down. He pushed his way free and stood warily in the field beyond.

Here the soil was too sparse and rocky for regular sowing. Left fallow, small trees and weedy scrub grew disconsolately between bare rocks and shadowed gullies. The wasteland was a sharp study of hard blacks and whites etched by the pale moon.

The tiger had halted just ahead, his belly flattened to the rocky soil. He sniffed the air, coughing a low rumble like distant thunder. Then his challenging roar burst from his throat, moonlight glowing on awesome fangs. Far away an ox bawled in far, and Lycon felt the hair on his neck tingle.

A bit of gravel rattled from the brush-filled gully just beyond. Lycon watched the cat's haunches rise, quivering with restrained tension. A man-sized shadow stood erect from the shadows of the gully, and the tiger leaped.

Thirty yards separated the cat from his prey. He took two short hops toward the blue devil, then lunged for the kill. The scaled creature was moving the instant the tiger left the ground for his final leap. A blur of energy, it darted beneath the lunge, needle-clawed fingers thrusting toward the cat's belly. The tiger squalled and hunched in mid-leap, slashing at its enemy in a deadly riposte that nearly succeeded.

Gravel and mud sprayed as the cat struck the ground and whirled. The blue killer was already upon him, its claws ripping at the tiger's neck. With speed almost as blinding, the cat twisted about, left forepaw flashing a bone-snapping blow against the creature's ribs—hurling it against a knot of brush.

The cat paused, trying to lick the stream of blood that spurted from its neck. The blue-scaled thing gave a high-pitched cry—the first sound Lycon had heard from it—and leaped onto the cat's back.

By misjudgement or sudden weakness, it landed too far back, straddling the tiger's belly instead of withers. The cat writhed backward and rolled, taloned forepaws slashing, hind legs pumping. Stripped from its hold, the creature burrowed into the razor-edged fury of thrashing limbs.

It was too fast to follow. Both animals flung themselves half erect, spinning, snarling in a crimson spray. A dozen savage blows ripped back and forth in the space of a heartbeat, as they tore against each other in suicidal frenzy.

With no apparent transition, the tiger slumped into the mud. His huge head hung loose, and bare bone gleamed for an instant. Blood spouted in a great torrent, then ebbed abruptly to a dark smear. The tiger arched his back convulsively in death as his slayer staggered away.

Lycon stared in disbelief as the blue-scaled killer took a careful step toward him. Blood bathed its bright scales like a glistening imperial cloak. Murder gleamed joyously in its eyes. Lycon readied his spear.

Another step and it stumbled, bracing itself on the ground with one deadly hand. The other arm hung broken, useless—all but torn away by the tiger's claws. It jerked erect and grinned at the hunter, its feral face a reflection of death. It lunged for him.

There was no strength to its legs. Its leap fell short a yard from the hunter. The beast skidded across the rocky soil. The claws of its good hand scored the dirt at his feet, then relaxed.

The moon glared down, drowning the stars with chilled splendour. Lycon shivered, and after a while he walked back to the road.

He felt old that night.

FRANK HERBERT's
11 MILLION-COPY BESTSELLING

DUNE

MASTERWORKS

__0-441-17266-0	DUNE	$4.50
__0-441-17269-5	DUNE MESSIAH	$4.95
__0-441-10402-9	CHILDREN OF DUNE	$4.95
__0-441-29467-7	GOD EMPEROR OF DUNE	$4.95
__0-441-32800-8	HERETICS OF DUNE	$4.95
__0-441-10267-0	CHAPTERHOUSE DUNE	$4.95